JONATHAN & MONICA

BOOK ONE - ONE NIGHT WITH HIM

CD REISS

THE

MIDNIGHT EDITION

FLIP CITY MEDIA INC.

One Night With Him - CD Reiss
Midnight Edition
Formerly *Beg Tease Submit* and *Submission*
Copyright © 2013
All rights reserved.

This book was previously published as *Beg Tease Submit* and *Submission*. Chapters from *Dominance* have been added inside the timeline.

That aside, the subtitle is the title and Jonathan & Monica doesn't mean anything at all. But some folks wanted a plain cover with a sexless title so they could read the book at work or on the train. I aim to please.

JONATHAN & MONICA

THE SUBMISSION SERIES

This is what you're reading right now.

Monica insists she's not submissive. Jonathan Drazen is going to prove otherwise, but he might fall in love doing it.

One Night With Him

One Year With Him

One Life With Him

THE GAMES DUET

Adam Steinbeck will give his wife a divorce on one condition. She join him in a remote cabin for 30 days, submitting to his sexual dominance.

Marriage Games

Separation Games

THE EDGE SERIES

Rough. Edgy. Sexy enough to melt in your hands.

Rough Edge

On The Edge

Broken Edge

Over the Edge

PART I
BEG

CHAPTER 1

*A*t the height of singing the last note, when my lungs were still full and I was switching from pure physical power to emotional thrust, I was blindsided by last night's dream. Like most dreams, it hadn't had a story. I was on top of a grand piano on the rooftop bar of Hotel K. The fact that the real hotel didn't have a piano on the roof notwithstanding, I was on it and naked from the waist down, propped on my elbows. My knees were spread further apart than physically possible. Customers drank their thirty-dollar drinks and watched as I sang. The song didn't have words, but I knew them well, and as the strange man with his head between my legs licked me, I sang harder and harder until I woke up with an arched back and soaked sheets, hanging on to a middle C for dear life.

Same as the last note of our last song, and I held it like a stranger was pleasuring me on a nonexistent piano. I drew that last note out for everything it was worth, pulling from deep inside my diaphragm, feeling the song rattle the bones of my rib cage, sweat pouring down my face. It was my note. The dream told me so. Even after Harry stopped strumming and Gabby's keyboard softened to silence, I croaked out the last tearful strain as if gripping the edge of a precipice.

When I opened my eyes in the dark club, I knew I had them; every one of them stared at me as if I had just ripped out their souls, put them in envelopes, and sent them back to their mothers, COD. Even in the few silent seconds after I stopped, when most singers would worry that they'd lost the audience, I knew I hadn't; they just needed permission to applaud. When I smiled, permission was granted, and they clapped all right.

Our band, Spoken Not Stirred, had brought down the Thelonius Room. A year of writing and rehearsing the songs and a month getting bodies in the door had paid off right here, right now.

The crowd. That was what it was all about. That was why I busted my ass. That was why I had shut out everything in my life but putting a roof over my head and food in my mouth. I didn't want anything from them but that ovation.

I bowed and went off stage, followed by the band. Harry bolted to the bathroom to throw up, as always. I could still hear the applause and banging feet. The room held a hundred people, and the audience sounded like a thousand. I wanted to take the moment to bathe in something other than the disappointment and failure that accompanied a career in music, but I heard Gabrielle next to me, tapping her right thumb and middle finger. Her gaze was blank, settled in a corner, her eyes as big as teacups. I followed that gaze to exactly nothing. The corner was empty, but she stared as if a mirror into herself stood there, and she didn't like what she saw.

I glanced at Darren, our drummer. He stared back at me, then at his sister, who had tapped those fingers since puberty.

4

"Gabby," I said.

She didn't answer.

Darren poked her bicep. "Gabs? Shit together?"

"Fuck off, Darren," Gabby said flatly, not looking away from the empty corner.

Darren and I looked at each other. We were each other's first loves, back in L.A. Performing Arts High, and even after the soft, simple breakup, we had deepened our friendship to the point we didn't need to talk with words.

We said to each other, with our expressions, that Gabby was in trouble again.

"We rule!" Harry gave a fist pump as he exited the bathroom, still buttoning up his pants. "You were awesome." He punched me in the arm, oblivious to what was going on with Gabby. "My heart broke a little at 'Split Me.'"

"Thanks," I said without emotion. I did feel gratitude, but we had other concerns at the moment. "Where's Vinny?"

Our manager, Vinny Mardigian, appeared as if summoned, all glad-handing and smiles. Such a dick. I really couldn't stand him, but he'd seemed confident and competent when we met.

"You happy?" I said. "We sold all our tickets at full price. Now maybe next time we won't have to pay to play?"

"Hello, Monica Sexybitch." That was his pet name for me. The guy had the personality of a landfill and the drive of a shark in bloody waters. "Nice to see you too. I got Performer's Agency on the line. Their guy's right outside."

Great. I needed representation from the The Rinky-dink Agency like I needed a hole in the head. But I was an artist, and I was supposed to take whatever the industry handed me with a smile and spread legs.

5

Vinny, of course, couldn't shut up worth a damn. He was high on Performer's Agency and the worldwide fame he thought they would get us. He didn't realize half a step forward was just as good as a full step back. "You got a crowd out there asking for an encore. Everybody here does their job, then everybody's happy."

I listened, and sure enough, they were still clapping, and Gabby was still staring into the corner.

CHAPTER 2

*D*arren took Gabby home after the encore, which she played like the crazy prodigy she was, then she blanked out again. Her depression was ameliorated by music and brought on by just about anything, even if she was taking her meds.

She'd attempted suicide two years before after a few weeks of corner-staring and complaining of not being able to feel anything about anything. I'd been the one to find her in the kitchen, bleeding into the sink. That had been terrific for everyone. She took my second bedroom, and Darren moved from a roommate-infested guest house in West Hollywood to a studio a block away. We played music together because music was what we did, and because it kept Gabby sane, Darren close, and me from screwing up. But it didn't even keep us in hot dogs. We all worked, and until I got my current gig at the rooftop bar at Hotel K, I had to give up Starbucks because I couldn't rub two nickels together to make heat.

Because Spoken Not Stirred had drawn more people than the cost of our guaranteed tickets, we'd made three hundred dollars that night. Fifteen percent went to Vinny Landfillian. Sixty-eight dollars paid for

Harry's parking ticket because he figured if he was loading his bass and amp, he could park in a loading zone on the Sunset Strip before six o'clock. We split the rest four ways.

Hotel K was a spanking new modernist, thirty-story diamond in a one-story stucco shitpile of a neighborhood. The rooftop bar thing in L.A. had gotten out of hand. You couldn't swing a dead talent agent without hitting some new construction with a barside pool on the roof and thumping music day and night. The upside of the epidemic was that waitress service was the norm, and tall, skinny girls who could slip between name-dropping drunks while holding heavy trays over their heads without clocking anyone were an absolute necessity. The downside for someone tall and skinny like myself was my replaceability. You couldn't swing a tall, skinny girl in L.A. without hitting another one.

Darren and I had taken too long discussing who would watch Gabby. He convinced her to stay at his place for the night, though "convinced" might not be the word to use when talking about someone who didn't care about where she slept, or anything, one way or the other.

I ran from the elevator to the hotel locker room, the fifty bucks I'd made for holding a hundred people in my palm light in my pocket. I peeled off my jacket and stuffed it in my locker, then pulled my shirt off. I didn't have a second to spare before Yvonne, who I was relieving, started chewing me out for stranding her on the floor. I yanked a low-cut dress that showed more leg than modesty out of my bag and wrestled into it.

"You're late," Freddie, my manager, said. He stank of cigarettes, which I found disgusting.

"I'm sorry, I had a gig." I kicked off my shoes and pulled my pants off from under my dress. I had no time to worry about what Freddie thought of me.

"Bully for you." Freddie crossed his arms, scrunching his brown pinstripe suit. He had a mole on his cheek and wore a puckered expression even when he looked down my shirt, which was almost every time we talked.

I didn't wait to argue. I slipped back into my shoes, slapped my locker shut, and ran toward the floor.

"Yvonne!" I caught her in the back hall as she folded a wad of tips into her pocket.

"Monica, girl! Where were you?"

"I'm sorry. Thanks for covering my tables. Can I make it up to you?"

"I don't get home in time, you can pay the sitter an extra hour."

"No problem," I said, though it was a big problem.

"Jonathan Drazen is at your table." She put her hand to her heart. "He's hot, and he'll tip if he likes what he sees. So be nice." She handed me the tickets for my station.

Drazen was my boss's boss. He owned the hotel, but we'd never crossed paths. Apparently, he traveled a lot, and he spent little or no time on the roof when he was in town, so we hadn't met. This development was more annoying than anything. I'd just gotten the ovation of my life at a really cool club and was bathing in the warm validation. I didn't need to prove myself all over again, and based on what? If it wasn't my music, I didn't care.

The place was packed: wall-to-wall Eurotrash, Hollywood heavyweights, and assorted hangers-on. The pool was a big rectangle in the center of the expanse. Red chairs surrounded it, and a large cocktail area with tables and chairs sat off to the side. Little tents with couches inside outlined most of the roof, and when the curtains closed, you left them closed unless someone looked as though they'd taken off without paying.

I stood at the service bar, flipping through my tickets. Five tables, two with little star punch-outs in the upper right hand corners. Put there by Freddie, they meant someone important was at the table. Extra care was required.

My first tray was a star punch-out. I put on a smile and navigated through the crowd to deliver the tray to a table in the corner. Four men, and I knew Drazen right away. He had red hair cut just below the ears, disheveled in that absolutely precise way. He wore jeans and a grey shirt that showed off his broad shoulders and hard biceps. His full lips stretched across flawless, natural teeth when he saw his tray coming, and I was caught a little off guard by how much I couldn't stop looking at him.

"H-Hi," I stammered. "I'll be your server." I smiled. That always worked. Then I thought happy thoughts because that made my smile genuine, and I watched Drazen move his gaze from my smiling face, over my breasts, to my hips, stopping at my calves. I felt as if I were being applauded again.

He looked back at my face. I stared right back at him, and he pursed his lips. I'd caught him looking, and he seemed justifiably embarrassed.

"Hello," he said. "You're new." His voice resonated like a cello, even over the music.

I checked Yvonne's notes and picked up a short glass with ice and amber liquid from the tray. "You have the Jameson's?"

"Thank you." He nodded to me, keeping his eyes on my face and off my body. Even then, I felt as if I were being eaten alive, sucked to fluid, mouthful by mouthful. A liquid feeling came over me, and I stopped doing my job for half a second while I allowed myself to be completely saturated by that warm feeling. In that moment, of course, someone, a man judging from the weight of impact, pushed or got pushed, and my tray went flying.

For a second, the glasses hung in the air like a handful of glitter, and I thought I could catch them. I felt the sound of the impact too long after three gin and tonics splashed over each guest. I was shocked into silence as everyone at the table stood, hands out, dripping, clothes getting darker at crotches and chests. A collective gasp rose from everyone within splash distance.

Freddie appeared like a zombie smelling fresh brains. "You're fired." He turned to Drazen and said, "Sir, can I get you anything? We have shirts—"

Drazen shook a splash of liquid off his hand. "It's fine."

"I am so sorry," I said.

Freddie got between me and my former boss, as if I would beg him for my job back, which I'd never do, and said, "Get your things."

CHAPTER 3

*F*uck it. Fuck that job and everything else. I'd get another one. I promised myself I was going to make it big, and when I did, I would come in here with my freaking entourage and Freddie was going to serve me whatever I wanted for no tip at all. Not even a cent. And Jonathan Drazen was going to sit by me and look at me just like he did before I spilled gin and tonic all over him, but like I'm an equal, not some little piece of candy working for tips.

I slammed my locker shut.

I had to find another job soon. I always paid my housing expenses first, but we owed the studio money, and I couldn't take another dime from Harry.

Freddie strode down the dim hallway, toes pointed out and walking like a duck on a mission.

"Fuck off, Freddie. I'm leaving, and by the way, you're an—"

"Mister Drazen wants to see you."

"Fuck him. He can't summon me. I don't work for him anymore."

Freddie smiled like a sly cat. "Sometimes he gives the short timers a severance if he feels bad. Nice chunka change. After that, you can get the hell out if you don't want to sleep with him. I'd like to see him not get laid for once."

He took a step closer. I didn't know why he'd get close enough to touch me, so I didn't back away, and when he slapped my ass, I was so stunned I didn't move. He ended the slap with a pinch.

"What did you…?"

But he was already waddling off, elbows bent, as if someone else's life needed to be miserable and he was just the guy to make it so. I stood there with my mouth open, seventy percent mad at him for being a complete molester and thirty percent mad at myself for being too shocked to punch him in the face.

CHAPTER 4

I had pride. I had so much pride that heeling at Jonathan Drazen's beck and call for a "chunka change" was the most humiliating thing I could think of doing. But there I was, in front of his ajar door on the thirtieth floor, knocking, not because I needed the money (which I did), and not because I wanted him to look at me like that again (which I also did), but because I couldn't have been the first waitress ass-slapped, or worse, by Freddie. If Drazen wasn't aware of Freddie's douchebaggery, he needed to be.

The office looked onto the Hollywood Hills, which must have been stunning in daylight. At night, the neighborhood was just a splash of twinkling lights on a black canvas. He stood behind his desk, back to the window, the room's soft lighting a flattering glaze on the perfect skin of his forearms. He wore a fresh pair of jeans and a white shirt. The dark wood and frosted glass accentuated the fact his office was meant to be a comforting space, and even though I knew the setting was manipulating me, I relaxed.

"Come on in," he said.

I stepped onto the carpet, its softness easing the pain caused by my high heels.

"I'm sorry I spilled on you. I'll pay for dry cleaning, if you want."

"I don't want. Sit down." His green eyes flickered in the lamplight. I had to admit he was stunning. His copper hair curled at the edges, and his smile could light a thousand cities. He couldn't have been older than his early thirties.

"I'll stand," I said. I was wearing a short skirt, and judging from the way he'd looked at me on the roof, if I sat down, I'd receive another stare that would make me want to jump him.

"I want to apologize for Freddie," he said. "He's a little more aggressive than he should be."

"We need to talk about that," I said.

He raised an eyebrow and came around to the front of the desk. He wore some cologne that stole the scent of sage leaves on a foggy day: dry, dusty, and clean. He leaned on his desk, putting his hands behind him, and I could see the whole length of his body: broad shoulders, tight waist, and straight hips. He looked at me again, then down to the floor. I felt as if he'd moved his hands off of me, and at once I was thrilled and ashamed. I wasn't going to be intimidated or scared. I wasn't going to let him look away from me. If he wanted to stare, he should stare. I placed my hands on my hips and let my body language challenge him to put his eyes where they wanted to go, not the floor.

Because, fuck him.

"Freddie's a douchebag." I could tell from his expression that was the wrong way to start. I needed to keep opinions and juicy expressions to myself and state facts. "He said you're going to try and sleep with me, for one." He smiled as if he really was going to try to sleep with me and got caught.

"Then," I continued, because I wanted to wipe that smile off his gorgeous face, "he grabbed my ass."

The smile melted as though it was an ice cube in a hot frying pan. He took his hungry eyes off mine, a relief on one hand and a disappointment on the other. "I was going to offer you severance."

"I don't want your money."

"Let me finish."

I nodded, a sting of prickly heat spreading across my cheeks.

"The severance was in case you didn't want to continue working here," he said. "Even though I can't stand the smell of the gin you got on me, I don't think you should lose your job over it. But now that you told me that, what should I do? If I give you severance, it looks like I'm paying you off. And if I unfire you, it looks like I'm letting you stay because I'm afraid of getting sued."

"I get it," I said. "If he said you'd try to sleep with me, then you've got your own shit to hide, and nothing would bring it out better than a lawsuit." I waited a second to see if I could glean anything from his eyes, but he had his business face on, so I put on my sarcasm face. "Quite a terrible position you're in."

His nod told me he understood me. His position was privileged. He got to make choices about my life based on his convenience. "What do you do, Monica?"

"I'm a waitress."

He smirked, looking at me full on, and I wanted to drop right there. "That's your circumstance. It's not who you are. Law school, maybe?"

"Like hell."

"Teacher, woodworker, volleyball player?" He ran the words together quickly, and I guessed he could come up with another hundred potential professions before he got it right.

"I'm a musician," I said.

"I'd like to see you play sometime."

"I'm not going to sleep with you."

16

"Indeed." He walked behind his desk. "I assume no one witnessed this alleged ass-grab?"

"Correct."

He opened a drawer and flipped through some files. "I hired Freddie, and he's my responsibility to manage. Your responsibility is to report it to someone besides me." He handed me a slip of paper. It was a standard U.S. Equal Employment Opportunity Commission flyer. "The numbers are on there. File a report. Send me a copy, please. It would protect both of us."

I stared at the paper. Drazen could get into a lot of trouble if enough reports were filed. I intended to tell the authorities what happened because I couldn't stand Freddie, but I felt a little sheepish about getting Drazen cited or investigated.

"You're not an asshole," I said.

He bowed his head, and though I couldn't see his face, I imagined he was smiling. He took a card from his pocket and came back around the desk. "My friend Sam owns the Stock downtown. I think it's a better fit for you. I'll tell him you might call."

When I took the card, I had an urge I couldn't resist. I reached my hand a little farther than I should have and brushed my finger against his. A shot of pleasure drove through me, and his finger flicked to extend the touch.

I had to get away from that guy as fast as possible.

CHAPTER 5

*L*os Angeles weather in late September was mid-July weather everywhere else—dog's-mouth hot, sweat-through-your-antiperspirant hot, car-exhaust hot. Gabby seemed better than the previous night, but Darren and I were on our toes.

Gabby said she was going for a walk and, trying to make sure she wasn't alone, I suggested she and I get ice cream at the artisanal place on Sunset.

We sat on the outside patio so the noise would mask our conversation. I poked at my strawberry basil ice cream while she considered her wasabi/honey longer than she might have a week ago.

"It's good money," she said, trying to talk me into a Thursday night lounge job. "And no pay to play. Just cash and go home."

"I hate those gigs. I hate being background."

"Two hundred dollars? Come on, Monica. You don't have to learn any songs; one rehearsal, maybe two, and we got it."

Gabby had spent her childhood getting her fingers slapped with a ruler every time she made a mistake on the piano. Her playing became so perfect she barely had to work at it. She was so compulsive her every waking moment was spent eating, playing, or thinking about playing, so the word "rehearse" couldn't apply to her because it implied an artist taking time out of their day to get something right, not a compulsive perfectionist basically breathing. She was a genius, and in all likelihood, her genius plus her perfectionist nature drove her depression.

"I only want to sing my own songs," I said.

"You can spin them. Just, come on. If I don't bring a voice on, I'll lose the gig, and I need it." That hitch in her voice meant she was swinging between desperation and emotional flatness, and it terrified me. "Mon, I can't wait for the next Spoken gig. I'm twenty-five, and I don't have a lot of time. *We* don't have a lot of time. Every month goes by, and I'm nobody. God, I don't even have an agent. What will happen to me? I can't take it. I think I'll die if I end up like Frieda DuPree, trying her whole life and then she's in her sixties and still going to band auditions."

"You're not going to end up like Frieda DuPree."

"I have to keep working. Every night that goes by without someone seeing me play is a lost opportunity."

Performance school rote bullshit. Get out and play. Keep working. Play the odds. Teachers told poor kids they might be seen if they busted their violins on the streets if they had to. Dream-feeders. Fuck them. Some of those kids should have gone into accounting, and that line of shit kept them dreaming a few too many years.

I looked at Gabby and her big blue eyes, pleading for consideration. She was mid-anxiety attack. If it continued over the coming weeks, the anxiety attacks would become less frequent and the dead stares into corners more frequent if she didn't take her meds regularly. Then it would be trouble: another suicide attempt, or worse, a success. I loved Gabby. She was like a sister to me, but sometimes I wished for a less burdensome friend.

"Fine," I said. "One time, okay? You can find someone else in all of Los Angeles to do it next time."

Gabby nodded and tapped her thumb and middle finger together. "It's good," she said. "It'll be good, Monica. You'll knock them out. You will." The words had a rote quality, like she said them just to fill space.

"I guess I need it too," I said. "I got fired last night."

"What did you do?"

"Spilled drinks in my boss's lap."

"That Freddie guy?"

"Jonathan Drazen."

"Oh…" She put her hands to her mouth. "He also owns the R.O.Q. Club in Santa Monica. So don't try to work there, either."

"Did you know he's gorgeous?"

A voice came from behind me. "Talking about me again?" Darren had shown up, God bless him.

"Jonathan Drazen fired her last night," Gabby said.

"Who is that?" He sat down, placing his laptop on the table.

"He didn't do it. Freddie did. Drazen just offered me a severance and referred me to the Stock."

"And apparently he's gorgeous." He raised an eyebrow at me. I shrugged. Darren and I were over each other, but he'd rib me bloody at the slightest sign of weakness. "I haven't heard you talk like that about a guy in a year and a half. I thought maybe you were still in love with me." I must have blushed, or my eyes might have given away some hidden spark of feeling, because Darren snapped open his laptop. "Let's see what kinda wifi I can pick up."

"I don't talk like that about men because I prefer celibacy to bullshit."

Darren tapped away on his laptop. "Jonathan

Drazen. Thirty-two. Old man." He looked at me over the screen.

"Do not underestimate how hot he is. I could barely talk."

"Earned his money the old-fashioned way."

"Rich daddy?"

"A long line of them. He makes more in interest than the entire GDP of Burma." Darren scrolled through some web page or another. He loved the internet like most people loved puppies and babies. "Real estate magnate. His dad lost a chunk of money. Our Jonathan the Third…" He drifted off as he scrolled. "BA from Penn. MBA from Stanford. He brought the business back. Bazillionaire. He's a real catch if you can tear him away from the four hundred other women he's getting photographed with."

"Lalala. Don't care."

"Why? It's not like you've had sex in…what?" Darren clicked around, pretending he didn't care about my answer, but I knew he did.

"Men are bad news," I said. "They're a distraction. They make demands."

"Not all men are Kevin."

Kevin was my last boyfriend, the one whose control issues had turned me off to men for eighteen months. "Lalala… not talking about Kevin either." I scraped the bottom of my ice cream cup.

Darren turned his laptop so I could see the screen. "This him?"

Jonathan Drazen stood between a woman and man I didn't recognize. I scrolled through the gossip page. His Irish good looks were undeniable next to anyone, even movie stars.

"He *has* been photographed with an awful lot of women," I said.

"Yeah, he's been a total fuck-around since his divorce, FYI. If you wanted him, he'd probably be game. All I'm saying." He crossed his legs and looked out onto Sunset.

Gabby had a faraway look as she watched the cars. "His wife was Jessica Carnes," Gabby recited as if she was reading a newspaper in her head, "the artist. Drazen married her at his father's place on Venice Beach. She's half-sister to Thomas Deacon, the sports agent at APR, who has a baby with Susan Kincaid, the hostess at the Key Club, whose brother plays basketball with Eugene Testarossa. Our dream agent at WDE."

"One day, Gabster, your obsession with Hollywood interrelationships will pay off." Darren clicked his laptop closed. "But not today."

CHAPTER 6

I think one could be at Hotel K, get blindfolded, taken to the Stock, and believe they'd been driven around and dropped in the same place they started: same pool, same chairs, same couches, same music, and same assholes clutching the same drinks and passing off the same tips. What was different was that there was no Freddie. The Stock had Debbie, a tall Asian lady who wore mandarin collar embroidered shirts and black trousers. She knew every superstar from just their face, and they loved her as much as she loved them. She could tell a movie mogul from an actress and sat them where they'd have the most professional friction. She coordinated the waitresses' tables according to the patron's taste and coddled the girls until they worked like a machine.

She was the nicest person I'd ever worked for.

"Smile, girl," Debbie said. I'd been there a week and she knew exactly how many tables I could handle, how fast I was compared to the others, and my strong suit, which appeared to be my magnetic personality. "People look at you," she said. "They can't help it. Be smiling."

It was hard to smile. We'd had three good shows in a row, then Vinny disappeared into thin air. We'd banged on his office door in Thai Town, went to his house in East Hollywood, and called four hundred times. No Vinny. Every gig he had lined up for us fell through. My momentum was slowing and I didn't like it.

"What's your freaking problem?" said one dude as he threw a dollar bill and three dimes on my tray. "You need a blast of coke or something?" He'd looked like every other spikey-haired, fake-blonde, Hugo Boss-wearing douchenozzle who namedropped from zero to sixty in three beers. But Debbie had put his name on the ticket, probably as a favor to me. His name was Eugene Testarossa, the one guy at WDE I'd wanted to meet for months. In my depression over stupid Vinny, I hadn't recognized him.

I stalked toward the bathroom on my break and bumped into a hard chest that smelled of sage green and fog.

"Monica," Jonathan said. "Hey. Sam told me he hired you." His green eyes looked down at me and I wanted to break apart under the weight of them. As he looked at me, his face went from amused to concerned. "Are you okay?"

"Fine, just a bad day. Whatever." I stepped toward the bathroom, but he seemed disinclined to let me go so easily.

"I got your report. Thanks. It was very professional."

"You assumed a waitress couldn't put together a sentence?" His glance down told me I'd been a bitch. He didn't deserve my worst side. I tried to think fast; I didn't want a barrage of questions about my life right then. "The Dodgers lost and I'm from Echo Park and all, so I got a little down."

"The Dodgers won tonight." His pressed lips and bemused eyes told me he understood I was half joking.

I shuffled my feet, feeling like a kid caught lying

about kissing behind the gym. "Yeah. Fucking Jesus Renaldo pulling it out in the ninth like that."

"He's got five good pitches in him per game."

"He tends to throw them in the bullpen."

"Or trying to pick a guy off." He shook his head. He looked normal just then, not like the guy behind the desk undressing me with his eyes.

"I'm sorry I was such a bitch just now."

"I'm used to it."

"No, you're not. Come on. People are nice to you all day."

He shrugged. "You lied about why you were upset. I get to lie about how people treat me."

"I'll keep that in mind."

"Yeah," he said, clearing his throat. "I have season tickets on the first base line."

I felt my eyes light up a little, and getting so excited over something someone else had embarrassed me.

"I could bring you sometime," he said.

"You haven't seen a Dodger game until you've seen it from the bleachers. Six dolla seats, yo."

He laughed, and I laughed too. Then Debbie showed up at the end of the hall.

"Monica!" she called out, tapping her wrist.

"Shit!" I cried out and ran back to my station, turning to give Jonathan a wave before rounding the corner.

I put on a smile and made myself as intensely personable as I could. I saw Jonathan at the head of the bar, talking to Sam and Debbie, laughing at some joke I couldn't hear. When I went to the station to pick up my tray, he looked at me and I felt his sight. He was gorgeous, no doubt. I could write songs about that face, those cheekbones, those eyes, that dry scent.

I wished he'd go away. I tried not to look at him, but he and Sam were still talking at one in the morning.

Debbie stood at the end of the service bar, counting receipts, when I came by with a ticket, and I couldn't take it anymore.

"I'm sorry I was talking to Mister Drazen in the hall," I said. "I used to work for him."

"I know."

"How often does he come around here?"

"He and Sam have been close since they went to Stanford together, so… once a week? Should I arrange for him to be here more often?"

My cheeks got hot. To Debbie, who read people like neon street signs, the blushing was visible even in the dim lights. I glanced at him across the bar. He was looking at Debbie and me. He lifted his rocks glass, a bunch of melting ice in the bottom. Sam had gone to take care of some late-night hotel business, and Jonathan was alone.

"Perfect," Debbie said to me. "You will bring him his refill." She hailed the bartender, a buffed out model who worked his body more than his mind. "Robert, give Mister Drazen's drink to Monica."

"Debbie, really," I said.

"Why?" asked Robert, pouring a glass of single malt from a shelf so high I would have needed a cherry picker to reach it. "I'm not pretty enough?"

"You're plenty pretty," Debbie said. "Now do it." She put her hand on my forearm and spoke quietly. "You need more practice dealing with his social class. For you, as a person. Getting used to it will only benefit you. Now go."

Being mothered was nice, I guess. My mother had been more or less absent since I went to high school, which was about when she and Dad moved to Castaic. I never felt abandoned, but I could have used a hand with the day to day bullshit.

Drazen watched me come around the bar with his

scotch. I wondered if he knew that made me uncomfortable or if he even gave it a thought. I wondered if the difference in our relative positions bothered him or turned him on. He was a bazillionaire and a customer. I was a waitress with two nickels making heat. This had to be a turn on.

"Thanks," he said when I placed the napkin and drink on the bar, a job Robert could have done in half the time.

"You're welcome."

We looked at each other for a second or ten. I had nothing to add to the conversation, but his magnetic pull made words irrelevant. I was stepping away to leave when he said, "I meant it, about seeing a game."

"I meant it about the bleachers."

"I like to get to know someone before they drag me out past centerfield." He clinked his ice against the sides of his glass. "The company has to be pretty engaging that far from the plate."

I wanted to mention the stunning color of his eyes. I wanted to touch his hand as it rested on the edges of the bar. Instead I said, "Your fellow fans keep you on your toes, especially if you wear red."

"Can I see you after work?"

The clattering noise in my chest must have been audible. It wasn't that I hadn't been asked out or the object of a proposition in the last year and a half; all of the men who wanted me were simply too easy to politely reject. If I had a brain in my head, I would reject Jonathan Drazen right out of hand. Politely.

"Maybe," I said. "Company's got to be pretty engaging at two thirty in the morning."

Sam showed up, and since I didn't want to be seen talking up my ex-boss, I walked away without confirming that he'd feel engaging at that ungodly hour.

CHAPTER 7

I spent the next hour and a half talking myself out of meeting with Jonathan after work, if he even showed. He was going to be a distraction, I could tell. I couldn't be in the same room with him without feeling like I needed to touch him.

I thought about Kevin. A fine specimen of a man, he'd had much the same effect on me as Jonathan Drazen, complete with fluttery stomach and tingling cheeks.

I'd been with Darren over six years when he admitted to kissing Dana Fasano. We were in the process of either breaking up or getting married. I went to a party downtown with a friend whose name eluded me right then, and there he was. Kevin was talking to some girl in the corner, and when he glanced over her head, his eyes found mine like he was looking for them. I froze in place. He had brown eyes and thick black lashes, and when we saw each other, the distance between us became a plucked cello string, vibrating, making a beautiful sound.

I didn't see him again for another half an hour, yet I had felt him circling me, tethered, even when we talked to different people. Finally, in the crowded kitchen, he was behind me, and I knew it because I could feel him before I even saw him reach over me to slide a beer from the sink.

"Hi," he said.

"Hi."

He held the beer bottle toward me, his hands slick on the glass, cold water pooling in the crevice between his skin and the bottle. "Is the opener over there?"

I took the bottle from him, overreaching, as I'd done with Drazen, so I could touch his cool, wet hand. Then I put the bottle cap on the metal edge of the counter and pulled down swiftly. The cap bent and popped off, clinking to the floor. I held up the bottle for him. "Here you go."

"Thanks." He considered the bottle, then me. "See that girl over there?" He pointed at a girl about my age with short, dark hair and striped leggings.

"Yeah."

"In twenty seconds, she's going to come over here and ask what I'm working on for my show. I don't want to tell her."

"So don't."

As if on cue, the girl saw Kevin and walked over. It was the first time I experienced him as a charmed person, and it would not be the last.

"It would be better if she didn't ask. My paintings are secret before a show. If I tell her, she'll own them. Her soul will own them. I can't explain it." The kitchen was crowded, slowing the striped leggings' progress and pushing us together, forcing us to whisper.

"I get it," I said. I would have gotten anything he said at that point. I would have claimed to understand quantum mechanics if he explained it to me. "They aren't born yet," I continued. "If she sees them while they're being made, she knows them as children. Their insides."

"My God, you get me."

I had no snappy reply. I wanted to get him. I wanted to get everything he said from now on. He touched my chin. "If I kiss you, she'll turn around and go away."

In retrospect, that was the lamest come-on imaginable from him. He'd done much better in the year following. But at the party, the word "kiss" breathed from his beautiful lips, was all I needed. I put my hand on his shoulder, and he slipped one around my waist. Our lips met, and I held back a groan of pleasure. I'd only ever been with Darren, and I loved him. I would always love him, but kissing that man, like that, with his taste of malt and chocolate, uncovered physical sensations I didn't know could come from a kiss. I felt every pore of his tongue, every turn of his lips. The world shut off and my identity became a glow of sexual desire.

I went home barely able to walk from wanting him and completed my breakup with Darren the next day. If desire was supposed to feel like that, I needed more of it. I felt awake, alive, not just sexy, but sexual. Thoughts of him infected me until I saw him again and we tumbled into bed, screwing like wild animals.

When I finally walked away from him, weeping, I realized I'd let my sexuality control and manipulate me through him. He took my music and crushed it under the weight of his own talent. He ignored what I created, dismissing it, degenerating it, so that within three months, I couldn't sing a word and any instrument I picked up became a bludgeon. I'd never felt so creatively dead and so sexually alive.

When I got the strength to walk away from him, I vowed never again.

CHAPTER 8

$\mathcal{I}$ snapped my locker closed, thinking about those Dodger seats on the first base line. A corporation gets a skybox. A real fan gets tickets at field level, luxuries be damned. I'd never seen a game from that angle.

Debbie came into the locker room, buzzing with talk and flirting and locker doors banging, and handed out our tip envelopes. "A good night for everyone," she said, then got close to me. "Someone is waiting for you at the front exit. If you want to avoid him, go through the parking lot, but be nice. He's a friend of the hotel."

"Can I ask you something?"

"Quickly, I have to count out."

"How many drinks did he have?" I asked as quietly as I could.

Debbie smiled as if I'd asked the exact right question. "Two. He nurses like a baby."

"I know you don't know me that well yet, but... would going out the front be a mistake?"

"Only if you take it too seriously."

"Thanks."

Debbie walked off to hand out the rest of the envelopes. What she said had been a relief, actually. It made the boundaries that much clearer. I could hang out, be close to him and feel the buzz of sex between us, but I had to be careful about climbing into bed with him. Fair warning.

CHAPTER 9

*J*onathan stood in the lobby, talking to Sam, laughing like an old buddy. I wasn't going to approach him with my boss right there. Sam seemed like a fine guy for the fifteen minutes we'd talked. With his white hair and slim build, he looked like a newscaster and had an all-business attitude. I just pushed through the revolving doors, figuring fate had lent a hand in deciding whether or not I'd see Drazen outside a rooftop bar.

I was three steps into the hot night when I heard him call my name.

"You stalking me?" I asked, slowing my steps to the parking lot.

"Just wanted company to walk to my car."

We strolled down Flower Street, the long way to the underground parking lot. Any normal person would have gone through the hotel.

"How do you know Sam?" I asked.

"He introduced me to my ex-wife, which I'm trying not to hold against him."

"You're a good sport," I said. "Have you always been blue?"

He tilted his head a few degrees.

"Dodger fan," I said. "I would've taken you for more of an Angels guy."

"Ah. Because I have money?"

"Kind of."

"I like a little grit," he said, that smile lighting up the night.

"Is that why you met me after work?" I asked, turning toward the parking lot entrance.

"Kind of."

He let me go first into the underground passage, and I felt his eyes on me as I walked. It was not an uncomfortable feeling. When we got to the bottom of the ramp, we stopped. I parked in the employee level and his car was in the valet section. I held up my hand to wave good-bye.

"It was nice to talk to you," I said.

"You too."

We faced each other, walking backward in opposite directions.

"See you around," I said.

"Okay." He waved, tall and beautiful in the flat light and grey parking lot.

"Take care."

"What do I have to say?"

"You have to say please," I said.

"Please."

"Where do you think you're taking me?"

"Come on. Text a friend and tell them who you're with in case I'm a psycho killer."

CHAPTER 10

The early hour guaranteed a traffic-free trip to the west side. I'd gotten into his Mercedes convertible thinking most killers don't drive with the top down where everyone could see, so I just let the wind whip my hair into a bird's nest. Jonathan drove with one hand, and as I watched his fingers move and slide on the bottom of the wheel, the hair on the back of it, the strong wrist, I imagined it on me. I grabbed the leather seat, trying to keep my mind on something, anything else, but the leather itself seemed to rub the backs of my thighs the wrong way. "So, you pick up waitresses a lot?"

He smirked and glanced over to me. The wind was doing crazy shit to his hair as well, but it made him look sexy, and I was sure I looked like Medusa. "Only the very attractive ones."

"I guess I should take that as a compliment."

"You definitely should."

"I'm not sleeping with you."

"You mentioned that."

So maybe the rumors were true, and he was a total womanizer. Well, I'd already told him sex was off the table, so he could womanize all he wanted. Didn't matter to me at all. I was driven by curiosity. Who was this guy? What was it like to be him? Not that it mattered, I told myself, because again, I had no time for a heartbreak.

"What's your instrument, Monica? You said you were a musician."

"My voice, mostly," I said. "But I play everything. I play piano, guitar, viola. I learned to play the Theremin last year."

"What is that?"

"Oh, it's beautiful. You actually don't touch it to play it. There's an electrical signal between two antennae, and you move your hands between them to create a sound. It's just the most haunting thing you ever heard."

"You play it without touching it?"

"Yeah, you just move your hands inside it. Like a dance."

"This, I have to see."

When he tipped his head toward me, I thought, oh no. He wants me to play it for him. Never gonna happen. For some reason, the idea of this guy seeing me sing or play made me feel vulnerable, and I wasn't in for that at all. "You can watch people play it on YouTube."

"True. But I want to watch *you* do it."

I didn't know where we were going, so I didn't know how much of a drive we were in for. I wanted to get off the subject of me before I told him something that gave him a hold over me. I had to remember he was my new boss's friend, and I really liked working at the Stock.

"What do you do besides own hotels and pick up very attractive waitresses?"

"I own lots of things, and they all need attention."

He pulled the car to the side of the road. We were on the twistiest part of Mulholland, the part that looked like a desolate park instead of the most expensive real estate in Los Angeles County. A short guardrail stood between the car and a nearly sheer drop down to the valley and its twinkling Saturday night lights.

"Let's go take a look," he said, pulling the emergency brake.

I got out, thankful for the opportunity to uncross my legs, and slammed the door behind me. I walked toward the edge overlooking the city. My heels kept hitting little rocky ditches, but I played it off. They were comfortable, but they weren't hiking boots. I stood close to the guardrail, leaning against it with my knees. I felt him behind me, closing his door and jingling his keys. I'd been to places like that before. There were thousands of them all over the city, which was surrounded by hills and mountains. Way back when, before I'd even kissed Darren, I'd been up to a similar place to squirm around the back of Peter Dunbar's Nissan. And after the prom, I'd come up to drink too much and make love to Darren behind a tree.

"Do you live up here?" I asked.

"I live in Griffith Park." He stepped behind me. "Those bright lights are Universal City. To the right, that black part is the Hollywood reservoir." I could feel his breath on the back of my neck. "Toluca Lake is to the left." He put his hands on my neck, where every nerve ending in my body was now located, following his touch as he stroked me, like the little magnet shavings under plastic I'd played with as a kid. When the pen moved, the shavings moved, and I arched my neck to feel more of him. "The rest," he said, "is hell on Earth. Not recommended."

He kissed me at the base of my neck. His lips were full and soft. His tongue traced a line across my shoulder. I gasped. I had not a single word to say, even when

I felt his erection against my back and his hands moved across my stomach, feeling me through my clothes. God, I hadn't been touched like that in so long. When did I decide men were too much trouble? A year and a half since I shed Kevin like a too-warm coat? I couldn't even say. Drazen's lips were more than lips; they were the physical memory of myself before I shut out sex to pursue music.

I twisted, my lips searching for his, my mouth open for him as his was for me. We met there, tongues twisting together, his chest to my back, his hands moving up my shirt, teasing my nipples.

I moaned and turned to face him. He pushed me against the car. The hardness between his legs felt enormous on my thigh. He moved his hand down and pushed my legs open, gripping tight enough to press my jeans against my skin. He looked down at me, and the intensity of the lust in his eyes was nearly intimidating, but I was way past sense. Miles. The thought of saying, "No, stop, I need sleep so I'm fresh for rehearsals tomorrow," didn't even occur to me. He pushed his hips between my legs and kissed me again. I was hungry for him. A white hot ball of heat grew beneath my hips. We kept kissing and grinding, hands everywhere. I pinched his nipple through his shirt and he gasped, biting my neck. I hated my clothes. I hated every layer of fabric between myself and his cock. I wanted to feel skin sweating above mine, his dick rigid and hot, his hands at my breasts. I wanted those hard, dry thrusts to be real, slick, sliding inside me.

The siren blast split my ears. I almost choked on my own spit. Jonathan looked over at the police car and the tension in his neck was the last thing I saw before the light got too bright to see anything. I lowered my legs, and when he got off me, he held his hand out to help me off the hood.

"Good morning," came a male voice from behind the driver's side light. The passenger door opened, and a female cop got out.

"Good morning," Jonathan and I answered like two kids greeting their third grade teacher. He wove his fingers in mine. The female cop shone her flashlight in my face. I flinched.

"You okay, miss?"

"Yeah."

"Can you step away from the gentleman, please? Come toward me."

I did, hands out so she knew I wasn't reaching for anything. The cop pulled me out of earshot.

"Do you know this guy?" she asked, shining a little light into my pupils to see if I was on anything stronger than pheromones.

"Yes."

"Are you here of your own free will?"

"Yes."

"That was pretty hot." She snapped her little light down. "Next time, get a room, okay?"

CHAPTER 11

*T*hings cooled on the way home. I kept my legs crossed and his hand stayed on the gear shifter. When I told Jonathan the lady cop said we should get a room, he laughed.

"If only she knew who she was talking about," he said. After a few seconds, he stopped at a light and turned to me. "So, what's up with you saying you're not sleeping with me, then pushing up against my dick on the hood of my car?"

I was a little annoyed with the question, because he brought me there and he started kissing my neck, but I also couldn't pretend I wasn't just as responsible for the raw heat of the scene.

"I just…" I had to pause and think. The light changed, and when he turned his head back to the road, I felt like I could talk. "I have things I'm doing. I can't be up all night fucking because my voice gets messed up. I can't think about a man, any man, nothing personal, when I should be writing songs. Carving out enough nights for song writing, between gigs and working, is hard enough without making time for a boyfriend. So, I mean, I had to give up something in life, and it's men."

He nodded and thought about it. He rubbed his

40

chin, which had a little bit of stubble. My neck remembered it very fondly. "I get it."

"So, I'm sorry I led you on. That was careless."

His laugh was loud and inappropriate, considering
what I'd just said, but he didn't seem embarrassed.

"What's so funny?" I asked.

"You're taking all my best lines."

"Didn't mean to steal your thunder."

"No problem. I enjoyed hearing it."

I leaned back and watched the scenery change
from the twisted forestation of Mulholland to the
expanse of the 101. How did I end up in this car, at
four in the morning, with a known womanizer? Yes,
he was gorgeous and warm and knew all the right
places and ways to touch me, but really? How
stupid would I be? How many women had fallen for
this crap, and I was going to be another one in
line?

The wind made it hard to talk until he pulled off
downtown. "What's with you and sleeping around?" I
asked.

"What do you mean?"

"All the women. You have a reputation."

"Do I?" He smirked, not looking at me as he drove.
"And that didn't chase you away?"

"I trust myself. I trust my instincts and my resolve.
You just make me curious is all."

He shrugged. "What do you think your reputation
is?"

"I don't have one."

"Of course you do. Everyone does. When people
talk about Monica, what do they say, besides that she's
beautiful?"

I let the compliment slide. Coming from someone
who had almost made his way into my pants, it didn't
mean much. "I guess they say I'm ambitious. I hope

41

they say I'm talented. My friend Darren would say I'm cold."

"Did he try to get you into bed, too?"

"Shut up." He glanced at me and we smiled at each other. "I was with him for six and a half years, so it's not like he had to try for a long time."

"Was it a hard breakup?" He stopped at a light and turned his gaze to me, ready to offer me sympathy or words of wisdom.

"No. It was the easiest thing we ever did." I couldn't discern what he was thinking from the way he looked at me, but he got serious, draining his tone of all flirtation.

"Easy for *you*?"

"Both. It was dying for a long time."

He looked out his window, rubbing his lips with two fingertips.

"You want to say something you're not saying," I said. "I don't want to be your girlfriend, so being honest isn't going to come back and bite you on the ass."

The Stock, and my car, were a block away. He pulled up to the curb. He put the Mercedes in park but didn't turn the key.

"You really want to know?"

"Yeah."

"Why?"

"Because you make me curious."

He smirked. "My wife and I were married that long. It wasn't easy." He rubbed the steering wheel, and I re-alized he regretted answering even the first part of the question. It was too late for me to give up on him now, so I waited until he said, "She left and took everything with her."

"I don't understand. Are you broke?"

He put the car into drive and turned to me. "She didn't take a dime. She took everything that *mattered*."

I felt sorry and then I felt stupid for feeling any kind of sympathy. I wanted to hold his hand and tell him he'd get over it someday, but nothing could have been less appropriate.

"I'm kinda hungry," I said. "There's this food truck thing on First and Olive. In a parking lot? You can come if you want."

"It's four in the morning."

"Don't come. Your call."

"You're a tough customer. Anyone ever tell you that?"

I shrugged. I really was hungry, and nothing sounded better than a little Kogi kimchi right then.

CHAPTER 12

*J*onathan was right in mentioning the time. Four in the morning was pretty late, as evidenced by the fact that he found a place for the car half a block away. We walked into the lot, against the traffic of twenty- and thirty-something partiers as they filtered out, one third more sober than they had been when they got there, carrying food folded in wax paper or swishing around eco-friendly containers. The lot was smallish, being in the middle of downtown and not in front of a Costco. The only parked vehicles lined the chain link fence, brightly painted trucks spewing luscious smells from all over the globe. My Kogi truck was there, as well as a gourmet popcorn truck, artisanal grilled cheese, lobster poppers, ice cream, sushi, and Mongolian barbecue. The night's litter dotted the asphalt, hard white from the brash floodlights brought by the truck owners. The truck stops were informal and gathered by tweet and rumor. Each truck brought their own tables and chairs, garbage pail, and lights. The customers came between midnight and whenever.

I scanned the lot for someone I knew, hoping I'd

find someone to say hello to on one hand and wishing Jonathan and I could stay alone on the other.

"My Kogi truck is over there," I said.

"I'm going to Korea next week. The last thing I need is to fill up on Kogi. Have you had the Tipo's Tacos?"

"Tacos? Really?"

"Come on." He took my hand and pulled me over to the taco truck. "You're not a vegetarian or anything?"

"No."

"*Hola,*" he said to the guy in the window, who looked to be about my age or younger with a wide smile and little moustache. "*Que tal?*" he continued. That was about the extent of my Spanish, but not Jonathan's. He started rattling off stuff, asking questions, and if the laughter between him and the guy with the little moustache was any indication, *joking* fluidly. If I'd closed my eyes, I'd have thought he was a different person.

"You speak Spanish?" I asked.

"I live in Los Angeles," Jonathan replied as if his answer was the most obvious in the world.

"You don't speak it?" Little Moustache asked me.

"No."

He said something to Jonathan, and there was more conversation, which made me feel left out. They were obviously talking about me.

"He wants to know if you're as smart as you are beautiful," Jonathan said.

"What did you tell him?"

"Prospects are good, but I need time to get to know you better."

"Anywhere in that conversation, did you order me a *pastor?*"

"Just one?"

"Yes. Just one."

"They're small." He made a circle with his hands,

smiling like an old grandma talking to her grand-daughter about being too damn skinny.

I pinched his side, and there wasn't much to grab. It was hard and tight. "One," I said, trying to forget that I'd touched him.

We sat at a long table. A few trucks were breaking down for the night. There was a feeling of quiet and finality, the feeling he and I had outlasted the late nighters and deep partiers. I finished my taco in three bites and turned around, putting my back to the table and stretching my legs.

He took a swig of his water and touched my bicep with his thumb. "No tattoos?"

"No. Why?"

"I don't know. Mid-twenties. Musician. Lives in Echo Park. You need tattoos and piercings to get into that club."

I shook my head. "I went a few times, but couldn't commit to anything. My best friend Gabby has a few. I went with her once, and I couldn't decide what to get. And anyway, it would have been awkward."

"Why?" He was working on his last taco, so I guess I felt like I should do the talking until he finished.

"She was getting something important. On the inside of her wrist, she got the words *Never Again* on the scars she made when she cut herself. I couldn't diminish it by getting some stupid thing on me."

He ate his last bite and balled up his napkin. "What happened that made her try to commit suicide?"

"We have no idea. She doesn't even know. Just life." I wanted to tell him I'd found her, and been with her in the hospital, and that I took care of her, but I thought I'd gotten heavy enough. "I have a piercing, though," I said. "Wanna see?"

"I can see your ears from here."

I lifted my shirt to show him my navel ring with its little fake diamond. "Yes, it hurt."

"Ah," he said. "Lovely."

He touched it, then spread his fingers over my stomach. His pinkie grazed the top of my waistband, and I took in a deep gasp. He put a little pressure toward him on my waist, and I followed it, kissing him deeply. His stubble scratched my lips and his tongue tasted of the water he'd just drunk. I put my hands on his cheeks, weaving my fingers in his hair.

It was sweet, and doomed, and pointless, but it was late, and he was handsome and funny. I may not have been interested in having a boyfriend, but I wasn't made of stone.

When Little Moustache had to break down the table, we had to admit it was time to go. The sky had gone from navy to cyan, and the air warmed with the appearance of the first arc of the sun.

We got to his car before he had to feed the meter. We didn't say anything as he pulled into the parking lot at the Stock and went down two stories to my lonely Honda, sitting in the employee section. I opened the door with a clack that echoed in the empty underground lot.

"Thanks," he said. "I'll probably see you at the hotel sometime."

"We can pretend this never happened."

"Up to you." He touched my cheek with his fingertips, and I felt like an electrical cable to my nervous system went live. "I wouldn't mind finishing the job."

"Let's not promise each other anything."

"All right. No promises," he said.

"No lies," I replied.

"See you around."

We parted without a good-bye kiss.

CHAPTER 13

*G*abby and I lived in the house I grew up in, which was on the second steepest hill in Los Angeles. When my parents moved, they let me live in the house for rent that equaled the property taxes plus utilities. I was sure I'd never need to move. I had two bedrooms and a little yard. The house had been a worthless piece of crap in a bad neighborhood when they bought it in the 1980s. Now it had a cardiologist to the west of it and a converted Montessori school that cost $1,800 a month to the east.

The night Jonathan Drazen took me up to Mulholland Drive, I returned to find Darren sleeping on my couch. We had agreed to not leave Gabby alone until we knew she was okay, and she'd gotten no better after a week on her meds. The first blue light of morning came through the drapes, so I could see well enough to step around the pizza box he'd left on the floor and get into the bathroom.

I looked at myself in the mirror. The convertible had wreaked havoc with my hair and my makeup was gone, probably all over Jonathan Drazen's face.

I still felt his touch: his lips on my neck, his hands

feeling my breasts through my shirt. My fingers traced where his had been, and my pussy felt like an overripe fruit. I stuck my hand in my jeans, one knee on the toilet bowl, and came so fast and hard under the ugly fluorescent lights that my back arched and I moaned at my own touch. It was a waste of time. I wanted him as much after I came as I did before.

My God, I thought, how did I do this to myself? What have I become?

I needed to never see him again. I didn't need his lips or his firm hands. If I needed to take care of my body's needs, I could find a man easily enough. I didn't need one so pissed at his ex-wife he'd make me fall in love with him before apologizing for leading me on. He wanted to hurt women, and nothing froze my creative juices like heartache. No, I decided as I went back out to the kitchen, anyone but Jonathan.

Darren was already making coffee.

"Where were you?" he asked. "It's six thirty already."

"Driving all over the west side with I-won't-say."

"Mister Gorgeous?" He said it without jealousy or teasing.

"Yep."

"He's nice to you?"

"He wants to sleep with me, so it's hard to say if he's being nice or being manipulative," I said. "How's Gabby?"

"Same." He got out two cups and a near-dead carton of half-and-half. "She's volatile, then deadened. She started shaking because she wasn't playing last night. Missed opportunity and all that. Then she rocked back and forth for half an hour."

"Did you sit her at the piano?"

"Yeah, that worked. We need something to happen for her."

"She'll still be who she is," I said. "She could play the Staples Center, and she'd be this way."

"But she could afford to get care, the right meds, maybe therapy. Something." I nodded. He was right. They were stymied by poverty. "And Vinny? I haven't heard a damn thing from that guy. I tried calling him and his mailbox is full." He was losing his shit, standing there with a coffee cup in his hand.

"We have six more months on our contract with him and we're out," I said.

"She doesn't have six months, Mon."

"Okay, I get it." I held him by the biceps and looked him in the face.

"She's like she was the last time, when you found her. I don't want—"

"Darren! Stop!"

But it was too late. The stress of the evening had gotten to him. He blinked hard and tears dripped down his cheeks. I put my arms around him, and we held each other in the middle of the kitchen until the coffeemaker beeped. He wiped his eyes with his sleeve, still holding the empty cup. "I'm working the music store this morning. Will you stay with her until rehearsal?"

"Yeah."

"Can I shower here? My water heater's busted."

"Knock yourself out. Just hang the towel."

He strode out of the kitchen, and I was left there with our dripping sink and filthy floor. The roof leaked, and the foundation was cracked from the last earthquake swarm. It had been nice to sit in that Mercedes and drive around with someone who never spent a minute agonizing about money. It had been nice to not worry about anything but physical pleasure and what to do with it for a couple of hours. Real nice.

Darren's laptop was on the kitchen table, set to some Pro Tools thing he probably hadn't gotten a chance to touch in the middle of taking care of Gabby. I fixed my coffee and slid into the chair, opening the internet browser. We stole bandwidth from the Montessori school during off hours, so I checked my email. I remembered my conversation with Jonathan about his ex-wife, so I did a search for her: Jessica Carnes.

I got a different set of pictures than Darren had shown us the other day. Jessica was an abstract and conceptual artist. Searching under Google Images brought back a treasury of pictures of the artist and her art, which despite Kevin schooling me in the vocabulary of the visual arts, I didn't get at all.

Jessica had long blond hair and an Ivory Girl complexion. She might have worn a stitch of makeup and maybe used hot rollers. She wore nice flats, but flats nonetheless. Her skirts were long and her demeanor was modest. She was my exact opposite. I had long brown hair and black eyes. I wore makeup, tight jeans, short skirts, and the highest heels I could manage. And black. I wore a lot of black, a color I hadn't given a thought to until I saw Jessica in every cream, ecru, and pastel on the palette.

On page three, I came across a wedding photo. I clicked through.

The page had been built by her agent, and it showed a beachside extravaganza the likes of which I could only aspire to waitress. I scrolled down, looking for his face. I found him here and there with people I didn't know or side-by-side with his bride. A picture at the bottom stopped me. I sighed as if the air had been forced out of my lungs by an outside force. Jessica and Jonathan stood together, separated from the crowds. Her back was three-quarters to the camera, and he faced her. He was speaking, his eyes joyous, happy, his face an open book about love. He looked like a different man with his fingertips resting on Jessica's collarbone. I knew exactly how that touch felt, and I envied that collarbone enough to snap the laptop closed.

CHAPTER 14

J tapped my foot. Studio time was bought by the hour and not cheap, yet Gabby and I were the only ones there. She was at the piano, of course, running her fingers over the keys with her usual brilliance, but it was only therapy, not real practice. Darren's drums took twenty minutes to set up. The chitchat and apologies would take another fifteen minutes, and I still had to practice some dumb standards for the solo gig at Frontage that night.

I sat on a wooden bench facing the glass separating the studio from the control room. The room stank of cigarettes and human funk. The soundproofing on the walls and ceiling was foam, porous by necessity, and thus holding cells for germs and odor. Though I thought I'd rubbed away the ache Jonathan had caused, I woke up with it, and a good scrub and an arched back in the shower did nothing to dispel the feel of him. I needed to get to work. Letting this guy under my skin was counterproductive already.

I whispered, "I've got you, under my skin." Then I groaned the rest of the lyrics like I was in heat. No. But yes. It was a good song. It was missing how I really felt: frustrated and angry. So I belted out the last line of the chorus without Sinatra's little snappy croon, but a longing, accusatory howl.

"Hang on," Gabby said. She took a second to find the melody, and I sang the chorus the way I wanted it played.

"Wow, that's not how Sinatra did it," she said.

"Play it loungey, like we're seducing someone." I tapped her a slower rhythm, and she caught onto it. "Right, Gabs. That's it."

I stood up and took the rest of the song, owning it, singing as if the intrusion was unacceptable, as if insects crawled inside me, because I didn't want anyone under my skin. I wanted to be left alone to do my work.

Having the guys here to record it so I could hear it would have been nice, but I could tell I was onto something. The back room at Frontage was small, so I needed less rage and more discomfort. More sadness. More disappointment in myself for letting it happen, and begging the pain away. If I could nail that, I might actually enjoy singing a few standards at a restaurant. Or I might get fired for changing them. No way to know.

I did it again, from the top. The first time I sang the word, "skin," I felt Jonathan's hands on me and didn't resist the pleasure and warmth. I sang right through it, and when Gabby accompanied, she put her own sadness into it. I felt it. It was my song now.

My phone rang: Darren.

"Where the hell are you?"

"Harry just called me. His mother is sick in Arizona. He's out. For good."

I would have said something like, *so no bassist, no band*, but Gabby would have heard, and she wasn't ready for any kind of upset.

"And you're not here because?"

He sighed. "I got held up at work. I'll be there in twenty. Tomorrow night, I have a favor to ask."

"Yeah?"

"I have a date. Can you get her home after your gig and make sure she takes her meds?"

"Yeah."

"Thanks, Mon."

"Go get laid."

I clicked the phone off and used the rest of the time to work on our performance.

CHAPTER 15

Thursday afternoon shift at the Stock was slow by Saturday night standards. I earned less money, but the atmosphere was more relaxed. There was always a minute to chill with Debbie at the service bar. I liked her more and more all the time. I tried to keep it light and hold my energy up. Just because this gig tonight wasn't my own songwriting, I still wanted to do a good job. But after Darren's call and the sputtering dissolution of the band, I lost the mojo, and I just sounded like Sinatra on barbiturates. I had no idea how to get that heat back.

Debbie got off her phone as I slid table ten's ticket across the bar. Robert snapped it up and poured my rounds.

"I think he likes you," Debbie said, indicating Robert. He was hot in his black T-shirt and Celtic tattoos.

"Not my type."

"What is your type?"

I shrugged. "Nonexistent."

"Okay, well, finish with this table and go on your break. Could you go down to Sam's office and make a copy of next week's schedule?" She handed me a slip of paper with the calendar. The waitstaff hung around waiting for it every week as our station placement and hours determined not only how much money we'd make over the next seven days, but our social and family plans as well. And here she was giving it to me two hours early. She smiled and patted my arm before walking off to greet three men in suits.

I went to the bathroom and freshened up, then headed for Sam's office.

It wasn't a warm, fabulously decorated place like Jonathan's at K. It was totally utilitarian, with a linoleum floor and metal filing cabinets. The copy machine was in there, and I put the schedule on the glass without turning the lights on. The windows gave enough afternoon light.

The energy saver was on, meaning the copier was ice cold. I tapped start and waited. Lord knew how long it would take. I stretched my neck and hummed, then whispered, the lyrics to *Under My Skin*.

I gasped when I smelled his dry scent. When I turned, Jonathan stood in the doorway with his arms crossed. That was the first time I'd seen him in daylight, and the sunlight made him look more human, more substantial, more present, and more gorgeous, if that was even possible.

"Jonathan."

"Hi."

I realized the deal with the schedule copying just then. "Debbie sent me up here."

"You didn't know she was a yenta?"

"You're very persistent."

"I just kept telling myself I didn't want you, but we said no lies, and I think that includes lying to myself. How about you?"

I didn't know what to say. I had shut out thoughts of him for almost a week. I thought about baseball, chord progressions, and getting a new manager whenever he came into my mind. So having him in front of me was like opening a closet door and having all the stuff come tumbling out.

I took a step forward, and he did, too. We were in each other's arms in a second, mouths attached, tongues twisting. He reached back and closed the door.

Okay, I was going to get this over with now. Me and him. Right there. Just get it done so I could move on. He thrust me onto the desk and I opened my legs, wrapping them around his waist. He was pushing against me again, like on the hood of the Mercedes, a million years ago.

He put his hands up my shirt, across my stomach and to my breasts.

"Yes?" he gasped.

"Yes," I whispered. "Yes to everything."

"Yes," he whispered in my ear, then pushed my bra up and cupped my tits, finding my nipples and rubbing them with his thumbs. My hips levitated from the desk, and I made some noise deep in my throat. Damn, he was good. Lots of practice. He knew exactly what to do.

He looked down at my chest, nipples hardening from his touch and the cool air. "My God, Monica, you are magnificent."

I laughed, because being admired like that made me nervous, but he shut me up when he put his mouth on one nipple and his fingers on the other, pressing and twisting. My legs tightened around him, hitching my skirt up to my waist. With only my panties between me and his jeans, he felt harder and more forceful. He pushed against me, and I flowed with him, my hips to his rhythm as I gripped his hair. I'd almost come like that, eons ago, with some guy in freshman year I couldn't even remember now, and it felt like it might happen again.

As if reading my mind, he pulled away. His own breathing was heavy as he looked at me, not as if he was undressing me with his eyes, but as if he was making plans for the body in front of him. He moved his hands down my sides and pulled my skirt up, bunching it at the waist. My underwear bottoms, which I hadn't given a thought to when I'd dressed in the morning, were the only thing between me and the world.

"Listen," I started, "I don't know if Sam would think this is ok."

He put his fingertips to my mouth, and I shushed. Let him explain to Sam. Let me get fired. I parted my lips and took two of his fingers in my mouth, sucking them down to the back.

"Ah, Monica," was all he said as he pulled them out, slowly, and pushed them back in at the same pace. I cupped my tongue around them and sucked. Not too hard, just enough. I knew I was doing it right when his eyelids closed just a little, and he opened his mouth for something between a gasp and an *aah*. He rubbed them over my bottom lip, curling it back, then put them back in my mouth. I took them eagerly, tasting his skin, feeling his warm breath on my face.

He slid his fingers out and stepped back, taking his crotch away from mine. I suddenly felt exposed and started to close my legs, but he pressed them apart. I reached for his buckle, but he pulled away.

"I want to touch you," I said.

"Not yet."

"I'm going crazy."

"No, you're not. Not enough."

With that, he moved the crotch of my panties to the side and put the finger he'd just removed from my mouth onto my wet folds. We both gasped. Then he slid two fingers into me. Slowly.

"Oh, God," I whispered.

He slipped them out without a word and put his thumb on the thin strip of cotton covering my clit. Lightly. Barely touching it. Just enough so I knew it was there, and he leaned over to kiss me, flicking his tongue in time with his thumbnail as it gently scratched the fabric of my underwear.

I thrust my hips forward. His fingers went deep into me, but the thumb wouldn't press down any harder. It just grazed the cotton as he glided his two fingers in and out.

"What do you want?" he asked.

"I want you to fuck me."

"What's the magic word?"

"Now?"

His fingers worked my body while he bent down to whisper into my ear. "You have three minutes of break left."

"I don't care."

"I'm going to spend hours fucking you."

My hips pushed against his hand, but he kept control: a light touch of the thumb and a slow grind with the fingers. I was on fire. I thought I had known what that meant, but I didn't.

"After your shift."

"I have a gig right after. We have to do it now." He might have considered it for the next three thrusts, but he didn't give my clit more than a stroke through fabric. I couldn't decide if that was pleasure or torture.

"After your gig," he said. "I have a dinner meeting anyway. Meet me at the hotel tonight. Room 3423."

"I have to take care of my roommate."

"Figure it out."

He pulled his fingers out of me. I felt the loss of them and his tormenting thumb so deeply I moaned. Sitting there, splayed and nearly naked on Sam's desk, I felt foolish and exposed, not to mention ravenously aroused.

"Don't." I didn't have anything more to say, except don't stop there; don't leave me like this. My eyes must have pleaded with him for some release, because his face, with its parted lips and heavy lids, shone with a lustful satisfaction. He knew I wanted him to fuck me for hours, starting on that desk. "You are despicable," I said.

He pulled my skirt down, and when he leaned down to kiss me, I returned it with no little anger on my lips. "Too true. And tonight, you're mine."

"What if I don't show?"

"You'll show."

After opening the door as little as possible, as if to protect my destroyed modesty, he was gone.

CHAPTER 16

*J*had another three hours to work, and I couldn't keep my mind on the task at hand: pouring drinks. A moron could do it. First example: Robert. A hunk by any measure, but dumb as a post.

He slid the tray over the service bar. Each had the requisite alcohol as listed on the order ticket, clockwise from twelve o'clock, where he'd put the ticket. My job was to fill each glass with mixers from the soda gun and juice bin.

Like I said, a moron could do it. But I stood there, with Debbie next to me checking stuff off the inventory list, and I put soda in a whiskey. I stared at the glass and watched it over flow and why? Because the pain between my legs was uncomfortable and exquisite, and I was counting down the hours before I could get home and release it.

"Whoa!" Robert shouted, waking me up. "You got soda all over the tray!"

"I'm sorry!"

"Monica," Debbie said, slipping her pen onto the top of the clipboard, "come sit with me."

She pulled me over to an empty table by the kitchen door. We tried to keep it clear until the bar got too packed. I pressed my legs together when I sat even though my skirt was long enough. I felt like she could see my arousal.

Debbie placed her clipboard in front of her and leaned forward. "What's happening? You took the wrong order to Frazier Upton; you stepped on Jennifer Roberg's foot. That's not how we do service here."

"Why did you do that, Debbie? Why did you set me up to meet Jonathan upstairs?"

"I saw you looking at him the other night. I thought it would be a nice surprise."

"If you could avoid doing that again, that would be great."

"Of course. I'm sorry, I thought I was doing you a favor."

"You were. It's just…" I looked at my hands in my lap. "He's… I don't know." I felt suddenly embarrassed talking about a man's hold over me with my manager. I should have been mad at her, but in the world I lived in, she had done me a kindness, and it wasn't like he'd raped me. I'd loved it. I hated it ending when it did. "I just don't need to be with anyone right now. Or ever. I had this boyfriend, Kevin, a year and a little ago. He wouldn't let me sing. It was awful, but what I'm trying to say is, I don't want to be that person again."

"Okay." Debbie sat up straight. She pushed her long, straight hair out of her face with a single, French-manicured finger and got down to business. "I am going to tell you things you need to hear, but don't want to. Are you okay with that?"

"Sure."

"Jonathan Drazen is not going to stay with you long enough to care what you do with your spare time. He is very attracted to you, that much I can see. But he is in love with one woman, and one woman only."

"His ex-wife."

Debbie nodded. "When Jessica left, he begged her to stay. She wouldn't. He broke down at a shareholder meeting. It was ugly. He was humiliated. He's *still* humiliated. He won't put himself in that position again, I promise you. So if you like him, I suggest you enjoy yourself with him. He will treat you very well, and then you'll go your separate ways. He can be a valuable friend."

I nodded. I got it. I felt comforted, in a way, that I could meet him later, have mattress-bending sex, then go home without worrying. I knew I wasn't getting involved, and if he had the same idea, I was safe.

Debbie gathered her things and started to stand, but I wasn't done.

"Why did she leave?" I asked.

"Another man," she said, "and everyone knew it."

"Ouch."

Debbie nodded. "Ouch is right. It should never happen to any of us."

CHAPTER 17

I hated gigs like Frontage. I had to sing songs someone else wrote to people who weren't there to see me. I had to sing through waiters taking orders and customers being seated. I couldn't sing too loud or I'd disturb everyone, and I couldn't improvise at all. Ever. I was background.

But it was money, if not a lot, and it was practice. It wasn't as if Vinny had shown up and booked anything fabulous. It wasn't as if he'd shown up at all in the past two weeks. I simply had nothing else going on.

We had a dressing room with a smudged mirror and filth on everything. Sometime in the eighties, a tube of lipstick had been jammed into the seam between the two pieces of plywood that made up the counter, and the red goo that was out of reach of a folded paper towel had turned brown and crusty. The carpet stank of beer vomit, and the bathroom had been casually wiped down a few days previous. I felt like a superstar.

Gabby was already out there, tinkling the piano. She had a jazzy way of rolling her fingers across the keys, creating a melody from nothing, building on it, and landing into something else without a hitch. Her bag was open on the counter, and I did what Darren and I always did. I took out her meds and made sure she had one less Marplan than she had last night. Ten milligrams, twice a day. Eleven pills in the bottle. Darren had texted me this morning with the number twelve. Good.

I called him. He was headed out for another date with this girl whose name he wouldn't reveal.

"Hey, Mon," he said.

"Eleven," I said.

"Thanks."

"What are you doing tonight?" I asked.

"Date."

"Are you going to tell me her name?" I sat on the torn pleather chair, letting my short skirt ride up since I was alone. My hair was up, and red lipstick coated my lips like lacquer. I looked like a 1950s pinup.

"Not yet," he said.

"Is it an early date or a late date?" I swallowed hard. I was about to ask a lot.

"Maybe both. Why?"

"I wanted to…" I drifted off, because I wanted to meet Jonathan and relieve the ache he created, but I didn't want to get into too much detail with Darren.

"Ask. I'm shaving and it's messing up the phone."

"I wanted to see Jonathan Drazen tonight. After the gig. Right after. I can be home to watch Gabby by eleven."

"Can't. My date's boss got us tickets to *Madame Bovary*."

Great. A date including a musical would go from dinner at seven p.m. to curtains at eleven thirty. He must like this girl.

"Sorry," he said. I heard the water running.

"No problem." I hung up.

Eight months before I ever worked at K, I found Gabby sitting at the kitchen sink, on the high stool I'd used to get cereal as a kid. Her head was on the counter and one wrist had flopped over, spilling blood onto the floor.

I'm so sorry I messed up the floor, Monica, she'd said the next day, in her hospital bed. That was what she was worried about: That I would be mad I had to clean up the floor. I'd just ripped up the whole thing and put in new press-on vinyl tiles. I couldn't find another way to think about something besides how dead and cold she looked when I pulled her off the stool, or the blood trapped in the drain catch, or the way I'd screamed at her the day before for eating graham crackers in the living room, or the way she'd wept when Darren and I broke up, eons ago. I cried over cracking linoleum flooring because the ambulance had arrived a full nine and a half minutes after I called, and I spent them slapping her because it made her groan and I didn't know what else to do to prove she was alive.

So though I wanted Jonathan to treat me like his own personal toy for a few hours, I had to get Gabby home and stay there until the next morning, when Darren would show up.

The lights kept me from seeing any of the diners. I smiled at a bunch of silhouettes because even though I couldn't see them, they could see me.

Gabrielle hit the first song, *Someone to Watch Over Me,* then went to *Stormy Weather.* I had my groove on then. I sang with the feeling she and I had practiced, but as I got to the middle of *Cheek to Cheek,* I caught a whiff of cologne I recognized: Jonathan's. Someone was wearing his cologne, and the weight between my legs came back from the memory of the afternoon. I sang about his cheek on mine, about the scent and feel of him. *Under My Skin* came out like a seduction. I sang the words, but all I could feel was sex, the need for it. I begged for it with the lyrics, the snappy little Sinatra tune gone, replaced by a moan for gratification.

When my voice fell off the last note, I was ready for that hotel room.

They applauded, quiet but earnest. You weren't supposed to clap at all at these types of gigs, and I said, "Thank you" with an embarrassed smile. I was convinced they could see my arousal like a dark patch soaking through my dress. I looked back at Gabby, and she gave me a thumbs up. I think I must have been a hundred shades of blush. I put the mike down and the spotlights went out. The diners started up their conversations again, and I headed back to the shitty dressing room.

Jonathan was in a booth, staring at me.

Of course that was where the cologne smell had come from. The source. It wasn't like he'd gotten it at Barney's. If it wasn't a handmade scent, I'd eat my shoe. But I hadn't even thought of that until I saw him in a booth at Frontage with a gorgeous redhead sipping a cosmopolitan. He tipped his glass to me.

He leaned toward the redhead and whispered something to her. Right into her ear. Like tipping his glass to me and breathing on her in any ten second interval was perfectly okay.

I was going to run and get as far from him as possible. I couldn't believe what I'd almost done. I wasn't kidding myself into thinking monogamy was on the table, but I'd think a day would pass before he'd put his hand up someone else's skirt, or that he'd take the trouble to not shove it right in my face.

But instead of running away like a sensible person, I walked up to the booth. "Hi, Jonathan."

"Monica," he said. "This is Teresa."

I nodded and smiled, and she held her glass up to me. "That was beautiful."

"Thanks."

"You were incredible," Jonathan said. "I've never heard anything like that." I stared at him. Something had changed in his face. I couldn't pin it down. Softer? Was he tired? Or did Teresa have a relaxing effect on him? His happiness made me feel evil and sharp.

"I've never heard of a man trying to sandwich another woman between fingering me and fucking me in the same day."

Teresa, who looked as though she was one hundred percent lady, almost spit out a mouthful of her cosmopolitan. Jonathan laughed too. I personally didn't find any of this funny. I stepped back, and Theresa stood as well. Maybe she was pissed. Maybe her laugh was the nervous kind or maybe I'd just shocked her. But she was as composed as possible as she turned to Jonathan and said, "I'm going to the ladies'."

He nodded, then scooted over once she was gone. "Would you like to sit?"

"No."

"For someone who doesn't want to get involved, you have a way of being involved."

"Even I have limits."

"She's a natural redhead." His look was full deadpan, and though what he said had a hundred filthy connotations, the one non-pornographic one became apparent with the straight-faced look.

"She's your sister," I said.

"Two years between us. She'd appreciate it if you assumed I was older."

"I'm so embarrassed," I said. "I have to apologize to her."

"Are you going to sit? Or am I just going to stare at your body without touching you?"

I slid in next to him, and he put his arm around me, his fingertips brushing my neck.

"What are you doing here?" I asked.

"I was having dinner with my sister. No, I was not stalking you, though I have to say again, I think you have a gift. I think I felt a half a tear, right here." He touched the inside corner of his eye.

"Are you making fun of me?"

"No. I promise you. You were… I don't have a word big enough." He looked at my face, and I noticed his eyelashes were copper, like his hair. I was overcome by his presence. "Now I know what you're protecting by not getting entangled."

"Thank you," I said. "I appreciate that. I really do."

He ran his finger over my collarbone with just enough pressure to make me breathe a little more deeply. "Am I seeing you tonight?"

I tried to stay cool, but I wanted him all over again. "I don't think I can. I'm not avoiding you. I have something else going on. Tomorrow?"

He shrugged. He must have thought I was playing games with him, which he'd probably be exquisitely sensitive about after the cheating wife. But I wasn't playing a game. Not at all.

"I have a flight out at five tomorrow. After two weeks, you might forget me."

"I should do to you what you did to me this afternoon," I said.

He let out a short snort of a laugh into his whiskey. "You don't have the self-control."

"What?"

"You heard me."

"You're wrong."

"Wanna bet?"

"Yeah. I wanna bet."

He pulled me close and spoke so softly I could barely hear him. "You get me to beg for it, and tomorrow I will take you to Tiffany on Rodeo Drive where you can pick out anything you want."

"Anything?"

"Anything."

"And what if I don't? Which I won't, but just for argument's sake."

"Then you cancel whatever it is you're doing, and I take you back to my house, where you will obey my every command until the sun comes up."

"I am not scrubbing your kitchen floor."

He smirked. "That's not what I had in mind."

I hadn't noticed the piano had stopped until I mentioned the kitchen floor.

"I'll be right back," I said, getting out of the booth before I had a chance to explain that I wasn't ditching him or manipulating him. I'd let Gabby go off by herself, and I didn't know if she'd seen me with him and taken a cab home.

I ran into Teresa in the hall on the way to the dressing room.

"I am so sorry," I said. "I was rude and unbecoming."

"My brother's an asshole, so I don't blame you." She said it with a smile, taking my hand and squeezing. "We both loved your voice."

"Thank you. I have to go. I'll try to see you on the way out."

I got into the dressing room just as Gabby shouldered her bag.

"I was looking for you," she said.

"I was talking to Jonathan. You ready to go? I want to see him on the way out."

"He's here? Oh my God, Mon, he can help us get an agent or something. Another manager. Anything."

"He's not in the business, Gabs, please come on."

She tugged my sleeve. "Wait. First of all, everyone's in the business, even if they're not. Okay? And what are you hiding from me? What?" She was a few inches shorter and looked up at me like she could pierce me with her eyes.

"Nothing."

"Monica."

"I want to go home." I took a step toward the door, but Gabby leaned against it. I dropped my bag, giving in. "Fine, he wants to make this bet, and it has to do with sex, and I'm not hanging out with him tonight, I'm hanging out with you."

"Cancel with me."

"No."

"Why not?"

"Because Darren would kill me."

"God damn the two of you!" she shouted.

"Gabs, please. Give me a break."

"No, you guys won't leave me alone to take a dump and you think I'm too stupid to notice? Now you have the chance to get the ear of a major fucking player—"

"He's not—"

"Shut up. Because you don't know anything. He teaches business at UCLA where Janet Terova heads up the Industry Relations board, and you know who that is, right?"

I sighed. I felt like I was taking a quiz.

"Arnie Sanderson's ex-wife?"

"Eugene Testarossa's boss. Right. Him."

"Gabby, if something happened because I went to have sex with some guy I barely even know…"

She put her hands on my arms and looked up at me with those big stinking blue eyes, the ones that had rolled to the back of her head and could only be brought back with a slap in the face, and said, "I promise I will not try to kill myself tonight."

"Your word is the last thing I should believe."

"I tried to kill myself because I felt hopeless. You do this, I have hope. Okay?"

"You're whoring me out."

"Am I taking a cab home or not?"

I had to admit, the temptation was painful, almost physically so. Here she was, not only giving me permission to leave her alone and promising not to hurt herself, but pushing me out the door.

The exquisite ache between my legs grew to a distracting level when I thought about being with Jonathan. The afternoon's frustration had turned into a longing that seemed bigger than my body.

Right then Darren's face showed up in my mind. He looked disappointed and angry.

I pushed past Gabby and went out to Jonathan and Teresa, who had moved to the bar. He put his hand on the back of my neck when I got close enough, and I whispered in his ear, "If I win, you cancel your flight and see me tomorrow night."

"And no Tiffany?" he asked, smirking.

"Yes, Tiffany. If you win, I'm at your command until sunrise. And after the sun comes up, I'll scrub your floors." He laughed. I didn't know exactly what he was laughing at, unless it was the presumption that he didn't already have a team of people to sterilize his house, but I smiled back at him because it was a stupid offer and I knew it.

Gabby situated herself at the end of the bar and ordered something. I hoped it was soda. Alcohol's a depressant, and she could assure me she had hope all she wanted. I didn't believe she had as much control as she asserted.

"You drive a hard bargain." He put his drink down.

"And you're funny. I never know what's going to come out of your mouth next."

I had a million jokes about what was going in my mouth, but I kept them to myself as I pulled him into the back room.

CHAPTER 18

*T*he dressing room was locked. I was momentarily stumped, but I remembered there was another one for men. I took his hand and led him deeper into the back, passing the kitchen and backmost hallway, to the least populated part of the club.

"I'm really liking this scrubbing idea," he said as I pulled him into the second dressing room, which was as gross as the first, and slammed the door behind me. If he had more wisecracks, they got swallowed in a kiss. I ran my fingers through his hair, pressing his face to mine, then ran them down the length of his body. I pushed him onto the chair, which squeaked when he fell into it.

I kneeled in front of him, the industrial carpet digging into my knees, and opened his fly. I stroked the hardness under his boxers until I teased out his cock. It was rock hard and gorgeous.

"You ready?" I asked.

"You are really cute."

He held his arms out as if to say *come at me.*

I pulled up his shirt and kissed his stomach, which was hard and tight, down the line of hair, until I got to his base. I put him between my lips, kissed it, sucking the length on one side, then the other, running my tongue up and down the taut skin, tasting the sharpness of it. He took a deep breath. I flattened my tongue against the underside and ran it up to the end, then put the head in my mouth, sucking it on the way out. I tasted a salty drop of moisture on his tip.

I looked up at him as I slid it into my mouth again. His lips parted and he looked straight at me, moving my hair from my eyes. Perfect. I moved down, sliding the whole huge length of him into my open mouth.

"Oh," he whispered as I took him to the bottom. I moved my head up and down, taking all of him with every stroke, sucking on the way out, rubbing him with my tongue on the way in. I looked up at him again, going slow, letting him see every inch of his dick going in my mouth. I picked up the pace slightly, then gave three really fast strokes. He sighed and thrust his hips forward, jamming himself down my throat. I had him. All I had to do was slow down and tease him so close he'd beg me to finish him.

But he put his head back and looked at the ceiling, groaning deep in his throat. It was such a position of surrender, I couldn't do it. I couldn't stop. I was going to make him come way before he begged.

He was going to have me at his beck and call until sunrise.

I didn't like jewelry that much anyway.

$\mathcal{H}$e'd smirked when he'd given me his address and tried to give me directions, but I knew where he lived, give or take. He was up in the park, where the lawyers and magnates play. I remembered Debbie's edict to just have fun, but the fact I'd failed in my mission to get him to take me to Tiffany rankled. Not that I really had anything to go with the carats I would have made him buy me, but failure wasn't something I took lightly, especially if it meant I'd been weak.

The valet pulled up with his dark green Jaguar. "Can I drive you to your car?" Jonathan asked.

"I'm in the lot," I said. "It's fine."

He put his face close to mine, until I could feel his breath in my ear. "If you don't want to go home with me, I won't hold you to it. We can wait, or we can call it off."

"A bet's a bet."

He brushed his nose on my cheek. "You sure? I can be demanding."

"So can I."

He stepped back and smiled. "Not tonight, you're not." He moved onto the curb. "I'll leave the gate open

77

for you." He got into the car and drove off. I watched it head down La Brea, swaggering just like he did.

When I went inside, Gabby had already called a cab. I could smell a vodka tonic on her breath, but she seemed relatively sober.

"Are you sure you're going to be all right?" I said.

"Monica, you want to go, so just go. I'm tired of being babied."

And that was that. I put her in a cab and walked to my car.

My phone buzzed as I got into my little Honda. It was Vinny. Fucking Vinny.

"Where are you?" I asked.

"Vegas, baby." He was somewhere loud and unruly, yelling into the phone.

"We've been looking for you. The band broke up."

"I can't hear you. Listen, Sexybitch, you did a gig tonight at that shithole on Santa Monica?"

"Fron—"

"Eugene Testarossa's partner was there. Testarossa himself wants to see you. So you text me when you're up next, and I'll call him back and he'll show up. Bang! You're in."

"Vinny, I can't—"

"Text me, baby. Love you."

He cut the call.

What an asshole. He goes to Vegas for how long and now he wants his fifteen percent because I got my own gig? Oh no. That wasn't going to work. I texted him.

—*You're fired*—

I was at my car when the phone dinged.

—*Fuck I am. You signed a contract*—

—The band signed a contract.
The band didn't play tonight.
I played solo—

There was a longer pause, and I sat in the driver's seat waiting to hear back, my night of subservience forgotten.

—Good luck getting WDE to
take your call—

I shut off my phone. I wanted to throw it, but I couldn't afford to replace it when I smashed it into a million pieces. He was right. No one at WDE was going to take a call or email from me. They'd contacted Vinny. I wouldn't get past the first round of assistants. Their job was to filter out artists. I could sing *Under My Skin* a hundred more times and never get another opportunity like this.

I think I looked out the window for fifteen minutes, resigning myself to the fact that I had a manager I hated and distrusted, and he was going to take a chunk of money from me from now until I accepted my Grammy.

I started the engine, but I had forgotten where I was going. Then that weight between my legs came back. Shit. I had an evening of wild sex planned with a rich womanizer who liked cute broke chicks. I was worrying about Vinny Landfillian. Fuck him. I hated Los Angeles.

All money and connections.
He can be a valuable friend.

All I needed was a lawyer to unravel that contract, and I was about to screw a guy who must have had a hundred sharky lawyers on speed dial. All I had to do was let him boss me around all night. The pleasure would be all mine.

I put the car in drive and headed east to Griffith Park.

It was wrong. My mother didn't raise me like that. She raised a nice girl who cared about her body more than her career. I didn't know who that girl was or what she wanted out of life though. I knew who I was. And the only thing I wanted more than Jonathan Drazen's body was an agent at WDE.

CHAPTER 20

The houses north of Los Feliz Boulevard aren't dream houses. A dream house in Los Angeles has four walls and a roof and maybe heat, but no one can afford it. The houses up in Griffith Park are scenery. They're owned by other people, the people who live on the other side. Not nouveau riche rock stars and actors. Old money. Generations' worth of trust funds. Three thousand square feet was a palace behind ten-foot hedges. I drove up the winding pass. Never having looked at the addresses before, I was at a loss to find them. It was as if you were supposed to just *know* where you were going because you belonged there.

I finally found the address under a gigantic fig tree with a brass plaque next to it, announcing the tree's status as a protected landmark. The gate opened for me, and I went up the drive and parked next to the Jag.

I sat in the car and looked at the house, convincing myself I still had a choice between going in or going home. The house was a craftsman, all warm lighting and dark woods. The porch was as big as my living room, leading to a wide, thick door. It was closed.

I took a deep breath.

Bottom line: He was hot, he was charming, and he didn't want anything out of me but the same thing I wanted. Unless he wanted me to clean his bathroom. I took hours to clean a bathroom, and I wasn't cleaning his.

I slid my phone out of my purse and called Darren.

"Hi," I said. "How was the show?"

"Fantastic. What's up?"

"I thought you should know…" I swallowed hard. "I sent Gabby home in a cab."

"You what?"

"She's tired of being followed around."

"And where are you?" He was pissed. He sounded like he was in the middle of a street, with people everywhere.

"Griffith Park. I can explain more later."

"No, explain now why you let a suicidal woman go home alone when her meds obviously aren't working and she's showing the same behaviors she did just before you found her bleeding into your kitchen sink."

"She's fine."

"This is completely irresponsible."

He hung up, which was a huge favor. I didn't want to tell him *why* I'd ditched Gabby.

I got out and walked up to the porch. Stained glass windows bordered the door. The light on the other side was soft and inviting. *This would be all right. Just fine.*

I knocked so softly, he couldn't have heard me unless he'd been waiting. I needed to see if he'd found something else to occupy him or if he was looking forward to seeing me. That could set the timbre for what I could request in the way of a warm call to WDE on my behalf.

The door opened immediately.

He wore the same button down shirt and jeans he'd

worn at Frontage. His feet were bare, and in his right hand, he held a glass containing whiskey on ice.

I stood with my bag in front of me, which didn't stop him from looking at me as if he wanted to eat me alive. He leaned on the door jamb and swirled his drink. "I thought you weren't coming. I was starting to think I was losing my touch."

"This is a nice house."

He paused, and I waited. Despite the distractions of the past half hour, I was back to wanting to put my tongue all over his body. "All bets are on?" he asked.

"I'm yours to command."

He took my bag and put it on a side table. "Turn around."

I put my back to him. My car sat in the drive, next to his, the gate to the street wide open. He clicked the button on a little handheld box, and the gate slid closed.

The ice in his glass clinked, and I felt the touch of his hand at the base of my neck, then a tug as he unzipped my dress. "Jonathan…"

"No one can see."

The zipper went down past my lower back, and he slowly pulled it open. The sleeves slipped off a little when his hand, cold from the drink, touched between my shoulder blades. He ran his hand up to my neck, then over my right shoulder, pushing the dress off. Then he ran his hand to the left shoulder, until the dress slipped off and pooled around my ankles. I felt a breeze over my body. He slipped his finger under the bra strap. "Take this off."

I did, dropping it to the porch floor. He stroked under my waistband. He wanted that off too. I knew it, and I complied. I was fully naked except for my shoes, with my back to him.

"Face me."

I did. I'd never felt so naked in my life as he took his time looking me over.

"Hands behind your back."

I think if anyone else had gotten to command number four, I would have started laughing, but he wasn't anyone else.

"You doing okay?" he asked, stepping up to me. He put the glass to my lips and tipped it. Warmth filled my chest. It was good whiskey. The single malt I'd suspected.

"It's warm tonight," I said.

He put his face up to mine and whispered, "Infield fly rule. What is it?"

He kissed my neck as I answered. "When there's a force play at third, any fly hit inside the baselines, whether it's caught or not, means the batter's automatically out."

"Why?" He bit the corner of my neck and shoulder, and I gasped.

"To prevent an intentional error that would manufacture a double play."

"You are very real." He enunciated each word.

He drank the last of the whiskey and took an ice cube in his teeth. He put his face to mine and pressed the ice cube to my lips. I sucked on it, then took it from him, holding it in my mouth.

He took half a step back. I must have been a sight: naked but for my heels, hands behind my back, with an ice cube in my mouth. "And you are stunning," he said, lifting his glass. He put the cold base of it to my nipple, and I groaned as it hardened. He touched the other one, chilling it to a rock.

He bent down and warmed my breast with his mouth, sucking on the hard tip, pulling on it with lip-blunted teeth. I gasped, but couldn't open my mouth farther or I'd lose the ice. I guess that wouldn't have been the worst tragedy, but I knew the game was to keep the ice in my teeth. His attention to my breast made me groan, awakening the warmth in my crotch. The ice in my mouth melted, dripping down my chin and neck, tingling a wet path to my stomach. He licked the droplets that found their way to my breasts, warming cooled skin with his tongue. When I thought I couldn't take another minute of his attention without falling down from the pleasure of it, he stood straight and put his mouth over mine, sucking the ice back.

He crunched it and said, "Come on in."

I stepped past the threshold, and he closed the door behind me. The living room was impeccable in dark woods and Persian carpets. The bookcases were full. The whole place was the exact opposite of the cold modernity of his hotels.

Jonathan stood in front of me, watching my eyes take in the details of his house. The paintings. The stained glass. The clean corners and fluffed pillows. He kissed me again and, having forgotten the edict about the position of my hands, I put my arms around him. His hands warmed my back, his touch solid and strong. He kissed my cheek and neck. "Go upstairs. There's a room with the light on and an open door. Sit on the end of the bed. I'm going to lock up down here."

"Okay," I said because I needed to hear the sound of my own voice at the end of so many commands. I backed up, and he watched me as I turned and went up the stairs.

The room he wanted was right in front of me. There were other doors, all closed. I heard him banging around downstairs with locks and lights. I could peek in one room, just to see, then say I was looking for the bathroom, but the idea lasted the time it took for me to step into the room with the single, glowing lamp.

I sat at the edge of the bed. It must have been a guest

bedroom. There were no pictures, no personal effects, just a hardwood bed and matching craftsman style dressers.

He seemed to take forever, and just as I was about to get up and see if he was all right, I heard him coming, one slow step at a time, up the stairs.

He was still dressed and had a bottle of water. He held it out to me.

"I'm good. Thanks."

"You look uncomfortable."

"You took a long time."

He kneeled in front of me and touched my knee. "I'm sorry, Monica. Can you forgive me?"

Before I could answer, he kissed inside my knee. "I think so," I said. "If you keep doing that."

He looked up at me, all green eyes and messy red hair. He moved his lips up my thigh, spreading my legs. A tingle went up the inside of my thighs as he ran his hands up them, the edge of his watch made a light scratch on sensitive skin. He picked my leg up, and I fell back as he lightly kissed the outside of my mound.

"Ah, Jonathan," I whispered, stroking his hair. He spread my legs farther, kissing between them. He slipped his finger into my wetness, and I gasped and remember the afternoon and Sam's desk. This time was different. When I looked down at him, his eyes were closed with intensity as he flicked his tongue over my clit. I think I said his name again. He flicked again. He was so light with it. Like he didn't want me to come.

As if he read my mind, he stood up, undressing so quickly I had only a second to admire his body, with its light hair and perfect angles. He flipped a condom out of his pocket and got it on without missing a beat, then lodged himself on top of me, his dick like a rock and everywhere it should be except inside me. We kissed. He tasted perfectly of whiskey and desire. I wanted him. I wanted every inch of him. He was right outside, pressing in, the head of his cock a tingle at my opening. I twisted my hips to move him in, but he backed off, picking his head up to look at me.

"Please," I said.

"Not yet."

He slid his dick up my folds without entering me, rubbing the length of him on my clit, sending waves of pleasure through me. I was so wet, he slid back and forth. I spread my legs as far as I could and moved with him. I could come like this, but I didn't want to. I wanted him inside me. This would feel like masturbation compared to his cock being where it belonged.

"Please," I said again.

"Not yet."

"Jesus, Jonathan. What do you want?" My sex ached for him. It didn't feel empty. It felt full to bursting, a throbbing, pounding hunger filling my skin.

"I want you to want it," he said.

"I do. My God, I do."

In response, he pushed harder, increasing the pressure without entering me. "No, you don't. Not enough."

I knew what he wanted, and I was willing to give it to him. "Please. I'm begging you. I'm begging. I'll do anything you want. I'll be anything you want. Just don't—"

He drove his dick into me with a ferocity that shocked me and turned the last word into a cry. He stopped for a second, as if he'd been shaken by the violence of his initial thrust.

"Don't stop," I gasped. "Don't make me beg again."

He buried his face in my neck and fucked me, pushing inside, pressing his body against my clit, his cock rubbing with each stroke, until I couldn't take it anymore, and then he stopped.

"What?" I groaned.

"You want to come?"

"Yes. Fuck. Yes."

"Beg for it."

"Fuck you." I pushed his chest. I was on fire, so close to orgasm, nearly unable to think complete thoughts. He pushed himself in me once, then stopped. It was a burst of sensation between my legs, then nothing. I looked up at him. He was enjoying himself, and he could keep going as long as he needed to.

"Please. Fuck you."

"Close." He stroked again, a taste of what I could have. He went slowly, too slowly, moving enough to keep me hot, but not enough to get me off. I put a hand between my legs and he grabbed both my wrists, holding them against the mattress with all his weight, rocking his hips back and forth just a little.

I had never felt anything like that. It wasn't an orgasm, because I had not an ounce of release, only the firing nerve endings and blasting heat between my legs. I was sweating everywhere. Tendrils of hair clung to my face, but his hands held mine down,.

"I want to come," I groaned.

"I want you to come."

"Let me. Please." I said it so softly I didn't even think he'd hear me. "Please. Please. *Please...*" With every *please*, I got more desperate and more quiet. On the last plea, he pulled out of me and pushed back in, all the way, and then again, until everything went hot red. I said his name over and over, going limp everywhere, and still the orgasm went on and on. His mouth was at my ear, and I could hear his groan as I finally stopped coming. His arms wrapped around me, tightening as he came, a guttural *ahh* rattling his throat with each slowing thrust.

"Holy fuck," he whispered into my neck.

"Thank you," I said. "Thank you."

He propped himself up on his elbows and kissed my face from my chin, to my right cheek, to my forehead, and back down my left cheek, and to my chin again. His eyes flicked to his watch.

"Sun rises at 5:38 a.m. You're mine for four more hours."

"I don't think I can take four more hours of that."

"Don't sell yourself short." He rolled off me, and we just stared at the ceiling, letting our breathing get back to normal.

I had never experienced anything like that, not with Kevin and certainly not with Darren. I didn't know I could sit on the brink for that long or just how many brinks there were. I didn't know I could give someone else control over what I felt.

It felt as though, after that orgasm, I should have to sleep for hours, or I wouldn't want sex for at least a month, but neither was the case. I was energized, and I wanted it again.

"Where are you flying off to tomorrow!" I asked.

"Korea. I'm putting a hotel up in Seoul."

"Can I ask you a question?"

"Uh oh."

"Your house. You have all the original everything in here, and the hotels are, like, white and chrome."

"This house was built for a family a hundred years ago. It was a home. People want to feel like they're *away* from home when they go to a hotel."

"Right. That makes sense."

"I thought you were going to bail on me."

"I got held up talking to my manager. Ex-manager. Jerk-off." I tucked my head on his shoulder and ran my fingertips up and down his chest. I couldn't keep my hands off him.

"This the guy who disappeared?"

I propped myself up on my elbows and kissed his

shoulder and down his chest. I could still smell some of the dusty cologne past the sheen of sweat built up from our sex. "This guy from WDE was at Frontage and called him. He wants his boss to see me. But I fired Vinny, and now he won't give me the contact."

"Why'd you fire him?"

"Because he's an asshole. I'll find a way to get Testarossa to take my call myself." I worked my way down his stomach, over his hip bones, with my lips and tongue. I was aroused all over again. He put his hands on my shoulders.

"WDE? That's Arnie Sanderson, right?"

Arnie Sanderson owned WDE and was the single most inaccessible person in the world. Even his own clients had to make appointments to get a call, and regular schlub WDE clients, who were some of the top paid people in entertainment, never met the guy.

"Arnie Sanderson. Yeah," I said. Jonathan's dick was hard again already.

"I'll call him for you."

"I'm not about to suck your dick so you'll make a call for me."

"And I'm not making the call so you'll suck my dick. So, now that we've cleared that up, can you get on with it?"

I looked up at him. He smiled from ear to ear and put one hand under his head. I licked his dick's length with the flattest part of my tongue. When I got to the top, I slid the entire length of it down my throat.

He breathed a deep *ahh* and said, "Where did you learn to do that?"

"Los Angeles High School of Performing Arts," I said. "They taught me how to open my throat to sing. Then Kevin Wainwright taught me how to put his dick down it."

He laughed. "I'd like to thank LA Unified and Kevin Whatever for this moment."

I couldn't help but grin, which kept me from engaging in the task at hand. "I like you, Jonathan."

"Feeling's mutual, Monica."

CHAPTER 21

*W*e collapsed from exhaustion around five thirty a.m. Two hours later, I woke up with a sore sex and a dry throat. Jonathan's arm was draped over me. His breath came in heavy, slow rhythms. I looked at him sleeping, closely inspecting him for the first time. His copper-colored lashes fluttered under soft brows. Faded freckles dotted his nose. He was truly beautiful, and seeing him with those eyes, I realized I could easily fall for this man. I was walking on a precipice even letting myself stare at him for this long.

I slipped out from under his arm and went to find my clothes.

My dress and underwear were draped over a chair by the door and smelled like last night's whiskey and fresh porch air. I slipped into them and went into the kitchen for water.

I looked onto the backyard, with its dark green furniture and bean-shaped pool, sipping my water. I ran over the night in my mind, which was hard, because after a certain point, it just became a blur of skin, sweat, and orgasms. I must have said his name a hundred times, starting with me begging him to fuck me and ending with an orgasm he'd delayed eternally. When he finally let me come, it must have lasted fifteen minutes.

The first time he had thrust into me with such force, it was almost like he wanted to shut me up. Like he was saying, "here, take it, but please stop."

Please. I'm begging you. I'm begging. I'll do anything you want. I'll be anything you want. Just don't—

I was going to stay *don't stop*, but in a different circumstance, when the love of your life was walking out the door, you might say *don't leave.*

The buzz of a phone brought me back to my senses. I was making stuff up. The phone buzzed again. I didn't know if it was mine, but I located the source on the kitchen counter, plugged into the wall. Jonathan's phone, and it was facing up.

The caller: *Jess.*

Ex-wife.

Fuck.

I threw the rest of the water down my throat and put the glass in the sink. I had to go. I didn't want to get in the middle of whatever that was.

"Good morning," he said, sleep all over his face, T-shirt stretched over his perfect body.

"I took the glass from the rack and got water from the little thing in the fridge door. Didn't even open it." He shrugged, and I relaxed. He didn't seem to feel invaded.

"Can I make you coffee?" he asked. "I can scramble eggs if you want."

"No, I'm okay."

As I rinsed the glass, he came up behind me and kissed my neck, fingering my zipper. "How about another go?"

"The sun is up," I teased. I wanted another go. On

the counter. On the floor. His lips caressed my earlobe, and I leaned my head back.

He slipped the dress's zipper down. "You need to beg again. You're good at it." He kissed my back. I wanted to. I wanted to cry for it, one more time, before he became a memory. He pushed my dress off my shoulders with a perfect touch that rode between firm and light, a touch on a collarbone, maybe, like the one caught on camera from his wedding day.

"Your phone rang," I said. Stupid. Another go would have been nice, but it was too late now.

"It's always ringing." He reached inside the dress and caressed my breasts, nipples hardening at his touch.

The phone buzzed. His lips left me, and I knew he was looking at it. His hands fell, and a palpable chill filled the room. I cleared my throat.

"I think I need to take this," he said, zipping me back up.

"Sure," I whispered. "My shoes are upstairs."

I walked to the door, and when I looked back, he was popping the cable from the phone. His hands might have been shaking. I couldn't tell.

I scooped up my shoes from the bedroom floor and went back to the kitchen. He was on the patio, elbows on his knees, looking at the flagstones with the phone pressed to his ear. His hands gestured, but I couldn't hear him. It wasn't my business.

"Good-bye, Jonathan," I said before I slipped out the front door.

PART II
TEASE

CHAPTER 22

*J*onathan was master of my nudity, my positions, and my orgasms, and though the first screw of the evening should have satisfied any normal woman for the night, minutes after it was done, I wanted him again.

His dick was beautiful: proportional, with a head just the right size and a straight and hard shaft. I'd only seen two other dicks in person, and though I'd seen those two a lot, I wouldn't pretend I had enough experience to judge if he was as huge as he seemed. But as we talked and he stroked my hair, his penis got hard again, and I couldn't resist putting it in my mouth. Minutes later, he twisted my hips around, and we became a gorgeous ball of sweat and heat, sixty-nining with me on top. I took the whole length of him while he put his tongue into my pussy. He grabbed my ass hard, digging his fingers into my skin, and drew his tongue out, then stuck it in again.

"Jonathan," I'd groaned, kissing the head of his prick, "I'm going to come if you keep doing that."

"No, you're not," he said, giving my clit a peck before turning me around. He guided my body around until I was on top and facing him. He grabbed my ass again, fingers in my crack where it was sensitive, and pushed me down. His penis went flush with my lips, and he pulled me toward him, then away, rubbing my lips against the length of his dick.

I put my face to his, breathing on his cheek, and said, "I want you."

"You want what?"

"I want you to fuck me."

He reached into the nightstand drawer and got a condom while I rubbed myself on him. I rolled it on, my hands shaking. When I started guiding him in, he said, "I want to see."

I moved my hips up so I squatted over him. He looked between my legs and watched as I slid his dick into me. I put my knees back on the bed and moved up and down. He put his hand between my legs to shift my hips. My ass stuck out, and the triangle between my legs pressed against his cock, making my clit rub right against it as I moved.

I shuddered from the heat and friction. I didn't think I could keep any kind of rhythm, but I did, because I had to. He moved his hand to my breast, but I knew what to do. The way I held my hips was everything, and I'd never forget it. The direct clitoral contact, him inside me, surrounded by his smell and his voice and his touch made me blind to everything outside my pussy.

As if he sensed how hot I was, he rolled over and got on top. "You're close."

I couldn't answer. If I agreed, he'd probably have gone to do the laundry. "Harder," I said in a breath.

He pulled my legs up and apart and pounded me. I cried out, clawing at his back. He pummeled himself into me until I was about to come. I tried to tell him, but I didn't have any words.

Then he slowed down.

"Oh, God no," I moaned.

"Take it easy," he breathed in my ear, rocking so gently, so slowly.

"You're killing me." I hovered at the edge of climax. Tension and pleasure tugged at each other inside me.

"I don't know how much longer I'm going to last," he said. But he lasted, at that pace, until the buildup almost pushed pleasure over the edge. I thought, for a second, *I'm going to come without telling him, because he won't let me.*

"Please," I gasped, my resolve gone, "I need to come."

"No, you don't."

"May I? Please?" As much as I wanted to come, I wanted to ask even more. I wanted to beg for it. I wanted him to make me lose myself in him.

He pushed against me, and I groaned. He didn't answer.

I was supposed to know what to do. "Jonathan, please. Please let me come. I can't…" He put his nose to mine and looked into my eyes. I felt surrounded by him and safe in his attention. "I'm going to lose it…please. Please do it so I come."

"Do what?"

"Fuck me hard. Please. I'll do whatever you want. I'll suck anywhere you want. I'll be yours. It's all I have, but please fuck me so I come."

"Come then." He pushed into me, slowly but forcefully, and I felt my world tip over as he grunted and heaved with his own fulfillment. My hands went over my head and clutched the headboard. My back arched, and I must have screamed, because I felt his hand on the side of my face, his thumb hooking into my open mouth. He kept moving, churning his hips and gasping, and every push sent a new wave of sensation through my lips, my pussy, my clit, everything.

Warmth had shot up the curve of my spine. The

feelings went on and on with changing breaths and sensations. My voice wasn't my own, but the expression of a built-up explosive detonating inside me. When he bit me hard, at the base of my neck, another point of gratification had been found. The pain was a counterpoint to everything else, bringing me back to consciousness and reigniting my orgasm. I cried out again, pushing myself into his dick, feeling nothing but wetness and hardness and shocks of pleasure between us. I'd entered a timeless zone, and when I realized he was softening inside me, I slowed down, even as my orgasm took on a life of its own.

"Monica?" asked Debbie's voice, not Jonathan's.

"Huh?" I was at work. Early afternoon, Thursday. I had five full tables and a tray of sucked-dry glasses in my hand.

Debbie, my boss, looked at me with concern and a little irritation. "Are you all right?"

"Yeah, I was just thinking."

"About what? You just stopped dead in the middle of the floor."

"Nothing. I'm sorry."

"You have Ute Yanix on seven. Please, if you need a sick day, let me know. Otherwise—" She twisted her hand at the wrist to let me know it was time to get moving. I ran to Ute Yanix's table with a smile and an apology. I took the actress's order with a temporarily clear head that got muddied by thoughts of Jonathan's belly hair just three minutes later.

Two weeks ago before I'd met Jonathan, I felt like a normal person. I worked. I sang. I bitched about my manager. I took care of Gabby and drank a little too much. I pleasured myself maybe once a week if I thought of it. I went from place to place, daydreaming about winning a Grammy or ruining my ex-boyfriend's life forever. I didn't realize how much time I'd spent plotting Kevin's demise, but when I stopped, I filled the spaces with Jonathan.

After Jonathan, my brain seemed hard-wired for sex. I walked around in a state of constant arousal. The past year and a half had caught up with me like a train crashing into a wall. After the initial impact, the rest of the train kept moving, pushing into that front car until eighteen months of desire got squashed into two weeks.

The afternoon following my first night at his house, he sent me a text message from some lounge at LAX. He thanked me for a great night and made promises I didn't believe he meant at all, and then… nothing. I didn't expect anything. He wasn't my boyfriend. He wasn't even my lover. He was some guy I used to work for who happened to get me into bed after I'd spent a year and a half intentionally celibate. He opened a jack-in-the-box of sexuality by turning a handle I didn't even know I had.

He'd done a whole list of little things before that, naturally. He'd been confident and charming and vulnerable all at once. He had a way of touching me that felt like static electricity without the shock, and he made me come like no man ever had before. Scratch that. I'd never even made *myself* come like that.

The hot heaviness between my legs was why I ran home from work most days, shut the bathroom door behind me and masturbated like a thirteen year-old. I had trouble functioning outside of work, too. I'd sent my band manager, Vinny, a termination notice littered with typos, fielded a call from Eugene Testarossa's assistant mid-masturbation session and stopped eating. My friend Darren had started cooking for me and watching me like a hawk.

The only thing I could do better than ever was sing.

Fuck, I was on fire. Rehearsals with Gabby, my pianist and best friend, were almost as good as the sex eating my mind. She and I could do no wrong. I could make changes on the fly, and she went with it. Two weeks ago, I'd been ashamed to sing old-time standards at a dinner club, but the performances of the past two weeks had drawn the attention of the agents at WDE. That night, they were coming to see us. Our version of *Under My Skin* would send Sinatra running and *Stormy Weather* would make it rain in L.A. In my life, I'd never felt better about my work.

I just needed to keep my mind on the paying job.

"You playing again tonight?" Robert asked as he poured alcohol into iced glasses.

"Yeah," I said. "Late set."

"I'm glad I saw you last week. You were hot."

"Thanks." The compliment was about the extent of Robert's vocabulary, and I accepted it with a smile.

"You been okay?" he asked. "You just stopped moving for a second earlier. I wondered if you were going to fall over or something."

"I'm fine. Just a little distracted."

"Probably the music. Got your mind in the game." He winked and clicked his tongue on his teeth. He was a nice guy but a bit of a douchebag.

I took care of Ute Yanix and the rest of my tables, making a concerted effort to smile and keep my mind on my job.

Toward the middle of my shift, I saw Debbie talking to a big woman by the door. The big woman wore grey, pleated pants and a matching grey jacket with darker velvet lapels.

"Who's that with Debbie?" I asked Robert as I handed him a ticket.

"She doesn't look like a customer," I whispered.

"She probably has a script under her shirt," he mur-

mured, keeping quieter than the white noise of the instrumental trip-hop.

I swooped up my tray and delivered my drinks, took an order, and checked on the rest of my tables. I forgot about the lady in the grey suit until I went back to the service bar and saw her standing with Debbie, looking at me as though I was the reason she was there. Robert arched an eyebrow at me, and I told him to shut the hell up with my pursed lips and narrowed eyes.

"Hi," I said when I reached Debbie and The Rectangle.

"Monica," Debbie said, "this is Lily."

"You can call me Lil." The Rectangle had a genuine smile and feminine voice.

"Hi, Lil." I slid my tray onto the bar and pressed a damp terry towel to my soda-sticky palms before offering my hand. She shook it, but only for a second, as if the familiarity made her uncomfortable.

Lil handed me a small beige envelope that seemed only wide enough for a check. My name was scribbled on the front in blue ballpoint.

"It's not a subpoena, is it?" I joked.

"Nah."

I looked from her, to Debbie, and back. Lil gave me a short nod and said, "Thank you," before walking out.

"What was that about?" I asked Debbie.

"Yeah," said Robert, appearing like a bad penny, elbow on the bar, peering at my envelope. I smacked him with it.

"Take your break," Debbie said to me. "Maddy has you covered."

I took my little envelope to the back room, which had a few long tables, a vending machine, microwaves, and our lockers. I was alone. I opened the envelope.

Dear Monica,

Can you meet me at the Loft Club after work? I'd like to talk to you, at length, until morning if possible.

Lil will meet you out front after your shift.

If you can't make it, let her know.

—Jonathan

The print was tightly written with the same blue ballpoint. As though he'd dashed it off without thinking, or as if he had been in a rush. For the billionth time that afternoon, I counted the days since we'd last seen each other. He'd said he was going to Korea for two weeks, and it had been just about that. I put the paper to my nose and got his dry smell full in the face. A controlled scent, it was truly original.

I had no idea how I would get through the second half of my shift. I had a gig that night, and it was an important one. According to the assistant's assistant I had spoken to at WDE, half of their talent agents would be at Frontage to see me and Gabby, though she and I were still a nameless pairing. I had four hours between my lunch shift and my gig. I could squeeze Jonathan in. Making plans with him before the gig was foolish and reckless, but I wanted to see Jonathan Drazen almost as much as I wanted to play.

CHAPTER 23

*L*il waited out front, leaning on a grey Bentley in a loading zone. When she saw me, she opened the back door.

"Hi. Uh…" I felt weird getting into the car without knowing where I was going or who was driving.

Lil spoke as if reading my mind. "I'm Mister Drazen's driver. I'll take you there and back. If you're going to be out late, you can give me your car key, and I'll take care of your car for you."

"How?"

"Take it back to your house."

"How would you get back to your car?"

Lil smiled as if I was a seven-year-old asking why water floated down, not up. "I'm not the only staff. Don't worry. Please. I do this for a living."

I smiled at her, broadcasting pure discomfort, and slid into the back seat.

I'd never been in a car like that before. Darren and I had taken a limo to prom, but it smelled of beer and vomit and the carpet was damp from a recent shampoo. I'd ridden in Bennet Mattewich's Ferarri down the 405 at two a.m. He thought the ride bought him a blow job, but it almost bought him a slashed tire. We'd stayed friends, but he never took me out in his dad's car again.

The Bentley was huge. The leather seats faced each other and it had brushed chrome buttons I didn't understand without a crumb or speck of grime anywhere around them. The paneling was wood—real wood, dark and warm—and though the ride took about ten minutes, I felt as if I'd been transported from one world to another via spacecraft.

The car stopped on a dead end street in the most industrial part of downtown, somewhere between the arts district and the river. Next to the car was an old warehouse with a top floor made exclusively of windows. The side of the building facing the parking lot was painted in matte black with modernist lettering listing each tenant. No mention of a Loft Club or anything like it.

I'd seen enough movies to know I should wait, and Lil was at my door in two seconds flat, as if I was incapable of opening it myself.

"Go on in to the desk, and the concierge will take care of you." She handed me a cardboard rectangle the size of a business card with a few numbers printed on the front. The word LOFT was printed on the top, in grey.

"Thanks," I said. I walked up the steps and inside. When I showed the card to the Asian gentleman behind the lobby's glass counter, I was still convinced I was either in the wrong building or the whole thing was a cruel joke.

He checked the card against something written in a leather book in a way that wasn't rude but was somehow officious. I shifted a little in my waitress getup: a black wrap shirt and short skirt, from Target and the thrift store on Sunset respectively. I felt as though my clothes exposed me as an outsider or worse:

a liar and sneak. But he looked up with a smile and said, "Down this hall behind me. Pass the first elevator bank and make a left. I'll buzz you through the doors. There's another elevator at the end of the hall. Take it to the top."

"Thank you."

My heels clicked on the concrete floors. I shrugged my bag close. I passed the first set of elevators and made the left. A pair of frosted glass doors stood in my way, and I noticed a camera hovering above them. A second later, a resonant beep preceded a click, and the doors whooshed open.

Beyond those doors, the hallway changed. The lighting was softer and came from modernist chrome sconces. The walls were a softer white, and when I got close, I saw the texture was silkier, somehow more nuanced. The oak and brass elevator didn't look like a refrigerator, as most do, and it hummed in D minor and dinged in the same key before it whooshed open.

I stepped onto the floral carpet and hit the button that said *Loft* in block letters. The door closed, and the elevator took off without a sound. I closed my eyes, focusing on the force under my feet. The elevator's movement somehow added to the pressure between my legs that maybe had more to do with the fact I was seeing Jonathan than the perfect speed of the vessel I stood in.

The doors opened onto a room made of glass overlooking the city. I could see the library, the Marriot, the whole skyline, and the miasma of smog hovering over it all. The marble floors had a gravitas all their own and were buffed to a shine that didn't look cheap. The woodwork seemed to have gotten seven extra turns of the dowel.

The lobby was lightly populated with people speaking quietly. A clink of laughter. A klatch of young men in perfect suits. Leather couches. A chandelier as big as my garage. I couldn't take it all in fast enough.

"May I help you?" The woman clasped her hands in front of her and bent a little at the waist. Her hair was twisted in an unremarkable bun and was an equally unremarkable color. She smiled in a way that was attractive but not stunningly so. Even though she wore a blue Chanel suit, her job seemed to be to appear as unthreatening as possible, and she was very good at it.

"Hi," I said. I smiled because I didn't know what else to do.

She noted the card I'd crumpled in my hand. "May I?"

"Oh." I was so nervous I was being an ass. I was entitled to be there. I was invited. I had no reason to feel unworthy just because I didn't know where I was. I handed her the card and stood up straighter, no thanks to my thrift store skirt and two-year-old shoes.

She thanked me and looked at the card. "Right this way. My name is Dorothy."

"I'm Monica. Nice to meet you."

She gave me a courteous smile and took me down halls and byways. When I noticed how many outer walls had windows, I remembered how the building had looked from the street. Places all over the city looked mysterious and inaccessible from the outside, and that warehouse was one of them.

Finally, Dorothy stopped in front of a door. "If you need anything, I'll be your concierge. My number is on the card."

She gave me a white card the size of a playing card, then opened the door.

"Thank you." I didn't know if I was supposed to tip her or say anything in particular, so I just slipped in. Dorothy clicked the thick wooden door shut behind me. Two walls were made of windows. A third wall made of shelves included wine, glasses, a bucket of ice, and a wet bar. The fourth wall had a huge oil painting that looked like a Monet or a damn good copy. The Persian carpet looked real. Antique couches flanked a six-foot long coffee table cut from a single tree.

I had no idea what I was supposed to do.

I spotted a bottle of Perrier and two glasses on a small table on the opposite side of the room, against a window, and walked over to it. The leather chairs next to the table were worn in the right places and their arms were bolted with brass studs. An envelope with the word "Monica" printed on the front balanced between the two glasses. I slid the note out. Printed on the club letterhead, which was embossed with silver, was,

Five minutes late – Jonathan.

I looked at my watch, then poured myself a glass of water and waited in the chair, humming and looking at the skyline. I was looking forward to seeing him and feeling his touch, the curves of his body, the heat of his mouth on mine.

When the door opened, it startled me. I stood up, still holding the short glass of bubbling water.

Jonathan tucked his phone away with one hand and carried a briefcase in the other. I'd only seen him at night, naked or in casual clothes and late day scruff. I'd never seen him clean-shaven and wearing a three-button herringbone tweed jacket with a windowpane white shirt and a tie the color of coal. A black silk square stuck out of his left chest pocket. Matte black cufflinks. All that was really nice. It brought out the shape of his body: straight, tall, with shoulders that didn't need padding and a waist that didn't pull his front buttons.

"Hi," I said.

"You came." He seemed genuinely surprised and placed his briefcase on the short table by the couches.

"Lil didn't tell you?"

He stepped toward me. "She doesn't answer the phone if she's driving, which is most of the time." He stood a foot from me, and I felt his gaze on my face. "And in a way, I didn't want to know."

I leaned into him, breathing a little heavier, just to take him in. "I have a gig later."

"How much later?" He seemed to lean forward, too, though I couldn't tell if it was a physical lean or the spear of his attention.

"Later."

"Would you like to sit down?"

No, I didn't. I wanted to put my body all over his. Instead, I sat when he did.

He poured himself a glass of Perrier and leaned back. "How have you been?"

"You had a driver pick me up to ask me that? You could have sent me a text and gotten the same answer."

"What's the answer?"

"I've been fine. Thank you."

"Just fine?"

He wanted more. He wanted a way into a conversation about what he and I did really well. At least, that was what I was reading. "Fine," I said, "and a little aroused most of the time."

He smiled a true and genuine smile. "I think I missed you."

"You think?"

He leaned forward, putting his elbows on his knees. "I'm not going to pretend I missed you the way I'd miss someone I know very well. But, okay, here's an example. I'm in the office of the Korean Minister of Tourism. This is the guy who can approve the hotel or send me packing if I say the wrong word. My Korean is fluent, but not nuanced, so I have to pay attention."

I leaned forward as well. "You speak Korean?"

"I live in Los Angeles. Do you want me to finish my story?"

I wanted him to bend me over and fuck me, but instead I said, "Yes. Finish."

"He's rattling off numbers, and somewhere in there is a mistake that will cost me a fortune if I only pay attention to the total, but I have to translate the numbers and find the flaw. Like he'll say the permit is one, the fees are two, something else is three, and it all equals ten, meaning the mistake is four. He considers that his bribe, which I'm not paying. But the numbers are bigger, and he's talking fast so no one else in the room will get it. I can't keep my mind on what he's saying or who I'm paying because all I can think about ..." He paused as if he'd reached the important part. "All I can picture in my mind is spreading your legs."

I cleared my throat to keep from smiling, but my face still split in a wide grin. For a second, I wondered if he hadn't been trying to be funny, but when I saw his pleased expression, I knew I hadn't insulted him.

"I wasn't even thinking about sex," he said. "I mean, I was, but just that moment when I put my hands on your knees and pulled them apart, and you leaned back and let me do it. I kept replaying it. That moment when you *let me*. Couldn't add and subtract worth a dime. I'm sure I overpaid the man."

My legs tingled, wanting the pressure of his hands between them. I pressed my knees together, waiting for him to do what he'd fantasized. "Well," I said, "I've started sucking on ice cubes all day."

"Ah. The porch."

"I just smile until it melts. Debbie thinks I've lost my mind."

He plucked a cube from his glass. "Maybe you have." He reached out and put the ice to my mouth, brushing my bottom lip. I opened my mouth and circled around the edge. I flicked my tongue out, but he wouldn't give it to me. A drop of cold water trailed down my chin, and he took the cube away, popping it into his mouth and crunching. "I want you," he said.

My spine felt like a piano someone had just done scales down.

"I want to have you in ways that surprise me."

"I'll take that as a compliment."

"But I think we need clarity first." Nothing followed but him looking into his glass.

I leaned back and sipped my water. "Go on."

He tapped his fingertips together and looked out the window, stalling. I wasn't about to interrupt.

"I've imagined a hundred ways to say this. They all sounded like I was trying to hurt you," he started.

"Unless your dick fell off in Seoul, it can't be anything that bad."

He laughed and rubbed his eyes. "I'll say it straight. I love my wife. My ex-wife. Nothing will ever change that."

"Okay."

"I can't love anyone else."

I got it. We could like each other forever, but he wouldn't cross that line into love even if I did. I considered myself fair-warned. I had to let him know I was good with that, but I wasn't his doormat either.

"I don't want your heart," I said. "I want your attention for a few hours at a time. I understand I'm one of many women you carouse around with."

He raised an eyebrow. "How much carousing do you think I do?"

"A lot."

"Based on what?"

"Rumor. And pictures on the internet." My face burned red hot.

"The rumors are based partly on fact, I admit," he said. "But carousing's only carousing if I take them out. The pictures on the internet, I had my clothes on?"

"Parties and stuff." I couldn't look at him. I felt silly accusing him of being a whore with so little evidence.

"I have seven sisters. Most of them have been there for me since the divorce."

How many women had been in the pictures? Not a hundred. But I assumed they were like roaches. If you see one on the counter, there are fifty more behind the cabinets. "How many times will this sister thing bite me in the ass?" I asked.

He smiled. "They're a slippery bunch. All older. And protective."

"You're lucky. I'm an only. I attach to friends."

He put his glass down and slipped his icy fingers between my knees, but he didn't part them. A chill went up my thighs, to my belly, where the heat I'd been tamping for weeks raged. I could have closed my mouth right then, said nothing, opened my legs, and let him do whatever he wanted.

"I have something else to say," I whispered.

"Tell me."

"I'm a musician. It's what I do. You can't interfere. Even for the best sex of my life, you can't get in the way of one rehearsal."

"That's the last thing I'd do," he said.

"That also means if I start feeling as though my heart's getting shredded, even if you're being a pure gentleman, it won't matter. We're done. Even if you haven't done anything wrong. I don't have time for it."

He ran his palms along my thighs, then back to my knees, his thumbs grazing the insides. I kept them closed. I wanted him to open me. I wanted the pressure of his fingers on my flesh, and I wanted to resist, just a little.

"I have another thing I've been thinking about," he said.

"Go."

He put his hands up my skirt and slid his fingers under my panties as if they weren't even there. The intrusion was delicious, and my cheap knit skirt rode up until the triangle of my underwear was exposed. When he looked down, I felt like I was being touched again.

"I own your orgasms." He pulled me forward to the edge of the seat before I could respond. His move was forceful, demanding, and left no room for questions.

"I don't know what that means," I gasped as he slipped my panties off. He put his finger under my right knee and placed it over the arm of the chair. I let him. I wanted him to. The less I resisted, the more aroused I became, especially when he did the same with the left leg. I was spread-eagled on the chair. My skirt rode up, leaving nothing between him and me.

"It means," he said, running his hands up the insides of my thighs, "you come when I say. Not before. If I send you home without, you just deal with it until I see you again." He looked at me as though he wasn't sure how I'd react. His green eyes darkened in the afternoon light.

"My fingers reach, you know," I said.

"Honor system," Jonathan said, running a thumb on each wet lip, leaving a vibrating hum behind them, like a plucked string.

I groaned. Had it only been two weeks? With my butt sliding forward, my legs over the chair's arms, and my pink wetness under his fingers, I felt as though I'd been pent up much longer.

"Ok." I would have agreed to anything.

"Ok, what?" He knelt in front of me and kissed the

inside of my knee before running his tongue up my thigh. I touched his shoulder, and he grabbed my wrists, placing my hands on my knees. "Say it."

"You own my orgasms."

"And?" He bit down, deep where my thigh creased into sex. The pain was sharp and perfect. I lost words for a second. "When do you come?" he asked. His hands gripped my thighs, spreading my legs farther apart. It didn't hurt. It felt like surrender. It felt like giving myself over to his control. It felt safe.

"I come when you say," I whispered.

"I've thought about nothing but this," Jonathan said and put his tongue on my clit. He warmed it with his breath, not moving his tongue. I gasped and gripped the back of his head. He pulled his tongue away, and when I tried to push him back, he held my wrists in one hand. He sucked my clit, keeping my wrists in his tight grip. I was helpless under his tongue, the gentle counterpart to his rough hand. The tip of his tongue traced a line from my clit to my opening, teasing it, then sucking lightly. Warmth coursed through me. I threw my head back, breathing hard.

"Part of this," he said, moving his tongue back to my thigh, "is you have to tell me when you're close."

"Okay."

"You're very agreeable today." His green eyes looked at me over my crotch. I'd agree to anything that face asked.

"Next time, ask when I'm wearing pants."

He crawled up and kissed me, and I tasted my juices on his tongue. My legs were still spread, and he was still fully dressed. He let go of my hands to brush his fingers over my breasts. I reached for his belt with one hand and felt the hardness through his pants with the other.

"Let me," I said.

"Later."

"Now."

"I own my orgasms, too," he said.

"God, you are a greedy bastard."

He kissed me again, then stood back, staring at me. I started to move one leg down, but he held my ankle.

"Don't move yet," he said. Then he stepped back.

I saw his erection under his perfectly fit trousers, and he seemed disinclined to hide it. All he did was stand there, smiling, and look at me with my pussy out. I knew he wouldn't fuck me, and I knew he wouldn't let me come. Despite how unfulfilled that made me, because my body wanted him without a thought to any kind of agreement or rule, I knew he would draw our encounter out until I peaked with desire. I wanted him, and I'd wait as long as he told me to.

"It was a long flight," he said. "I could use a drink."

"And after that?"

"You said you had a gig." He kneeled again.

I hoped for a second he would put his tongue back between my legs and finish the job, but he gently took my knees off the arms of the chair instead.

"Oh, man," I said. "This orgasm thing is going to break me into a million little pieces."

"What if it's worth it?"

"I'm counting on it."

Jonathan scooped my panties off the floor and held them open while I put my toes through, then he slid them back into place when I stood. He was still kneeling, with his hands up my thighs, when he said, "Pick up your skirt." I did. He put his hands on my ass and kissed between my legs, through the fabric of my underwear. Nerve endings I didn't know I had fired like rounds of ammunition.

A million little pieces, for sure.

CHAPTER 24

"*W*hat do you drink, Monica?" Jonathan asked, as if realizing for the first time he had no idea. My mother would not have approved of our intimacy so soon, but Mom had never been at the raw wood bar in the lobby of Loft Club, either. She'd never seen the view of Los Angeles facing west, from downtown to the water, never been with a man besides Dad, never served drinks to seventy-five people a night or sung a note outside church. I stopped taking life lessons from my mother right about when I left my first love and started sleeping with Kevin.

"Same as you, actually," I said. "Single malt if they have it."

"I presume you'd like some ice to suck on?"

"You presume correctly."

The bartender, an old guy who looked as though he could mix a bull shot or Harvey Wallbanger without checking the book, scooped ice into two glasses and poured two fingers of MacAllan into each.

The room was huge and not too crowded. Mostly, the members wore creative class outfits, movie executives, talent agents, entertainment lawyers, ad agency people, and they all sat in square-cushioned armchairs around low tables. The waitstaff flitted between them, making as little fuss and being as unassuming and invisible as possible. I checked to see if everyone was out of earshot.

"How long have you been a member here?" I asked.

"My father got me a membership to the Gate Club when I turned eighteen. I moved over here a few years later."

Iggy Winkin, the sound guy at the studio, had a girlfriend who worked at Club KatManDo. It was probably the same kind of thing, and he said memberships ran about 35 grand a year. Obscene, for sure, but who was I to say? I was trying to get around to a different point entirely, and bringing up money would sidetrack the conversation indefinitely.

"They must know you in here," I said.

"Pretty much. The old guys. Like Kenny over there." He indicated the bartender. "He used to work at the Gate. Knew my dad. Told me stories I didn't want to hear."

"Like what?"

"You're full of questions."

"I'm trying to keep my mind off this feeling between my legs."

He leaned close. "Describe it."

I sipped my drink. I didn't have a single word or even phrase to describe the raw hunger of the physical sensation. I whispered, "Kind of like someone hooked me up to a bicycle pump and put too much air in. I feel overfull. It's your fault. Now, tell me. Kenny and your dad. Make something up, I don't care."

"Does it have to be true?"

"Honestly? No."

"My dad's a drunk. A passive, pathetic drunk, and Kenny poured him a few thousand gallons of vodka over three decades. His stool was at the end of the bar, right there." He pointed at a space occupied by a thirty-something year-old guy in a cream suit and blue tie.

"I don't believe it."

"That hardly matters. I want to hear more about what's going on between your legs."

"It's eating my brain. Your body just looks like a bunch of surfaces I want to rub against. I can't think in this state. IQ points are dropping off me. I can only speak in short sentences. Back to Kenny. How many times has he seen you here with a woman who wants to rub herself up against you?"

"Does it matter?"

"No, because it doesn't. And yes, because I want to know if I should steal a matchbook now or next time."

He laughed softly, covering his mouth. "I want to kiss you, but there's a guy here from acquisitions at Carnival Records and I don't want to embarrass you."

"Who?" I brushed my hair behind my ears and tried so hard not to look around that I must have looked everywhere at once.

"Eddie, hey," Jonathan said to a man behind me. He was Jonathan's age, bulky and handsome with receding black hair he brushed forward in a way that suggested he did it for style, not to cover a balding head.

"Jon, what's happening? Did you watch the game? We got killed."

"I can't watch anymore," Jonathan answered.

"Falling down on the job, as usual," Eddie said before he looked at me. "I'm Ed. We played for Penn together."

"Played what?" I was embarrassed I didn't know, but not too embarrassed to ask.

Eddie looked at Jonathan, then back at me. "You're not one of the sisters?"

Jonathan smiled, so I knew Eddie wasn't implying

anything terrible. "This is Monica. No relation," Jonathan said.

"Ah," Eddie said, holding out his hand to shake mine. "Sorry then. Nice to meet you. Jonathan pitched. I played the bench."

"Nice to meet you, Ed."

"Monica's a singer," Jonathan said, "but she finds time to follow the Dodgers."

"My sympathies to both of you," Eddie said.

"I'm from Echo Park," I said. "I don't know this guy's excuse."

Jonathan took mock offense, looking at his watch. "Don't you have a gig?"

I sipped the last of my scotch. The ice cubes were huge, so I couldn't hold one in my mouth for Jonathan's benefit the way I wanted to. "I do. The late dinner crowd at Frontage awaits. Ed, it was nice to meet you."

"Oh, that's *you*," he said.

"Maybe. I guess that depends on what you heard."

"I heard someone's taking the house down over there."

"I doubt it was me."

Jonathan put down his drink. "It's her. She's not as modest with a microphone in front of her." He addressed me, "Come on, let me get you down to the car."

We said our goodbyes, and when Jonathan walked me out, he put his hand on my back. My skin shivered where he touched.

"Thanks for that," I said in the hallway outside the elevator. "That guy, he's important in my world. You put my face in a good context."

"My pleasure, and just so you know, I wouldn't have said anything if you didn't sing the way you do."

The elevator was empty. I kissed him on the way down, not as a lead into sex, but because he'd moved me by talking about me the way he did. His arms went around my waist and cradled my back, his mouth returning my affections, matching the tone and substance of what I was trying to say. That he wanted my body was enough for me, but supporting my work was a new and different thing, and it required a different kind of kiss. I wished there were more floors, because the doors opened before I'd appreciated him enough.

Lil got out when she saw us approach. I had enough time to make it back to my car and get to Frontage early enough to get made up.

"After your gig," Jonathan said, "text me?"

"I usually go out after with my friends."

He looked me up and down as if he was eating me raw, just like he'd done and tried to hide the first time we'd met. Only now he didn't have to conceal it. "If you don't mind unfinished business, it's okay with me," he said.

I got into the Bentley, and he walked back into the club.

CHAPTER 25

*T*he dressing room at Frontage hadn't improved a single bit since my first night there two weeks earlier, but my attitude toward it had. We'd begun on a Thursday night, and they'd asked us back for Sundays and Tuesdays as well, until we dried up or found something better to do. Bitch and moan though I might, they paid in cash and didn't suck us dry for incidentals. After that first show, we brought people in, so they started feeding us dinner and slipping a few drinks our way after the set. I enjoyed being treated like something besides a piece of drink-slinging eye-candy or a desperate whore singing for nickels.

Gabby was already there, smearing beige under her eyes. Tonight was our night. WDE had booked a table. Rhee, the hostess, confirmed it was true, and at my request, she put them by the speaker on the left, which had the warmest sound.

"Did you check your seat for gum?" Gabby asked.

"No gum," I replied, clicking through the bottles and tubes in my makeup bag.

"Vocal chords attached?"

"I hope you get carpal tunnel."

"Bitch," she said.

"Snob," I replied. We smiled at each other through the mirror.

I'd met Gabby during my first day in L.A. Performing. I was tall but gangly and awkward. Glasses and braces, the whole thing. All the other kids seemed to know each other. They'd all come from a music charter on the west side, slipping into ninth grade at the exalted magnet as planned. I'd filled out my application and bussed myself to the audition behind my parents' backs. I informed them of where I was going to high school when the acceptance letter came.

So in that first week, while I was getting my bearings, Gabby and her crowd had themselves completely together. Totally unprepared for the competition, I was subjected to laughter that may or may not have been directed at the fact that I was off half a key, fell victim to broken guitar strings, and found a blue gum wad on my drum skin. During last period on my first Thursday, when I sat down on a stool and it broke under me to the music of everyone's laughter, I ran out crying.

The last person I'd expected ran out after me: Gabrielle. She laughed the loudest, stared the hardest, flipped her blonde hair with the most vigor. Before she fell apart at twenty-two, she was the most together girl I'd ever met.

"What do you want?" I'd shouted when she followed me into the bathroom. "Why are you all so mean to me?"

"What are you talking about?"

"You laughed when I fell."

"It was funny. I mean, you've been here a week, and if there's a broken chair or a guitar with a busted string, you pick it. The guys have a pool about when you're going to break your glasses in P.E."

I'd wanted to fight harder with her. I'd wanted to blame her for a week's worth of misery, but the fact was, I had chosen that guitar because it was blue, and I didn't check the strings. The gum did look pretty old, but I'd blamed them anyway, and I'd sat in that chair because it was far away from everyone.

"Everyone says you're a snob," said Gabby.

"I am not a snob. I'm a bitch."

I'd chewed the inside of my cheek for a second, because awkward girls weren't supposed to risk saying things like that to cool girls. After a second, she laughed, and I did too.

"Come sit with us at lunch," she'd said. "I think my brother has a crush on you, so… gross. Okay?"

She'd folded me into the in crowd from that lunch on, like a complementary voice in a symphony, just adding me as if I was naturally in the same rhythm and key, and my entrance simply hadn't been arranged for the first few measures.

"You calm?" I asked Gabby in the dressing room as she poked at something nonexistent on her face. She had to be. Since my night with Jonathan when he'd promised to call Arnie Sanderson, she'd been blissed out. The call had been totally unnecessary, but any light at the end of her tunnel was a positive.

"No, I am not calm." She giggled. "Look!" She held her hands out. They were shaking. Generally, one wouldn't want that in a pianist, but in Gabby's case, as soon as she sat down, her fingers and body would quiet, and she'd be completely on top of it. "I got everyone from school in. I called in every favor. And the whole gang from Thelonius? All here. Darren, too."

"He bring his new girl?"

"I have no idea. Do you feel strong on *Cheek to Cheek*?" We'd worked on a rendition that sounded as though Gershwin had been talking about more than a little facial contact. All the songs were shaking out that way, and it brought them in.

"We're good on *Cheek to Cheek.*"

"It's happening, Mon. Really happening."

"This is a long process." I took out my makeup bag and smeared back on what Jonathan had kissed off. "We're not signing any contracts in the morning. We don't even have a disc or anything."

"You said not to worry about that."

"I didn't worry about it until Jonathan introduced me to Eddie Walker as if I didn't know who he was, and if he'd asked me for a disc, I wouldn't have had one."

I watched her in the mirror and saw her eyes go blank. She was doing a calculation in her head, and she took a second to come up with the answer.

"Penn," she said.

"Yes, they went to University of Pennsylvania together, but do you know what sport they played?"

When Gabby didn't know something, she didn't pretend she did, so her answer came quickly. "No."

"Baseball."

She pushed her mascara stick into the tube slowly, staring at it. I could almost see her filing the information and cross-referencing it with every other piece of Hollywood intelligence in her head.

"Thanks for doing this," she said. "I know you didn't want to do a restaurant gig, but I feel really good about it, and I couldn't do it without you."

"Well, I was wrong. I should have said yes right off. I mean, the thing about performing is you have to perform, otherwise you're all talk, right?" I said.

"That's exactly what I'm saying. If we get WDE behind us, we can maybe start doing *your* songs."

I shrugged. My songs were rage-filled punk diatribes and wouldn't translate into the loungey thing I was doing with Gabby. If we landed an agent as a piano-driven lounge act, I had no idea what I would do with him. I couldn't go from eXene to Sade on a dime.

As a keyboardist, Gabby could play anything at any time, but I would be in a world of shit at the first hint of success working at Frontage. I had zero songs ready.

"I didn't tell you something about meeting Eddie today," I said, trying to sound flip.

"He cute?"

"Yes. And he'd heard about us."

"He was trying to get into your pants."

"No, he didn't know it was me singing here when he mentioned it. I mean, he did, but he could have just said something polite like, *oh, how nice*. But he didn't. He was all, *Oh, that's* you?"

"What did he say, exactly?"

"He'd heard someone was bringing down the house at Frontage."

"Some*one*?"

I got defensive. She'd gotten me through high school. I'd never abandon her. "He didn't phrase it like it was just one person. Could have been a swing ensemble from the way he said it."

Gabby tossed her sticks and tubes back in her little bag. "I'd better get out there," she said. "I have to warm them up."

We hugged like sisters, and I went back to making my face presentable.

When I told Jonathan he was lucky to have sisters, I'd meant it. I hated being an only child. I hated when my mother looked at me as if I'd somehow disappointed her by being her first and last, as if it was my fault they found cancer during the C-section. I hated being the only kid in the house. I hated being responsible for every success and failure of my parents' children. The attention was great, except when I wanted to die from it.

If anything happens to the only child, there's no backup. If she's a drug addict, all the kids are drug addicts. If she dies in a car accident, suddenly the family is dissolved.

In one way, I never felt right around people, and in another, I craved their company. I needed them too much. So I had tons of acquaintances, maybe four hundred people in a loose music-scene around Echo Park and Silver Lake. I could fill a club when I needed to, but outside the guys who wanted to screw me, I inspired no closeness in anyone besides Darren and Gabby, who were orphans and needed me as much as I needed them.

CHAPTER 26

I poked my head out into the restaurant. Darren was at the bar with a huddled group. I recognized them: Theo, Mark, Ursula, Mollie, and Raven. Darren was Mister Popularity. He could bust out an inside joke with anyone he met on the east side. He had an ear for language and a way of listening that gave him a vocal "in" with whoever was in earshot.

I didn't see a girl I didn't recognize, so he either came without her or I knew her. I deliberately didn't look at the table by the warm speaker. I didn't want to see if they'd shown or if it was a table full of assistants getting drunk on the company dime. I didn't want to see an empty table with a big "reserved" card on it. I didn't want to see anything at all; I only needed to feel.

I'd been drawing off the energy from my night with Jonathan for two weeks, and after that afternoon at the Loft Club, I felt renewed and concerned. I couldn't let myself depend on him getting me all hot and bothered so I could sing to the throb between my legs. I had no idea how much longer he'd drag me around by the panties, but it surely wouldn't be long enough to make a career.

Rhee stood by the door at the opposite side of the

room, hair up, a big smile her default setting. A black woman in her forties, she didn't look a day over thirty. She winked when she saw me and tilted her head to the table by the warm speaker, which I couldn't see from where I stood.

It was go time, as my dad would say.

The management always put fifteen minutes at the beginning of the schedule for the talent to walk around doing a meet and greet. My disdain for that type of gig had evaporated when I realized what shrewd businesspeople ran the operation. My job wasn't to fade into the background as I'd originally thought, but to make the diners feel as though they'd walked into a place where they were known, and special, and wanted. The goal was repeat business, and though new customers were encouraged, the management found people who came back regularly were better tippers, better customers, and better friends than a constant stream of trend followers.

Gabby was already improvising something on the piano in the center of the dining room. Her eyes were closed. She wouldn't even know it was time to start until I put my hand on her shoulder in twelve minutes. Darren was in the middle of an earnest discussion with Theo and Mark, and I broke in to greet them.

"You guys," I said to Darren, Theo, and Mark as a group, "please look like I'm cheering you up when I sing, okay? You're talking like you're at a funeral."

Theo, who had Maori tattoos crawling up his neck despite being a skinny Scottish dude, pointed an unlit cigarette at me. "You tell him to get his sorry ass over to Boing Boing Studios. He's a man without a band. It's a crime."

Darren rolled his eyes, and I put my hand on his arm, speaking for him. "He told you he wants to mature as an artist before selling his ass to the man, right? He told you he wants to develop his process before he starts playing for other people's glory?"

"Oy," Theo said. "My ears hurt with this."

Mark cut in. With his narrow-lapel jacket and horn-rimmed black glasses, he couldn't have been more Theo's opposite. "You need to get in your ten thousand hours, buddy. That's the rule. You can't master an art in under ten thousand hours. Documented. You can't develop a process in a vacuum. Bank on that."

Darren looked at me with his big blue eyes. Poor guy. He and Gabby had enough to live on from their inheritance, but they couldn't do much more than live. The cash flow they enjoyed seemed to keep them from doing the things they needed to do in order to grow.

"Darren, try it," I said. "Be a studio musician for fifteen minutes. You're making a big deal over nothing."

Over Darren's shoulder, I saw a face I recognized, and though I took a second to put a name to her face, she knew me right away and waved, smiling.

"Thank you," Theo said. "Nicely done, lassie."

But my mind was on the woman in the green dress. "I have to go," I said, making my way to her.

Before I got half a step away, Darren grabbed my arm and whispered in my ear, "Behind you, at a deuce up front. Kevin."

"Fuck."

"Bad idea," he said.

"Can you get rid of him?"

"Nope." He smiled at me, our faces close enough to kiss. I'd left Darren for Kevin almost two years before, and though he forgave me, he'd never forgotten.

"Fuck. What do I do?"

"You go and act like this is your room."

Right. This was my room. Kevin was the interloper. I stood up straighter and continued toward the woman in the green dress: Jonathan's sister.

"Theresa," I said, "hi. I'm so glad you came."

She kissed each of my cheeks. "I had to, of course, since I was the one who told Gene about you."

"Oh, it was you," I said. "Thanks again, then. I had no idea you worked at WDE."

"I run the accounting department. Not glamorous, but it keeps me busy. This is my sister, Deirdre."

Deirdre stood close to six feet tall, and she wore jeans and an Army surplus jacket. Her auburn curls stuck out everywhere, and her eyes were as big and green as the emerald isle itself. They were also glazed over, with lids hanging at half mast. She was drunk, and dinner hadn't even been served yet.

"Hi," I said. "Nice to meet you."

She looked at me, then made a point of looking away. I was being ignored, and somehow it was deeply personal. I turned back to Theresa with a big fat smile. "I hope you enjoy the entertainment tonight."

Deirdre made a huffing noise, and Theresa and I looked at each other for a second. She seemed as embarrassed as I was as she said, "I'm sure I will. Come by the table after."

I thanked her and left. I looked at Rhee. She spoke with a customer, nodding and serious, her dark skin a flawless velvet despite her knitted brows. If she wasn't on me, I had a minute. Scanning the room, I saw Kevin sitting with his buddy Jack. Kevin waved me over with one hand and pushed Jack's shoulder with the other. Jack gave me a quick wave and vacated the seat. Apparently, I was supposed to sit there. I glanced to Rhee again. She held up five fingers. Five minutes left. Perfect. I slid into Jack's empty chair. Kevin didn't get up or pull the chair out for me. He never did.

"Nice to see you," I said.

"You changed your number." He gave me the sorry eyes. They used to put me in a state of panic that I'd done something to hurt him. His huge brown eyes, big as saucers, hung under eyebrows that arched down at the ends. He had the textbook cartoon sad face. His hair had that greasy hipster look, a perfect complement to the ever-short beard that broadcast he was above such trivial concerns as looking nice in company. I used to think that made him smarter, more intellectual, more spiritual, but really, he'd just hit a lucky triple in the looks department and made it to home plate on a force play.

"I'm sorry," I said. "You know where I live." I smiled because I wanted Rhee to see me engaging a new person, not looking like an alley cat about to defend a fishbone.

"That's stalking," he explained. "The fact that you didn't want to talk to me was enough of a message."

"Yeah, well. We're grown-ups, and that was a year and a half ago. So, I have four and a half minutes. It is nice to see you." I plastered my friendliest smile across my face as I delivered the last line, and he bought it. He took a sip of his beer and relaxed.

"I heard about you singing here. Everyone's talking about it. 'This girl at Frontage will make you cry.' As soon as I heard it, I thought it was you. My canary." I think I blushed a little. No. I *know* I blushed a little. With all his degradation of my music toward the end, I'd forgotten his pet name for me. The memory of the time he did honor my talents went straight to my heart.

"And once I thought about you..." He stopped himself and reached into his pocket. "I thought, man, I'd like for her to see what I'm doing too. Thought we could hook up again. Artistically. You know? As creators in this mad city."

He handed me a brochure. The Los Angeles Modern Museum had a Solar Eclipse show every time there was a full eclipse somewhere in the world. It was a group show of the moment's hottest visual and conceptual artists, and an invitation to show could open doors to new artists, reinvigorate the careers of established artists, and solidify stars in the historical lexicon.

Kevin's name sat in the middle of the list.

"Congratulations," I said. "Tomorrow night, huh? Have you hung it already?"

"Did it today. It looks amazing. This is my best work yet. I have one last invite, and well..." He made his deep artist face, where he looked away and made a pained expression before he blanked it off his face. "You contributed to my work. You were my muse. I want you to be there."

Either he had a new expression or he really meant it, because his face was nothing if not completely sincere.

"I'll try to come. I'm happy for you."

He smiled, and I remembered why I'd loved him. Not for the serious crap, but the smiles that lit up his face and my heart at the same time.

I caught sight of Rhee out of the corner of my eye and stood up.

"I'll put you on the list," he said as I walked away.

I walked to the piano and touched Gabby's shoulder. She opened her eyes.

I gave the flyer one last look before slipping it onto my music stand. Jonathan's ex-wife, Jessica Carnes, was at the top of the list. I folded it over.

Gabby started *Stormy Weather*. The room quieted, though I could still hear the occasional fork or clinking glass. I had to close my eyes against the spotlight. I sang it the way we'd rehearsed, of course, with the sexual longing intact, but something was missing.

Jonathan's ministrations that afternoon had done their work on my body, but my mind was on Kevin, and everything he said to me and didn't, every expectation I couldn't meet, every time I'd failed him with my own ambitions. My disappointment at the inadequacy of his love came in a flood.

I had nothing to do but use it because I started *Someone to Watch Over Me*. I growled it from my diaphragm. I used the breakup I'd caused, cutting me off from friends I depended on because I was the aggressor. I wasn't allowed hurt. I wasn't allowed to grieve. Without Gabby and Darren, I had had no one to love me during that time. No guarantees. No sisters to protect me from bad decisions or whatever predatory lover followed. No Deirdre to defend me. No one would shelter me or worry about me. When I found that emotional place, I roared the last notes of the song, getting rid of all the accumulated junk feeding the angry girl in my heart.

Then I felt clean. I went through the rest of the songs the way we'd planned, with the dynamics and inflections coming from the right place. We culminated with *Moon River*, our gentle send-off from the emotional roller-coaster of the set.

I breathed. And they applauded. I was getting used to that. I didn't get filled-up like a balloon anymore, probably because they weren't my songs. What they applauded over their dinners was my craft, not my songwriting, and that artistic distance made all the difference.

I nodded, glancing behind me. Kevin's table was empty. Typical. I thanked everyone, and just like every time before, I slipped into the dressing room. Gabby came in right behind me.

"What happened to you?" she demanded.

"What?"

"I thought you were falling apart at *Stormy Weather*."

Ah. I remembered. Gabby the perfectionist. "I pulled it out, I think."

"Every. Song. Counts."

"Thanks. No pressure, right?"

"This was not the night to find your footing, Mon." She pointed at me, accusing me of ruining the set.

"Hey, you know what? Lay off. And you might consider pulling your weight at the meet and greet. The Gabby I knew in high school didn't hide behind a piano."

I didn't wait for a reaction. I just walked out. I'd been underhanded and cruel. The Gabby I knew in high school wasn't coming back, not after the depression and suicide attempt. That Gabby hadn't shown up for years, and bringing her up was unfair. I was fighting with some core, self-fulfilling loneliness that made me push people away.

The room was crowded, with the bar area customers bleeding into the dining area. The servers had trouble navigating the people and tables and mislaid chairs. I made it to the table by the warm speakers and found it full of men in fitted suits with colorful ties and women in button-down shirts and spiked heels. Agentwear. Theresa had her back to me, and Deirdre, with her dismissive glare, was nowhere to be found. The eleven of them were having so many heated conversations in groups of two and three that I was going to pass the table and pretend I hadn't been on my way over.

"Monica Faulkner!" I heard my name and almost had a heart attack. Eugene Testarossa, who I'd been a creep to a couple of weeks before at the rooftop bar of the Stock, called out to me.

"Hi," I said, waiting for him to recognize me. From his expression, he either didn't remember me or didn't care.

"Nice set."

"Thanks."

"I'm Eugene. I'm a recording talent agent at WDE. You've heard of us?"

"Yes, of course." I was spinning smiles into gold, trying to keep from hugging a guy who, without his job and connections, wouldn't have gotten more than a courteous rejection.

"I'd like to sit and talk with you about something. Not a big deal. We're headed out to Snag. Can you come?"

A dream invitation. But no. I wasn't talking business over drinks. And if it wasn't business, I didn't want to be trapped at a douchebag bar on the west side.

"I have plans, I'm sorry."

He handed me a bright red card I knew had the WDE logo on it. "Call me then, and we'll set something up."

"Thanks. We hoped you'd come tonight."

"We? You've got representation already?"

"No, me and Gabby." I indicated her at the bar, next to Darren.

"Oh, the piano player? I thought she came with the club. Huh. Well. You don't gotta bring her if you don't want." My face must have been dragging on the floor, because he stood up straighter and held his hands out. "But no problem. Yeah, sure. Both of you. A set. We can talk."

"Great."

"Okay, you call tomorrow," he pointed at me, then put a phone to his ear. I smiled, but I knew more douchebag representation was in my future.

I started walking backward out into the aisle. "Will do," I said, nearly crashing into Iris, the waitress who'd been there long enough to be considered furniture. With one last wave, I went to the bar as fast as I could which, after the kind words and handshakes with everyone between Eugene Testarossa and Gabby, took about seven minutes.

"What happened?" Gabby was all over me. "What did he say?"

I showed her the card. She hugged me as if I'd just told her it was a healthy baby.

"Nice work." Darren held up his beer.

"Don't all huddle around the card, guys. Act cool, okay? It's not a big deal," I said.

"Ah, lassie," Theo said, "there's nothing coolish about you." He took my chin in his thumb and forefinger and shook my face. I playfully slapped his hand away.

"Let's go out," Darren said. "We can take every word you two said and give it major surgery."

Oh no. That wouldn't be good at all. I'd have to tell Gabby she was an optional part of the set or make something up I'd get busted for later. If she found out I'd had to rescue her before she'd even met Testarossa, she would spiral into Shitsville, and I didn't want Darren and me following her around again. Our recent freedom had been delicious.

"I made other plans," I said, glancing from face to face, landing on Gabby's last.

"Uh oh," Darren said. "Kevin's back."

"It's not Kevin," I said.

Gabby's eyes narrowed. "Cancel them."

"I don't want to. Tomorrow, you and I can call WDE. Testarossa's assistant will pick up. We'll make the appointment during lunchtime so he takes us out. Until then, you guys go out and have a good time. Come on. Give me a hug."

She did. Thank God, because I didn't know how much more convincing language I had in me.

CHAPTER 27

I texted Jonathan as soon as I got outside.

—*Are you up?*—

—*I'm on Asia time. Wide awake.*—

—*Me too*—

—*So, why aren't you here?*—

—*Coming*—

—*!*—

—*j/k*—

I'd been debating seeing Jonathan when a late night with the crew was the standard procedure. Testarossa had handed me the perfect incentive, but I'd almost wished he hadn't. I'd rather tell them I was ditching them to get laid than that Gabby's dream agent wanted to rep her as an optional attachment, or not at all.

I wouldn't abandon her.

I couldn't. I didn't know how.

She wasn't just my first lover's sister. They'd both become my family. We'd been through *stuff* together.

CHAPTER 28

I remembered where Jonathan lived, up by the historic fig trees. I had no idea how many cars he owned, but the little Fiat in the drive didn't look like his style at all. At ten p.m., he shouldn't have had any guests, but he stood on the porch with his arms crossed, talking to a blonde a few years older than me. She wore a printed, ankle-length dress and a loose jacket. He saw me pull in and waved. The blonde kept talking. I didn't know if I should get out or hide until she left.

That was ridiculous. I had a right to be there. I gathered my things and got out of the car. As if on cue, the woman turned and stepped off the porch, tapping something into her phone. As we passed each other, she glanced at me, but she got the phone to her ear in time to avoid greeting me.

"That was awkward," I said as I stepped onto the porch.

"Not really," Jonathan replied. "Or, I mean to say, not yet." He wore a sweatshirt and jeans, but not old, grey things. He wore designer clothes that were new at the edges and fit as they should, bringing out the beauty of his body without showing an inch of skin.

He looked behind me at the Fiat as it pulled out.

"Your assistant?" I asked.

"One of them." When the Fiat got into the street, he clicked a button on his remote box, and the gate slid shut. He leaned on the door jamb. "How did your gig go?"

"Fantastic. We're about to land a very good agent." I suddenly felt exposed, standing out on the porch again in a sleeveless, button-down shirt dress and heels.

"Oh, really." He put the remote on a table by the door.

"Really."

My dress had a fabric belt on sideseam loops. He pulled the bow loose and yanked the belt off. "Can you unbutton that thing and tell me the rest?"

"Is there some superstition about me entering your house with my clothes on?"

"I prefer you without them. And I like fresh air. Come on, I want to hear about your career." He wrapped the belt around his hand, which was muscular and square with a little hair on top.

I slipped my top button through the hole. "You want me to undress or tell you about the agent?"

"Yes to both. Tell me how it went."

I slipped the next button through, exposing the space between my breasts. "I almost screwed up the entire thing. I wasn't in the right frame of mind for the first song."

"My fault?"

"No. Actually..." I didn't want to bring up his sisters or my ex-boyfriend. Not with me getting down to my belly, and him watching the buttons' progress. "The agent wanted to go out tonight and talk about things." I finished the last button and stood in front of him.

"You could have gone." He stepped out of the doorway, reaching for the split in the dress. When he touched my throat, I lifted my chin. "We didn't have definite plans."

"He wants to ditch Gabby. I can see it. I'm not ready to tell her, and if we went out with him, she'd know."

He ran his hand down my body, only touching what the open dress revealed. "You think you can protect her from getting ditched?" He slipped his hand into the front of my panties. He stopped before he hit my growing wetness, but the electricity of his touch under my clothes made me gasp.

"Probably not for long." I stepped toward him. He pulled the dress off me. I unhooked my bra and let it drop to the floor.

Again, I stood almost naked before him. He unwrapped my belt from his hand, put it around my neck, and used it to pull me toward him. Our tongues and lips met. He let go of the belt, leaving it draped over my shoulders, and moved his hands under my panties, onto my bare ass. He grabbed it, pulling me to him, grinding me against his erection. I slipped my hands down his shirt, and he pinned them behind my back.

"I have a call with Seoul in seven minutes," he whispered in my ear.

"You couldn't make *yourself* come in seven minutes."

"That a challenge?"

"You tell me."

We kissed again, and he let my wrists go to hitch my legs up around his waist. He pushed me against the doorjamb, moving our hips together in a rhythm.

"Actually," he said, "I don't think I can get you upstairs in seven minutes."

"Don't sell yourself short."

He smiled, his face close to mine, where I could see every crease in his skin, every freckle, every thorn of stubble. His scent was everywhere around me. I wanted to fall into him. As if hearing my thoughts, he pulled away from the doorway, carrying me with my legs still around his waist. He shut the door behind us as he carried me to the stairs, kissing me. I wound my fingers in his hair. He bumped into a chair, then a bannister. We fell onto the soft wool carpet of the stairs, him on top of my nearly naked body, our hands everywhere, our hips joined in a fabric-sheathed tease.

His phone rang.

"Oh, no," I said.

"There wasn't going to be a good time."

"Don't answer it."

He looked right at me as he slipped the phone out of his pocket, smiling as if he knew he was tormenting me and felt nothing but sweet delight. He answered the thing, right there on the stairs, after putting his finger to his lips.

He said something I'd never be able to repeat, his Korean was so fast. His face hovered so close to mine I tasted his breath as he had a conversation I couldn't understand. The corners of the stairs bit my back, and the pressure of his hips on mine hurt, sending shocks of pleasure up my spine.

He put the phone to his chest and lifted himself off me. "I'm on hold. Get upstairs."

We ran up the stairs and into the room we'd been in two weeks before, laughing like teenagers. He landed on top of me on the bed, still fully clothed against my naked skin. He kissed me with his phone to his ear, putting his free hand on my breast, groaning into my mouth when I ran my hands under his shirt.

"Hey, Tom," he said into the phone. He put his finger to my lips and got off me, leaving me spread out like a bear-skin rug. I sat up.

"Yes," he said, his eyes on me. "I heard. Janice told me half an hour ago." I considered getting up and making myself a sandwich or something. I closed my legs. Who knew how long he would be? From his tone, it sounded urgent, but that could mean an hour or five minutes. If I left, I could still catch the guys for a drink, and I could glaze over the thing with Testarossa if Gabby was tipsy enough.

Jonathan put his hand on my shoulder and pushed me back down. He grinned and spoke into the phone. "They're insane. The Seoul Hilton is two miles away. If the North Koreans want a target, they already have one." He put his knee between my legs and parted them. I gasped, and he put his finger to his lips. Part of me thought he was being rude, disrespectful, and deserving of a desertion, but part of me found the third person in the room exciting, yet safe.

I reached for his belt, and he let me feel his erection through his clothes, but no more. "I am not taking five stories off it," he said. "I'm taking exactly zero stories off it. This whole Pyongyang alarm is a scam. Tandy Burton from the Hilton paid them off to give me a hard time." He tucked the phone between his shoulder and ear and used both hands to spread my legs wider, bending them at the knees. He nodded at something Tom said. Tom couldn't see us, but he was there. Jonathan lay beside me and slipped his fingers under the crotch of my underpants, sliding his finger along the length of my wetness. I bit my lip so the man in Korea wouldn't hear me.

"No, don't do that." He ran his thumb along my clit. "You'll have to back it up, and I can't." I gasped. I'd entered the room on fire, and his touch was charged with electricity, just hard enough on my bump before he put two fingers inside me. I was wet and ready, and after the past weeks of longing, and an afternoon with my legs spread over the arms of a chair, I was already close to coming. He would give me my orgasm. He had to.

We had all night. Except for Tom, who could be a real wrench in my works.

"What you need to do," he said, eyes on me, fingers inside me, thumb rubbing my clit under the fabric, skin to wet skin, "is get a council of Koreans. Natives. Have them work up numbers, odds, and projections. See what they come up with on a North Korean attack."

His thumb circled me. I wanted to moan but couldn't, or I'd be heard. I just spread my legs wider, hitching my hips forward and into his fingers. Tom babbled. It sounded like gobbledygook. Jonathan said, "yes, yes," periodically as he spoke to Tom, but he looked at my face as he fingered me. With his phone tucked at his shoulder, he grabbed my nipple with his other hand and turned it absently as if he was fiddling with a pen on his desk, except the "pen" was connected to my sexual center.

My back arched. My breathing got short. I mouthed to him, *Let me come.*

He tilted his head as if he didn't understand me.

I mouthed again, *Please let me come.*

He took his hand off my nipple and put it behind his ear, mouthing, *I can't hear you.*

"No," he said into the phone, "we're paying them. Tom, listen. The hotel is not a target, okay? Seoul is a major city. Everything's a target." He rolled his eyes as if Tom was just some annoying employee, and he and I were watching TV on the couch. Oh, funny guy.

His fingers left my hole and ran up to my clit and back. Once, then twice. I mouthed, *Please let me come please let me come....*

He made the *I can't hear you sign,* and I got the game, but I was about to explode into his hand hours after I'd given him control of my orgasms. I couldn't show so much weakness so early.

I rolled off the bed, letting his hand slip out of me, and ran out of the room.

I stood in the hall, back against the wall, and tried not to make a sound, but I started laughing. I couldn't help it. I crouched, balled my fists up in front of my mouth, and just laughed.

I saw Jonathan in the doorway, phone to his ear, fist in the same position in front of his mouth as he tried not to crack up in the middle of a business call.

"Okay." He cleared his throat. "Tom, I have to go." The last word came out in the squeak. Tom, however, wouldn't shut up. "I get it," Jonathan said.

I got myself together, but I knew I could burst into audible laughter any second. I went back into the bedroom and hooked my hand in his waistband before I kneeled in front of him.

"Okay, that's fine," he said. "Just let me know if you hear anything else." I unbuckled his belt and got his dick out of his pants. He leaned back against the wall. "Yes, and keep your ear to the ground on the other thing."

I gave him a taste of his own medicine, licking the underside of his dick with the flat of my tongue from base to tip, then throating him.

"It's an expression, Tom. It means listen hard." He put his fingers in my hair and pulled my head into him. "Yes, okay. Really, it's late here. Let me know tomorrow." He hung up and threw the phone on the chair. "You," he said, looking down at me, "are very naughty."

I couldn't respond. I had a dick in my mouth. When I pulled back, leaving it slick with my spit, he bent down and caught me under the arms. I laughed as he threw me on the bed, and I tried to get away until he crawled over me.

"No, you don't." He grabbed my arms. We laughed together as I tried to wiggle away, but he flipped me over onto my stomach and pinned my wrists behind my back.

"You shoulda let me come while the coming was good," I said.

"Oh, you're going to come." He slapped my ass, and the sting made me catch my breath.

"You didn't just …" I said, knowing he did and wanting him to do it again.

He did. One hand held my wrists behind my back and the other thwacked my ass as if I was a wicked, naughty child. I made some noise, like a breathy cry, that might have sounded something like "yes."

I felt him bend down and whisper, "Have you ever been tied up, Monica?"

"No."

"Why not?"

"Never came up."

I waited for him to ask, maybe a formal request for permission, but he just bent backward while holding my wrists. I felt the pressure on the bed change, and I knew he wasn't asking for permission or anything else.

He let go of my wrists and laid his body over mine, slipping his forearms under my face. I saw him holding the belt of my dress. It had fallen on the floor at some point, and he was making sure I saw it.

He kissed the back of my neck as he said, "I understand words like *no* and *stop*. Outside of those, your body is my playground."

"Yes, sir."

"You're like a prodigy at this."

Before I could answer, he pulled me up to my knees. I felt him behind me, still clothed, as he stroked me from my neck to my crotch and back up again. He ran his hands from my shoulders down my arms and placed my hands on the wooden headboard. The railings and runner across the top were roughhewn. He

CD REISS

looped the belt around my wrists, binding them together, then around the railing. It was a good knot, firm and tight.

I wasn't frightened. Nervous. I was nervous in the best way possible as he got off the bed and stood there in his jeans and sweatshirt, staring at me. Me, on my knees with my wrists tied to his headboard, hair in my face, ass out; him with his arms folded, checking out his work.

"Well?" I said.

He smirked a dangerous smirk. I felt the tingle of liquid dripping down my leg.

He pulled his shirt off, and when his face was covered and I only saw his body, another shiver went through me. His tight torso, with its patches of light hair, was a feast for the eyes, and when he got his shirt over his head, messing up his hair, he smiled as if he knew I was admiring him.

He took his time getting the rest of his clothes off. The condom went on, and he put his knee on the bed, tilting the mattress, and put his arms around my waist. One hand landed on my breast and the other between my legs. He found where I was wettest and rubbed gently, then harder. I rotated my hips, my tethered hands a fulcrum I rocked against, his dick waiting against my ass.

"Jonathan." My voice was husky. Breaths without a voice. I didn't know what I was trying to say. Just his name, as if that would tell him what I wanted. As if that would connect us to my pleasure. As if him binding my hands wasn't enough for me to feel possessed, owned, protected.

He stopped rubbing my clit, pulled my ass up, and put the head of his cock at my pussy. I felt as if it would be sucked inside me by the sheer force of my desire. But no, he let it hover there, just touching the skin. I pushed back, but my tied hands held me. He kept himself just out of my body's reach.

"Go," I said with a squeak of desperation.

I thought I'd have to beg him to fuck me, but I didn't. He slid in easy and sweet, pulling my ass up. The slow slide was good, the wet inches rubbing inside me and pushing against my hole. He moved so my wrists felts trapped and burned, the feeling of being held still almost stronger than the feeling of his stomach hitting my ass. He was doing everything right. He was fucking the hell out of me. But something was missing. He was holding back.

"Jonathan," I said.

"Monica."

"Hurt me."

"What?"

"Do it so it hurts. Break me apart. Make it hurt so I scream. I want everything. All of it."

He paused and slid his hands down my back. "Say it again."

"Hurt me, Jonathan. Hurt me. Please."

After a long exhale that sounded like a decision being made, he started moving faster, but that wasn't the half of it. He gripped my ass, a hand in each cheek, and spread me apart until I thought he'd rip me. When he pummeled me then, he was in my pussy so deep I felt the head of his cock hitting the end of me. But he didn't ease up. His fingers dug into my skin. My ass became dough in his hands. My wrists kept me steady against him. I wanted to scream, but I couldn't, or he'd stop. I didn't want him to stop because the pain was exquisite, focusing me on his pleasure as it peaked my own.

He took a hand off one cheek and grabbed my hair. I moaned so loud it came out as a bark. He pulled my ass up again, his fingers digging into my skin, as he fucked the shit out of me. I was damp all over from sweat and juice.

"Say my name," he gasped.

"Jonathan."

"Again."

"Jonathan, Jonathan, oh God, Jonathan."

He came as if he'd hurled himself off a cliff, with a long grunt and a longer groan. He pumped at me from behind, still groaning, going on forever. Nothing had ever given me more satisfaction than hearing him come so hard.

He stopped and fell on top of me, his chest to my back, his dick falling away from me. We breathed together for a minute, our bodies still in tune.

"Are you okay?" he asked, brushing the hair away from my face.

"Never better."

"Give me a minute. You'll be even better."

He kissed my neck, then between my shoulder blades, down my back, then to my ass cheeks, which hurt. I groaned and arched my back.

"Stay still," he said. I dropped down. "Very still."

"Okay."

The skin of my slit was sore and bruised from his fingers. The sting felt wonderful as he licked the insides of my thighs, then my soaking pussy, which throbbed with the hurt and pleasure of him. His tongue went up and down my folds, landing on my clit, teasing the tip with tiny, imperceptible motions. Then he drew his lips around it and kissed, ending in a light sucking.

"Oh, Jonathan…"

"Don't move."

"Please let me come when I'm ready. Please don't make me wait more."

"Only if you stay still. Move, and I take you out for coffee."

"Yes."

He spread me apart, which hurt until he slipped his tongue inside me, then drew it out, along the slit, which was so sore, and over my clit, slowly. Then back, into my hole and down until he sucked on my clit one last time. I went rigid, crying out with everything I had. My back wanted to arch, but I couldn't let it. My hips wanted to thrust, but my mind overrode the impulse. I became a vessel for my pussy and my clenching ass and the pressure on my wrists. My body's stillness drew out my orgasm, because I couldn't surrender to it until the final moment when I lost all sense to his touch and tongue, screaming his name at the top of my lungs. He sucked gently on my clit until I was a shuddering mess, way past the point of agony.

CHAPTER 29

*K*evin had been the fuck of my life. That didn't mean much as he'd been one of two. Darren had been serviceable, but we were young and inexperienced and *in love,* so we had no idea how boring it was.

Kevin had seemed like a white hot ball of fire. He was all hands and lips. He masturbated in front of me, and I tried not to giggle because I thought hot people would be very serious. He told me I was pent up and repressed in a way that made me want to get unrepressed, but I didn't know how. I tried to get wilder by wearing lingerie and groaning louder. I sucked his dick more. I danced for him. All that seemed wonderful at the time, like really being grown up and sexual. But he didn't know how to take my repression, wring it out, and throw it out the window. He didn't know how to fuck it out of me or quietly tell me to get undressed in the night air while he watched in such a way that wouldn't make me laugh. I couldn't have given Kevin my orgasms, because he didn't want them. I could never have asked him to hurt me, because he would have.

I watched the sun come up through Jonathan's window, felt his breath on my neck, and thought *don't fall in love don't fall in love don't fall in love.* I didn't look at him while he slept. I didn't stroke the top of his hand where it rested on my belly. I didn't think about him. Nothing. Not his scent or the sound of his voice. Not his sharp wit or his easy smile. My job there was to enjoy him, and sense sooner rather than later when it was time to move on. That was the only way I would get out intact.

I heard steps in the hall, and some loose, non-English muttering between a man and woman, which alarmed me. But then I heard a broom on the hardwood. The staff. They probably lived in a house out back and were like furniture to him.

My bag was on the floor. The second and last time we'd fucked, I went downstairs for it because he ran out of condoms. I'd rooted in the pockets and found a little latex sack a month from its expiration date.

I had to grab that, and my clothes, which were probably still on the porch. That would be tricky. It was broad daylight, and I couldn't leave the room naked with the cleaning staff around. Or maybe I could. Who knew how people with money lived?

I closed my eyes and tried to sleep again, but Jonathan's phone buzzed. When I looked at him, his eyes were open.

"You gonna get that?" I asked.

"No."

"Your cleaning staff's been knocking around."

The phone stopped buzzing. Jonathan stretched as if two hours of sleep had left him refreshed. "I have to go get your clothes. You don't want to flash Maria, or she'll start sprinkling holy water all over the place. Makes a mess."

He kissed me and swung his legs over the side of the bed. I sat up, aching everywhere. I was so sore I could barely sit straight. Jonathan looked down at something and didn't move.

"What?" I said.

"I don't want you to think I'm prying or that I was looking in your things."

"Okay, I won't think that."

He picked my bag up off the floor. It was open, and Kevin's flyer for the Solar Eclipse show stuck out. I showed him the name list. I knew the only name he would see was Jessica's, so I pointed out Kevin's.

"Kevin Wainwright," he said. "The guy with the dick."

"He came to Frontage last night."

"And invited you to a show for tonight? Late notice, don't you think?"

I shrugged. "It's Kevin. He thinks courtesy is for non-creatives."

"Like me."

"You're plenty creative." I slapped his arm with the brochure. "With your body."

"You going?" he asked.

"I don't know. You?"

He sighed and ran his fingers through his hair. "I have to. It's unbecoming if I don't. The divorce looks anything but amicable, and people are watching."

"What kind of people?"

"She got custody of most of our friends. I do business with some of them. Others have just been in the same circles too long."

"Which sister you taking?"

"Deirdre, I think. Are you going to pretend you don't know me?" His phone buzzed again.

I slid off the bed. "We'll see if I even go."

I went into the bathroom, a huge white room with a separate shower and tub. Every corner was clean, as if little gremlins lived under the sink and scrubbed the place while he flattened women on the bed.

I had no idea if I was going to L.A. Mod. It was a black tie thing, and I didn't have anything to wear. And there was the Kevin issue. Jonathan would be there with Deirdre, who had given me dagger eyes just the night before. If I were being honest with myself, I would admit I was just making excuses. I didn't want to be in Jonathan and Kevin's line of sight at the same time. I couldn't stand any unmanageable drama just as my career was rousing itself.

I heard Jonathan through the door, mumbling. Not a business call. Then it went quiet. I peeked into the bedroom. He was gone, but my dress was laid out on the chair. I put it on and fished my underwear and shoes out from under the bed.

I went downstairs. Though I'd been to Jonathan's before, I hadn't paid attention to what he had on the walls.

One couldn't go through music school without an immersion in all the arts, and Kevin had continued my education with his passion for all things visual. So once I was fully clothed and paying attention, I recognized a Kandinsky in Jonathan's living room. I saw the Holbein over the mantle and the Mondrian studies in geometry in the corner. I didn't linger though, because I heard him in the kitchen. I didn't want him to think I was prying.

I followed his voice to the kitchen, realizing he wasn't speaking English, Spanish, or Korean. A middle-aged, dark-skinned woman with Asian features and wearing a cleaning smock smiled at me.

"Do you drink coffee?" Jonathan asked when I walked in.

"Not really." I leaned on the counter. "I like it with

milk, and dairy's not good for my voice. So, let me guess. The lady you're talking to is Filipina?"

"Good call."

"I do live in Los Angeles." I smirked. "You speak, what is it called?"

"It's called Tagalog, and yes—"

"You live in Los Angeles."

He smiled. "Ally Mira washed your dress."

"That was very kind."

"She is. So, seriously, are you going to this thing tonight?"

"Kevin dragged me to a thousand art shows when we were together, and I'm just not into another one."

"That was Teresa on the phone," he said. "She says you met Deirdre last night?"

"Briefly. Very tall. Big curly red hair."

"She got alcohol poisoning."

"That's terrible."

"That's Deirdre. Theresa was watching her, and she didn't know Deirdre had a flask. So Theresa's counting drinks and Deirdre's off to the bathroom twelve times. Do the math on that." He came toward me. "They have her on a B vitamin IV drip, and she's already cursing the nurses." He put his thumb on my cheek, and I raised my face to kiss him. "You sure you're not going?" he said. "I can give you a lift."

"That would be like us going together."

"Would that make you uncomfortable?"

"No." I put my hands on his chest to caress him through his T-shirt. "I think it might make *you* uncomfortable."

He wrapped his arms around my waist. "Tell me more about me."

"You take your sisters out, and you meet your women in private. You said you and your wife, sorry, ex-wife, still hang around the same circles. You don't want her to see you with an actual woman. And don't make a crack about your sisters being women."

He looked up for a second, and I got a full view of the muscles and veins in his neck. I was right, or at least close.

"I can go alone," he said, looking at me. "I'm a big boy. But I don't want to. So if you're going, this non-creative wants to go with you, courtesy be damned."

The offer was compelling. I hadn't planned on going because I didn't want to stand in a corner and watch Kevin work the room. I didn't want to make small talk with his friends, and I didn't want to get the death-eye from whatever little hipster groupie was chasing him. Jonathan would be a nice buffer.

"Fine," I said. "I'll let your handsome ass drag me to a black tie thing at L.A. Mod. But you'll owe me."

"What exactly will I owe you?"

"You pick." I stepped away. The call Gabby and I had to make had started worrying the back of my mind. "Whatever it's worth to you. If it makes me scream and yell your name, even better." I kissed him quickly. "I have to go."

I walked toward the doorway, but I didn't get past it before I heard him say, "What are you wearing?"

I stopped and turned. "Why?"

"Because you're a beautiful woman, and what you wear is important."

"If I'm going to embarrass you, I can just stay home."

He stepped forward and grabbed me around the waist. "Jessica makes art because she has so much money she's bored and because she has the sharpest eye I've ever known. If she's going to see me with you, she's not going to see you wearing Target."

I looked him in the eyes. "Really, Jonathan? You never seemed like the catty type."

"*I* also want to see you in something better. I'm

sorry. Come on. Go to Barney's and talk to Lorraine. She'll fix you up and bill me."

"Now I'm the one who's really uncomfortable."

"Please? Just go. And if you spend less than three thousand dollars, I'm spanking you and sending you back to Wilshire Boulevard."

"I'll come in *just* under three large then. And not because I have any intention of returning to that side of Wilshire."

CHAPTER 30

I stood under the shower head with my hands on the wall, letting the water scald my back. My head drooped, and my hair fell in front of me. I couldn't move without aching, and when I opened my eyes, I saw the insides of my thighs through the steam.

At first I'd thought they were dirty. When I touched them and felt a sharp pain, I knew they weren't dirty. They were bruised.

I got out of the shower and looked in the mirror. My ass, the area just below it, and between my legs were black and blue. It hurt to move. My pussy was so sore, it had hurt to clean myself. I heard a soft tap at the door, and Gabby asked, "Mon? Is that you?"

"Yeah. You need to pee?"

"Yeah." She started to open the door. Gabby and I saw each other naked and stood in the same room to pee all the time, but I couldn't let her see me that way. I looked as if a shark had tried to bite me in half. I grabbed the door handle and pulled it closed. "Are you okay?" she asked.

"I'm fine, I just…." I had no excuse. "Give me a minute."

I wiggled into a tee and jeans I pulled from the hamper, cringing from torn muscle and broken blood vessels. I snapped the door open. Judging from her clean clothes and brushed hair, she'd been up a while.

"Where did you go last night?" she asked.

"I saw Jonathan." I brushed my wet hair while she peed.

"Oh, really. Well? How was it?"

"He knows how to fuck, that's for sure."

"Better than Kevin?"

"It's the difference between a man and a boy." I slid my toothbrush out of the cup and got to the point. "I figure we should call WDE at about ten-thirty. Those guys don't get in until ten, and I want to give him a chance to get his jacket off and bang his secretary, but I want to catch him before he goes into a meeting."

"I'm nervous. Are you nervous?"

"Yeah. Actually, I am." I lathered up my toothbrush, and Gabby leaned toward the mirror, picking some nonexistent crud from the corner of her eye. "But you know how it is," I continued. "You get all nervous for a call, and you make it and they're not available. Then they call you back when you're going eighty on the 101."

"Since when can you go eighty on the 101? Give me a break." She held up a tube of aloe moisturizer I got from the farmer's market. "Can I try this?"

"Go ahead," I said, brushing my teeth. After I spit, I said, "I want to be clear we come as a set. You and me. Okay?"

"Why?" She seemed unfazed by my suggestion.

"Suppose he can't get a keyboardist for some band, and then you're off touring, and what am I supposed to do?" I pulled my hair into strands so I could braid it.

"We should give ourselves a name." Gabby pushed me onto the toilet. I winced, but she wasn't looking.

God, sitting was going to be torture today, and maybe tomorrow.

Gabby had braid mojo. Our first year of Colburn, we made ninety percent of our friends because she could braid like a magician. She picked up the strands I'd started. I turned my head so she wouldn't see me grimace at the pain in my behind.

"I really liked Spoken Not Stirred," I said. "But Vinny reps them."

"That wasn't the last cool name we have in us," Gabby said.

"I guess it depends on what he wants out of us. Am I recording my own stuff? But how could he want that? He doesn't even know if I can write a freaking song." I gestured with my hands and saw the bruising around my wrists. Fuck. I slipped them between my legs, wishing I'd worn long sleeves.

"You can, Mon. Your songs are amazing."

I let her ministrations tickle my scalp. "What I'm saying is, if it's my stuff, then that's one name, but we'd need a whole band. If it's just you and me, that's a totally different sound. Which is fine, but even then, are we writing new material? Or are we doing Irving Berlin?"

"He might not even know what he wants." She concentrated on the strands, looping one around the other, tugging and pulling, straightening and separating the lengths with a black comb.

"He knows," I said. "Those sharks don't start swimming around unless they've smelled blood. Some label is looking for a specific something he thinks we can do. Otherwise he wouldn't have come out. Trust me."

She pulled my hair off my neck. "Whoa, Monica."

"What?"

"Hickey City back here."

I stood and looked in the mirror. Gabby held up a

handheld mirror so I could see the trail of bruises at the back of my neck.

"Fuck," I said. "Can you braid it to cover it?" I sat on the toilet again and Gabby undid her work. My ass, my wrists, and now my back. If it hadn't felt so good, it would have been assault.

"Sure, but what's the diff?" Gabby asked. "It's a phone call."

"I'm going to the Eclipse opening at L.A. Mod tonight."

"Fancy. Did Jonathan invite you?" Gabby moved my hair around in a way that soothed me, and I wanted to purr like a kitten.

"No, Kevin did. But Jonathan is taking me."

"Kevin?"

"This is such a long story."

"Are you wearing your little black mini with the bow on the shoulder?"

God, no. Even in my mind, that thing looked cheap and worn. Jonathan had been right, despite my hurt feelings. I had a closet full of black and nothing nice to wear to a black tie function.

"How about this? It's almost nine. You go take your meds. Come back in here and braid while I tell you everything about last night without the dirty parts. Then, at ten-thirty, we make a call on the speakerphone in the kitchen."

"Deal."

CHAPTER 31

*B*arney's New York was on the best part of Wilshire, close to Rodeo Drive and near all the big agencies. WDE was half a block away, in its own slick black phallus of a building.

Jonathan had given my name to an apparently very difficult-to-get personal shopper. She called me, and we made an appointment.

A valet drove my shitty Honda behind a Bugatti and a Jaguar and treated me like a princess when, as Lorraine instructed, I asked for the elevator that went to the fifth floor. I was handed off to a guy in a burgundy jacket who led me right down the hall, then right again, and pressed the button for me as if I was too good to lift my arm.

The elevator doors opened into a room rich in wildflowers and tapestries. The white leather couches were empty, but the antique desk was manned by a woman about my age with smooth skin and a ready smile.

"Good afternoon, Miss Faulkner," she said.

"Monica's fine."

"My name's Shonda. Lorraine will be right with

you. Would you like some coffee? Or we have herbal tea?"

"If you have a green or a white tea, hot and plain? I'd love that."

"Great." Shonda seemed genuinely pleased to get me tea. She didn't have the same face I wore when I wanted to seem genuinely pleased to get someone their drinks, but I really wasn't. Or maybe that was exactly what I looked like.

I didn't sit but stood at the window, staring at the WDE building. Our call with Eugene Testarossa had been as quick as a hot fuck. Our meeting was in four days at twelve-thirty. High lunch. Location TBA. That meant we were important to him. He wanted to be seen with us. One day, I'd walk into that big black building from the parking lot and take the elevator up as if I belonged there. I'd be a moneymaker, a golden ticket, their canary.

"Ms. Faulkner?"

I turned to see Lorraine, a sixty-ish woman a few inches shorter than me with pixie cut white hair and not a stitch more makeup than was appropriate.

"Hi," I said.

"So nice to meet you." She held her hand out, and I shook it.

"I'm sorry," I said. "I want to be honest. I don't know exactly how to do this. I mean, usually, I'd just go shopping, so, if you could kinda guide me through?"

"Of course," she said, folding her hands in front of her. "You're looking for something for the Eclipse show?"

"Yes."

"Follow me." She smiled slyly and winked at me. "This will be fun. I promise."

We walked into a room with mirrors and a white

carpet. My tea waited for me on a little marble table. Lorraine closed the door behind us.

"I set up some possibilities for you," said Lorraine, pointing to a rack of garments on hangers. Four mannequins wore other dresses. All of the clothes were black eveningwear. "You probably won't need any alterations. I pulled from size six per Mister Drazen's recommendation."

"He knew my size?"

"He said you were perfect. I had to draw conclusions from there."

I didn't want to know how many women he'd sent up to Lorraine for her to know that. It wasn't a productive line of thought, and I had a bunch of clothes to look through. I usually loved shopping, but that was nerve-wracking. I felt like a Dodger's fan at Wrigley Field.

"If you sit," Lorraine said, indicating a chair, "I'll show you what I have."

I sat slowly when her back was turned. I didn't want her to see the pain in my face. She pulled things from the rack, one at a time, and laid them out. I rejected most as too dowdy or too slutty, which made her laugh. I didn't know exactly what I wanted, which didn't help. As she got to the last frock on the rack, and I knew from the length it wouldn't work, I imagined myself walking into the L.A. Mod. Who would I see? How did I want to present myself? I'd be with Jonathan, but who would see me besides him?

She didn't seem impatient or put out at all when I rejected the last thing and said, "I think I decided something."

"Oh, good."

"I want to look like an artist."

She looked at me for a second, hands folded in front

of her again, and winked when she said, "I know just the thing."

She left and came back in a second flat. The dress was black, naturally, and soft to the touch, yet stiff enough to hold a shape. The skirt hit at the knee, with a raw edge and strips of fabric dropping from below the hem, like a deconstructed fringe. The bodice was plain, but the shoulder straps crisscrossed each other along the back and front, making an asymmetrical web of lines across the shoulders.

"It's gorgeous."

"Try it on."

I went into the dressing room. The dress felt like magic on my skin. The difference between a Target dress and a designer dress brought to me by a personal shopper wasn't the way it made me look, though I looked like the best version of myself. It was the way I felt inside it. I felt like a queen.

Until I got out of the dressing room, turned around, and saw the bruises on the back of my neck.

"Crap." My face went hot red.

Lorraine waved the concern away. "We have something for that down at the makeup counter. I'll get it for you. Don't you worry. I've seen much worse. And I've seen wealthy brats who wanted something that showed those marks off." She shook her head. I smiled at her. She made me feel comfortable, which I guessed was her job, but it was a gift. If she wasn't there, I'd be very, very ashamed.

"I love this dress," I said.

"You look lovely," she said. "Do you have shoes?"

I hadn't even thought of that. "I guess not."

"And something nice to wear underneath?"

"Oh, I don't need anything like that."

Lorraine looked at me in the mirror. "It's not about what you need, dear. And it's not for *you*."

"I guess I should spend a little something on him then?"

"Exactly."

CHAPTER 32

*A*fter shopping the fifth floor at Barney's, my room looked messy and dim. My mirror made my body squiggle. The walls were cracked, and the floor was scratched down to the raw wood. Even through that, the dress was perfect on me. The bracelets I'd bought to cover my bruised wrists clinked and clanked when I spun hard enough to make the skirt wave. I'd tried to protest that the red soles of the shoes didn't go with the black dress, but Lorraine insisted they were fine, and since she'd rejected so many things on my behalf before that, I felt pretty sure she wouldn't bullshit me.

The bill came, and though I wasn't responsible for paying it, I had to sign off on what I was taking out of the store. Lorraine had slid it across Shonda's little desk with a smile. I checked the items and then the price. It came to two thousand, nine hundred, ninety-nine dollars.

"I know I spent more than this," I'd said. "I saw the price on the shoes."

"Well, you caught me," she'd said. "You're not supposed to see the price tags. So if you don't tell anyone

168

you saw it…" She paused and smiled to let me know it really wasn't that big a deal. "I'll tell you. Mister Drazen asked that the bill say this number no matter what. He said you'd get the joke."

"I get it all right." I'd signed, trying not to smile too wide. But as I looked at myself in my bedroom mirror, I smiled again.

Gabby had done my hair to cover the bite marks, tsking the whole time and making me giggle. I'd told her what I could about the night before, leaving out the parts that made my thighs black and blue. She did a church lady voice that made me laugh so hard I thought I would break a rib. We were in the bathroom playing with my makeup bag when the doorbell rang.

"God," I said, "this is ridiculous. I feel like I'm going to prom."

"You didn't go to prom." Gabby ran some hand cream over her fingers. "You and Darren stayed in the limo making out."

"And you and Bennet Provist? In Elysian Park?" I popped tubes and pencils into my little makeup bag.

"Yeah. Excellent prom."

"Mon!" Darren shouted from the living room. "You have a gentleman caller!" Oh God, was Darren going to embarrass me? I ran out to do damage control.

Jonathan was by the doorway, looking too big for the space, wearing a tuxedo cut for him and no one else. He and Darren were smiling.

"Yes, sir," said Jonathan, "the dance is chaperoned."

"I want her home by eleven."

I stepped into the living room before the joke got old, and Jonathan saw me in my new black dress. He liked it. He pressed his lips together to suppress a smile that would have mortified me in front of Darren and Gabby.

"You clean up nice," I said.

"Obviously you were intending to clean up in that old thing as well."

I snapped my bag shut. "Good thing the Salvation Army was open late."

He held out his hand, and we laced our fingers together.

"You met Darren, I guess?"

"Yes. He mentioned his shotgun."

"This is Gabby."

"Nice to meet you," Jonathan said.

"Hi."

"Okay, great," I said. "Let's go." I pulled him out the door. I saw Lil standing outside the Bentley, which looked damn near vertical parked on my hill.

Darren stood in the door and wagged his finger. "Remember what we talked about. Not a minute later, young man."

Jonathan walked backward a step and waved to Darren. "Eleven tomorrow morning, yes, sir."

"Hi, Lil," I said. "How did you enjoy my hill?"

"Quite a ride," she said. "I want to try it in the Jag."

"Be careful."

"I was born careful, miss." She opened the door for us. I slid in, and Jonathan got in right after and sat facing me. Behind him, the partition between us and Lil was shut. We sat quietly for ten seconds. My eyes must have eaten him alive as much as his undressed me. By the time the car started rolling, we were on each other, lips searching, tongues twisting, hands testing how far they could get before we risked wrinkles and stains.

He put his hands up my skirt, and when he felt the garter, he whispered *oh* into my ear. But I cringed because he'd gone up high enough to touch the bruises. He pulled back and said, "Let me see."

I pulled the skirt to the top of the stockings.

"Monica, are you shy all of a sudden?"

"Don't freak out."

"I guarantee you I'll freak out." His tone told me he didn't mean "freak out" in the same way I did.

I pulled the skirt up to reveal the black silk garters, and though the fronts of my legs were fine, he could definitely see the damaged insides.

"I did this?"

"We did it. I shouldn't have worn garters, but they were so pretty."

"Turn around."

I turned to face the back window, my knees on the seat cushion, my hands on the back of the seat, steadying me. He touched me when he pulled my skirt up, his fingers barely grazing my skin. He didn't hurt me, but the anticipation of pain made me flinch anyway. He kissed where I hurt, lips soft and yielding. "I'm sorry," he said as he kissed the backs of my thighs.

"Don't be. It was worth it." He pulled my dress down and gently guided me back to sitting. I took his hands. "I just got a little bruised, but I was never scared."

"I feel terrible." His elbows rested on his knees, a posture I remembered from the morning I saw him talking to his ex-wife on the back patio. His eyes searched mine, looking for any hidden anger.

"Okay, stop it. Really. I've never had sex like that in my life. The bruises will heal. My brain chemistry is what's totally fucked."

"That's a high compliment. I should say thank you first."

"You're welcome."

He held his hands over my thighs. "I'm afraid to touch them."

"Do it."

"I'm going to San Francisco for a few days. By the

time I get back, these should be healed enough I won't have to worry about hurting you."

"I remember asking for it."

"God," he whispered, "so do I."

He put his hands on my neck and kissed me all the way to the museum.

CHAPTER 33

We walked hand in hand to the L.A. Mod from the parking lot, taking an extra turn around the block. His dry palm against mine, the tracks of his thumb drawing circles on the base of my wrist, and the sound of his voice seemed to have a direct line to the heat in my crotch, which pulsed to its own beat after the make out session in the car.

The museum had been built on one of the busiest streets in the city, set back to leave room for a granite courtyard flanked by steps on either side that led to a patio a flight up. The gathering began in the courtyard. Jonathan introduced me to thirty people, none of whom stuck in my mind. Gabby would have had a field day drawing connections between everyone, but all I saw were the expensive dresses and cufflinks. I saw why Jonathan had insisted I go to Barney's. I would have stuck out like a sore thumb in my cotton shirtdress.

"When you sent me to Barney's, you were saving *me* from embarrassment," I whispered after another introduction. I held Jonathan's hand, leaning into him as if he was a string bass.

"I just wanted you to fit in."

I squeezed his hand and looked over the crowd, my eyes scanning the staircases.

"Why are you nervous?" he asked. "I'll introduce you to anyone you want."

"I'm not nervous."

"Yes, you are."

"Kevin." I looked right at Jonathan when I said it. I was a little ashamed to have my eyes peeled for my ex-boyfriend while I was with my current lover, but I had no illusions about my future with either man. "I'm looking out for Kevin. I'm sorry. I don't mean to be rude. I just suddenly want to avoid him."

"Monica, when you're with me, you don't need to be nervous about seeing Kevin or anyone else." He led me up the stone stairs.

"I'm not nervous."

"You better keep the truth on those lips."

I shook my head and looked away. I saw her at the top of the stairs: Jessica Carnes. She didn't photograph well. She looked gorgeous on film, but in person, she was exquisite. She wore a long white dress over her straight, slim figure and low heels on small feet. She saw us, or rather Jonathan, and excused herself from the couple she was speaking to.

Jonathan squeezed my hand. I looked in his direction and spoke close to him, keeping my lips as still as possible. "And this is who makes *you* nervous."

"I hate this," he said.

"We can lean on each other. Then you can take me home and bruise the rest of me."

"The things that come out of your mouth."

"They please you?"

"Yes." He looked at me and took one long blink before facing his ex-wife. "Jess, how are you? Congratulations!" His smile was so wide I thought his face would snap. It wasn't a happy smile. They kissed each other's cheeks, his hand on her bare shoulder.

"Thanks," she said. "I'm glad you could come." She made a quarter-turn so she faced me completely, her sky-blue eyes twinkling with icy delight. "We haven't met." She held her hand out.

Jonathan spoke before I could get out a word. "This is Monica."

I shook her hand, and to my surprise, it was warm. "It's nice to meet you," she said. "Very, *very* nice to see you here."

"Thank you," I said. As I tried to pull back my hand, Jessica put her left hand over our clasped hands for a second, then let go.

"Where's Erik?" Jonathan asked.

Her expression didn't change. Not a hair nor muscle moved. "He didn't come."

"Ah, too bad. Well, we're about to sign in. We'll see you in there?"

"Sure."

Another half turn and she was speaking to someone else. Jonathan put his arm around my shoulders and guided me away.

"Who's Erik?" I asked.

"The man she left me for."

I shook my head. "You people are too fucking mature for me."

He chuckled as if he had so much to say, but he didn't know how.

CHAPTER 34

The galleries were designed to change. The vast space was chopped up by permanent-looking temporary partitions that still left enough room for huge sculptures. The lighting was flat, warm, and consistent, flattering the people in it. The space was so big, I stopped looking for Kevin and looked at the work.

Lynn Francis was still doing huge, photorealistic canvases of branded stuffed animals. Star Klein put out a bucket of meat encased in Plexiglas. Borofsky was still counting from one to a billion in ball point pen. Elaine Slomoff knitted pullovers with the names of the war dead. Jessica Carnes exhibited three sculptures thirty feet high that could only be accommodated by removing pieces of the modular ceiling and making the sky visible above them. The bottoms were shaped like Popsicle sticks and the tops, which reached into the night sky, were living trees. She'd cut them to look like a bomb pop, a fudgesicle, and one of the double flavor jobbies that had two sticks you broke in half and shared with your sister if you had one.

"Any insight?" I asked Jonathan, standing next to him under the leafy fudgesicle.

"She glorifies nature against popular culture. It's

what she does. She's cut the trunks, so these are designed to die, like everything."

I turned to face him, feeling ornery and out of my depth. "I think its bullshit on a stick."

"The ability to talk about modern art is the sign of an educated mind." His voice was smug, yet inviting. He wanted a comeback.

I faced him but stood to the side and laced my fingers in his, speaking quietly into his ear. "Jeff Koons's grandiosity, plus Damien Hirst's embellishment of the mundane, divided by Coosje van Bruggen's extremity of the unremarkable … equals bullshit. The presence of the stick is unimpeachable."

We regarded each other for a second. "Suitably erudite," he said. "And you pronounced van Bruggen's name right. What other tricks do you have up your sleeve?" He stroked the inside of my forearm, leaving trails of tingling nerve endings in their wake. I wanted to kiss him, but I was a stranger there, and I had no idea who I'd upset.

"I can throw a guy out at second from home plate," I said. "Arm like a rifle, as long as the pitcher gets out of the way."

Our noses sat next to each other, and my lips felt the heat of his. I smelled his sagey cologne and fennel toothpaste.

"Monica?" I knew that voice. It had uttered my name in the dark of night, with moonlight coming through the window, and had screamed it in the bright light of day with heat coming off the asphalt. My name had been on those lips between laughs and tears and rage and humility.

I turned my face away from Jonathan's. "Kevin."

"I'm sorry, I, uh … didn't mean to interrupt, but I didn't know if I'd catch you again tonight." He was in a brown suit for a black tie event, with a lavender tie and a blue striped shirt. It should have been a mess, but he looked gorgeous, like he was *in* the world of the reception but not *of* it. The scarf in his pocket was folded into a peeking triangle, and his pants fit him as though they'd been custom made. He'd apparently been shopping for the event as well, and unless he had a rich girlfriend, the business of being Kevin Wainwright had been brisk.

"Hi, Kevin. This is Jonathan."

Kevin held out his hand. "Drazen?"

"That's me."

Of course Kevin knew Jonathan, at least by name and face. He made it his business to know anyone who could afford original art.

Kevin turned back to me. "Did you see my piece yet?"

"No, where is it?" Of course he was worried about himself. Of course he thought nothing of interrupting an intimate moment to ask me if I'd seen *his* piece yet.

"No rush," he said. "It's around that corner. I just wanted to see you first. I want to say…" He glanced at Jonathan, then back at me. "I hope you like it. Excuse me." He fell back into the crowd.

"That was awkward," I said.

"Looks like we'd better go see if it's bullshit on a stick." Jonathan held his arm out, and we turned around the next corner.

"Kevin Wainwright puts his bullshit in a box."

Kevin was known for installations. Two dimensions could not contain him or his big stinking ideas. His first set up was in a ten by ten storefront he rented in the worst part of downtown. When his parents moved to a one-bedroom apartment in the center of Seattle, he got shipped a basement full of every toy, game, and fetish object from his childhood. But to him, it wasn't crap. To him, it was media. He spent a month in that storefront hanging, pinning, pasting, and strapping things to the walls; setting up tables for *mise-en-scenes* with army men and action figures; deconstructed board games and decks of cards, mixing up the pieces to make new things. I hadn't known him then. I shared his bed after he was already an agented comet streaking across the art-world's night sky. I had heard of his downtown store-front, which had been titled *Arcade Idaho* and had spawned a hundred imitators but not one other suc-cess story.

Kevin was a shrewd businessman as well. Installa-tions left nothing for the artist to sell. His art wasn't a painting a rich person could put in their living room or a sculpture for their yard. He sold the preparatory sketches and worked closely with a little hipster book-binding outfit on Santa Monica Boulevard to create limited edition booklets containing silver halide prints of the installation, along with his wordy, over-modified prose describing what it all meant.

I knew his exhibit would be crap. I knew it would be manufactured meaning, and exasperating, and it would remind me of all his drama. But when I turned the corner and saw the doorway to the installation, I got a little nervous. Metal signs hung outside. CAU-TION. HARDHAT AREA. NO TRESPASSING. The signs were typical Kevin overstatement, but the sign at the top concerned me.

FAULKNER COAL MINE

"Isn't that your last name?" Jonathan asked.

"Yeah."

"You sure you want to go in?"

"No."

But I pressed forward anyway.

From just outside, I heard a canary singing, a lone bird at top volume. The doorway was little more than five feet high. I bent a little to get in, and Jonathan bent a lot.

The room was dark, with spotlights to point where he wanted you to look. At first, I hadn't adjusted to what I was seeing. He'd scribbled a lot of words, floor to ceiling, on two facing walls and the other two facing walls had eight and a half by eleven copy paper pinned to them. Piles of objects were on the floor with papers on music stands, which I couldn't read because people stood in front of them.

Then, like a gunshot, the canary turned into the honking of a disconnected number. Everyone flinched, and some people got angry at the intrusive noise. Except me. I knew what the noise was about. I knew what the canary was about, and I knew, for damn sure, what that installation was about.

The phone noise drove out the people standing in front of one pile of about nine small objects. A black chalk line had been drawn around them. A music stand stood in front. The stand had a piece of paper clipped to it, and engraved on the paper:

1 (ONE) 13.5 oz bottle Purell shampoo. 50% empty. Current value - $2.39

1 (one) 13.5 oz bottle Purell conditioner, dry hair formula. Unopened. Current value - $4.79

5 (five) Tampax brand tampons, regular. Current value - $1.34

1 (one) Recyclable toothbrush, soft bristles. Used. Current value - $0

1 (one) 16oz bottle Kiehl's Crème de Corps moisturizer. 75% empty. Current value - $12.50

I remembered a conversation over that tube. He'd questioned me about that and everything else, because he assumed I was too incompetent to manage my skin.

"How much do you spend on this stuff?" Kevin had asked, putting a blob of Kiehl's into his palm.

"This bottle will last me a year if you don't take that much."

Then he'd rubbed it on my thighs, and we did it on the bathroom floor. The bottle was 75% empty because that wasn't the last time.

I felt Jonathan behind me. "What is it?" he asked, just as the canary came back on.

"This is the stuff I left at his place."

Someone moved to my right, and I saw a pile of clothes. The pockets of my jeans and the T-shirt I slept in were folded neatly under a pair of simple cotton underpants. I didn't read the little menu. I knew what those jeans were worth. Any normal person who wasn't terrified of getting sucked back into their ex-boyfriend's life would have gone back for them.

To my left, a pile of hair accessories: a brush and a scrunchy. And a disk of birth control pills. Open. Half-used.

"Are you sure you're taking these right?" he'd said one month when I was a day late.

"It's easy enough."

"Not if you're knocked up."

The lights changed and illuminated the walls, making the little piles of my things disappear in the darkness. The scribbles became legible, and more than my things on display, more than the exact value of what I'd left behind, those words, written as one long, run-on sentence, brought months of sidelined emotion to the back of my throat.

I didn't say she was more important why do you have to make everything about you she needs me she tried to kill herself, Kevin, what the fuck do you think is going on in your life that's more important right now how can you tell me I can't practice how can you try to silence me again I've put everything on hold for you I can't do this I can't take care of everyone I can't be there for everyone I need to go I need to go I need to go I need to go.

"Bullshit in a box?" Jonathan asked from a safe distance, as if he knew coming closer would be inappropriate.

"These are the last things I said to him."

I walked to the other side of the room. More scrawled words on the wall.

I'm not telling you not to work I'm telling you to stay with me when I'm with those guys they make me feel inadequate and stupid and you're the only one I trust you're the only one I know who doesn't make me feel small without you I'm not a man you don't understand I need you I need you I need you I need you I need you.

I walked out as fast as the low-hanging entrance would let me.

CHAPTER 35

*H*aving been inside the relationship described in the Faulkner Coal Mine, I knew how brave Kevin was to create and display it. We had been impeccable together. We looked good. We never fought in public. No one heard a word from him or me that anything between us was less than perfect. He dragged his confidence around like a skin he seemed to own. That installation fearlessly let his friends and admirers know that not only was our relationship imperfect, but he himself lacked confidence and swagger.

But that was Kevin. Mister one hundred percent. When he'd loved me, it was with all of his heart and soul. I never worried about his commitment or his fidelity. I never found a leak in his passion. I was his everything, and as suffocating as that was, I never wondered where I stood. That in itself was liberating.

But now all our friends would know our last straw. Tuesdays had been his poker night. All the guys would sit in Jack's loft smoking cigars and talking about didactics in postmodernism, or definitions of folk art from the twentieth century's cultural diaspora. The girlfriends would sit in the kitchen talking about sex and drinking wine. It was like the fifties.

Gabby and I had finally put together a band because playing music made her feel better. That burned his ass. Because ever since Gabby had tried to kill herself, I got less available. Harry got us free studio time on Tuesday nights, for rehearsals. Perfect. He could go play poker so I could rehearse. But he threw a fit. He needed my support. He needed me *there*. Why was I abandoning him for Gabby? And you know what? I felt *bad*. My first reaction was that he was *right*. Because that was the whole relationship. His needs, and they were plenty.

In the sculpture garden, behind a little pagoda, was a spot the lights didn't reach. I knew about it because I'd given Kevin a blowjob back there the night he helped his mentor hang his retrospective.

I was headed there when Jonathan grabbed my arm on the patio. "Monica?"

I took his hand and pulled him along with me until I caught a glimpse of Jessica. She smiled at us. I was trying not to burst out crying, so I nodded and let Jonathan do all the smiling.

He let go of my hand.

I glanced back. He and Jessica were talking. He half-faced her, one foot still pointing in my direction, like he wasn't committed to either one of us. I had no time for that. I didn't need him anyway. I ran down the stairs.

I was halfway to the courtyard when I heard his shoes tapping behind me. "Monica, wait up."

I slowed, and he took my hand again without another word.

When we got to the ground floor, I turned into the sculpture garden. It was empty, mostly, so I slowed down. I wasn't breathing well. That was how I cried: breathing badly. Then fat tears would come. I was a ladylike bawler, more or less, which was why I let

Jonathan put his arm around me and slow me down. If I was a messy blubberer, I would have run away and gotten the bus home. He sat me on a quiet bench, slowly, as if remembering the damage he'd done to me.

"Are you all right?" he asked.

I put my finger to his lips, then I put my arms around him and rested my head on his shoulder. "I'm so sorry about all this."

"It's okay."

"Tonight was supposed to be your drama."

"I prefer it to be yours, to be honest."

I picked my head up. "That was why he invited me so late. He wasn't sure if he wanted me to come. And that was why it was a single space on the list and not me plus one."

"But you tricked him." He took a hankie out of his pocket and handed it to me. It was thick, possibly silk, and monogrammed.

"God, I feel like such a bitch leaving the way I did. What kind of person just leaves all their stuff and—" I took a hard breath, and the fat tears came every time I blinked. I dabbed my eyes with the hankie.

"Someone who's scared," Jonathan said. "Come on, he made that thing from his perspective. You didn't expect it to be fair, did you?"

I shrugged and dabbed, trying to get control of myself and not lose too much makeup. I sniffed hard.

"I just walked out on him," I said. "I had no closure. I know the way I did it was the only way, because I could be strong once and leave, but he had a way of making me forgive him. We would have been the couple that was always half broken up, and I knew I couldn't be strong another hundred times."

I dabbed the insides of my eyes with the hankie, but I didn't want to get mascara on it, so the wet blobs stayed on the outside of my eyes. Jonathan stroked the back of my neck and waited patiently.

"I don't know what this will make you think of me," I said.

"That any man who's with you better pay attention, or they'll find you gone."

A short exhale of a laugh shot out of me. I shook my head. If I wanted more from Jonathan than a casual fuck, my chances of getting there had just shrunk to nil. Who would want to be with such a psychopath?

"See, I was keeping you on a need to know basis," I said. "And now you know too much about me. I'm going to have to kill you. Sorry."

I looked up from the hankie. He was gazing at my mouth as if it was the most interesting body part he'd ever seen. He touched my lower lip with his thumb and brought it down to my chin.

"I know you're trying to be guarded, but you're too real for that." He brushed my lips with his fingertips, and I kissed them. "I think that piece up there wasn't bullshit. I think it's the most unkind thing I've ever seen. And to sell off the pieces to a stranger is a dirty trick."

I looked back down at my lap, where my hands sat. My wrists were covered in bangly bracelets to hide the bruises. I felt beat up.

"Thanks for listening," I said. "This can't be attractive."

"If you have never seen beauty in a moment of suffering, you have never seen beauty at all."

"Who said that?"

"Some German poet. Now, blow your nose. The sniffling's making me crazy."

I held up the hankie. "I can't. It's too nice." I sniffed again.

"Are you serious?" He snapped the hankie from me

and draped it over his palm. He put it over my nose. It had his dry, foggy smell. "Blow," he said.

I looked at him over the silk fabric, and he looked back at me, tilting his head as if waiting impatiently for me to blow my nose into his hankie-covered palm. The corners of his mouth curled ever so slightly. He was trying not to laugh.

"Come on now," he said, squeezing my nose.

I couldn't hold it in. I burst out laughing.

He laughed too, even as he said, "Blow already."

"I can't when I'm laughing."

"Stop laughing then." He was a poor salesman for not laughing, of course, as he was mid-crackup.

I took the hankie back and turned away from him. I blew my nose right into that really nice, embroidered accessory, folded it, and blew again before turning back to him. He leaned back on the bench, his arm around the top of it. Streetlamps reflected blue on his cheeks and the tips of his hair. His finger brushed my bare shoulder.

"Do you want this back?" I said, trying not to laugh all over again.

"Keep it."

CHAPTER 36

I waited in the back seat as Jonathan spoke to Lil outside. I wanted to see him naked again. I wanted his cock and his lips. I wanted his hands on my hurting parts. But I couldn't stop thinking about Kevin. After I'd left him, I thought he'd forgotten about me. I sometimes thought he might have been hurt, but I took only gleeful satisfaction in that thought. He had always been the strong and confident one, and I was the doormat.

Jonathan slid in across from me, and Lil slammed the door after him.

"You going to tell me to spread my legs?" I asked.

"I'll get to it."

He didn't. He just looked at me. My knees were pressed together. My nipples were hardened from the fierce air conditioning, and my hands lay folded on my lap. Once he was done with my body, he looked at my face.

The car moved, and the view of the parking lot turned into L.A. at night.

"I want to do things to you," Jonathan said, "but you're not in any physical condition for that right now."

"I'm not made of sugar." I tried to keep the disappointment out of my voice and feared I'd failed.

"Indeed." He touched my collarbone and drew his finger down, under my dress, pulling it down below my breast. The knit of the straps strained and held as he extracted my nipple. "Shift forward again." I pushed my hips to the edge of the seat, flinching with pain. He pulled the other side of my dress down and, getting off his seat, kissed the nipple he took out. I groaned and held his head to me. He sucked it hard, then bit on it, and I gasped.

"I want to tie you to the bed in a hundred positions and fuck you everywhere, but I want those bruises to heal first. I want a clean ass to bruise again."

"I shouldn't ask this."

"Then don't." He brushed his finger against my nipple.

"I need to know if you're like this with everyone. All the women."

He looked in my eyes for a second, silent, then cast his gaze downward. I didn't know what I wanted him to say, but the curiosity burned me from the inside out.

His fingertips touched my lips, and I opened my mouth for him. "Make these wet," he said. "You're going to need it." He slid two fingers in.

I put my tongue against them, and I felt them rub my tongue and slide down my throat. He pulled them out, then shoved them in again. I sucked hard, trying to get my saliva going.

"Come on, Monica, you can do better." He slid his fingers in and out of my mouth, hovering just at my lips then pushing them back in. I was sore. Pounding with heat.

I wanted him, despite the pain, or because of it.

His fingers were in my mouth up to his hand. My

lips curved around them, and I was sucking. He used his fingers to pull my head up until I faced the ceiling, and his fingers fucked my mouth from above.

"Pull your skirt up. Gently." I heard the smirk in his voice as he pulled his fingers out then back. I shifted my skirt around my waist.

"Ah, this is gorgeous." With his free hand, he stroked under the garter at the tops of my legs where the pain wasn't so bad. "Now spread these beautiful legs."

A war raged in my pussy between the pain of soreness and bruising, and the intense fire of need. When I opened my legs, I groaned into his fingers, because I got warmer when exposed to him.

"More, Monica. Don't be shy." I moved them out a little more, but my muscles burned. With his free hand, he yanked my legs apart. I gasped with pain and pleasure. He pulled his soaking fingers out of my mouth, and with his left thumb pressed under my chin, he kept me facing the ceiling.

"You don't want a relationship," he said. "But you keep asking about other women." He put his fingers under the crotch of my underwear and stroked my clit. "Why is that?"

"I can't say." I didn't know how I made words instead of just sounds. The pressure between my legs was so distracting.

"Yes, you do."

"Ah, that's so good, Jonathan."

He put his two fingers in my pussy. They burned all the way in, and I thrust my hips forward. His thumb rubbed my clit, and I went with his rhythm. His left thumb stayed under my chin almost painfully, keeping me from moving freely.

"Yesterday," he said, "you mentioned something about rumors, and you asked how many women I brought to the club, and now, another question. Do you want to fuck or not?"

God, had I been so childish? "I want to fuck."

"So what's your intention? Why do you keep asking?"

"Curiosity."

He took his fingers out and moved my panties back in place. I thought *ok, now he's going to tease me all night, and let's face it, I'm going to love it.* But he did something that surprised me. I couldn't see it because he held my chin up, but it felt as if he flicked my clit the way he might flick a crumb off the table, with his thumb and middle finger. His thumbnail hit my engorged clit like a pebble tossed on a water balloon. I felt it as exquisite pain followed by sharp pleasure. I made a vowel sound in my throat, still looking at the ceiling.

"Tell me, Monica. Why so interested?" He flicked me again.

"Oh, Jonathan...." I moaned. Flick. I started to squirm.

"Tell me what's on your mind."

It was gorgeous torture. I had no idea when the flicks were coming, and they were sharp, excruciating, and beautiful. I'd never, ever be able to come even if he did it twenty thousand times.

"If I tell you," I said, "you tell me everything."

He flicked me twice in quick succession. I cried out. "No deals," he said.

"Don't make me scream," I said. "Lil will hear."

"Then talk," he said, flicking me again.

"Fuck you."

"Talk, baby," he said softly, as if cajoling me.

I breathed heavily, feeling the light pressure of his hand on my throat. I could have stopped him. My wrists weren't bound. I could have pulled his arm away. Honestly, I wanted to tell him. "I want you."

"And?" He rubbed over the now wet fabric of my underwear. It soothed the heat but not the arousal.

"I want you all to myself. I want to know what they didn't do so I can do it. So I can keep you longer."

"Ah." He took his thumb away from under my chin. My legs were still spread, and his knees prevented me from closing them. I looked at him, feeling ashamed. I was sure he'd drop me like a foul ball, right there in the back of his Bentley in a designer dress and new garter. "Three times is my limit. We're one fuck to our expiration date," he said.

"I hope it's a monster because I'm going to miss it."

He smiled at me, then pushed himself back. He closed my legs, and I pulled my skirt down, smoothing it against my thighs, pensive.

"I'll tell you what," he said. "I can't promise you anything long-term. I can't get past my marriage. But I like you more than I care to, and I'm not interested in anyone else right now." He pressed my hands in his and looked at them, then back at me. "Let's do it. As long as you understand where I can't go. Jess talked me through a lot of shit. She rescued me in ways you can't even fathom."

Asking him to explain would have been aggressively intimate enough to break whatever we had. Whatever indefinable thing that was, short-term monogamous relationship, friendly fuckery, exclusive fling, it was not what he had had with Jessica. Our connection didn't have the bandwidth to sustain the pain buried far enough in our past to cause the grind of our present. His past belonged to her, even though she'd cut the line, taking it with her, tugging at him, leaving no one else for him to give it to.

"I get it," I said, "and I'm okay with that."

"Not for long. That's what I'm afraid of."

I stared at him for a second, then down at our hands. "I didn't get into this car wanting anything more from you."

"Yes, you did. You just don't tell yourself the truth all the time." He put a finger on my chin. "You're a goddess, Monica. Never be afraid to ask for what you want."

Our faces were a breath away. I kissed him gently, minutes passing while the city zipped by outside the windows. I heard my phone bloop, and I ignored it. His dinged, and he ignored it. Our devices were like a chorus of bells in the wrong church. I felt the car drop from the nose to the back, as if it were falling off a cliff.

I looked out the window as we stopped. "You drove me *home*?"

"You're black and blue in just about all the places I want to fuck, and if you come back with me, I'm fucking them."

"The things that come out of your mouth," I said.

"Do they please you?"

"No, actually."

"Come on, Monica. I'll be gone for a few days. When I get back, we can pick up where we left off."

"You're leaving me like this for *days*? I feel like I'm carrying a baseball between my legs."

"No touching either. That orgasm's mine, and I'm trusting you to hold it for me."

I put my face to his, kissing his cheek, his nose, his lips. "It weighs ten pounds. Just release me."

"I'm going to release you when I get back," he said into my ear. "Repeatedly." He reached back and knocked on the window between us and the driver.

"You have a serious cruelty streak."

He smiled at me as though he knew good goddamn well what his streak was made of. Lil opened the door, and we stepped out. He kissed me by my porch steps, and my phone blooped again. From my porch, I watched the Bentley dip down the hill as if it was a feather thrown from a tall building. Inside the house, I heard the piano getting the attention I wished I was getting.

CHAPTER 37

JONATHAN

I watched Monica close the door behind her and felt the car dive off that cliff of a hill. Her house would be a deathtrap in an earthquake, and the hill was probably already falling into the backyard. I considered rectifying it. She was no good to me under forty tons of clay and detritus. She was only any good writhing under my hips like a pinned kitten. God, she was one big nerve ending, that girl, and those big brown eyes got just a little wider when she was close. And those bruises. And how she begged for them.

I knew she was special the night I met her, I just didn't know how special.

I'd gone up to K with Eddie and two other guys from Penn. I was meeting Wendy afterward in one of the hotel rooms. I had one foot in LA from a disaster of a trip to New York, and the other in Seoul for a trip that could not, under any circumstances be anything but a roaring success, or I was going to have to answer questions. I hated answering questions.

So I'd just done the easy thing and took them to K. There had been plenty of nonsense before the tall girl with big, black eyes and long brown hair twisted into braids brought our drinks. The guys were bullshitting about ball and women, when we all stopped to watch waitress come toward us. The night was over. I couldn't take my eyes off her. Everything was in the right place, naturally. My staff has to look as stunning as the guests. But this girl wasn't just beautiful, because they all are, she was something else entirely. I was trying to figure out what it was, and she just looked right back at me, as if daring me to make an even bigger ass of myself.

Then she spilled gin on me, and Freddie fired her. The guys tried to reason with Freddie, but the waitress was gone and I had to let him do his job however he saw fit. I was an hour to Wendy with her legs up in the air and I suddenly found the idea depressing. She was gorgeous and shrill and shallow. She blew too much coke and giggled at all the wrong times. She exhausted me. The thought of another night in one of my hotel rooms drained the life out of my limbs.

Freddie told me the waitress's name, and that she was a sexual harassment case waiting to happen. But I couldn't let the ebony-eyed girl walk away. I had to look at her again. Five minutes. I'd give her a severance. Whatever.

I heard her outside my office and I seized up a little. I wanted to look at her, but had to be discreet. She slipped in, and I wanted to fuck her immediately. She was so long, so curved, so smooth. Her skirt cupped her ass, and her heels brought her to a couple of inches shorter than me. As my eyes dragged over her breasts, and over the length of her neck, I realized she'd seen me looking again. She put her hands on her hips. Definitely a harassment case waiting to happen, especially considering she was telling me about Freddie's fucking stupidity. I looked into her eyes. Fire, and pride. Not an ounce of fear. What was going on with that gaze was ten times more interesting than the curves of her body.

"I was going to offer you severance," I'd said.

"I don't want your money," she'd shot back.

"Let me finish."

She obeyed not just with her mouth, but her heart. Her face got red and she cast her eyes down. Her fingers twitched, but didn't move otherwise. Holy fuck. I almost lost my breath. This gorgeous, proud creature was submissive.

I couldn't let her walk into Los Angeles and disappear.

And it had only gotten worse since. Of course, I couldn't fall in love with her, even if I tried, but I could pass a lot of time with her. A lot.

I wanted to know every twitch, every growl, every moment of desperate need, and eat her alive. If she needed me to be exclusive, I could do it. I'd just put Sharon on ice and stop looking around. How long could Monica last? A month? Two? How long could she make me laugh before she started asking for more? How many things could leave her lips that would make me want to put my face on hers? She couldn't stay so attractive for long. She'd burn herself out soon enough, but for the time being, I could not have created a more flawless woman.

I felt bad about bruising her, but I hadn't done half the damage her ex-boyfriend's piece had done. What a dick. And as soon as I saw that guy, what he'd done, and the way he looked at her, I wanted her for myself. I knew she was going to ask for exclusivity, I could see it in her face, and once I saw that piece, I was ready to give it to her. The thought of her getting hurt bothered me. It wasn't her personally as much as it was wrong to make their private business so public. It wasn't that hearing her cry made my fist clench, or that I felt as though I saw some shameful part of her she'd wanted to keep hidden. It was an overall, amoral wrongness. Could have been anyone, and I would have been just as mad.

Well, maybe not as mad.

Damn. I should have taken her home. I had a weird compulsion to reach out to her.

> *—Thank you for tonight. I'll call you during the week to check on that baseball—*

—You're welcome—

A flat, emotionless response. Odd. I regretted letting her out of arm's reach.

> *—Speaking of...They're playing the Mets the day after I get back—*

—Ok good night—

I sat back. Not even a joke or wisecrack. I shouldn't have cared, but I did. My phone dinged again, but it wasn't Monica loosening up. It was Jess.

Interesting that Erik wasn't there. He usually followed her around like a little beta puppy. Exactly what she needed. Half a man. I took a calming breath and called her.

"Jess."

"Jon. Where are you?"

She didn't sound good, and if I judged the whooshing background right, she was already home.

"Coming up LFB." Our shortcut for Los Feliz Boulevard, from when I was whole and had someone to make up little acronyms with.

"Are you alone?"

"Lil is driving. What's wrong, baby?" I could have guessed it was Erik, but she'd never admit it.

"Can I see you?"

I looked at my watch. My plane was scheduled out of Santa Monica at six. I could make it if I left Venice by four. If history was any indication though, I'd be out of there in an hour. I wished I could tell her no, but we had too much history, too much intimacy to just turn my back. So I let Lil take me home, then I got into the Mercedes and went to Venice.

Again.

* * *

JESSICA LIVED ON THE BEACH, as her publicly sunny demeanor demanded. I parked and walked up the long stairway to the back, where the pool overlooked the ocean. The furniture was gone, as was the barbecue. She stood alone at the half empty bar with her glass of white wine, still wearing her flowing white dress. It outlined the shape of her body in the breeze, making me think immediately of pulling her legs open, but gently. That brought my hot little goddess back to mind, because with her, gentle was optional. I should have nailed her in the car, bruises or no. I wasn't any less aroused than her, and now I was in a dangerous position. I wanted to fuck. I had a weight at the base of my cock that needed to drop, somewhere, somehow.

"Jess," I said when I could see her puffy eyes. "Wasn't there a party or something? After the opening?"

"I couldn't take it any more. Smile, talk about popsicle sticks and culture's effects on childhood memories. Smile. Answer process questions about keeping dead trees alive. Smile again. How are you?"

I snapped a glass off the rack, and Jessica poured me some wine. "I'm fine, really. You called me over here to ask me how I am? It looks like I should be asking you the question."

She barely paused before getting to the point. "Erik."

"I thought you were engaged."

"So did I. Do you want to sit?" She indicated the indoor patio behind sliding glass doors.

The thought of going inside and lounging on a couch with her, which I'd done a hundred times, somehow seemed too risky, so I slid onto a barstool. "Where's everything? Those hideous fucking lamps are gone."

She took a deep breath and swished her wine around. "Three days ago, he took them. They were his."

"Figured." I didn't know what she wanted. Was I supposed to sympathize? She had dozens of girlfriends, each with two shoulders to cry on. What the hell was I doing there?

"He found out you were coming to the opening. And he just went off. 'Why's this guy still hanging around? Why can't you cut him loose?' Blah blah." She downed her wine. "He doesn't understand. Or didn't understand. As you can see, he decided to stop trying, which I guess is for the best."

"I'm sorry to hear it, but I'm not taking the blame for it."

"Jon. You don't have to get defensive."

"Jess. What do you want, if not to blame me?"

She was a bundle of nerves, which no other person would notice because she never wasted a movement. She didn't have a set of sweet little tics like Monica. Jessica was still water, her tension revealed in her gaze, which sat in the middle distance.

"I should be frank," she said.

"You be anyone you want."

"Not funny."

I waited until she was ready, because she'd get to it if I stopped cracking wise, and I had the feeling I would want to hear it.

She took a deep breath. "I think Erik had something. I think he was seeing something I was pretending wasn't there."

She was squirming. Oh, this was good. Delicious even. I didn't say a word. I didn't want to assume she was going where I thought she was because I didn't want the rug pulled from under me again. It wouldn't be the first time she'd implied she wanted me back and then turned the conversation back on itself.

"You've always been there for me." She looked up, right at me.

"We were married," I said. "I told you, I take that seriously."

She took half a step toward me. I'd been through that before with her, and I wouldn't lean into her half a centimeter I didn't have to. I hoped with the same fervor, but I was gun shy. Even when she put her fingers on top of my hand, which she hadn't done in a while, I was torn. After the divorce, she'd still touch me, but she'd back off like a hosed down cat as soon as I went for her. I was impatient with the games and horny as hell from being around Monica. I felt like a caged animal.

So when she touched my face, I froze, convinced I would spin her by the hair and bend her over. That wouldn't do at all. Not if I was going to have her again.

"You're being shy, Jon. That's not like you."

"You going to push me away?"

"No. Not this time."

Fine. I put my hands on the sides of her face so she

couldn't turn and pushed her against the bar. I choked off her squeak with a kiss. She kissed me back. She really did.

My stomach tightened. To have my life back. To be back to normal again. With my wife at my side, a sealed unit, unbreakable. I touched my old self when I put my hand on her breast. The old me, at my fingertips.

I wanted light to see her, to believe it. Oh, anything could go wrong between us if I actually got my dick in her. I remembered my promise to Monica, but I could explain the next day. I'd be sorry to see that sweet thing go, but she shouldn't tolerate infidelity, and I cared too much about both of them to sneak around. Jessica had to be my choice. I'd taken a vow, begged for it to be honored, and waited so long that turning away the possibility of a reunion seemed ludicrous.

"Are you sure, Jess?" She'd better be sure.

"Yes, baby. Make love to me like you used to. In the beginning."

Yes, I wanted to. And I might have. If she hadn't asked for the old me back, I might have been as sweet and gentle as our first night. But in my ear, as if she sat right next to me, I heard Monica moan, "Hurt me, Jonathan. Tear me in two." I got even harder, if that was possible, and I was at the point where I could expect to walk out of there with a pair of ten pound weights between my legs. I was too old for that shit.

I faced Jessica. She was beautiful. Exactly the girl I remembered. Her lips were parted, her breathing shallow as she pushed her hips into me. So close. I was so close to having her again.

"I'm sorry, Jess."

"For what?"

"This." I pulled myself away from her.

"What? Why?"

I stroked looked in her face, half cast in the moonlight. "Because. It's been too much. I just... I can't."

She touched my face, and I saw her hurt. She had a deep fear of loneliness. Leaving her alone would undoubtedly be the hardest thing I ever did. "I don't understand," she said. "Is this spite? Or revenge?"

I owed her honesty, at least, after everything we'd been through, after all I'd promised her, after all the times we'd hurt each other. "It's too late. I'm sorry. I'm not the same man."

"Is it that girl?"

"Which girl?" I knew exactly who she meant. I was suddenly sorry I'd brought Monica to the show. Had I known Erik had walked out, I would have kept her home and writhed around with her all night, just to shield her from my ex-wife's eyes. The thought of that bruised ass, and her attitude about it, even the guilt I'd felt at giving it to her, made my dick twitch to the point of pain. "It's a dalliance, Jess. Don't try to read more into it."

Jessica didn't answer. She just stared at me as if she was reading a book. She must have seen right through me.

"Just go, then," she said quietly.

I wanted to say more, to apologize again or offer some comfort, but in a quarter of a second, I thought better of it. The door. I just had to make it to the door. I took long strides, looping my fingers in my keyring as I stepped into the night air. My Mercedes was five steps away. It had been her favorite. That's why I'd brought it. Maybe it was time to get rid of it.

"Jon," she called out. I took another step, getting my hand on the car, not looking back. I didn't want to change my mind. I didn't want another argument. I thought maybe I could get back to Echo Park in time to not make a rude ass of myself in front of Monica.

I couldn't pretend I hadn't heard Jessica. I looked back, just to say good-bye. I didn't see her immediately, but once my eyes scanned the flagstone walk, I saw her, balled up on the ground.

The visit was getting more dramatic than I'd anticipated. Did she feel this way when I'd gotten on my knees and begged her to stay? I'd been such a mess of tears I couldn't remember her expression. God, I'd never do that again.

She cradled her arm. I went to her, and from the way she looked at me, I knew I wasn't getting to my little goddess of Echo Park that night.

* * *

DR. FUHR WAS IN ARUBA, but a few phone calls and he'd managed to get us skipped ahead in the emergency room if we could get to Cedars in twenty minutes. It was late enough that the 10 was clear, and we zipped along with the top up, an ice pack on Jessica's arm and a sulk on her face.

"She's pretty," Jessica said.

"Who?" I asked as if I didn't know.

"The girl from tonight. Are they all that pretty?"

"Mostly," I lied.

She looked out the window. "Do they all let you fuck them the way you like it?"

The foul language brought my breath in. That wasn't her way of speaking, and her tone prodded. I took the bait because it was late, my balls ached, and Dr. Fuhr hadn't been available.

"How do I like it, Jess? Maybe you can just repeat back to me what you told all your friends?"

"I needed to tell someone!"

"Everyone. You told everyone that I wanted to beat you. Beat you?"

"You changed, Jon. I was scared."

We'd been through it so many times, the tracks of the argument were smooth and well worn, but that felt different. It felt like the last time.

"I changed because you changed me. And I'll always be grateful. You made me right with myself."

"And right with yourself means you want to tie women up and hurt them."

"I don't want to hurt anyone. You're so fucking vanilla, Jess. It's like a religion. You can't see outside it."

I turned into the ER at Cedars, not facing her until I parked. Tears dampened her face. I hadn't heard her crying in the white noise of the freeway.

I put my hand on hers, but she shook it off.

"I wish we could go back to the way we were," she said.

"I don't."

* * *

ERIK CAME AN HOUR LATER, as she was in the x-ray room. We shook hands like gentlemen.

"Nothing happened," I told him. "She's all yours."

The blonde lock drooping over his forehead swayed. He owned a surfboard company, but his face was permanently tanned from twenty years on the waves. "She never was."

"Well, honestly, this is the last time I'm coming running. I'm done. And I'm sorry I had my foot in your yard for so long."

We shook hands again, and I put my hand on his arm because I was really, terribly sorry I'd caused him grief over a woman who was completely wrong for me.

* * *

IT WASN'T until I got on the 10 that I started to feel as if a weight had been lifted from my shoulders. I pulled off on Mulholland to feel the Merc take the curves like a lumbering behemoth for the last time. I hated that goddamn car. I would get rid of it immediately. A smile spread across my face, and I laughed so hard I had to pull over. Laughter overtook me, turning to tears and back to a deep, silent laughter in my chest again. From relief. From a break in tension. From sheer joy. I was free. Fucking free.

The car was too small to contain me. I got out and sat on the railing, looking over the city, quiet, tearful bursts overtaking me. I looked at my phone, wanting to say something, connect with someone, but I couldn't conceive the words.

When I recognized where I was, I sobered up. I'd kissed Monica for the first time there. I felt a stabbing twinge in my twisted balls. Oh God, I could have her. I could own her. She could be mine, without hesitation or reservation. Mine. The relief turned into excitement.

I looked at the time. I'd have to wait.

Thinking of Monica, I got calm and focused on my phone.

To: Matt.reynolds@harrywinston.com
    CC: KristenK@drazeninc.com
    Fr: Jon@drazeninc.com

SUBJECT: open a new account

MATT –

. . .

LONG TIME.

I need a favor. I need a diamond navel bar. Not a ring. The other kind. Platinum with a 1.25 to 1.375 carat stone. As perfect as you have on hand. Can you deliver it to the east side before noon tomorrow?

Address to come. Let me know.

J DRAZEN.

TO: KristenK@drazeninc.com
   Fr: Jon@drazeninc.com

SUBJECT: Kevin Wainwright/Faulkner Coal Mine

KK –

IVAN SINCHOT IS on the board at the L.A. Mod. I need him on the phone first thing. I want to buy Kevin Wainwright's piece from Eclipse. All documentation. All copyrights. All assets, period. Do it through the Ibiza trust, immediately. Drop everything.

-JD

                        . . .

MY FINGER HOVERED over Monica's number. I wanted to talk to her.

No. I didn't want to hear her talk. I wanted to hear her scream my name. Hours. I wanted her for hours, and time was one thing I didn't have. I had real business in San Francisco that couldn't wait, and I had to break it off with Sharon if I was going to be honest. I texted my pilot, Jacques, telling him I was on my way.

I looked out over the city, feeling as though I owned it.

Beautiful goddess, when I get back, you are mine.

CHAPTER 38

*G*abby was up. No one else could play like that. She didn't stop when I came in, but she nodded to me.

"It's eleven at night," I shouted over the music.

"So?"

"Can you play something a little less bombastic so the neighbors don't call the cops again?"

She stopped playing entirely. "Why are you home? Did you guys have a fight or something?"

"No. Where's Darren?" I dropped my bag and kicked off my shoes, draping myself across the couch. Even lying still on the couch made me think about sex, adding to the throbbing between my legs. Damn Jonathan.

"Fucker's on another date." She tinkled a fun little tune on the keys. I'd never seen her like that before, with so few words and a tone of such pent up anger. I wished I could have my old high school friend back. She was fun. The person I'd spent the last two years watching had a new personality every few weeks.

"So? We set you free. You should be happy."

"I am. I'm meeting Theo for a midnight show at Sphere."

"Scottish Theo of the tattoos? He's all right." As excited and approving as I tried to sound about her new fling, she seemed disinclined to take the bait. She'd always been that way, which I'd liked about her, but over the past two years, the trait had become less charming and more alarming.

"So," she said, "Darren has a mystery lady. You have mister bazillionaire."

"I don't have anyone. It's completely casual."

She ignored me and my half truth. I was falling for Jonathan, and she knew it better than anyone. She turned to the piano again and played something sweet and sexual that made me want to run to the bathroom and finger myself to orgasm just so I could sleep.

My phone blooped, and I finally looked at it. The number wasn't in my contacts, but I recognized it anyway.

—*see me*—

Scrolling revealed five more of the same.

—*see me*—

—*see me*—

—*see me*—

—*see me*—

—*see me*—

"How did Kevin get my number?" I asked.

"Darren. I told him not to."

"God. Fuck him. Is that a man thing? We're all too butch to admit something would be a problem?"

I held the phone out for Gabby so she could see the six texts. "You should see him," she said. "He met us after our show. I think he's over you."

"And these texts prove it." I held up the phone for her to see, then I texted him back.

—*leave me alone*—

"I'm going to bed," I said. "Did you take your meds?"

"Yep."

I stood behind her for a second. I didn't believe her, and I didn't know if I should say something or not.

I trudged to the bathroom and took out her bottle of Marplan. She'd just gotten a refill that past Monday. There were a lot of pills, and a month ago, I would have counted them. I would have checked Darren's text with the last number he counted and counted the number of hours since to see if she'd taken two per day. Then I would have texted Darren the results, and all would be well with the world.

But I knew I wouldn't count all those pills. Darren hadn't texted me a pill count in a day and a half, and I was tired, and horny, and my phone blooped again.

I put the top on the bottle and put it away. I brushed my teeth and went to bed, taking my phone under the covers.

—let me explain, pls. I needed to make that piece. I'm not trying to get you back I know you're happy with someone else—

Happy. Sure. Kevin had only known the Monica who was never casual about sex. He'd only known the fully-committed me. I was suddenly miserable with Jonathan. Two fucks and a few illicit fingerings, and what would it ever be? A few more fucks and some more denied orgasms. In the end, we'd move on. He didn't have space in his heart for me. He'd made that clear. I'd never felt so empty in my life.

—good night Kevin—

Another text came in.

—Thank you for tonight.
I'll call you during the week
to check on that baseball—

—You're welcome.—

—Speaking of…They're
playing the Mets the day
after I get back—

I had snappy comebacks ready, but they turned to ice. Every bit of attention he gave me made me sad because it was fleeting and meaningless. I didn't have the will or the energy to play his game.

—Ok good night—

Bloop.

—see me—

I shut the phone and closed my eyes. The baseball between my legs shrunk into an olive, and I fell asleep.

CHAPTER 39

*I*mpossible as it seemed, I was more sore the next morning. Gabby was already up when I trudged into the kitchen. She stared into the corner with a mug of coffee in her hands. If someone had put a gun to my head and asked, I'd have said her coffee was cold.

"Gabby?"

"Should we practice a new set for our meeting?"

"At WDE? No. It's a meeting, not an audition. Are you feeling okay?"

"Yeah." She looked at me as if I'd woken her from a nap. "We have rehearsal in an hour. Let me shower first."

We'd moved the rehearsal venue from the studio, which cost money but was necessary with a band of four people, to the living room, which was free and was fine for two people. We were as diligent about our appointments as we would have been if we were meeting at a studio.

I boiled water for tea as I heard the shower go on. The slap of metal on metal from the gate outside was barely audible over the noise. It was way too early for the mail. I got to the front door just in time to see a green Jaguar going up the hill and a bulky figure in the front. Lil, for sure. I got out onto the porch quickly enough to see the backseat was empty. When I turned to go back inside, I saw a little navy box with a silver ribbon. I scooped it up and ran into my room, clicking the door shut behind me.

I sat on my bed and undid the ribbon, revealing the silver HW on the top of the box. A little envelope had been attached to the bottom, and when the ribbon slipped away, the envelope dropped into my lap. I opened it.

DEAR MONICA—
Please take this as a token of my appreciation.
—Jonathan

I SLID THE BOX OPEN, then the box inside that. It held a three quarter inch long bar, silver or platinum, with a circular diamond set in the bottom.

A navel ring. A real one to replace the fake ring I'd gotten from the piercing place on Melrose. I held it up to the morning light, and I was again distracted by how shabby and cheap everything in my room looked, the mess of laundry in the corner, the old frames on my pictures, the smudges on my mirror.

I peeled my shirt off and replaced my crappy navel ring with that gorgeous thing. As I looked at myself in the mirror, loving it, I wondered what it was for. I read the note again. Appreciation for what? Me, generally? Or something else? The card was too small to write more, but I wasn't sure what to make of those nine words.

The shower went off. I held my concerns. I had to shower, dress, drink my tea, and show up in the living room ready to go. I couldn't be burdened by my worries about what Jonathan meant to me and what I did—or didn't—mean to him.

CHAPTER 40

JONATHAN

*H*aving lots of money beat the alternatives, for sure. But having a plane didn't mean more privacy. It meant less, because everyone on board was there to serve me. I ended up in the bathroom taking care of the dead weight at the bottom of my balls, as if I'd taken a 727 like everyone else. On my mind was Monica, our first night, when we were so sore and tired I didn't think we'd have another go. She came out of the bathroom, naked, her dark hair a mess, mascara and lipstick worn to nothing. I sat on the edge of the bed waiting for her. She kneeled in front of me, looking up with those big, black eyes. Without a word, she kissed my dick, licking up the shaft, bringing the blood with her until it got hard again.

"Jesus, really?" I'd said.

"It's been eighteen months since I had sex. It might be another eighteen months before I do it again. I'm stocking up."

I'd laughed. I did that a lot with her. I pulled her up,

sitting her on my lap, her back to me and my fingers between her legs and on her breast. Since she was stocking up and I thought I'd never see her again, I fucked her hard, bouncing her on top of me while our hands met between our legs. We connected, feeling each other sliding together. When her back arched, she lost her balance, and we wound up on the floor, laughing, her on her stomach and me coming at her from behind. She turned her head, and I saw the pleasure in her face, her eyes rolling up. She was a gasping, moaning mess, crying and begging for release without being asked.

In the tiny closet of a bathroom on my six-seater plane, my imagination replayed her brown eyes looking up at me while she took my cock in her mouth, then her lips saying *please please, don't stop* from underneath me... My use for the bathroom concluded soon after.

I texted Monica a few times, just a couple of pokes to let her know I wasn't running off and to let myself know I was really doing it.

* * *

SHARON HAD BEEN EXQUISITE. Attractive, willing, discreet and far away, she'd do what I told her without question, talk to me about anything, and never open her mouth about who she screwed four or five days a month. Exactly what I needed, when I needed it, and I had been the same for her, but in the end, she needed to make a lifestyle out of her sexuality, and I was just a tourist.

I'd texted her when I landed, but I was two hours early thanks to Jacques answering calls during his morning jog and my desire to clean up business before returning to Los Angeles. She didn't expect me until after my meeting, so I figured she wouldn't be in ready position, and we could talk.

She lived on a high floor of one of my buildings by the Embarcadero. When we'd started screwing, she was a wreck from a string of abusive, boundary-free masters who beat or fucked her confidence away, and I was broken from Jessica's complete rejection of my needs. We were two complete disasters trying to teach each other the meaning of safe, sane, consensual kink. Putting her in one of my apartments seemed like the kindest thing to do, considering she was teaching me as much as I was disciplining her.

The lobby was spare, in dark woods and chrome, with an Italian stone tile floor. I nodded to the doorman and went upstairs.

My phone dinged. It was Sharon.

—*I'm ready for you, Sir.*—

Shit.

Sharon had three ready positions. That confused her initially. I liked a little surprise. I wanted her to choose, and she was used to being told what to do from how she brushed her teeth, to what she wore, to which route she took to the grocery store. Having a choice of ready position was unheard of in her sexual life, which was why Debbie had set us up in the first place.

But I didn't want her in a ready position. I wanted her clothed and ready to talk.

I opened the door. The place was impeccably clean, every inch made of glass and steel. I could never live in such a space. The apartment was too cold and impersonal, but it was easy to rent or sell, and it was just fine for fucking.

The living room was a big open area with a leather sectional and a shag rectangle under a teak coffee table. Sharon had both hands on the low table, palms spread, arms straight. Her ass was in the air, perched on top of a pair of beautiful legs planted in heels high enough to make a lesser woman fall over. Her blond hair hung over her face, and I knew she was watching me in the mirrors and chrome all over the apartment. Besides the stilettos, she was naked. Naked or underwear was her call, unless I stated otherwise. She was a lovely creature, with curves in the right places and smooth skin she carefully maintained.

Normally, depending on my mood and demeanor after travelling, I'd taunt and touch her until she begged, or I'd slap her ass and fuck her without a word.

I held my hand over her ass, because touching it was the first thing I'd usually do, then I stopped myself. I couldn't tease her because I wouldn't finish what that touch would start. Or worse, I would finish it and make the whole thing a hell of a lot worse.

"You can get up, Sharon."

"I'm sorry, Sir?"

"Get dressed."

"Have I displeased you?"

Fuck. Her voice squeaked with nerves. Bad start. I should have told her to be dressed when I texted her. Total miss on my part.

"No, baby. You're fine. We have to talk, and it's hard to do that with your beautiful ass in my face."

I held out my hand and helped her up. Her face was a blank slate of fear. She had no reason to look scared with me. When we met, any implication of my displeasure was greeted by her acceptance of punishment I had no intention of meting out. It wasn't my thing, but history was hard to shake. She held onto my hand, then pulled it toward her mouth. I twisted away and cupped her cheek. Her grey-blue eyes were full of questions, and her lips were pressed tight, not a position I was used to seeing them in.

"Where do you want to go for breakfast?"

"Wherever you like, Sir."

"Can we not play right now?"

Her posture changed from erect to relaxed. "So," she said, "who is she? Or did the wife come to her senses?"

I smiled. She couldn't have dropped character like that two years ago. "Are you going to get dressed or is the whole town getting a look at you?"

* * *

JESSICA HADN'T UP and left a perfectly happy marriage. This took a year or more for me to sort out. As I'd become more comfortable with my past, and the man I was, I changed. I became sexually dominant and emotionally controlling. I wanted her to submit to me in bed, which she wouldn't have any of. I wanted her body to be available to me more often, which annoyed her. I wanted her to dress for me, even if I wasn't there. I wanted her to do things during the day, when we were apart. Simple things. Touch herself. Roll her sleeves up. Open her legs. Say my name. It made me feel as though we were connected, but she didn't want to play the game, at all. I became frustrated and unsatisfied. We both dug in, and by the time I was willing to cave on both points to keep her, it was too late.

It had been my fault. I had no idea what I was doing. I didn't know what to ask or what I wanted, I only knew I had new ideas, new excitement, new desires. My requests sounded like demands, when they should have been demands that sounded like requests. I became, in two words, a controlling asshole.

To Sharon, however, I was a sweetheart, and through her and Debbie's stories, I learned just how kinky the kinky world was. I learned how her past men had done things and adjusted what I did to suit me and show her a life that wasn't based on fear, where her needs weren't just important but pleasurable for both of us. It was a shame I couldn't work up an emotion outside general tenderness in the two and some years I'd known her.

Sharon chose a place we'd gone to a hundred times before, with coffee handpicked by college graduates, roasted in the sun only during working hours, trucked in on fuel-efficient vehicles, and made onsite with organic water.

She had her hair tied back with a black velvet twist I'd used to bind her any number of times. No doubt she wore it on purpose. She was used to getting by on her looks and had little to recommend her in the way of conversational skills, but she wasn't stupid. She leaned on her elbows over her skinny latte.

"So?"

"So." I sipped my black coffee. "I wanted to tell you what you've meant to me. You helped me define things I thought had no definition. You've had a big part in making me whole again. I want to thank you for that."

"You never answered my question. The wife or someone else?"

Our relationship was built on honesty and trust but not on fidelity. She'd been on the lookout for a more permanent, full-time Dom, and I'd been searching for what I wanted out of a woman at all. "Both," I said.

"The wife's going to share? I thought she was vanilla?"

"No. Jessica's not going to share, but she did almost get me in the sack. I resisted."

"No *way*! And you turned her down? Why?"

Sharon was rapt. My life's dramas always interested her, yet she'd never betrayed a confidence. "Because I just didn't want her. Honestly. Just didn't. And also, there's someone I promised myself to, at least for the time being."

"Tell me."

"I probably shouldn't."

"What does she look like?"

I shrugged. "Nothing special."

"Oh, please."

I slipped my hand into hers and squeezed it. "You going to be okay without me?"

"You only show up once a month, and you're too gentle anyway."

"Without the tasks and the discipline and knowing I'm there. Are you going to be okay?"

"I think so."

"No assholes."

She took my hand in both of hers and looked me in the eye. "No assholes."

"The apartment. Do you want it?"

"I have some modeling things coming up. I'll pay you for it." I cocked my head at her. She knew what that place cost. "Installment plan."

"Fine."

"Is she short? Tall? How old?"

There is nothing like a woman's curiosity about other women. She'd never imply or even admit to herself she felt an ounce of competition between herself and Monica, yet she had to know so she could compare herself and decide if she was okay with it.

"I meet a lot of beautiful girls," I said. "She's... I don't know. The first time I talked to her, in my office, she was a waitress at my hotel. I looked at her, trying to figure out why she looked so tangible, so *present*. Every curve looked exactly right. Even her skin is this perfect color... Not even color. The texture of it. I wanted to touch it like I'd never wanted to touch anything before. She saw me looking, and she stood with her hands on her hips, daring me to get an eyeful. No fear. She filled that fucking room." I sipped my coffee.

"She took my breath away. I was too stunned to even ask her out."

"So?" Sharon might have been watching the last fifteen minutes of a Lifetime movie, her attention was so focused.

"So I got her a job at the Stock, where Debbie works. I figured she could check her out, tell me if I was crazy."

"So smart, you. What did she say?"

"You know Debbie. She won't rest until everyone's happily coupled off but her."

I sensed rue in Sharon's smile. I rested my hand on her forearm. "You'll find someone, baby."

She shrugged. "Maybe. I don't think it matters. Can you stay for one last fuck?"

I checked my watch as if it was a possibility. "Got a meeting with Tim LaShaun from District 34. Then a tenant's advocacy group that wants my head on a stick. More bullshit tomorrow and the next."

She nodded. I always had at least that much bullshit when I came to San Francisco, but things was different, and she knew it. There wouldn't be one last fuck. I'd done it. I'd come out unscathed and true to my word. I was less confident about Sharon. She had a way of putting a nice face on everything until she decided the pain was too much to bear.

We parted outside. I gave her a hug and a kiss on the cheek. I felt that relief again, but unlike the previous night, when I'd walked out on Jessica, it felt less like getting hit in the head by a two-by-four.

My phone rang as I put Sharon in a cab.

"Hi, Debbie," I answered as I handed the valet my ticket. "Speak of the devil. I was just with Sharon."

As usual, she wasted no time getting to the point. "Jessica met Monica last night?"

"Correct."

"She came here and insisted on sitting at her station."

Ugly. It was just like Jessica to highlight any class difference she could tease out. Having Monica serve her would be a way to humiliate her with a smile.

Debbie continued, "I don't expect you to do anything about it. Except your wife—"

"Ex-wife."

"She said something to Monica. I don't know what, but now the girl looks like she's been slapped."

My fingers got ice cold. Jessica could have said a hundred things, secrets she could have revealed or implied. A million half-truths. Without a man to lean on, she was a cornered animal. I'd forgotten how dangerous she was when I was busy choosing another woman over her.

"Did you ask Monica?" I asked.

"She won't repeat it."

Apparently, my beautiful goddess was also a woman of honor. "I'll call her."

"She's working the floor, so her phone is off. Fix it, please. I don't like it. The power trip. It's sneaky."

"I will, Debbie. I will."

I hung up. My car came, and I parked it around the corner to give myself a minute to think. What did Jessica know? Everything. What was she willing to share? Or imply? Or use? I had no idea. I knew for sure I wasn't ready to share everything about my past with Monica, not a word or deed I didn't have to, because I'd lose her. Any woman would run for the hills.

I texted Monica before I drove away.

—*Can you call me?*—

* * *

WHEN I GOT out of my first meeting, she still hadn't called. She'd gotten the text, so her silence was intentional.

If I were her, what would I do?

Whatever Jessica had said, I'd be finding out if it was true. So I had to make the investigation impossible to complete. That meant moving Rachel, touching base with each sister, Deirdre especially, and stressing their silence. And Thomas. And the hospital. And dad, who would laugh in my face. And... Fuck. There were too many fires to put out. Too many pieces to move across the chessboard.

I put my phone in my pocket.

It occurred to me that I'd longed for Jessica because she knew all the ugliness of my past. I didn't have to reveal a thing to her. I didn't have to bear the uncertainty and loneliness of wondering what someone thought of me. But if she loved me through it, couldn't someone else? Couldn't someone else keep a secret or ten? Maybe, but I was getting ahead of myself. I was letting my excitement get ahead of my sense. I had to finish up here and get back to LA without panicking.

I made my way to my meeting with the tenant's rights group. That bunch would use that information to take me down, even if I gave them what they wanted. I had to deal with Jessica at some point, no matter what, unless I was willing to live without intimacy the way I wanted it. Or I would risk losing Monica before we even started.

CHAPTER 41

*I*f my unease came through during rehearsal, Gabby didn't say anything, but I could tell it was an off day. I'd texted Jonathan a thank you for the gift, hoping my uneasiness didn't come through. He didn't respond, and I was sure he was on a plane. I didn't want to hear from him right away anyway. I was too busy worrying. Nothing had changed. He'd given me everything I'd asked of him and more.

> *—Thank you for the gift. It's really too much—*

Especially for a meaningless fling. Way too much.

"How was your night last night?" asked Debbie. "I heard you went to L.A. Mod?"

Debbie, Robert, and I stood at the service bar. It was the slowest part of my shift, toward the end. All of my candles had been lit for the next shift. All of my chairs had been put into place, paper napkins twisted, and trays wiped. The sun got about its business of setting orange over the Los Angeles skyline, a sight I took for granted during the early shift.

"It was good. My ex-boyfriend did a whole piece on

me, basically eviscerating me as a heartless bitch in front of everyone. Not sure what I'm going to do about that."

"Is that legal?" Robert asked.

"Only if I'm a heartless bitch. But I figure if it's not bad for my career, I should just close my eyes and pretend it didn't happen." Robert drifted off to make drinks.

"And how was the company?" Debbie smirked, a little wink flicking the bottom of her low-hanging bangs.

"Fine."

"He took you out in public. That's good. For both of you."

I shook my head and rearranged the lemon and lime trays. "I don't know."

Debbie didn't even hear the last word I said. She was up like a shot and already approaching a woman who'd just walked in by herself. She was tallish and blonde, and her skin glowed with health.

It was Jessica Carnes.

Debbie did her thing, smiling and double kissing, spinning conversation out of nothing. I was frozen in place. I didn't want to serve her drinks. Nothing in the world could make me serve that woman drinks for tips. Nothing except needing my job.

Debbie indicated the bar to her. I loved Debbie with a bursting heart right then, because Robert served the bar. I was the only waitress for the next twenty minutes. If Jessica sat at a table, I'd have to serve her.

Another woman came in behind Jessica, and more kisses were doled out. She had wavy brown hair and a face shiny with plastic surgery. A buffer? Or a team?

"I'm going to be sick," I said to Robert.

"Bathroom's that way."

Debbie led them to a table and handed them the

drink menus. When she walked back toward the service bar, her face betrayed nothing.

"I tried," she said when she was in earshot. "You'll have to do it."

"I can't. I met her last night."

"That's probably why she's here." Debbie took my hand and squeezed it, her grip cool and firm. She looked me in the eye, unflinching. "Be a woman of grace."

I swallowed hard, glancing at Jessica. She and her plastic surgery buddy spoke closely. The couch they sat on left their arms exposed, and I saw Jessica had a slim nylon cast on her right wrist.

"Fine." I put my notepad in my pocket and strode over there as if I owned the place.

Jessica and Plastic watched me approach, two beige ovals with eyes seemingly in sync as they looked me up and down, much like Jonathan had when he first met me. I put a little lift in my step and smiled with closed lips.

"Hi," I said, "I'm Monica. Can I get you anything?"

They just stared until Plastic broke the silence. "You are just as cute as a button, aren't you?"

I smiled, showing my teeth, wishing for the pressure of Debbie's hand on mine. "Thank you."

"We met," Jessica said, "last night."

"Yes," I said, "that's right. I wasn't a hundred percent sure, so I didn't want to say anything. It's nice to see you again."

"Of course. Same here."

The awkward moment was broken by a phone ringing. Plastic reached for hers. "I have to take this." She smiled to me. "Grab me a mojito, would you, dear? Easy on the sugar." She pressed the phone to her ear and headed to the hallway.

"Can I get you something?" I asked Jessica.

"Yes, I'll have the same." She shifted in her seat. I was about to escape when she said, "You really had me scared last night."

"Why is that?"

"I thought you were an eighth sister."

Her gaze held me, and I felt just walking away would be rude. Debbie had told me to be a woman of grace, and I didn't know a better way to do that than to show I was interested in her. "What happened to your arm? You didn't have that last night."

"Hairline fracture. I spent half the night in the ER. I'm actually wiped out."

"Oh, wow. How did that happen?"

Jessica pursed her lips and looked away, then back to me. The movement was so smooth and quick, I almost missed it. "You know how it is," she said. "Jonathan can be a little rough."

My mouth went dry. I couldn't even swallow. I think I shook a little because I felt my knees knock once. I had to get away. I had to be somewhere else.

"Sure," I choked out. "Of course. I'll get those drinks."

I made it to the service bar. Debbie's eyes widened. "What happened? You're white as a sheet."

"I have fifteen minutes left in my shift."

"What did she say?"

"I'm not repeating it. I have to go home."

Debbie took both my shaking hands in hers, slipping the notepad away. "You finish your shift. And you smile. Another table just came in. Take care of them, but do not linger. Do you understand?"

Her face broached no arguments. My nod was so slight and forced, I was surprised she even saw it.

"Robert," she barked, "make two mojitos, *no* sugar." She looked back at me. "Let them ask for the sugar. Make them wait. Take care of your other tables. Smile.

Maddy's here to relieve you, but you have to finish your shift. Grace, Monica."

Robert put two drinks on my tray.

"Yes," I whispered.

"Go."

When I went to their table to drop the drinks, Jessica and Plastic were deep in conversation. I made a nice face for them, and though Plastic opened her mouth to say something to me, I turned away before she'd engaged her vocal cords, giving me the opportunity to service my other table.

Twelve and a half minutes later, I came back to the service bar with a drink order and handed it to Robert. Maddy was made up, bright-eyed, and ready to go. I briefed her on the tables.

"Are you okay?" she asked.

"Fantastic. Where's Debbie?"

She shrugged. I didn't care. I went into the back without looking behind me to see if Jessica saw me leave.

I got to the break room and turned my phone on. I had to turn it off when I was on the floor, but now I would give that motherfucker a piece of my mind. He couldn't even keep it in his pants for me for how long? How many *hours*? They must have arranged to meet while I was busy running down the stairs. He'd promised fidelity and dumped me home with a lame excuse about not wanting to hurt me. What a joke. He went and got himself laid.

By his ex-wife.

Who he loved and would always love.

Because she talked him through a tough time.

'Til death do us part.

I had no idea what I would say to Jonathan, but something had to be said. If he wanted her, then fine, but why play with my clit while demanding I ask him for whatever I wanted? Why push me to tell him I wanted to be his only one, for however long, if he would turn the car around and fuck his ex-wife so hard he fractured her wrist?

I stared at my screen. He'd sent me two messages a few hours before.

—*I'm glad you like it*—

—*I still owe you a spanking from Barney's*—

And another one just three minutes previous.

—*Can you call me?*—

Darren:

—*Have you seen Gabs?*—

I replied:

—*Try Theo*—

There were another two messages, sent rapid fire an hour before. They were from an emotional fuckup, but one who had been open, sincere, and vulnerable with me. Someone who never, in the two years he had me, ever cheated on me. He'd never even looked at another woman. Never gave me a reason to doubt his devotion.

—*last time I'm asking*—

I'd forgotten what a persistent pain in the ass Kevin was. I replied because it wouldn't be his last text, no matter what he said. I'd opened the door a crack, and he was intent on barging in.

—What—

I waited for his answer. I didn't feel a hum between my legs at the thought of him, nor did he make me grin with anticipation. I didn't want him as a boyfriend, lover, or fuck—not that he would find the latter two acceptable. I wanted to just talk to him, to see the devotion and fidelity I'd slaughtered so heartlessly. I didn't want him back. I wanted to surgically remove the viable parts, label them, and put them in a case so I would recognize them if I saw them again.

—see me—

I answered it.

—Where?—

PART III
SUBMIT

CHAPTER 42

I was on my hands and knees at Jonathan's front door, my palms inside the house, my knees still on the porch. The smell of sage and dry morning fog surrounded me. The air was cold enough to harden my nipples even though the sun baked my bare back. I wanted to touch my breasts, but I wouldn't because I'd been told not to move my hands from the floor. I obeyed, though I didn't know why. My pussy was wet. I felt the weight of my arousal hanging between my legs like the clapper on a bell, heavy and swinging.

I wanted Jonathan, but he'd gone somewhere, leaving me here like *this*. I wanted to press my legs together to squeeze my aching clit, but I'd been told to keep my knees spread.

A voice called my name. Darren. Then Gabby. God, no. They couldn't be here until Jonathan finished.

Then, I felt his dick pressed up against me and hands on my hips. I didn't have a second to gasp before he was inside me, pounding mercilessly. Hands gripped my ass, pressing hard enough to bruise, and the pain was a counterpoint to the pleasure, making it sweeter, wetter, hotter. I moved with him, slamming onto his cock. He pulled my hips up and pressed down the arch of my back, stroking my clit with his shaft. I was this close to exploding in a burst of moans and cries when I saw a mirror in the house that hadn't been there before, and Jonathan wasn't fucking me, but Gabby. She was moaning, and the bedsprings were squeaking.

I woke up, sweating. In the room next to mine, the bedsprings squeaked, and Gabby let the neighborhood know Theo was fucking the life out of her. God bless them.

I was not in a clear emotional state. Two days before, Jonathan had left me with a promise of fidelity and a swollen nodule between my legs that I pledged not to touch. A day later, his ex-wife had shown up at my job, apparently to tell me he fucked her so hard the night before that he fractured a bone.

Yet, despite the fact that he may well have been a stinking liar, I kept my promise to save my orgasm for him. And I would, until I dumped him, at which time I was going to run into the nearest bathroom and relieve myself.

Theo finished with a Scottish-accented grunt. Thank God. I wasn't sure if they were making me uncomfortable or horny. Seeing them in the kitchen for morning tea was going to be awkward.

I went into my bathroom to shower and dress. Afterward, I walked out the back door so I wouldn't have to say good morning to anyone.

I felt constantly on the verge of an assault on something or someone. I got angry at the chair leg I stubbed my toe against. Traffic went from the cost of living in Los Angeles to a singular attack by a spiteful God. Mostly, I was angry at myself. I knew I wasn't capable of having a serious relationship because I got too involved and lost myself in the other person's needs. Nor was I capable of a casual encounter because I couldn't bear the thought of anyone I was screwing being with another woman in the same space of time. My only alternative was celibacy, a fine and viable option, but I'd broken a perfectly good sexless streak to be with Jonathan. So I was stuck. Our relationship was too serious to forget and move on and too casual to get upset over him fucking his ex-wife. I was a fool. A damned fool.

I got in the car and realized I hadn't put on any makeup. I looked in the rearview. Did I need any? I was only going to see my ex, Kevin. If I went in without makeup, it would be a sign that I wasn't trying to impress him, that I didn't want him back. I just wanted to talk, and I didn't need lipstick for my mouth and ears to operate. I didn't need mascara to see if I'd been crazy to leave him.

Kevin used to have a place Downtown, but when the market for crap industrial spaces exploded, his rent tripled, so he'd split for the strip of land between Dodger Stadium and the L.A. River called Frogtown. I'd helped him move there four months before I left. The building had changed drastically in the interim. The broken brick façade had gone from a soot-encrusted dark red to a multicolored mural, corner to corner, of a huge young girl peeking into the front door as if it were the entrance to her doll house. The side of the building had been painted to look like the wall was see-through, with depicted trees and buildings that matched the real landscape of the L.A. River, like a Road Runner cartoon where the bird painted a single-point perspective road on a brick wall.

Those were not Kevin's work. The girl looking at the door was definitely Jack's style. The *trompe l'oeil* thing on the side looked like Geraldine Stark, one of his contemporaries. She was a quite prolific whore in the art scene, and I found myself wondering if Kevin had fucked her at some point.

I rang the bell. I waited. I rang again. Waited. Just like him to beg to see me then get so involved in something else he couldn't answer the door. God, men were such fuckups. Every damn one of them.

The door finally opened, and I stood straighter so he wouldn't see me arched with annoyance.

"Monica," he said. "You came."

"I said I would."

He grinned his most gorgeous grin, straight-ish teeth a crescent of white in the pink dust of a set of lips that God himself must have used as a template for the perfections of the human face. I remembered kissing them. I remembered them running over the insides of my thigh, brushing against my pussy, bookends for his flicking tongue.

"Come in," he said, stepping to the side.

"Thank you." I grasped the strap on my shoulder bag for something to hang on to as I caught his scent of malt and chocolate. Jonathan left me with a throbbing ache of desire unquenched because he thought it made me think of him, but he couldn't have had any idea how dangerous that was. A different person would have been fucking anything that moved.

The hall was narrow, and I had to brush by him to enter. He closed the door behind me with a metallic *thunk*. I passed doorways on either side of the hall. At the end, the hall opened into a warehouse space with a forty-foot ceiling and a cement floor he'd had poured himself. Waist-high tables stood all over the room in what looked like a random pattern but wasn't. They were set up in an emulation of Kevin's process. Each table was inaccessible without passing a necessary step before it, so the visual story of whatever he was working on could be told from the start every time.

The pattern would never make sense to an outsider, but in his mind, it brought his installations together.

"Can I get you something? Tea?" He seemed tiny in the huge space. His white T-shirt looked insignificant and plain. "I put in a kitchen."

"Wow," I said. "Can I see?"

He led me to the far end of the huge space, weaving past the tables down a path he'd left for that purpose. The kitchen had glass block windows to the outside and a wall covered in magazine pictures of food stuck on with silk straight pins. The cabinetry was white, the surfaces embellished here and there with perfectly placed stickers or an odd tile in an incongruous color that a person with anything less than exquisite taste would have screwed up.

"Green okay?" he asked, reaching for a box of tea on a high shelf. His T-shirt rode up, exposing the path of dark hair on his belly, and I shuddered with the memory of touching it.

"That's fine."

He nudged the box, and it fell, bouncing off his fingertips. He caught it and smiled like a shortstop fielding a chopper to left. He put a two-pint saucepot under the faucet, and by the time he got it on the stove, I noticed his eyes hadn't met mine since we'd walked into the kitchen.

"So," I said, pulling up a fifties-style chrome and pleather chair, "what the hell did you think you were doing with that coalmine bullshit?"

His back was to me, and I could clearly see the muscles there tense. His shoulder blades drew close, and he looked toward the ceiling as if pulling strength from the heavens.

He turned his head only slightly to answer. "I entertained every idea of what you'd think for the year I worked on that fucking thing."

"Did you ever consider sending me a letter and asking me what I thought?"

He turned and crossed his arms. His biceps were hard and lean from building, hammering, and climbing. Kevin's work was motionless in the gallery but very physical in its creation. "Yes, but honestly, Monica, once I decided to make the piece, what you thought was irrelevant. It wasn't about you."

Of course it wasn't. My stuff, my words, and our intimacy were his to use as he pleased. It was as if I'd never left. I didn't know what I thought I'd see by going to him, but he was the same old Kevin.

As if he could read my mind, his shoulders slackened and his hands dropped to his sides. "That's not what I meant," he said.

"Yeah."

"What *do* you think?"

"I'm really pissed I left those jeans behind."

He smiled again, a barely audible chuckle issuing from his perfect mouth. He dropped his eyes to the floor, black lashes shining blue in the fluorescent light. I wished I didn't have to look at him. He was screwing with my head.

"There were other things," he said. "I really struggled with what to put in."

"Did you miss a maxi pad?"

"Oh, Monica. Always ready with a joke when you feel uncomfortable."

"At least I don't flirt."

He looked me in the eye for the first time, and the gaze lasted long enough to make me shift in my seat. I looked away.

"I deserved that," he said. "Can I show you what I wanted you to come for?"

I stood up and turned the heat off the tea water. "Yes."

We wove back through the tables in the big room. Most were empty, as he'd just shown something, but as I went by, I noticed nudes in charcoal and ballpoint pen: men and women, some alone, some twined together in scribbled couplings. They were illustrations of what was on his mind, and what was on his mind was much the same as what was on mine.

The wall facing the front of the building had a row of doors, and unless something had changed, the rooms were meant to house draft installations. He opened one and flicked on the light.

The room was windowless and similar in size to the one in the Eclipse show, and it was a disaster. A quilted comforter hung on one wall, a table with more pornographic scribbles on the other wall. Stacks of boxes littered the floor.

"What am I looking at?" I asked.

"Early draft. But I really struggled with one object because I thought I should return it, but then, I got mad at you again, and I almost burned it. I had the barbecue going in the back, but I couldn't."

"What is it?"

He reached between two boxes and pulled out a hard plastic case with a handle. I noticed a pink and red Dirty Girls sticker by the buckle.

"My viola!" I held out my hands. He handed it to me then shifted some sketches so I could put it on the table. "I thought I left this up with my parents in Castaic the last time we went."

"Yeah. It was in the trunk. I… uh…" He put his fingers through his hair. "I didn't want you to play for me. It kept me from thinking straight about you."

Things between us hadn't been perfect before I left. I had no idea it was as clear to him as it had been to me. I opened the case. My viola was in there, exactly as I'd left it, with the bow tucked in the lid and a pocket with rosin, extra strings, and a pick I liked to use when I was feeling experimental. "Those last few months," I said, "I was very lonely. I could have used this."

He sat on a box. "I think hiding it was a mistake."

I should have been angry. I should have smacked the case across his face and run out with my instrument. But I couldn't. It all seemed so long ago. I touched the wood, running my finger over the curves. The gut core strings were dried out and would probably snap before I finished a song, and the fingerboard still had little grease spots from my hours of playing.

"That was really dickish of you, Kevin." I pulled the viola from the case. "You're an unscrupulous ass."

"Is that why you left me?"

I felt a sinkhole open in my diaphragm. I didn't want to discuss it. I had just wanted to break up with him, so I did. How did I get manipulated into going to his studio just to discuss an eighteen-month-old hurt?

Because I'd done it wrong. I'd done what was right for me, telling myself I'd just do without all the discussing and crying. I was just going to avoid all the emotional illness, but there were two of us, and Kevin hadn't been part of the decision.

I popped the bow from the clasps. The case was cheap, student-grade. The viola, however, was professional quality, purchased at a West Hollywood pawn shop for my fifteenth birthday by my father, who approved of me.

I tucked the viola under my chin and ran my fingers over the strings. They were loose. I tightened a couple of pegs, but the sound would only be barely acceptable. Barely. "I left you because I needed you," I said.

"That makes no sense."

I drew the bow over the strings and adjusted the tension, waiting for one to break in a snapping curlicue, but it didn't happen. I got the tension close and played something he'd know, dragging that first note across the bow as if summoning it from our collective past.

"You weren't capable of being needed." I played the next note.

"Don't." His whisper came out husky, as if the command had caught in his throat.

I didn't listen to him, but played the song my mind would never have recalled but my body knew.

Kevin didn't sleep well. Unlike workaholics and TV addicts, he wanted desperately to sleep a full night, and unlike most insomniacs, he fell soundly to sleep at a decent hour. But about four times a week, he awoke in the early hours of the morning with a pounding, anxious pain in his chest. I woke up when he shifted. I held him, stroked his hair, hummed, but nothing put him back to sleep except me playing the viola. We had a tune we shared, a lullaby I wrote for him with my fingers and arm. I never wrote it down because it became as real as the bond between us, and it ceased to exist when that bond broke.

So I played it for him in that first-draft installation that looked more like a storage room than a homage to a breakup. And he watched me with his butt leaning on the table, and his ankles and arms crossed. I let the last note drift off. The song had no end; I'd always just played it until his breathing became level and regular.

"Sounds like shit," I said.

"I don't know what you were doing, playing that."

"Maybe you can tell me what you were doing putting my shit in a museum without telling me."

"I was scared."

I laid the instrument in its case. "Of?"

"The piece was happening, and I wasn't fighting about it."

"I want my jeans back." This was ridiculous. I didn't

give a rat's ass about my fucking jeans. I just wanted to provide him with the exact thing he didn't want. I wanted to fight him.

"The whole thing is sold. Even the books and catalogs are sold out. You'd be after me and some collector on a Spanish island. Our lawyers would have lawyers."

"This is not fair," I whispered, stroking the brittle strings of my lost viola.

"I know. None of it was."

I knew he didn't just mean his piece. He meant everything from the minute we met to the moment I finished playing our lullaby. I felt emotionally dehydrated and raw at the edges.

"I should go." I snapped my case shut. "Thanks for not putting this in the piece."

I turned to walk out, and like a cat, he jumped in front of me, putting his hands on my cheeks. "You're happy? With this new guy?"

"Jonathan. You know his name."

"Are you happy?"

"It's casual."

"You? Tweety Bird? I don't believe it."

I'd forgotten that. He called me his canary when he was feeling warm and affectionate. How convenient for me to overlook that when he felt confronted in the slightest, or distant, or overwhelmed, he called me Tweety Bird. I never knew if he even realized the name he used for me said more about him than it did about me.

"Take your hands off my face," I said. His fingers fell off my cheeks as if they melted away. "I don't mean to be callous, Kevin. I don't want to fall into life unintentionally any more. Jonathan has a purpose." His eyebrows went up half a tick. That had to be answered. "Get your mind out of the gutter."

Out of the gutter meant one thing to the rest of the

world and the opposite to us. It meant, *Stop thinking it's about money*.

"You know, I didn't ask you to come here to talk about us. If you could give me another ten minutes, we can sit in the kitchen, and I'll make you some tea. Properly. I want to pitch something to you."

I looked at my watch. I had the night shift. "You have half an hour."

He leaned down a little to look me in the face with his big chocolate-coin eyes. "Thank you."

He walked quickly back to the kitchen. He made tea with efficiency and grace, speaking with a catch of thrill in his voice I hadn't heard in a long time. I couldn't have gotten a word in edgewise if I'd wanted.

"We all make art about these big concepts. We feel like we need to put it all under a cultural umbrella if we want to get into the lexicon, but I haven't cried in front of a piece of art since I was in college. It's because the whole scene is up in its head. Banksy's scribbling culture, Barbara Kruger's still yelling about consumer culture, John Currin's talking about sex and culture, and Frank Hermaine is ... I don't even know what that guy is talking about. No one's doing anything about the stuff that matters, stuff that gets us up in the morning and rocks us to sleep at night. When I realized this, I started being thankful you walked out. I mean ... not really, but it made me realize that nothing I was doing made a damn bit of difference or touched anyone, and I thought if I could take that pain I felt and put it in a room, so when someone walked into that room who was going through the same thing, they'd recognize it. They'd say, *yes, I'm connected to this. I'm feeling it.* Can you imagine it? The bond? The potential? The power?"

In the middle of his pitch, he'd sat down and, like a coiled spring, perched on the edge of the seat, his legs splayed, heels rocking his seat back onto the corners of the legs. His elbows were angled to the tabletop, hands gesturing.

How young I'd been to fall so deeply in love with his enthusiasm. "So this is what you were trying to do with the Eclipse piece?"

"I was trying to exorcise you with that, trying to figure it out so I could get rid of you. But it made me think about what something truly personal could mean as a visual narrative, and then I thought, maybe it's not a visual narrative. Maybe it's a multi-media narrative, with one party speaking to the visual and another to the aural." As if reacting to my expression, he leaned forward even farther. "Before you think anything, both narratives need to fight each other. There needs to be an aesthetic tension until it all goes black and silent. It's an experience of fullness before death. *Pow*."

I sipped my tea. He needed to wait for me to think. I wasn't fucking him anymore. I didn't have to jump like a brainless fangirl on every idea he pitched me. Except it was a good idea. Everything about it could be beautiful, a truly moving experience, a three-dimensional cinema of tone.

"You're not talking about a linear narrative," I said.

"Of course not."

"Yeah."

"Yeah, what?"

"You should do it. But without my toiletries."

"Fuck your toiletries. I want *you*."

I took a long breath through my nose and closed my eyes. I needed to avoid lashing out. He couldn't have meant it sexually. Couldn't.

"Let me rephrase that," he said.

"Please."

"It's a collaboration. You do the aural, obviously."

I pursed my lips and stared into my tea. "Kevin, I can't."

"Why not?"

"For one, it would be awkward."

"Only if we let it be."

He leaned on the wall, his posture relaxed now that the pitch phase of the process was ended and the artistic seduction phase was about to begin.

"And two," I said, "I haven't been able to write a word or make two notes together make sense. I'm stuck."

"Getting stuck is part of the process."

"It's a no."

"So you'll think about it?"

"Your thirty minutes are up, Kevin." I stood. "It was nice to see you."

"Let me walk you out." He smiled like a man who hadn't been rejected but had just gotten exactly what he wanted.

ifteen minutes after Jessica Carnes implied Jonathan's roughness in bed had broken her wrist, Jonathan had texted me.

—*What did she tell you?*—

I didn't answer, and I didn't hear from him again. Debbie, my bar manager and a friend of Jonathan's, had seen but not heard the exchange and had alerted him while he was in San Francisco. She'd admitted it with no guilt.

"If you saw your face," she said, "you would have called him too."

"Sometimes I think you're more invested in this relationship than either of us," I'd replied, arranging drinks on a tray.

"I like you both. Jessica, not as much. Now go serve those before the ice melts."

But I was glad I didn't hear from Jonathan again. I didn't want to have some drawn-out phone conversation about what Jessica had told me and why it upset me, whether or not he fucked her. I didn't want excuses. I didn't want conflicting stories. I just wanted to do what I was supposed to be doing: making music, being at peace with it, watching Gabby, doing my paying job without a sad look on my face or clumsy spills.

So when I got another call from Jonathan, I sent it to voicemail. I was driving. And I didn't want to talk to him. I knew he was back, because for all my posturing, I was counting the days until his return. He texted, and I ignored it. But when I got to a red light, I had to read it. I was only human.

—*If you're ending it with me*
just tell me, ok?—

Fuck. He had to go there. He had to undercut my delicious spite. I pulled the car over and drafted and re-drafted a text. If I saw him before our studio time for WDE tomorrow, I could cut it short. No twelve-hour fuck sessions. Perfect. I needed to avoid hurting myself on his body.

—*Tomorrow afternoon to talk?*—

My screen told me he was typing, and I imagined his thumb sliding over the glass, the way it had slid over my body, and I shuddered a little as the car idled in a red zone.
—*Public space?*—
I started typing, then stopped myself. A public space meant I couldn't show that I was upset, and if I were honest with myself for a change, I *was* upset. The problem with a private space was that being alone in a room with him meant the conversation could only end one way.

—*Private*—

—*Would the Loft Club be ok?*

Not exactly neutral—

—It's fine. 1pm. Gotta go—

I tossed the phone onto the passenger seat and put the car in drive. I'd scheduled Jonathan three hours before a recording session in Burbank. The session had been set up by Eugene Testarossa at WDE because Gabby and I didn't have a track between us.

The lunch meeting with Testarossa had gone smoothly and lasted exactly one hour. We were stroked, complimented, and offered gigs and contracts that could never be delivered. I'd become convinced some time during college that the most valuable skill one needed in Los Angeles was the ability to tell the bullshit from the real shit. Only one piece of reality entered the conversation.

"Carnival has a new label," Eugene said as he finished his salad. He'd taken us to Mantini's and spent the whole meal looking at the door. "Singer, songwriters. Not folk, but a kind of trip-hop poetry. Lyrically heavy lounge."

"I don't have a lot of songs ready," I'd jumped in. I didn't want to say I didn't have *any* songs, but I couldn't lie completely without getting busted.

Eugene waved his hand. "We have a songwriter. We need your pipes." As an afterthought, he turned to Gabby. "And your compositional skills."

So we'd agreed to cut two songs written by a WDE client at DownDawg Studios in Burbank. Gabby and I were hip-pocketed, meaning they could take a portion of any money we made without committing to represent us over the long term. Gabby giggled the whole way home, but I felt as though I'd just had a fist removed from my ass.

The songs had been messengered the next day. For all Eugene's pretentions about lyrically driven vocals, they were lame garbage. I was going to have to work twice as hard to make them sound like anything. The last thing I should have done was make a date with Jonathan just before the recording session, but I'd been compelled. It was good timing. I'd have an excuse to leave.

When my phone blooped, I didn't look at it. If Jonathan and I were on, then we were on. If he had a change, he was going to have to wait for me to accept it. I wasn't playing games with him. I really needed to get to Darren's if I was going to talk to him and still get to Frontage on time.

I parked in my driveway and walked down the hill and right on Echo Park Ave. Darren lived in a two-story apartment building with a courtyard in the middle of a giant U. It was exactly like thousands of other buildings in Los Angeles: poorly thought-out, carelessly built, and hopelessly ugly. But the tall hedges and trees in the front gave it the appearance of a quiet hideaway, and its proximity to his damaged sister, who he had to watch if he was going to sleep at night, made it the perfect place for him.

The front gate was chocked open as always by the kids running in and out. I was thinking about how to ask him what I wanted to ask him and what answer I wanted as I trudged up the steps. I passed his window. The TV was on, so he was home. The front door was open, the screen was shut, and inside, Darren leaned on the kitchen doorframe and laughed. It was a relaxed laugh, done with his arms crossed, as an answer to something, and I felt as though I was eavesdropping. I raised my hand to knock, but a man with short sandy hair got up from the couch, and Darren laughed harder as he was engulfed in arms and kisses—wet and passionate—and four robust male arms tangled around each other.

I couldn't keep silent. "A*ha!*"

They pulled off each other and looked at me.

"Musical theater!" I shouted. "You're the mystery woman taking him out to shows!"

"Which one is this?" Sandy Hair asked.

They looked at each other, and Darren said, "You coming in or what?"

I went through the door and held out my hand. "I'm Monica. It's nice to meet you."

"Adam. Same here."

We shook. His grip was tight and dry. He was hot, with a little blondish stubble and grey eyes I knew would change color depending on what he wore. I tried to stay calm, but inside, I was giggling with delight. I was happy not only to uncover Darren's secret, but that he was only hiding happiness.

Adam picked up his jacket. "I gotta go." He approached Darren and went in for a kiss. Darren kept his arms crossed and turned his face to catch it on the cheek. Adam took him by the cheeks and turned his face, kissing him wetly on the lips. Darren was non-responsive.

"Oh, come on," Adam said. "Look at her. She's smiling."

"Kiss him! Kiss him!" I said.

He did, and it was such a lovely sight to see my friend happy that I had to clench my hands to keep from clapping.

Adam finally pushed him away. "God, slut. You're making me late." He winked at me on the way out.

I knew I was smiling again. It was the uncontrollable type of grin that hurt my face.

"You're embarrassing yourself," he said.

"I don't care. Are you going to tell me everything?"

He threw himself on the couch and turned off the TV. "We met in the Music House. He comes in all the time. I thought he was asking for me because of my expertise."

"But it was your hot body."

He threw a pillow at me. "Would you stop?"

I buried my face in the pillow. "I'm so happy. I worried about you all the time because you rarely went out with anyone."

"I was confused, as they say. And Lord knows I couldn't burden Gabby."

I flung the pillow back at him. "Why didn't you tell *me*?"

"We have a past. I didn't want you to feel like I was... I don't know, like I didn't love you the right way."

"You didn't, you fucktard. Now you do, but then you didn't. And why don't you tell Gabby now?"

He sighed. "Adam's last name is Marsillo. Which means nothing to you. But the CEO of Foundation Records? That's her maiden name."

"That's his mother."

"Gabby would know that," he said, "and freak out. She'd start making marriage plans. He's nice, but I'm not ready for her to start hovering."

I looked away, fondling the crease in my jeans. Gabby would handle her brother's homosexuality just fine, but he was right. Any connection to the music industry could send her spinning in either direction.

I jumped up and dropped into his lap, hugging him for all I was worth. I kissed his cheek.

He laughed and pushed me away. "Sorry, baby, you're not my type."

"I'm heartbroken."

"Did you come here to snoop or did you have something to say?"

"I saw Kevin."

"Uh oh?"

"Nothing like that. He wants to collaborate on a project. I'm totally stuck, and I thought if the three of us worked on it, I'd get unstuck, and we could be together again." I looked at my watch and bounced to my feet. "But now I have no time to even discuss it. Are you coming tonight?"

"Adam and I have tickets." He smiled. "Musical theater."

"You're a cliché."

He shrugged. "Don't tell Gabby yet. I don't like this thing with Theo."

"Why not?" I was annoyed that he'd deny her happiness just when he'd found his own.

"He deals scrips. He's the last person she should be messing with."

"How did I not know that?"

"Your head hasn't been in the game since you spent the night up in Griffith Park. Speaking of, did you see the pictures of you and Mister Gorgeous at the Eclipse show? They were all over the internet."

"God, no."

"Do you want me to pull them up? You look amazing."

"Absolutely not. I don't want to hear what anyone has to say about my life. Living it is hard enough." I went to the door but thought better of bolting out. I hugged Darren again and kissed his cheek. "I'm happy for you."

He pushed me toward the door. I felt closer to him than I'd felt since we were in high school. "Get out of here," he said. "Knock 'em dead or whatever."

*a*t first, I wore the outfit least likely to land Jonathan's dick inside me. My jeans were tight enough to cut the curve of my ass and accent the space between my skinny thighs, but so difficult to get off in a heat of passion that I'd have plenty of time to think about what I was doing and deny him access. I wore a bra with three hooks in back and a woven shirt that couldn't be pulled over the head without unbuttoning it. I looked hot and physically inaccessible.

I realized that made me very easy to lie to, because I'd walk into the room, he'd make plans to remove my clothes, assess the difficulties, and say whatever he had to in order to soothe my mind. I didn't want that. I wanted the truth about what had happened between him and Jessica the night he dropped me at my house. I wanted it in all its ugliness and gritty detail. I wanted all the pain and all the hurt. I owned it for trusting him and for asking more of him than he could give, even though I'd been warned. If he hurt me enough, I wouldn't make those mistakes again.

Despite the bruises that still stained the backs of my thighs, Jonathan wasn't the kind of guy to revel in hurting me, at least not emotionally. I was going to have to pull it out of him, and my suit of armor wasn't going to cut it. I had to weaken him. I had to make him tell me everything, even against his better judgment. I had to make him beg.

It was a garter, then, and a dress with a flared bottom. I got aroused just putting on that outfit. I'd go to the studio in Burbank directly after, so I stuck a pair of spare undies in my bag and called myself done.

CHAPTER 45

$\mathcal{A}$s I stepped out of the elevator into the club's lobby, a throbbing ache developed between my legs, and with each step down the hall, I got wetter just from being aware of the garter under the skirt. The upcoming conversation was going to be very difficult if I didn't get a handle on my sex drive.

I towered over Terry, the hostess, in four-inch heels. They made me about six feet tall, but I'd wanted to be looking Jonathan in the face. I needed to catch lies and half-truths before they dropped.

The room was a different one, smaller, with two sets of cocktail tables and a leather loveseat and coffee table in the center of the room. He stood by the wall of windows, and when he looked at me, my heart stopped for half a beat. It was the work clothes: the charcoal suit, maroon tie, and the cufflinks. The glass of Perrier in his fingertips.

But when I got close, something had changed. His scent wasn't the dry one I remembered, but something like sawdust, leather, and wet earth. The aroma was less beautiful, but sexier, and I felt the effects of it in the weight and wetness between my legs.

"Hi," he said.

"Hello."

The door closed behind me. I wanted to hold him, to forget everything. If I could only pretend Jessica hadn't come into the bar, I would have wrapped myself around him. I stepped close to him, until we were eye to eye.

"Can I get you a glass of water?" he asked.

"No, thanks."

"Flat water? I can get it without bubbles."

"No, thanks."

"I can order up some cookies."

"I don't want anything."

"Can you just tell me what she told you?"

"You're all aquiver, Jonathan. What do you think she told me?" My tone was sharper than I'd intended.

He swirled the ice around in his glass. "Something that upset you." He was going to dance around indefinitely. He was guarded and undoubtedly ready to be dishonest about something.

I had come prepared to make it very difficult for him. "Yes. She said something that upset me. A lot." I hooked my finger in his waistband.

"Did she say you looked fat? She can be very catty."

"Funny guy." I pulled his belt from the loop, yanking the tongue from the metal hook. "I'm going to ask you a question, and I want it answered in detail." His belt fell open with a metallic clank. I took the glass from his hand and placed it on the table. His fingertips went for my face, but I pulled them away. "Hands at your sides."

"You're joking."

"Do I look like I'm joking?" I unzipped his pants. "I'm going to be on my knees. No touching."

"Was there a question? You said there was a question."

I dropped to my knees and rubbed his organ through his underwear, hardening it. I put my lips to it and breathed a hot breath, then rubbed my teeth through the cloth covering his growing stiffness. He groaned.

I pulled out his cock, the gorgeous thing, and licked the tip. "Are you ready for my question?"

"No."

I put the head in my mouth to get it wet, sucking on the way out. "You stop talking, I stop sucking. Okay?" I looked up at him.

He reached for my hair, but I pushed his hand back.

"Okay," he said, and I could hear the smile on his lips.

I gave the head another suck, then said, "Tell me where you went after you dropped me at my house and what happened there."

"I don't need a blowjob this bad, Monica."

"I want your guard down, and I want your dick." I slid my mouth all the way down then, lips dragging along the length of him, tongue following, my throat open. I let it feel the whole of me for a second before drawing it slowly out.

"God damn." He reached for the back of my head, and I pulled his hand away again. "I'm tying your hands behind your back next time," he said.

"You went which way on Vestal Street?"

"I'm just going to cut to it," he said. "Jessica's. I went to see Jessica."

"An hour after we agreed to be exclusive?"

I didn't want to look at him when he answered, so I took his dick in my mouth and worked it while he spoke.

"She texted me. She wanted to talk. I was always there for her because she was there for me. I didn't see any harm in it. I didn't think anything would happen." He must have felt a hitch in my throat, because he added, "Wait. I don't want to phrase it like that."

"Phrase it any way you have to," I said, stroking his dick with my hand. My saliva made it slick enough to work, and his sharp intake of breath told me he could slip up anytime. A drop of pre-come oozed from his red tip, and I caught it with my tongue. I licked down to the base, his skin paper thin against my tongue, and what I was looking for, the scent of another woman, was nowhere on him.

"Monica, I like you. I don't want to—" He gasped as a tooth grazed his shaft.

"Speak. I can take it."

"I didn't fuck her. I don't know what she said, but I'm not telling you anything else while you're sucking me off." He grabbed my wrists and placed them on my head like I was being arrested. "Now, finish the job."

I looked up at his smiling lips. I didn't know what he'd done. Undoubtedly, there was more to the story, but was I going to swallow a load of his come to find out?

I opened my mouth. He held my wrists in his right hand, gripping them tightly. With his left, he guided his cock into my mouth, and unlike a second ago when I had controlled the situation, the taste and tautness of his skin sent a bolt of pleasure through me. I couldn't resist it. My pussy bulged when he tightened his lock on my wrists. Jesus, the motherfucker sucked away my resolve and turned it into orgasms.

He put his left hand to the back of my head and gently thrust himself down my throat, letting out a groan on the third thrust.

"You okay down there?" he asked.

I made a noise that indicated I was.

"Take it. All the way."

The act of obeying his command engorged my clit. It throbbed, demanding I notice the tone of his voice, his new smell, his hand tugging the hair at the back of my head.

"Flatten your tongue along the bottom. Ah, like that."

He pushed into my throat, my tongue stroking the underside of his throbbing, hot cock. He squeezed my wrists and thrust hard and fast, holding my head still. I opened my mouth wide to keep from biting him as he went down my throat to the base. The hairs of his stomach tickled my nose. All the concentration it took to keep my mouth open and take his cock only brought my own orgasm closer.

"I'm coming," he whispered. It was a statement, not a question, and I was meant to prepare to swallow.

He grunted and came, sharp and sticky down my throat. I breathed through my nose, taking him without gagging and letting his juice run out as he finished. When he came to a stop, I kissed the end of his cock. He released my arms.

When I put them down, I caught a shooting ache in my biceps. "I better not find out you're lying," I said. "That was the best blowjob I ever gave anyone."

He put himself back in his pants and zipped up. "You have a funny way of showing a guy you're pissed off." He reached for my hand to help me up, and I took it. He steadied me as I wobbled on my high heels.

"Welcome home," I said. "Now, I've been upset for days."

"I'm sorry about that. If you had called me, I could have told you sooner."

"But you did *something* with her."

He touched my chin with two fingers, then slid them over my jaw and down my neck, down my chest, stopping at my nipple, which was rock hard under my dress. He brushed his thumb against it and leaned his body into mine, kissing my lips softly while he stroked my breast.

"Why do you want to know?" he asked.

"I hate secrets."

"I have secrets I may never tell you."

"I only want this one today. I know she's yours. I know she has your heart, but you promised me your body, so I have the right to it."

He kissed my neck, finding the sensitive spots. "She has nothing of mine."

My hands went under his jacket, finding his waist. I stroked the shape of him while he moved off my breast and down to my ass.

He gasped in my neck when he felt what I was wearing under my skirt. "Monica."

"I was ready to do whatever I needed to so you'd tell me."

He stepped back. "Pick up your skirt."

"We didn't get to enjoy this the other night." I pulled up my skirt so he could see the garter, minus the panties. "So you're telling me, right?"

"No."

I put down my skirt.

He stepped closer and brushed his finger against my collarbone. "No games. I don't want to tell you because it's better that way. But I'll tell you this: I spent the past three days thinking about you, how much I wanted you, and realizing I was free to have you." He kissed me, a slow, soft grind of his lips and tongue, and I yielded to him. "Tell me you're mine," he whispered. "Say it."

I wanted to. I almost did. I almost promised him whatever he wanted, but the anxiety of the last few days nagged at my chest and throat. "Tell me what happened with Jessica."

"I'm afraid I'll chase you away, and I don't want to

do that."

"I can take it."

"Fine then. Turn around."

I let go of my skirt and faced away from him. He put his palms on my ass, then moved closer and drew them up my back until his newly erect penis was pressed against me. He unzipped the simple black dress and pressed his hands to my shoulders in such a way as to turn me around to face him.

"Take it off," he said.

I let the dress slip over my shoulders and onto the floor. I stood in the black garter, black heels, matching lace bra, and a wet pussy. I stepped out of the dress and pushed it to the side. He watched me, and I could almost see his brain working. He stepped back to me and kicked my legs open with his foot, then stroked my forearms, down to my hands. He laced his fingers into mine. His eyes were not unkind, but hard and focused.

"I'd fuck you senseless," he said, "but I never got more condoms."

"You'll make it up to me."

"What did she say to you?" he asked.

"I asked her how she broke her wrist, and she said, 'Jonathan can be rough sometimes.'"

He made a little snort that might have been mistaken for a short laugh if the rest of his face hadn't been so hardened. "First of all, that's a typical Jessica contextual lie." He moved my hands behind me. "Lean back." He held my arms steady so I wouldn't fall, until my back was arched enough for my hands to lean on the back of the love seat. His body curved with mine, his breath on my shoulder as he drew his hands up my arms. "It's true as a statement, but false in context. Second of all, she doesn't know from rough. You, my darling, got me rougher than she's ever seen."

He stepped back from me, an artist working on a

piece. I stood, legs apart, back arched, arms behind me leaning on the back of the sofa. I felt exposed, vulnerable, and turned on. He'd called Jessica a liar, and one with her own brand of lying. I noted the change in attitude. He put his hand on the small of my back and pushed up, arching it further, exposing me to him, and forcing me to look at the ceiling.

"She lives in Venice, on the water," he said as he lifted my bra, exposing my tits so he could stroke the rock-hard nipples. "And she was waiting. As soon as I drove up, she was in the doorway. She hadn't acted happy to see me in two years or more. And yes, I thought about you, but I figured only a few hours had passed. If I needed to get out, you'd understand. Or not. I wasn't on ethically shaky ground."

A drizzle of wetness dripped down my leg.

"She hugged me and pulled me into the house. I kept asking her what was wrong, and I mean, I shouldn't have been surprised, but there was so much shit missing."

"Her boyfriend left and took his stuff," I said.

"I was happy. I was excited. I felt like I'd won some kind of war." He reached down to part my thighs more than I thought physically possible. His finger grazed the drip. "A war of patience. She poured us some wine, and as soon as she started talking about how great she felt that he was gone, I knew something was wrong." He brushed his wet finger against my lower lips, and I tasted myself. "This is turning you on."

"What you're doing. Not what you're saying."

"She put her hands on me. I can't tell you how long I waited for her to touch me again." He put his hand between my breasts and moved it down my belly, touching the diamond in my navel and circling it before he drifted down to my crotch. He brushed against my crotch only long enough to feel the dampness then moved to my thighs again.

I moaned and pushed against him.

He pressed his hand flat against my pussy, letting me do the work of grinding against him. "And I kissed her. I admit it. I couldn't have stopped myself. She said, 'Make love to me, Jonathan, like you used to.' So I threw her on the couch."

I scrunched my face because I didn't want to show I was upset. I wanted to enjoy him and his touch and not hear what happened that had kept him from making love to his ex-wife. Had she pushed him away at the last minute? Or had the boyfriend walked in? I didn't care anymore. "I don't want to hear it," I said, staring at the exposed beam on the ceiling.

"Too late." He picked up his glass of Perrier and placed it on my chest. "Don't let this fall."

I couldn't look at him or the glass would tip. An icy cold patch formed at the center of my sternum.

He kneeled between my legs. "She smelled like I'd always remembered. Like cut grass." He kissed the inside of my thigh, licking away the juices from my pussy as he made his way upward. "And I thought, ah, I remember this smell. And I was kissing her, but…" He stopped and kissed my clit once. "I realized I didn't want her. And the cut-grass smell?" His tongue went from my pussy to my clit and back.

I moaned again, louder. He pulled me open. The air itself was a physical pressure on me, and I wanted him, just this once, even if it would be the last time.

"The cut grass smell wasn't love. It was gratitude. I felt like I was kissing one of my sisters." He gave my clit a suck, a fast, light thing that got a cry from me. "Then I thought of you, and I knew I had to get out of there. That was the end of that."

With that, he put his tongue on my clit, breathing

hot breaths, wiggling his tongue until I thought for sure I was going to tip the glass. I felt gratitude, too, and it smelled nothing like cut grass.

"Kissing is cheating," I said. "Even if you had to do it to get over her."

"Yeah. But I figured if I got my lips on your cunt before I told you, you'd forgive me. I think we walked in here with the same strategy." He slid his fingers into me. "If that glass drops, I stop, and you go home with a baseball."

"I don't forgive you." Cold condensation dripped off my chest and down my sides.

"I know." He pushed his fingers in as deep as they'd go and used his other hand to expose the hard nodule of my clit. "You have a beautiful cunt, Monica."

I had not a second to think about how that word was foul and disgusting from anyone else's lips before he put his tongue to my clit and all thinking disappeared. Three strokes with the tip and a suck. Four strokes and a longer suck. Pushing fingers in and out, stretching me, while he licked me again, then he jammed his fingers all the way in and gently used his teeth on my clit.

"Oh, *God!*" I shouted. The pain was sharp but immediately followed by a pleasure I'd never experienced, as if the nerves were exposed raw by the bite and made more alive by the gentleness that followed.

"That a good 'oh, God' or a bad 'oh, God'?"

"Great, good, fucking *God.*"

He did it again, pressing his teeth a little harder and adding a suck to the grind of his teeth. The pain and pleasure coexisted, moving from opposite poles to the center of me. I writhed enough to shake water from the glass and onto my belly but not tip it.

He sucked my clit through his teeth, and I filled his mouth with stars.

"I'm coming. Fuck. Jonathan...."

He moaned into me, and I knew that meant I was allowed to come. And he didn't stop or pause long enough for me to stop the freight train of my orgasm. I tried to keep my body still, but toward the end, as the sucking felt as though his mouth was pulling every last bit of pleasure from me, I lost control of my body, and the glass tumbled, rolling along the floor. My back arched even more. The top of my head wound up on the loveseat cushions, and Jonathan stood to keep his head between my legs. He kept sucking even after I tried to push his head away, his pussy-wet fingers holding my thighs.

He moved his mouth away when I was a hot, shuddering mess. I breathed heavily, getting my bearings again. He put his hands around my waist and lifted me to standing. I still couldn't speak. He lowered my bra gently, then picked up my dress from the floor. I fell on him, and he laughed, holding me up.

"You all right?"

"I don't think all my parts are attached."

"You look just as perfect as you did ten minutes ago."

I breathed into him for a second, taking in the new, musty scent. "I don't think I have the coordination to get my clothes on." I got my bearings, feeling sexually satisfied in a way I knew wouldn't last. I could be ready for another go in minutes.

Jonathan found the neck opening of my dress and lifted it over my head.

I wiggled my arms through the sleeves. "What did she do for you that you're so grateful about?"

"I'm about to be cryptic," he said.

"Great."

"I went through some stuff when I was younger, and I was treated like it all happened *to me*. I was this victim. She showed me that I was responsible. She gave me my manhood back. That too heartwarming for you?"

I caught the sarcasm in the last sentence but also the defensiveness. I turned my back and moved my hair out of the way so he could zip me up.

"How did she break her wrist?" I asked.

He slowly zipped up the dress. "I said I was sorry and that I couldn't do this with her anymore, this whole dance we've been doing. She ran out after me and tripped on the walk. Fell on her wrist. I couldn't get my doctor on the phone, so I took her to the ER and waited with her. The only four words she said to me? 'Is it that girl?'"

"She was talking about me?"

"I assumed so."

"What did you say?"

"I lied."

I turned around. "You said I wasn't a girl?"

He smiled. "I said you were nothing to me. I think I used the word dalliance."

"Am I a dalliance?"

"Not for me. Not anymore." Looking pensive, he smoothed my dress. "But you see what she did when she thought you were. Made a special trip up to the Stock just to hurt you. If she knew I think about you all the time ... well, she's possessive. Even after she left me, she made it a point to find out who I was with and what I was doing with them. I thought it meant she still loved me, but actually, it means she's crazy." He kissed my hands, then my cheek. His face smelled like my pussy. "Do you have a few more minutes?"

"Some. I'm going to record something in a few hours. I set it up so we couldn't be together too long."

"Clever girl."

"Well, now I just want to eat you alive."

He turned me back around and kissed me. The taste of our tongues was a mix of sex and sweat. I fell into him, a groan rising in the back of my throat. I wanted him again, and again.

He moved his mouth to my nose, my chin, and spoke into my cheek. "I need to wash up. Can you meet me downstairs in the bar?"

CHAPTER 46

$\mathcal{I}$ carried a toothbrush in my bag because I knew, at the very least, his dick would be in my mouth, and I didn't want to hit the high notes at DownDawg Studio with blowjob breath. I washed my face, readjusted my dress, and slipped on my panties. They made my pussy feel gagged, but if any part of me needed to shut up for a minute, it was the sopping cup of sensation between my legs.

He was waiting at a small table near the window, a bottle of Perrier and two glasses ready. He saw me come in, and I noted the appreciation in his gaze.

"How long do I have?" He scooped a couple of beige pistachios from a porcelain bowl. A metal bowl sat next to it, a couple of empty shells nesting inside.

"About ninety minutes. No time for another round." I sat. Our chairs faced the windows and were so close our knees touched.

"That's fine. I just want to talk to you."

"You smell different," I said.

He smiled. "The last cologne … Jessica got it for me for Christmas seven years ago. I had something new made up north. Do you like it?"

"It's the other side of you."

He removed the meat from a nut and placed it to my lips. I glanced around. The bar was empty except for Larry, who was wiping glasses to an optic shine. I took the nut into my mouth like an offering.

"Which side is that?" He looked at me with those tourmaline eyes, his copper hair glinting at the edges from the afternoon sun.

I didn't know if I was allowed to fall for him, since he'd shed Jessica like an old skin. I didn't know if I was allowed to believe she was gone, or if that much had changed between us. "The side that makes me beg."

"You like that side of me?" He cracked another pistachio, tossing the shell into the metal bowl with a *plink*.

"You can't tell?"

"I want to make sure you're not tolerating it for other reasons." He placed the nut to my lips again.

I took it, letting the wet part of my lips graze his thumb. "If I were, I'd just lie about it."

"True."

"What do your instincts say? Am I a liar?"

"You're as real as anyone I ever met."

He turned his attention to the pistachios, popping another one open and dropping the shell with a *plink*. He ate that one, then another. *Plink, plink.* "I had business in San Francisco, but also, there's a woman up there."

The cold metal feeling that went up my spine must have made a sound loud enough for him to hear.

He glanced up at me and spoke in the voice he used when he was telling me to put my hands behind my back. "Wait. Let me finish."

That calmed me enough to remove the ice from my veins. "Go on," I said.

He fed me another nutmeat, *plinking* the shell with his other hand. "Her name is Sharon. We've been fucking on and off for a couple of years. We're very honest with each other, and she likes some of the same things in bed that you and I have done, but she's more experienced with it. When I got there, I saw her, and I told her about Jessica and you. I ended it with her, of course. Judging from your face you needed to hear that?"

"Sorry. I don't mean to be possessive."

He smiled. "You're fine." *Plink.* He put his face close to mine and brought his hand under my chin, a thumb on one cheek, and pressed lightly, opening my mouth.

My eyes went half-mast and a burst of pleasure blossomed between my legs.

With the other hand, he fed me the nut. "I want you, Monica. I want you on a regular basis. Constantly, actually. I don't think about much else." He let go of my cheeks and brushed his thumb against my bottom lip before taking his hand away and letting me chew. "I'm on the brink of being completely infatuated with you. I need to know if you feel the same."

I swallowed. Did I want him? Jesus fucking Christ, I'd never wanted anything so badly. I took a sip of water. "While you were away, and the last words I heard were Jessica's, I felt emotionally heightened. Sometimes, I just shook with rage. It doesn't matter that you didn't do anything, or didn't do much, or that you had to kiss her to get over her. The fact was, I had a hard time functioning. That's why I don't want a relationship. And the trouble is, you can't promise me I won't feel like that again."

"No, I can't." *Plink, plink.*

"But how am I supposed to walk away?"

"You can't. You're mine. The minute I told you to spread your legs and you did it, you were mine. When I told you to beg for it and you did, you were mine. When you put your hands behind your back without being told, I owned you. You never had to say a word. You're a natural submissive."

Plink. When he turned away from the bowl to look at me, he had a nutmeat in his fingers, ready for my lips. His face, which had been so close to mine, slid half a step away. "Why the look?" he asked.

"What did you say?"

He smirked and got his face close again. "You are a natural submissive, Monica. You enjoy being obedient. You cede control with both hands. It's exactly right."

I was shaking. I wanted him, and five minutes ago, he was mine. He'd given up on his wife and wanted me, and the ache of holding back my feelings for him was quelled, if only for a moment. Until he called me a submissive.

I took my own fucking nut and cracked the meat out. "What were you thinking about us? You gonna put me on a leash?"

"You just turned into stone."

I chewed, not commenting. I wanted an answer. He stalled, pouring himself half a glass of Perrier, and I was immediately reminded of the glass I'd spilled on the floor.

"Women I take to bed, mostly they defy me, or act cute, or overdo obedience but don't mean it. Many pretend to like getting tied to the bedpost. One was so pliable it was disconcerting."

"And this Sharon person?"

"She's a submissive. That's what she does. So she nailed it, but it's not that kind of relationship. I could talk to her about what I liked, and we could try things together, but it's not like you. I want you. I can't get enough of you. You're strong. I want to see how you look with your wrists tied to your knees. I want to spank you red in the ass. Because you can take it." He paused, looking at me. "And I think I scared you. It's not what you think. I don't want anything from you that you already haven't offered."

"With both hands, apparently."

"It's beautiful, Monica. Don't make it ugly." He tilted his head, as if trying to see through me.

I tossed my pistachio shell into the bowl with a *plink*, feeling surly and confused. "Was Jessica submissive?"

"No. I think it's what drove her away."

I couldn't help but think Jessica's refusal to be dominated meant she was respected more than I would ever be. I'd always be the child, the one who could be bossed around, dismissed, belittled, and abused.

"Monica, what's on your mind?"

"No," I said.

"No, what?"

"No. Just no." I grabbed my bag. "But thanks for asking."

I took big steps in my high heels, nodding to Larry, who I'd probably never see again, and went out to the hall, where the elevator waited. There was an image in my mind, a thought, and I was keeping it at bay. Something about the nuts and the things he said was bringing a memory back to me.

He caught my elbow as I pressed the elevator button. "Monica."

"Don't touch me."

"What is it?"

The doors slid open. I didn't think he'd follow me in, but he did.

"Leave me alone."

"No. Fuck no!"

The doors closed him in, and we headed down.

He took me by the biceps. "What is it? Is it the word? We'll pick a different one."

"It's not what I want. Please. Just forget everything. I'm sorry. I can't."

"Why?"

I didn't want to think about why. I didn't want to answer. I looked up at him, thinking maybe I'd find some words to string together that would be reasonable or acceptable without letting through the image I held at bay. His face, his posture, everything told me I'd hurt him.

"I'm sorry," I said as the doors opened. I ran out, into the hall, through the lobby, and into the parking lot. Lil sat with the other drivers and got up when she saw me, but I ran past. I got into my car and put it in drive before the engine was even engaged.

The downtown streets jogged the car. I couldn't drive correctly. My mind was a soup of images I wouldn't acknowledge. I pulled over in front of a set of bay doors on an empty dead end street and put the car in park.

My hands were shaking. I had to calm down. I had to cut a song in an hour. In Burbank. Who knew what the traffic would be?

Breathe. Breathe.

As I relaxed, I felt a cord of arousal under my skirt. I closed my eyes, thinking about the silly junk I was going to have to sing, the clichés and simple chords. I had to add *me* to it. I had to breathe life into something dead. That was all I should be thinking about.

I heard a *plink* on the roof of the car. Then another. It had started to rain. *Plink, plink.* Through my relaxation, the memory came. The one I'd tried to shut out.

A club. Kevin and I went places and did things at night, in the odd hours, in the corners of the city, seeking out subcultures and twisted paths. Because we were artists, nothing was beneath our understanding or experience.

The club was dark. I'd been there before. There was nothing at all special about it. We sat at the end of the bar, by the wall. I'd been drinking something, and Kevin had my hand in his. His fingertips were cold from the ice in his glass, and I enjoyed the way he drew circles inside my wrist with them. I felt delicious and loved.

I heard a creak of old hinges above me. I looked up. The wall above seemed to have a hidden door, and a shelf and false wall swung out. A blindfolded woman about my age was tied to the shelf, on her hands and knees, hands and head facing the room. She wore a configuration of leather ties that bound her wrists to her knees. A silver ring with the circumference of a castanet kept her mouth open and her head raised. The leather harness holding it in place was strapped around her head and connected to a hook on the wall.

The bartender slapped a metal bowl under the shelf holding the girl and got on with his business, as if girls were tied to the wall all the time. Kevin barely glanced up, and though I tried to keep my mind on the conversation we were having with Jack and his girlfriend, my eyes kept going to the girl. She wore pink cotton panties that didn't go with the black leather garter pressing her tits to her ribs, but when I noticed a carefully placed mirror, I knew why. Her panties were soaked through at the crotch, and the pink showed off her arousal in a way leather wouldn't. I turned back to some conversation about process art in the 1980s.

I heard a *plink, plink* and followed the sound to the metal bowl. I craned my neck. It contained a few drops of clear, whitish fluid. I looked up. The girl, her mouth forced open by the ring, was drooling spit and semen down her chin and into the bowl. *Plink, plink.*

I caught sight of her eyes in the crease under the blindfold. She looked away when we made eye contact.

I realized then that she could see through it. The blind-fold wasn't there to protect her identity, nor was it to protect her from seeing us look at her, but to protect us from seeing how turned on she was.

I wasn't her.

That was submissive. I wasn't that. No, no, no.

Kevin and I had gone home, and neither of us ever brought up the drooling girl. We never judged. We were too sophisticated and cosmopolitan for that. We were too fucking cool to even let on that we'd noticed. I hated us. The people we were had been hateful snobs who never asked questions about anything real. Like why a woman would want to drool her master's load into a metal bowl and show her wet cunt to everyone.

So there I was, shaking in my Honda, because Jonathan had seen that girl in me. On his command, I'd opened my mouth as big as a castanet so he could fuck my throat.

Stop it.

I had to stop. I had to sing. But every time I heard the *plink* of rain on my hood, it was a pistachio shell, and I was drooling Jonathan's load into a metal bowl.

CHAPTER 47

On the way to the 101, I realized I still had that stinking diamond in my navel. It felt like a harness. I'd drop it at Hotel K after my session. My phone danced on the passenger seat. It could be Jonathan, but it wasn't as though he was the only thing I had going on. I was really glad I looked at it—WDE.

"Hey, Monica," Trudie said.

"Yeah, I'm on my way up there."

"We had a change. The set's at DownDawg in Culver City, not Burbank."

"Oh. Did you call Gabby?"

"Yeah, I talked to her. Here, let me give you the address."

I pulled over and wrote it down. I was glad I didn't need to call Gabby because it would probably take me an hour to get there without yacking with my pianist for twenty minutes, dissecting all the possible reasons for the venue change.

I did take a second to scroll through my recents. Nothing from Jonathan. Both my relief and disappointment were palpable. Then the phone dinged and buzzed in my hand.

—*I'm calling you now. Answer.*—

Oh, wasn't that just a juicy command? Answer the phone. Spread your legs. What was the difference?

When my cell rang, I rejected the call and sent a text.

> —*I have to go to Culver City. I can't talk*—

—*Let's talk about it again. I'll use different words*—

—*Not that way. I mean I won't offend you*—

He was no one to me, really. If I never saw him again, my life would be no different than it had been a month ago. No, that wasn't true. My life would be the same in all the surface ways. I'd live in the same house and have the same friends. But somehow I'd changed. He'd woken me from a dreamless sleep, and I couldn't roll over and close my eyes, because in my wakefulness, I'd started dreaming.

I read his text again. I could think about what he said, but I couldn't answer him. I couldn't be who he thought I was, but if I couldn't be that, then who would I be? I couldn't go backward, and somehow, in such a short time, he'd become the conductor of my forward motion.

I am not submissive.
I am not submissive.
I am not submissive.

I chanted the mantra all the way to Culver City, deaf to the buzzing phone and any thought for where I was headed or what I was to do there.

I didn't get my head back until I parked the car.

My name is Monica, and I am not *submissive. I stand six feet tall in heels. I am descended from one of the greatest writers of the twentieth century. I can sing like an angel and growl like a lion. I am not owned. I am music.*

CHAPTER 48

*D*ownDawg Studios wasn't some little grunge house with egg-carton Styrofoam on the walls. It didn't smell of tobacco and fast food, and it most certainly wasn't a place we could have afforded on our own. There were three in Los Angeles. Burbank, which spent a lot of time servicing Disney, Santa Monica—home base for rich kids and middle-class rappers of the west side—and Culver City, where Sony did their ADR and apparently where WDE had their scratch cuts done.

The building was on Washington, in downtown Culver City. The renovated industrial box had the original casement windows in the front half, where they matched the three-ton metal-frame door. The back half was bricked in, a windowless green box with orange trim, the perfect modernist nonsensical combo.

A valet parked my car. A receptionist with more earrings than a Tiffany window pillow guided me to the back. I was seven minutes late. My excuse was the venue change. Right.

I opened the door and entered the engineering room with its bank of dials and window looking into the sound room. A man about my age with sandy hair and a linen shirt with the tails hanging below his sweater spoke to a guy with dark skin and a stiff-brimmed Lakers cap.

Linen Shirt held out his hand. "I'm Holden, your producer. This is Deshaun."

Deshaun offered a hand. "Sound engineer. My lady heard you play Thelonius a few weeks back. Said good things."

"Oh, thanks." I blushed a little. "Seems like ages ago."

"You got the song?" Holden asked. "What do you think?"

I thought it was a piece of shit, but honesty would get me nowhere. "We have a couple of takes on it. Gabby's on her way."

Holden got off the stool and threw himself on the couch. "Tell me how you're doing it."

I clutched my song sheet. I could do this. I could talk about the music. I knew what I had to do, and I was good at it, but the conversation with Jonathan had infected my mind, and I kept talking to Holden and Deshaun about dynamics and harmonies while thinking they somehow knew I was submissive. They were going to walk all over me and tell me how to sing the notes, how to breathe, how to open my mouth wide enough to take a cock. I knew they weren't laughing at me and my pretensions of vocal control, but I also knew they were.

Holden glanced at the clock. "It's getting late."

"Let me text Gabby," I said, slipping my phone out of my pocket. "She's probably in the parking lot."

—*Where the fuck are you?*—

—*With Jerry, waiting for you*—

I started getting a really bad feeling in my guts. I turned to Holden. "You know a guy named Jerry?"

"He does some production at the Burbank studio."

"Does he know Eugene Testarossa?"

"Yeah. Works with him all the time."

I typed fast.

> *—There's been a mixup, I'm in*
> *Culver City—*

There wasn't a text for a minute or more. "She's up in Burbank. She'll never make it here on time." I glanced toward the sound studio. A keyboard was already set up in there.

As if reading my mind, Holden said, "If you play, we're a go."

I did play. I generally didn't have to bother because of Gabby, but I played piano just fine. My phone blooped.

> *—It's not a mixup it's a fucking*
> *set-up Jerry never got an engineer*
> *and he's been talking about the*
> *fucking weather do you have*
> *an engineer there?—*

I glanced at Deshaun, who was tapping away at his phone. I didn't know what to do. If I played, she'd never forgive me, and if I didn't, I was a back-bending little sheep who walked out with nothing. A nobody. A disappointment.

"We have time for a few takes," I said, turning off my phone and stepping into the sound room.

CHAPTER 49

The sun was dipping below the skyline when I got back in the car and turned on my phone. There was no use pretending I didn't see Gabby's messages, and there was no use listening to them. I just called her.

"Moooooooniiiiiiicaaaaaa….." She was drunk. The white noise whipped like wind cut with the sound of music and laughter.

"Gabby, where are you?"

"I'm with Lord Theodore at the Santa Monica Pier. We're on the Ferris wheel."

"Are you okay?"

"You do the scratch cut?"

I rubbed the bottom of the steering wheel and stared at the building as if it could exonerate me, but the big green cube did nothing besides look squat and hip. "Yeah."

"We were set up, you know. I was. He don't want me, so they made it so you did the cut without me. You know that, right?"

She seemed okay with it, but she was wasted and on a Ferris wheel, so I couldn't take her forgiveness for granted. "Don't assume it was malicious, Gab."

"Oh fuck, when did you become such a …whassa word? When you believe the best in people? Like you never lived in L.A. your whole life."

"Is Theo drunk too?"

I heard the phone muffle and Gabby say, "Hey, baby, you drunk?" Then her voice got clear again. "He says he's a little bit o' this and a little bit o' that."

"Great. Do you want me to come and get you?"

"Go fuck yourself, Monica."

The line went dead.

CHAPTER 50

My car was the only one in the driveway, but the house lights were on. I got out and went inside.

"How did it go?" Darren was in my kitchen, wiping the counter. He had a key. He might as well have moved in. Fucker. I hated him and everything. He looked up at me when I didn't answer. "What happened?"

I had no words. I slipped my arms around his waist and held him tightly. He smelled nice.

He leaned his cheek against my head and stroked my back. "Is it the rich guy?"

"Yes and no."

"Where's Gabby?"

I let my hands drop and banged my forehead against his chest. "WDE set us up. It could have been a mistake, but it wasn't. I can feel it. We ended up in different studios, and she's with Theo right now, self-medicating."

"At least she's not alone. Theo's a fuckup, but he won't let her kill herself." He put his hands on my shoulders and pushed me away, looking into my face. "Did you do the scratch cut?"

"Yes."

"Oh thank God, Mon."

"I feel like I ditched her."

He shook his head. "They'd never reschedule, but if the cut's good, they'll send it out, and then you have a leg to stand on."

I dropped my bag on the floor and plopped onto a kitchen chair. "Well, we won't have to worry about that. It was the single worst performance of my life."

"Come on."

"Really."

"Because of my sister?"

I leaned on the table, lacing my fingers in my hair. "No."

"Do you want some tea?"

"Yes, please." I stood. "I'll make it. You don't even live here."

He pushed me back into the chair. "I can boil water." He pulled the teabags down. "I'm sure it wasn't that bad, Mon. Think about it. Are you just fighting the fraud men?"

The fraud men were the creatures that lived inside every artist's brain, rearing their ugly heads any time something good happened and telling them that they were useless, talentless hacks who had only gotten lucky. "No, I really blew it. Couldn't hold a note. I was … distracted."

"By?" He plopped the teapot on the stove and turned to me, leaning on the counter with his arms crossed.

Could I tell him? And if I didn't, who *would* I tell? I took a deep breath and got ready for the red heat to rise in my face. "Jonathan's a little kinky."

Darren raised an eyebrow. "Oh, dear."

"Please don't embarrass me."

He yanked a chair out from the table, sat, and put his elbows on the table. "Kinky billionaire meets hot waitress. It's a cliché of a cliché. I love it. Does he make you spank him?"

The prickly heat finally hit my cheeks. "It's the other way around."

"*No.*"

I nodded while scratching a nonexistent piece of crud from the tabletop. "I mean, we haven't gotten that far yet, but basically, that's the nature of us in bed. He tells me to do stuff, and I do it. And he's rough. Really rough. He wants a more, I guess, *intense* version of what's been happening, and I'm freaked out."

"Does he have a dungeon?"

I buried my face in my hands and gave a muffled "No" from behind my palms. I opened them. "I don't think so."

He paused, rubbing his chin, then leaned even farther across the table. "And he wants you to be his *official* fuck toy?"

"Oh God, Darren!"

"I haven't heard you say that in years."

I got up so fast the chair dropped behind me. "I'm really upset, Darren, and all you want to do is make jokes." I turned off the burner and set about making tea. "He thinks I'm a natural submissive, which is code for, like, doormat and beneath him, and yeah, it's code for Jonathan's little fucking fuck toy. And I know what you're going to say. You're going to say I'm no man's whore. And you're right. I'm not. I'm not some submissive little kitten or his god damn punching bag. What the fuck is he thinking? And you *know* what I'm thinking."

"I have no idea what you're thinking."

I held up the teapot. "Do you want some?"

"Sure."

"Sugar?"

"Monica?"

"What?"

"You were saying something about what you were thinking."

I poured the tea. Darren didn't take sugar and neither did I, but I'd needed a second to avoid saying something stupid. "I can't say it."

"You're no man's whore."

I stared at the tea as it steeped. "I know."

"But you're falling for him."

The strength went out of my spine. I hated Darren for bringing it up and for seeing through me, yet I was grateful he'd said what I couldn't. "He's witty," I said. "And confident and affectionate. And he looks at me like I'm the only woman in the world. And you can make fun but … the sex is …" I searched for the right word and came up with nothing adequate. "I'm a fuck toy whore, aren't I?"

Darren got up for his tea, since I was falling down on the job. "I'll tell you the truth. I don't like hearing someone is treating you like that. It upsets me. I'd actually like to punch him in the face a little." He poured the hot water. "You've been alone too long. You're vulnerable. You're doing things you wouldn't normally do."

"Yeah."

"If you want to date again, you should have tried dating, you know?"

"I want to rib you for not dating forever, then turning up gay. But I can't. It's right for you. This … I don't think this is right for me." I pulled the bag out of my cup and pressed it until it was a sack of damp leaves. "Too bad."

"Gabby was triangulating him against every other person in Los Angeles, and she said she came up with something she wanted to show you. It didn't sound good."

"Great. Secrets. Love those."

"Come on," Darren rubbed my shoulders. "Let's go watch a stupid movie and talk about Kevin's thing. I'm bored, and I've decided I'd love to make that guy crazy."

We never did speak about Kevin's thing. We never even watched a movie. We lay on the couch and watched a string of shows about rock stars with debilitating drug addictions who redeemed themselves in their fifties. I fell asleep on Darren's chest, where I felt as safe and comfortable as when I was with Jonathan.

I dreamed of some nether desert where the sky spoke in narrators, laugh tracks, and commercials, and I kneeled in the sand and put my hands in my pants to relieve the ache that had become water to me.

I woke up to the sound of Darren on the phone. Morning Stretch was muted. Darren's voice squeaked, but I thought nothing of it. The fullness of my bladder pushed against some sexual part of my insides, making me feel engorged and ready. I wanted to fuck.

I went to my room, crawled into bed, and pulled the legal pad I used for middle-of-the-night ideas from the nightstand. I wrote:

What if he collars me? Slaps me? Spanks me? Bites me? Fucks me in the ass? Whips me? Hurts me? Displays me? Gags me? Blindfolds me? Shares me? Humiliates me? Ties me down? Makes me bleed? Fucks me up?

I couldn't write any more. My imagination kept coming up with new things to do, and they got more and more horrible as I dug deeper.

I went to the bathroom and sat on the bowl, in the dark, trying not to wake up too much. I'd defined something about Jonathan during my conversation with Darren, and though I was comforted at having come to a conclusion, I was saddened at the decision.

There was a tap on the door.

"Mon?" Darren whispered.

"Use the other bathroom."

"They found Gabrielle." He sounded so calm I thought he meant something innocuous. "I have to identify the body."

I stood up, my pants around my knees. "What?"

He asked softly, "Can you come with me?"

$\mathcal{I}$n my life, I'd experienced grief like I experienced love. Deeply and with very few people.

My father had been taken from me when I was nineteen. I didn't see much of him, even when he wasn't deployed. My mother owned him, up in butt-fuck Castaic, two hours north of the den of sin and temptation I called home. The news came through her, icily framed as a happier existence with a benevolent God. I didn't want to talk to her about how it happened. I ended up on the phone with his supervisor at Tomrock, who told me he'd taken mortar fire while escorting a Saudi prince to the central mosque in Kabul. I had told Dad he should have stayed in the military, that privatizing himself would leave him unprotected, but he was tired of listening to politically motivated orders dressed up as patriotism. If he was walking into death, he wanted it called that, and he wanted to be paid to take those risks. No fanfare. No dressing up in the flag. Dad was real. He wanted life so real it hurt. He'd been shot twice, stabbed once, and had his bell rung more than a few times in neighborhood brawls. He still held the door open for my mother after twenty years of marriage and loved her like a queen, even though she didn't deserve it.

When he was killed, I thought I'd go insane. I felt unmoored, unsafe, orphaned. I found myself pulling the car over and checking directions to places I'd been to a hundred times. I called Darren twice as often, just to hear the voice of someone who loved me. I didn't want to go outside if I could avoid it. The only thing that saved me, besides Darren and Gabby, was music. Dad had taught me piano. He approved of my pursuits. So when I played, especially when I played in front of people, I felt safe again. As the years passed, I found other ways to feel secure and loved, and grief slipped away so slowly I didn't notice when it became a dull ache of memory brought on by some corner of the house or Dad's mandarin tree in the backyard.

Grief had been hiding, ready for the next time. So when Darren and I listened to the lady cop tell us that Gabby had been found, drowned, two miles north of the Santa Monica Pier, I listened, but I was too busy trying to keep the bucket of grief from tipping. Darren needed me, and if I fell into a cacophony of emotion, I wasn't going to be there for him.

We stood by a Plexiglas window, watching a sheet-covered gurney get wheeled into the adjacent room. I felt that bucket of sorrow tip and empty, dropping its contents from my throat to my heart. It sloshed around when I moved, and I thought I would be emptying it with a teaspoon.

I didn't know what Darren was feeling, initially. He identified his sister, who looked bloated and blue, then turned to leave. He collapsed into my arms, weeping. I did my best to hold him up, but the lady cop with the inky curly hair had to help me get him to her desk.

Lady Cop brought us water and a box of tissues. "Was she on any medication?"

"Marplan," Darren whispered.

"Did she mix it with alcohol?"

He grabbed my hand. "We should have gotten her. We shouldn't have trusted Theo. Fuck. Of all people."

I wasn't buying it. "She was drinking, sure, but I thought she drowned," I said to Lady Cop.

"Technically, yes. But what happens is people overdo, and because their judgment is compromised, they go for a swim. Their breath is shallower, and their coordination is poor, so they succumb." She paused in a way that felt practiced and professional. "I'm sorry."

We signed some papers. They wanted to know where to send the body. I gave the name of the funeral home my dad went to because I had no room in my brain for anything else, and Darren was too emotionally brutalized to make any kind of decision. I didn't know how we were going to walk out of there, but we did, slowly, because the farther away we got from the police station, the farther behind we left Gabby. We stopped dead in the parking lot, holding hands, immovable.

"I don't think I can go home," he said.

"You can stay with me."

"No."

"What about Adam?"

Darren just stared into the distance, his face a blank. I didn't know what to do next. He had no family except Gabby. I was *it*, and I had no idea how to help him. His gaze fixed on something, and I followed it. Theo closed the door on his Impala and came toward us, his gait a little crooked. I squeezed Darren's hand tighter.

"Let's just go," I said. "Don't try and deal with anything today." I pulled him toward the Honda. "Please."

He looked down at me, big blue eyes lined with webs of red.

"We have so much to do," I said. "I need you. Please."

He blinked as if some of what I said got through.

Theo was getting closer, waving and trotting as if he thought he might miss us. I pulled Darren away and tried to shoot Theo a warning look. I wasn't a praying person, but I prayed there would be no fights. No accusatory words. No defenses. No excuses. I shoved Darren into the passenger side just as Theo reached us.

"Lassie..." he said.

"Back up, Theo." I strode to my side of the car.

"I have feelings about it too. I stopped her from jumping off the Ferris wheel."

"I'll let you know when we have the funeral if you have the balls to come," I said as I opened the door.

"You're the one who betrayed her. You did that scratch track without her."

I slammed the door before Darren could hear another word.

"I'm going to kill him," Darren said.

"Not today."

I knew that I had a limited time to figure it all out. I felt the thoughts I didn't want to have push against the defensive wall that kept me functioning. I needed that wall. It was the percussion section, keeping the beat, organizing the symphony of reactions and decisions that needed to happen. Without it, the whole piece was going to shit.

I pulled out of the parking lot. Theo got small in my rearview. "We need to make arrangements," I said. "Are you up for it, or am I driving you home?"

"I don't know what to do."

"Do you have money?"

He shook his head. "There was a life insurance policy. For both of us. In case. I checked it when she tried the last time."

"Okay. Let's take care of it. Then, I don't know." I

took his hand at the red light. "Let's just keep our shit together until the sun goes down."

"Then what?"

"We fall apart."

We made it home before sunset. The funeral home had dealt with worse, and we did what the bereaved often did. We dumped everything in their laps and let them tell us what we had to do. Darren signed the forms to allow them to retrieve the body. We let them arrange a cremation. There would be no big funeral, no open casket, just a thing at my house. I didn't know what you called such a thing, but the funeral director seemed to know and nodded, letting it slide.

Then we ran back to my house and made phone calls, sprawled on the couch together. I'd called three people I knew weren't around, leaving messages and moving on, when I heard Darren weeping Adam's name into his phone. I felt glad enough to leave him alone. He needed someone besides me. He'd lost his sister, his only family. He deserved to have someone else to love him.

But my gladness was shouted down by something darker, more insidious, more selfish. A deep, evil stab of loneliness that I would have done best to ignore. I should have stayed in the living room to have Darren's warm body next to me, but he needed to be alone. He wouldn't want to go to Gabby's room, and I didn't feel right forcing him onto the porch. So I slipped into my room, crawled under the covers, and hugged my pillow, wondering who was going to braid my hair tomorrow.

CHAPTER 52

I texted Debbie, asking for a few days off and explaining that my best friend had died. She called, but I rejected it. I got dinged and blooped and buzzed a hundred times over by everyone we had ever known. I answered some, thanking people for their condolences, but I just wanted to be left alone, so I shut off the phone and cocooned myself under the covers.

I got out of bed the next night. The house was empty. I showered, ate a few crackers, and went back to bed.

I turned my phone back on, got under the covers, and scrolled through all the kind words and long messages. I resented them. I was grateful for them. I wanted to be around people and eviscerate the longing, lonely hole in my body. I'd earned the isolation and wanted nothing to do with another living soul. Fuck everybody. I needed them. I hated them.

I tried to remember things about my friend, nice stories to cheer me under the dark, damp covers, but my brain wouldn't jog anything loose. I could only remember our most hackneyed scenes. Graduation day. The last time I had seen her, the last time I spoke to her. Everything else was scorched earth, as if it had never happened, or like some mature, godly part of me was protecting the weak, repellent part of me from more hurt by refusing to release painful data.

Someone knocked on the door at some point, maybe just some delivery person, but it woke me up. I scrolled through my messages. *So sorry/That's terrible/Can I bring you something to eat?* Et cetera, et cetera. Everyone was so sweet, but I didn't know how to accept their kindness. The phone vibrated in my hand, and though I'd been ignoring it for however many hours, I looked at this message.

—*Debbie told me*—

I didn't know how to respond to Jonathan. We weren't in a place in our relationship where I could ask him for anything or expect him to intuit what I needed. His text made me feel lonelier than any other. I answered, feeling as if I were shouting down an empty alley.

> —*Tell her I'm going to work day after tomorrow*—

—*What are you doing now?*—

> —*I'm under my covers*—

—*Alone?*—

> —*yes*—

—*A crime*—

I smiled, and the feeling of levity cracked the brittle shell of sorrow, if only for a second, and tears streamed down my face.

> —*Don't make me laugh, fuckhead*—

*—May I join you under those
lucky covers?—*

When I read the message, I didn't feel his request in my loins but on my skin. I wanted him to touch me. Kiss me. Breathe on me. Talk to me. Hold me for hours. The desire wasn't just between my legs, but in my rib cage, my marrow, my fingertips. Could I give up the consuming protection of loneliness and indulge in a few hours with Jonathan? Was I worthy of a little comfort? Probably not. And I hadn't forgotten the submissive thing. No. He was going to drag me into a pit of defilement and humiliation. Seeing him would only draw him closer to me than he should be, ever.

—I need you—

I hit send. I shouldn't have. I should have made a much cooler, more distant statement. At the very least, I should have been witty in admitting I was a filthy, repugnant mess of need. But I didn't. Three words and I'd debased myself.

I felt hopeful for the first time in days. I got out of bed and crawled into the shower, setting it for hotter than it needed to be. I had no idea how long I'd been in bed, but it was seven in the morning according to my clock. I hadn't seen or heard from Darren, and I assumed he was with Adam. I should have called him, but the idea of reaching out, even to the only person in the world who would understand my sense of failure, made me flinch as if my face would get slapped.

My skin was raw and pink from heat and friction when I stepped out of the shower. I dried my hair and pulled out my brush. A twisted black hair tie was wrapped around the handle. Gabby had put it there when she worked on my hair for the Eclipse show. I put my palm on my wet hair and stroked downward, curling my fingers to gather a strand, just enough to string a bow. The sensation was nothing like when Gabby did it with her care and artistry. And all that was gone. All that talent went into the nothing and nowhere. All the music she would have made would never exist.

I hurled myself under the covers, naked and half wet, grabbing my phone on the way.

—don't come nevermind—

I heard a phone ding from the living room and, soon after, a voice so close it shocked me.

"Too late," Jonathan said. "Your front door was open."

—go away—

A blast of cold air hit me as the covers were moved, and in the next breath, I caught his new scent. He pulled the covers over us just as his phone dinged. He pressed his front to my back, spooning me, his clothes taking on the dampness I hadn't gotten around to toweling off.

"I'm sorry, Monica." He put his face in my wet hair and draped his arm around me. "Ah. What's this text I have here? It says *go away*."

I sniffled.

He slid his arm under my neck and held the phone in front of our faces with both hands. His breath tickled my ear. "Let me text back. Hang on."

—I'd rather be here for you—

I waited for it to appear on my phone. He nuzzled into the hair pooling at the back of my neck as I typed back.

—And then what?—

His fingers flew across the glass.

*—And let's talk about the rest
later. Today, you are the goddess
my universe revolves around.—*

In the seconds it took my phone to bloop, I had a million thoughts, not the least of which was that he was crazy. Out of his mind. Didn't he see who he was curled against? For fuck's sake, I'd killed my best friend, first with carelessness and then with ambition.

I started texting back:

—you have the wrong…

But then I felt his lips on my shoulder and his warm breath on my skin, and my sorrow dropped out of me. I couldn't finish. My chest hitched and heaved, and the tears came so hard I couldn't breathe. His arms held me tight from behind, and his voice twisted itself into little nothings of comfort. I went into a timeless blackness where I let everything spill out, because he'd catch it. I knew in every cough and sob, every hitched breath and chest spasm, that he'd hold me together. Whatever fell apart, he'd put right. I couldn't curse him for not being everything I needed or failing to commit to me completely. I didn't have space to reject his idea that I was submissive or the will to deny him control over me. He was there, and he was exactly what I needed.

When the crying slowed, I turned to face him. In the dark, I found his lips by following his breath and kissed him. He opened his mouth, stroking my tongue with his in a gentle dance. I wove my legs into his.

"Thank you," I whispered, breathing it without a voice.

He started to answer, but I kissed away whatever

came next. I pushed my hips into him. He was hard, and I was ready. I kissed him again, so I wouldn't hear any objections when I pulled his shirt from his waistband. I wanted him naked against me. I wanted to feel good, if only for a minute, and to forget everything for as long as it took us to bind together and fall apart. I hadn't earned it, but I wanted it.

A little light went on under the covers, and a bloop preceded a ding, but we ignored it. He rolled on top of me, mouth attached to mine, and stroked the length of my body. I gasped. The touch was so comforting, so distracting, a bow suddenly dragged across silent strings.

"Hello? Mon?" The voice sounded far away.

Jonathan and I separated.

"What was that?" Jonathan asked.

I twisted around. My phone was lit up under me. I must have rolled on top of it and answered the call by accident. Too late to reject the call.

"Hello? Darren?" I whispered. For some reason, I couldn't engage my vocal cords.

"I'm downtown."

Jonathan pulled the covers off us, and the light seemed as blinding as the air was cold. I already missed his warmth on my body.

"I need you to post bail, or I'm going to miss the wake." He sounded dead, emotionless. "I found Theo. I hurt him. There are bail places all around here. So can you come?"

"Yes, I'll come."

"Thank you."

I glanced at Jonathan as Darren started giving me the details. He was still fully clothed in a blue polo shirt and jeans, sitting up against the wall. I was naked and crouched beside him. He stroked my shoulder.

"What happened?" he asked when I clicked off.

302

"Darren beat up Gabby's boyfriend. I have to bail him out."

"Why are you whispering?"

I shrugged. I had no idea. All I knew was, I could whisper fine, but I couldn't speak out loud.

"You're not speaking at the wake, I guess?"

I shook my head.

"Where's it going to be?"

"Here."

He looked at his watch. "In seven hours? Are you prepared? How many people?"

"It's tomorrow."

"Debbie said it was Saturday. Today."

Oh God. Darren had said he'd miss the wake, and I thought he meant he'd miss it tomorrow. How long had I been under the covers? Had I slept more than I thought? I stood up, panicked. It was Saturday. I had to put out food. Clean the house. Make myself emotionally presentable. And I had to bail Darren out of jail? With what money? And what time?

I must have been a sight, naked in the middle of my room, hands out, not knowing what to do first. Jonathan got up and grabbed my wrists. I had no words.

"Calm down."

I nodded.

"I'm going to take care of it."

"No," I whispered. "It's my job."

He held my hands, pressing them together between his palms. He spoke in the voice that broached no questions, but he didn't tell me to spread my legs or come. "I have to work for a few hours today. I'll send a crew here to clean up, and I'll get food in. How many people?"

"Jonathan. Please. I don't want it to be like this, like I'm using you."

"You're not using me. You're mine. You are my own personal goddess. It's my job to make sure you're happy. And if I can't make you happy, I won't feel right if you're not taken care of as best as I can. So please, tell me how many people so I can feel right."

"A hundred?" I whispered.

How was I going to fit a hundred people in my thousand-square-foot house? Jesus, what were Darren and I thinking? Jonathan squeezed my hands and brought my attention back to his face. He seemed un-fazed by the size of the guest list.

"I have this," he said. "I can take care of it between doing ten other things. Lil will take you downtown. I don't want you driving. Do you have enough to get him out?"

My mouth opened, but not even a whisper came. Did I have enough to bail Darren out of jail? I had no idea. How much did something like that cost? And how was I going to actually take money from Jonathan? I'd get my mother to mortgage the house if necessary. I'd supplicate myself before her, promise to stay on the narrow path, and eat four tons of shit on a hot tar shingle to get Darren out in time for his sister's funeral, but I wasn't taking money from Jonathan.

I nodded. "I have it."

He kissed me tenderly, stroking my cheek with his thumb. "I'll be in touch. Pick up the phone, okay?"

I nodded because I didn't want to whisper again.

CHAPTER 53

*J*onathan left gingerly, as if turning his back on me long enough to get to work making arrangements to prepare my house for a wake was going to give me enough time to fall apart again. He walked backward to the Jag, watching me, the red in his hair catching the morning sun. I waved and even managed to smile a little. I was determined to get through this, even if it meant pretending my shit was together long enough to restore his faith in me. When he drove down the hill, I felt as if he pulled part of me with him.

Lil showed up in Jonathan's Bentley spaceship thirty minutes later.

"Ms. Faulkner," she said. "How are you holding up?"

"Fine."

"Something wrong with your voice?"

I shrugged. I didn't know what was wrong with me, whether it was my voice or my mind or something else entirely, some trick of the universe. I was getting frustrated. The condition I'd initially attributed to too many tears and hurt was starting to feel like something more intractable.

"I wanted to say," Lil said, "and I hope I'm not being

inappropriate, but my wife's brother took his own life. So my sympathies. It can be hardest on the family."

I screwed my face up, trying not to cry again, because she'd called Gabby family. She was exactly that. My sister. And having that recognized was like a bucket of cold water. "Thanks, Lil," I whispered.

"Where are we going today?"

"Going to bail my brother out of jail."

CHAPTER 54

Five thousand dollars.

Apparently, Darren had gone after Theo with a broken bottle, which according to the State of California was a deadly weapon.

So, five large. Cash.

I swallowed hard.

The big lady with the skinny glasses behind the bulletproof glass seemed sympathetic. She'd tolerated my whispering and slid a notepad under the glass once she realized I could hear fine but couldn't speak.

"There's three bondsmen across the street. You pay five hundred, and they forward us the rest. But you don't get it back. Kaylee. That's the one I like. Best with first-timers and ain't no glass in between you so she'll hear that little voice you got. All right, young lady?"

I nodded, ripping the page from the notebook. I took the papers and forms she gave me that detailed Darren's infractions and went outside.

Lil stood by the car, which was perched in a loading zone, pretty as you please. She handed me a paper cup of tea. I didn't know how she knew I liked tea. I didn't know if Jonathan had detailed all my foibles and preferences to her or if she just paid incredible attention, but I took it and thanked her.

"I have to go to the bondsman." I pointed across the street at a yellow and black sign marked Kaylee's Bailbonds.

Lil opened the car door.

"It's just across the street." I had to lean in close to Lil so she'd hear me over the din of rush hour traffic.

"I told Mister Drazen I'd take care of you. So just get in. I have to drive around to the parking lot anyway."

I got in, feeling silly and childish. I could have run across the street in half the time, quarter-time if I jay-walked. But Lil was doing her job with sincerity and kindness, and I didn't have the heart to disrupt her. I sipped my tea in the backseat, hoping the hot liquid would reconnect my voice to my lungs, but when I tried to make a sound, there was only breath.

I felt that there was a choice at the deepest parts of my being not to speak, some fear that my voice would break the world or call up beasts that would rend me and everything I loved to tatters. But I couldn't locate that dark place and explain that it was doing more harm than good, that I needed the fear to go away, that everything in my life would be torn to shreds by simple inaction if I couldn't function as an artist and member of society.

I breathed. Panic was going to get me nowhere. I had to get through the day and bail Darren out in time for the wake. Sleep. Eat. Go to work tomorrow. Breathe. I would figure it out if I could keep the anxiety at bay.

Lil pulled in behind the bondsman place and let me out as if I were a celebrity arriving at a red carpet event. "Mister Drazen said if you needed anything, I should let you know he'll take care of it."

"Thanks."

"You should let him help you." She gave me a meaningful look that said she knew I had reservations about taking help from Jonathan.

I nodded to her and walked through the back door.

The space had no aesthetic pretentions whatsoever. The grey industrial carpet was worn in the high-traffic areas. The fluorescent lights buzzed behind the dropped ceiling, yellowing the piles of papers lying on every surface, every metal shelving unit, veneer desk, and unoccupied black chairs. The occupied chairs, three of them, held people of varying ages and ethnicities, all talking on phones or tapping into aged beige computers. Out the front windows, downtown Los Angeles hummed by.

A middle-aged woman in big dark glasses shuffled past in slippers and a multicolored shift. Her coffee cup was one third full of sludge.

"Hi," I whispered. "I'm looking for Kaylee?"

"Cat got your tongue?"

"Laryngitis." It was the only answer I could come up with that would make any sense. Telling her a part of me thought using my voice would shatter the world might have seemed a little crazy.

"You putting up a bond?"

"Yes. I don't know how."

"You got cash?"

"Some."

"Go on and sit by the desk at the front."

I did, slipping into the cushioned office chair placed in front of it. The bronze plaque that was really made of plastic had the name KAYLEE RECONAIRE cut into it. I had about two hundred dollars on me, which was more than usual because I'd never emptied my bag from my last shift at the Stock.

The lady with the sludge coffee placed herself on

her chair with a sigh. "Do you have the forms?" She held out her hand.

I handed over the stack. She had exactly enough clear space on her desk to look at them, spreading them into three neat piles. The pink stub, the stapled and clipped form, all had a place.

"Any relation?" she asked.

"No."

"Boyfriend?"

"No."

"So?" She leaned her elbows on the desk. "We have to assess if he's a flight risk. It's our money you're talking about, so there will be personal questions. Like, does this gentleman care if you're responsible for him? This is not just assault." She indicated the papers. "It's battery with a deadly weapon, honey." She raised an eyebrow as if I were some girlfriend battered into bailing out her own personal douchebag.

I leaned in so she could hear me. "We broke up a long time ago. He's like a brother to me. He's not some ex I can't stop fucking because I'm insecure."

Kaylee looked at me for a second before laughing. "You nuts, girl. You got a job?"

"I'm a waitress at the Stock downtown." I swung my thumb behind me since it was about five blocks north.

"How much cash you got?"

"I have two hundred on me."

"You're short three."

"I can go to the ATM," I said.

"You can only get two hundred from the machine." She blinked. I blinked. Then she said, "I ain't letting you off the hundred. I'm running a business here."

"You take collateral?"

She gave a knowing, snorty kind of laugh. "Whatever collateral you got, I gotta hold in my hand, and it's gotta be worth ten times what I need. I don't see any jewelry on you I'd take."

I stood and picked up my shirt, showing her the Harry Winston navel ring. I was stepping in a pile of shit, and I knew it. Using my current boyfriend's gift to bail my past boyfriend out of jail was the stuff Jerry Springer shows were made of.

Kaylee leaned forward, dropping her glasses low on her nose. "That real?"

"Yes."

She held out her hand, her face a mask of disbelief. I took out the diamond and handed it to her. She snapped open the top drawer of her desk, pulled out a jeweler's glass, and used it to inspect the diamond, which to me, looked like the hugest, most sparkly thing ever dug from the earth. I sat back down as she made little humming noises, turning the rock around under the glass.

She slid it back to me. "I can get in big trouble, young lady. I don't think you understand I'm running a business here. I don't take stolen merchandise."

I gasped. How could she? Was she insane? I was absolutely stunned wordless by the implication.

A lone, male voice cut through my distress. "Whose Bentley's in my spot?" A man with a crutch and a leg of his jeans rolled up over a missing calf wobbled in.

I raised my hand, whispering, "Sorry."

He sat at a desk. "Well, have that driver move it."

I looked back down at Kaylee. She was already slipping my diamond navel bar into a baggie. "You come back with the rest soon, you hear? Or for the love of three hundred dollars, your new man's gonna be pissed."

CHAPTER 55

I hadn't realized how big the Bentley was until
Darren sat on the other side of the backseat
as if he wanted nothing to do with me. It had taken me
hours to get him out. Money had to be wired, forms
shot over the internet, phone calls made, signatures
garnered, and he had to be driven from a holding area
two blocks away.

When they'd brought him, he looked tired but made
a funny face when he saw me waiting, as if to let me
know he was okay. When they took the cuffs off and
released him into my custody, he hugged me so hard I
thought he'd break something.

"Thank you, thank you," he said into my neck.

"You're welcome. Now we have to go, or we're
going to be missed."

He nodded, and I wondered if he'd gotten himself in
trouble to avoid the funeral.

"Why are you whispering?"

"Laryngitis."

"What? You weren't sick—"

I pulled him into the hallway, wanting to be away
from the bulletproof glass and linoleum flooring. Then
I stopped and moved my wrist like Debbie so often did

to let him know it was time to get moving on the story.

"I went to Adam's," he said. "He stayed with me all night, but he had to go to work, and I just walked around Silver Lake. I sat at a table at Bourgeois for half the day. Fabio knew what happened, so he just kept bringing me new cups."

The elevator doors opened, and a carload of people got out. I pulled Darren to the side.

"He should have called me," I whispered.

"He did."

Right. I'd rejected calls and ignored texts while I lay in my undercover cave.

We got into the elevator with twenty other people.

Darren spoke softly into my ear. "I realized while I was in there that I left you alone. I'm sorry about that."

I shrugged and waved his concern away. I was unhappy about it, but I didn't have the heart to hold it against him. And it had brought Jonathan to me.

Darren continued, "Theo came in for coffee, like he always does. I knew he went there all the time. I didn't realize I was waiting for him. But anyway, some girl at the table next to me had one of those pomello sodas. I smacked the bottle against the floor and went for his throat."

"Holy shit, Darren!" I managed to whisper loudly and with emphasis. I glanced around at the people in the elevator. No one was staring, but they must have been listening.

"He's fine. I got his cheek. I aim like the fag I am."

I pinched his side, and he cried, "Ow!" We laughed. The rest of the elevator population seemed relieved to get away from us when the doors slid open on the parking lot level. Lil was parked in an Authorized Vehicle Only spot, reading the L.A. *Times*.

When Darren saw the Bentley, he stopped in his

tracks. "Where'd you get the money to bail me out? Five grand? That's a lot of cash."

"I put up a bond."

"Did one penny of that come from *him*?"

"Stop."

"I'm not having any part of you being a whore."

I didn't know what came over me, maybe the stress of the past few days, maybe the insult, or maybe the fact that I couldn't speak properly to defend myself. But a ball of kinetic energy ran from my heart and down my right arm, and in order to release it, the only thing I could do was slap Darren across the face.

The *clap* of it echoed through the parking lot. Lil looked up from her paper. Darren crouched from the impact. The feeling of regret dropped into my belly even as my hand wanted to slap him again and again.

I folded it into a fist and stuck out my index finger. "Get in the car. If you are one minute late for your sister, Theo's face will look handsome in comparison." My throat was getting sore from all the harsh whispering, but I was sure I could lecture him for another half-hour if I had to.

He looked enraged with the red marks across his cheek, and his mouth was set in stone, the muscles of his face making tense lines in his jaw. I was a little afraid. Just a little, because I could fight, and I could take a hit. I would do both if I had to.

"The car is ready," Lil said, suddenly standing beside us with her calm, professional demeanor. She held out her hand toward the open back door of the Bentley. "Please."

I thought for a moment he'd opt for the bus, but I knew he had no money on him, because it had come back to me in an envelope of personal effects, along with a pocket knife he wasn't allowed to carry and a few credit cards. He also knew that public transportation would take hours on a Saturday. Despite his self-sabotage, he didn't want to miss Gabby's wake.

I nodded at Lil and walked toward the car, not looking behind me to see if he followed. My shoes clonked on the concrete, made louder from the enclosed space. I climbed into the back seat of the car and slid over, looking out the window so I wouldn't see if he was coming or not. If he saw me watching him, he would be more likely to turn around and take the bus out of pride.

I heard him get in, and the door snapped closed. That was when I discovered how wide that car really was.

Lil dropped him in front of his house. He didn't wait for her to open the door for him. There was a pause. I didn't look at him, but I held out the yellow receipt from Kaylee as I whispered, "Three hundred. Cash."

I felt the paper get snapped from my hand and heard the door close with that satisfying, low-pitched *thup* you get with expensive cars. I only dared to look when he was walking up his steps, head down, yellow receipt crumpled in his hand. I wanted to run up and hug him. He couldn't be held responsible for acting like an ass after what had happened with Gabby, but I wouldn't apologize. Yes, he'd insulted me, but he'd also insulted Jonathan, and somehow, that rankled me even more.

CHAPTER 56

The house was transformed. The front yard was trimmed like a poodle, hedges cut back, fallen oranges picked up and put into bowls at the porch railing, weeds and dead things gone.

"I'll let you know if I have to go anywhere for Mister Drazen," Lil said as she blocked the driveway behind a catering truck with chocks under the wheels.

I nodded, my throat too wrecked for one unnecessary word.

"Monica!" Carlos, our neighbor from two doors down, ran toward me holding a manila envelope. He was a cop and very protective of everyone on the block. "Hi, I heard what happened. I'm real sorry about it."

"Thanks."

"She had me look stuff up for her sometimes. About people. Celebrities and agents."

"Really?"

"Yeah," he smiled sweetly. "She took me out to dinner or something in exchange."

I wondered what "or something" meant and decided I was fine not knowing.

He handed me the envelope. "This was the last thing."

I took it and patted him on the arm. "Will I see you later?"

"Yeah. I'll come by."

We parted, and I headed for the house. I walked up the steps to the porch, which had been swept. Potted plants had appeared, giving the sense that the porch was a well thought-out, finished space. Yvonne, who I hadn't seen since the night I stopped working at Hotel K, almost knocked me over as she strode out to the catering truck.

"Whoa! Monica!" She smiled and kissed my cheek. "You working this gig? Double time. Boo-ya."

Shit. I was going to have to explain, and I didn't have the time, inclination, or vocal capability.

"I live here," I said in breaths.

Yvonne opened her mouth, then snapped it shut, cocking her head. "Girl, they said it was Drazen's girl-friend." Her eyes were wide and her face accusatory in a good-humored way. "I saw a picture on TMZ from that art show. I thought that was you."

"Hello!" Debbie called from inside the house. "Let's keep it moving."

"Later. I'll explain."

"I want *details*," Yvonne said before kicking up the pace to the truck.

The living room had been transformed as well, with chafing dishes on long tables, new lamps, and clean corners.

Debbie took my hands. "How are you doing?"

"You work at the Stock. Jonathan owns K."

"You do sound terrible. No more talking. I volunteered when I heard. No one from K could do it but Freddie, and he's on probation. Can't get within arm's reach of a waitress, or he'll be cleaning toilets, or so I hear. You know how the rumor mill works. You. Now.

We had the bathroom cleaned, so don't leave a mess. Go."

She pushed me across my own living room. I knew three of the people working the wake. All were dressed in catering formals, and all looked at me an extra second before getting back to it. I was mortified. They all thought they were doing an emergency party for the hotel owner's girlfriend, and it was *me*.

I went into my room and closed the door behind me. My closet was full of black. I chose a pair of pants and a sweater. I didn't want anything fancy or special, no bows, sparkly buttons, or short skirts. It didn't matter that Gabby liked it when I went sparkly; I didn't feel sparkly. I felt shitty, and I was going to respect her by wearing something so down and boring I'd be invisible.

I stripped down for a shower, catching a glimpse of myself in the mirror. I was naked, sure, but without that diamond in my navel, I had a worried pang. I couldn't let Jonathan see me without it. I'd have to explain or lie, and I wasn't ready to do either.

I took my shower, dressed, and made up in nudes and neutrals in twenty-four minutes, then texted Jonathan.

—Thanks for everything—

The answer shot back in seconds.

—My pleasure. In a meeting. See you there—

There? He was coming? I didn't know why I hadn't expected that. He'd come to me in minutes when I needed him; he wouldn't sit out my best friend's wake. I kicked off the sensible shoes I'd chosen and slipped into the red-soled pumps from the Eclipse show.

Carlos's envelope lay on my bed. I cracked it open and slid out a single sheet of paper. The heading was for Westonwood Acres, an exclusive retreat that was actually a mental institution. The paper was an admission form, and I froze when I saw the name of the admitted.

Jonathan S Drazen III

His age was right next to the date, so I didn't have to calculate that he had been sixteen. Everything else was blacked out with thick lines.

That was what Gabby had to tell me. I shoved the paper back in the envelope and stuffed it in my drawer with shaking hands.

CHAPTER 57

$\mathcal{D}$arren shuffled up the hill on time. He glanced at me as he passed into the house. I didn't know what he thought of the house's transformation, but I didn't care, and I was ready to defend Jonathan again.

People came, east-side hipsters, west-side musicians, and a few teachers from Colburn who would express sympathy for the vaporized talent. They were all going to want to talk to me. I knew about seventy percent of them by name at least, but the thought of talking to all of them and explaining my "laryngitis" was going to make it ten times the drag it had to be.

I put on my customer-service face. I cleared my throat, which hurt, and smiled at the first person who entered the gate. I nodded, said "laryngitis" while brushing my fingers across my throat, and moved on. After the first few people, it got easier. I just didn't think about anything at all except making the person I was speaking to comfortable. The outward focus helped.

As with the past days of constant calls and texts, I was surprised at how nice people were. They wanted to help, mostly. I left Darren to the inside of the house, and I stayed on the porch, shaking hands and kissing cheeks, smiling as if I were taking drink orders. I stopped seeing faces. I loved them all, *en masse*, without discernment. I was struck by an unexpected, sudden feeling of well-being. By the time Kevin rested his hand on my shoulder, I was at the maximum dose of endorphins.

I threw my arms around him and whispered, "Thanks for coming."

"I'm so sorry, Monica. I know what she meant to you." His hands rubbed my back, and I thought nothing of it.

I spoke softly in his ear. "The thing. The piece. I'm in. Just give me time."

He squeezed me harder. I remembered how he did that in the past, tensing his biceps until I thought my ribs would crack.

He let go, but we still stood close, and he spoke softly so no one else would hear. "I pitched it to the Modern of British Columbia in Vancouver. For Christmas. They had an unexpected opening. Can we make it?" He pulled back and looked into my eyes, keeping his hand on my neck, a touch too familiar, too intimate, but I didn't pull away.

"Let's talk about it," I whispered.

"Once you can talk," Kevin said, smiling.

His scent alerted me to his presence. The new one. Sawdust and leather with light harmonies of an ass-bruising all-night fuck. I turned and found Jonathan behind me in a black suit built for him, a grey shirt, and a black tie. The dark colors brought out his sleek ginger hair and jade eyes.

He held out his hand to Kevin. "Good to see you again," he said, voice tense and overly polite. His eyes were hard stones, and he smiled in a way that could be mistaken for baring his teeth. I'd never seen that look on his face before, and I didn't like it. Not one little bit.

I remembered the piece of paper in the manila envelope. Could I be seeing a symptom of whatever it was that had sent him to a mental hospital? Fuck, I knew I couldn't ask him about it, and now I'd always wonder.

"Of course," Kevin replied. Then he looked at me and did something that he had no right to do. He touched my arm and said, "I'll call you about the piece," before walking into the house.

Jesus fucking Christ, was I really being subjected to a male pissing match at Gabby's wake? Really? I missed the luxury of celibacy for a moment, then looked at Jonathan, whose face had softened. "What the hell was that?" I asked.

"Forget it. How has it been so far?"

"I have my game face on." I pulled away and showed him my stage smile.

"Gorgeous. Debbie said there's no casket?"

I shook my head and did everything to make my look tell him I thought the very idea was absurd.

"As a good lapsed Catholic," he said, "I feel the need for an open casket somewhere."

"Not me, and I'm lapsed, too."

He put his arm around me. "My mother is going to love you."

I swallowed hard through a ravaged throat. I had no idea how his parents fit in with me being his submissive whore fucktoy, or if that meant I was to be kept as far away from his family as possible. It was too much to absorb under the circumstances.

I looked away from him. My eyes found Darren and Adam, who were speaking softly in a corner. Darren looked up, and our eyes met. He came over, and I hoped Jonathan wasn't about to have another pissing match.

As if he thought Darren was no threat at all, while Kevin somehow was, Jonathan excused himself to the interior of the house.

"I'm not sorry," Darren said.

I shrugged. Neither was I.

"Adam's going to pick up your thing. Whatever it was."

"Okay." I wanted to ask how long it would take because I didn't want Jonathan to see me without it and end up giving Darren the same ice-cold stare he'd just given Kevin.

I looked at Darren's face. I'd slapped it just two hours ago, and it seemed healed. Gabby'd had bruises on her left cheek when I went to visit her in the hospital, and my hand hadn't fared much better for the nine and a half minutes I'd hit her, because I thought it kept her alive. Maybe it had. I'd never found out because she was in her hospital bed with apologies, and I'd done everything I could to distract her. Everything. There was nothing more I could have done.

I asked, "Did Gabby ever tell you what she had to say about Jonathan?"

"No, but it wasn't good. Why?"

I was suddenly exhausted. My eyes hurt. My shoulders felt as though they were carrying a huge weight, and my beautiful shoes pushed me too far forward.

"Monica?" Darren said, putting his hand on my arm.

I felt Jonathan's presence and stood up straight, shaking it off and putting on my stage smile. Jonathan put his arm around me and guided me to the backyard. I don't know if a look was exchanged with Darren or not, and I didn't care.

Dad had designed the small backyard with private spaces and fruit trees. He'd placed flagstones to make paths and let them get overgrown where they needed to be, bordering hard lines with low jade plants and rocks. I led Jonathan to the back, against the cinderblock wall that kept the hill from sliding over our house. I hadn't looked at the bench in months. It was dirty with leaves and dust. Jonathan wiped it off, and we sat.

"How are you holding up?" he asked, stroking my hair.

I put my arms around his shoulders and kissed the place where his cheek and neck met. "What was that with Kevin?" I needed to know who I was dealing with, and every new piece of information I got pointed to the fact that I had no idea.

"I'm not good at hiding when I'm pissed. I don't like what he did to you." His lips touched my neck and his hand pressed me to his mouth.

"Possessive and jealous are real turn-offs, Jonathan. If you can't trust me—"

"I'm not possessive. I'm protective."

I sighed deeply, forgetting everything as his tongue found the most sensitive place on my throat. "Jonathan ..."

"No talking."

The arm behind the bench brought me closer to him, and the hand at my cheek slid down my chest, landing over my breast, which reacted by getting tight, stiffening the nipple through my sweater. He dragged his fingernail over the hard lump, first lightly, then harder. He slid his face across mine until our noses touched, and I could see the blue specks in his eyes.

He squeezed my nipple hard through my sweater and bra. My mouth opened, but no sound came out. I reached between his legs, where I could feel his erection through his pants.

"No, Monica. This is for you. Put your hands to your sides."

I shook my head.

"I get off on this," he said. "You obeying me is what turns me on. Don't deny me."

I did as I was told, as always: submissive whore fucktoy to someone who neglected to tell me where he'd spent his sixteenth year. I decided to think about it later.

He put his thumb to my lips. "Make this wet."

I took his thumb, and he moved it against my tongue as I sucked, pulling the juices from my mouth to give him what he asked for. Anything he asked for. The tidal wave between my legs demanded it as much as he did.

Our noses still touched as he slid his hand up my sweater, pushing the bra up so he could cup my breast. I panicked a little as he went past my navel, where the diamond should have been, but he went right by it, taking the nipple between his first finger and his moist thumb. I let out a *hah* when he squeezed and twisted.

"Keep your eyes open," he said. "Look at me."

I did as I was told.

He filled my vision when he pulled the nipple. "This is who we are." As if seeing my objection through my arousal, he continued, "You and I. You know that."

He dragged his thumbnail over the stretched nipple, and I opened my mouth, but no words came.

"Your legs are crossed. Spread them."

I did, cursing that I'd worn pants. I wanted his touch on me. I wanted him to feel how wet I was for him. A pang of guilt shot through me for being so turned on at Gabby's wake, but it was drowned out by the roar between my legs when he twisted my nipple again.

"Open the pants."

I unbuttoned and unzipped, keeping the sweater down over my bellybutton.

"Put your hand between your legs," he whispered.

"I can't." Somehow, feeling his touch on me would

be all right. Touching myself would seem too self-indulgent.

"Yes, you can. And you will. For me."

I slipped my hand into my panties then stopped.

"Please," he said, not like a plea but a mandate.

My middle finger found my wetness first, gathering over my engorged clit like dew. Jonathan sighed when my expression changed. I put my hand down to my opening, dragging the tingle and heat with it, and circled, gathering the juices between the two fingers, like a metal ball around a roulette wheel.

Jonathan kissed my cheek and stroked my breast, keeping the nipple stiff as I pulled my hand back up to my clit, which was as hard as a marble and soaking wet. I was so close already. My body remembered I'd been lying under the covers with Jonathan, even if my mind had moved on to other things.

"May I come?" I whispered. Things may have changed between us, but one thing did not remain undefined. He owned my orgasms, and I wanted him to have them.

"You are such a good girl."

"May I?"

He waited before answering, kissing my nose, my cheek, caressing my breast. I kept stroking while he surrounded me. My orgasm pushed against me, a pressure inside, asking to get out, begging, needing. I kept telling it, *not yet, not yet* until, all at once, he grabbed my nipple hard enough to hurt and said, "Come."

The tension released like broken strings, everywhere. My body straightened under my own touch, pulsing and clenching from pussy to ass. I opened my mouth, and though I screamed inside, only air came out.

"Don't stop," he said.

I kept my hand moving, and the orgasm continued.

My knees bent, and my body crouched and again, like a shot, I went rigid, breathing *ah, ah, ah*. It hurt, and just as I thought I couldn't take it anymore, he said, "Stop."

I fell into his arms like a shuddering mound of jelly.

He laughed. "I think you needed that."

I just leaned my head on his chest, gasping for air.

"You didn't use your voice," he said, stroking my hair. "I thought for sure that would do it."

I shrugged.

"We need to get back inside," he said, "before all your ex-boyfriends come out here, and I have to kill them." He drew his hand over my belly and stopped. He picked up my sweater so he could see my naked navel. "Did you lose it?"

I put purest innocence on my face with a hint of lack of surprise. "Inside." I indicated the direction of the house, but downtown was in the same general direction, and unless it was in transport or being stolen, there was a good chance it was indoors.

He nodded and pulled my sweater down, then watched as I buttoned up. He seemed pensive, and I wondered if he'd become sensitive to contextual lies.

CHAPTER 58

*W*hen we got inside, much of the wake had broken up. The wait staff cleaned and put away, making beelines for the catering truck. Only a few people remained. Darren, in particular, looked lost, milling around the leftovers. Adam wasn't anywhere to be seen. Jonathan and Debbie spoke quietly at the door.

A man of about fifty, with round plastic glasses and long straight hair, approached me. "Are you Monica Faulkner?"

When I nodded, he held out his hand. "Jerry Evanston. I saw Gabby that afternoon."

I tilted my head. No memory had been jogged.

"Eugene at WDE asked me to go to DownDawg in Burbank to keep an artist company. It was crazy, but he got me my next gig, and I kind of owed him. I didn't question it. I wanted to say I'm sorry. I didn't know this would happen. Eugene's an asshole, but I knew him in college, and he's always got a favor lined up when I need it."

I nodded and pointed to let him know I knew he was the one who had kept Gabby company while I fucked up the scratch cut by myself. She'd been right. It had been a setup.

"I'd understand if you're pissed."

"It's okay," I whispered. "You didn't know."

"Your partner played for me, and she was brilliant. Eugene said you were really good."

I shrugged. It seemed the simplest way to communicate paragraphs worth of feeling. I was good. I was worthless. I was mute. I was music.

"Your voice okay?"

"Laryngitis."

"I have a proposition for you, because I feel guilty about what happened."

I nodded. The room suddenly seemed stifling with too many people around, and Yvonne giving me the old eyebrow as if I were her source for interesting news.

"Tell me," I said.

"I got this job. It's through Eugene, but that's not going to matter. Carnival Records. I'm working with the EVP to develop new talent."

"Herman Neville?" I asked, feeling like Gabby with her magic hat of names.

Jonathan came up behind me, and I took his hand. I wanted to lean on him more than anything. He and Jerry nodded to each other.

Jerry continued, "Yes. And I have this studio time I booked for Thursday. In Burbank. The talent cancelled this morning, and I thought, if you wanted to do something low production value, all you, we could put something decent together, and I could bring it to him. No promises. But I'd feel better."

"Could it be my song?"

"Well, it would have to be. If you have the voice to sing it, of course."

"Yes." My agreement came out in a breath, and I wondered what the hell I was doing. I had no song. Shit, I had no *voice*. What the fuck was I thinking?

"Great, here's my card."

"Thank you." I stared at it. It just had his name and number. Could have been anyone. And as he left, I thought, he was probably the last person to hear Gabby play.

Jonathan came up behind me as Jerry left, stroking my back, his touch electric even through my sweater. I glanced at Yvonne, who seemed to find our intimacy fascinating in a very "you go, girl" sort of way.

"Are you going to be all right?" he asked softly.

"Tired."

"Do you want to stay with me for a few days?"

My knees almost lost the ability to hold me up. I wanted nothing more than to crawl into the bed of his spare room, where we'd done all our fucking, and let him stroke and spoon me for days. His voice as I drifted off to sleep, the soft touch of his lips on me, and the feeling of being cared for, safe, partnered, were exactly what I wanted with all my heart. I looked into those jade eyes, which expressed none of the smug dominance of the club, only concern, and said, "I can't."

"Why not?"

"You're not a prince, Jonathan. You're a king. But I'm not ready." I touched his face and looked right at him, as if that could transmit the depth of my feelings for him, or my doubts about their prudence.

"I'm trying hard not to be a controlling asshole."

"You're doing a good job."

He left me with a tender kiss that Yvonne saw, and then Darren was gone, too. The staff and all their accoutrements disappeared with Debbie telling me I didn't have to come in tomorrow if I didn't want to. Then it was me in my clean house, alone. The door to Gabby's room was closed. I opened it.

My best friend's knowledge of Hollywood's web of relationships came from hours and hours of hard work. Her dresser was piled with manila envelopes, each with a name. Colored bars in felt tip pen decorated the bottom of each envelope, cross referenced by name, education, job, and personal and family relationships. Stacks of *Variety*, the Calendar section of the *LA Times*, the *New York Times*, and the *Hollywood Reporter* rose in towers around the perimeter of the room. I'd asked her repeatedly to make use of the recycle bin, but she always thought there might be one connection she missed, so she couldn't throw away a shred of paper. In the end, she'd just relegated the mess to her room and closed the door.

—*You ok?*—

Jonathan's text came in just as I was considering locking Gabby's door for good.

—*Feet hurt. Fine otherwise. I'm going to bed*—

—*Good night, goddess*—

—*We still need to talk*—

—*When you can talk, we will. Now get to bed. No touching. I'll know...*—

I was sure he would, somehow. The same way I was sure he knew about the diamond sitting in a baggie downtown.

CHAPTER 59

I wanted to stay in bed for days after Gabby's wake, but I couldn't skip work. I hustled in for the lunch shift dry-eyed and made up. I put on my stage smile for Debbie, who pursed her red lips and seemed generally unimpressed.

"Can you talk?"

I shook my head.

"So what do you think you're going to do?"

My face must have been a complete blank because I had no answer. Debbie sighed and called Robert over from the other side of the bar where he was flirting with two women who looked like cover models. She took my pad from my hands and said to him, "Monica's at the service bar tonight."

"Why? It's lunch."

"Question me again."

Robert was immediately cowed. The tone in Debbie's voice triggered something in me as well. A recognition. A wakefulness. When she glanced over at me and indicated I should go around to the other side of the bar, I knew what it was because I'd heard it from Jonathan's lips. Debbie was a dominant.

The fact that I recognized that told me more about myself than I wanted to know. I'd spent the morning and afternoon in busy sequester, puttering around the house, picking up Gabby's things, and putting them in boxes. The copies of *Variety* on top of the piano. The shoes by the door. The metronome she left by the TV. Music sheets. I'd separated them into *Keep* and *Toss* and then kept everything for Darren anyway. All that time, I heard not her voice in my head, but her music. I sat at the piano and played one of her compositions, the one she played when she was feeling threatened and powerless, the bombastic thing she'd been at just the other night, and I stopped mid-way. I didn't sound as good as she had. Some keys were off, but she never wrote down her own stuff. She only did notations on pieces she heard and was trying to figure out. I'd snapped up a few sheets of the notepaper abandoned in the *Toss* bin and played again, writing down the notes as I went. And then, as if the notes could not be contained as simple sounds, words flowed through them. I had to run for the legal pad by my bed.

What if he collars me? Slaps me? Spanks me? Bites me? Fucks me in the ass? Whips me? Hurts me? Displays me? Gags me? Blindfolds me? Shares me? Humiliates me? Ties me down? Makes me bleed? Fucks me up?

That fucking list. I could have added another hundred things.

Chocks my mouth open. Pulls my hair. Fucks my face. Calls me whore. Tells me to lick the floor. Destroys me. Makes me hate myself. Turns me into an animal.

And that was it, wasn't it? I was afraid of turning into something subhuman, not just to him or to the people around me, but to myself.

I'd remembered the tone in Jonathan's voice when he demanded something of me. The calmness, the surety, the note itself. A chord. I played it, toying with the sounds until I came up with something in D, and I checked the notations I'd made of Gabby's piece. I could do it. I could keep her alive. I could figure out how to continue with him, if at all.

Hearing that tone in Debbie's voice threw me for a second, and I stood silent. She raised her eyebrow and made a motion with her hand, indicating that it was time for me to go under the service bar and do my new job. As I passed her, she said, "You need to get to the doctor."

I smiled, not because I agreed, but because I knew it wasn't something a doctor could fix. I didn't know if I'd be able to sing in time to record with Jerry on Thursday, but at least I had the beginnings of a song.

I poured for the girls, dancing around Robert to get to the bottles, refilling the ice when necessary, and replenishing the beer. I was definitely stepping on his territory and his tip total for the shift, so I tried to be nice to him.

I was having a fun time just smiling and nodding as forms of communication, until I saw Darren at the bar, looking sullen.

"Hey," he said. "You're back there?"

I indicated the service part of the bar just as Tanya came up with a ticket. I filled glasses with ice, then the liquor, and stuck her ticket at six o'clock. It was still slow, so I leaned over the bar, wiping the space in front of Darren.

"Can you get me a beer?" he asked.

I shook my head. Robert was already giving me the devil eye. I pointed at the beers. Robert slipped it out of the case, poured it, and opened the ticket.

"I got your thing," Darren said. "Pretty big fucking rock."

I held out my hand.

"I left it on the piano."

I nodded and glanced at Debbie, who was on the phone and watching me.

"I'm not sorry," he said. "I shouldn't have called you a whore, but that doesn't change anything."

I had so much to say, starting with the fact that I had no use for his non-apology and ending with the fact that I didn't need his judgmental attitude. But I'd also evened it all out by slapping him good and hard, so it wasn't resentment I held as much as impatience. He needed to get over it so we could work on the Vancouver piece, whatever that would be.

Angie, another waitress, came by with a ticket, and I poured her drinks. Then Tanya. Then the new girl, whose name I'd forgotten. They were all working harder because I wasn't on the floor, and Robert was making less, so I tried hard to pull my weight. By the time I turned around, Darren was gone, and two hundred-dollar bills sat under his empty bottle. Robert went for them, but I snatched them first.

"What the fuck, Monica?"

Not being able to talk was getting on my last nerve. I showed him the money and grabbed him by the back of the neck, whispering as clearly as I could, "Paying back a loan." I looked him in the eye with all the intensity I had. I wasn't taking an argument for an answer. I pushed him away.

Then I saw Jonathan at the end of the bar. It was the same seat he'd occupied the night I'd kissed him overlooking the Valley on Mulholland and again at the food truck lot. He leaned on both elbows, talking on the phone and watching me. I hadn't seen him at the Stock since the day he'd left me hungry and begging for him on Sam's desk. I assumed he was intentionally and respectfully avoiding my shifts. I approached him. He opened his hand, and I took it just as he finished his call.

"Hello, goddess."

I mouthed, *Hello, king.*

"Still not talking?"

I shook my head, just staring at him. I was used to him, the curve of his jaw and the color of his hair. He was a familiar thing I was getting to know deeply, line by gorgeous line. I wanted to crawl over the bar and drop into his arms.

"When do you record with that guy?"

Thursday, I mouthed. He watched my lips move with an unnerving intensity.

"And what were you intending to do about this problem?"

I shrugged. I was anxious about the non-talking. I didn't think about much else, but I didn't have a cure. I knew it wasn't physical; fear kept my vocal cords from connecting.

"Do you have plans after work?"

I shook my head again. Yesterday, I would have been able to answer, but this thing had been getting worse. His concerned look told me he noticed. I caught sight of Sam approaching and slipped my fingers from Jonathan's and went back to the service bar.

Jonathan didn't make an appearance at the bar again, which was just as well. The dinner crowd was larger than usual, and we were busy enough for me to get a few grateful looks from Robert. My shift seemed to end in no time at all, but it was dark, and the heat lamps had just been turned on when relief arrived.

Debbie handed Robert and me our envelopes. "Nice night," she said. "Thank you both for working together. You—" She pointed at me. "—get that throat looked at. You did fine, but we don't need you at the service bar. We need you on the floor, acting witty and charming."

I nodded, mouthing *okay* while keeping my eyes downcast. She'd been very kind not to send me home as soon as she realized I couldn't talk, and I was grateful.

At my locker, I got out my clothes and stuffed my envelope in my pocket. I felt it then, a hard piece that was too rigid to be cash. I tore open the envelope. There was far less than I was used to, as seemed just under the circumstances, and a key card for one of the rooms in the Stock hotel.

My phone blooped right then.

—*room 522 be naked*—

A ripple of electricity coursed between my legs. Despite the fact that he and I had so much to discuss, despite the fact that I couldn't speak and should go see a doctor, despite everything, I wanted him immediately. I grabbed my bag and shuffled to the elevator, texting on the way.

> —*Honestly, why bother if I can't scream your name?*—

—*You'll scream*—

> —*I think I'll just go home and wash my socks*—

I was getting out on the fifth floor when I realized the one thing that should get me home right away. I cursed myself. I should have put him off with an honest rescheduling, if for even an hour. But now my jokey, sarcastic texts meant I was on my way up, and my diamond navel ring was on my piano. Fuck.

I stood outside the elevator, staring at my phone. I had to just do it.

—*Actually, can I...*

I never finished the text. Everything I considered typing sounded like a complete fabrication. I'd already told him I didn't have any plans. He'd already seen I wasn't sick or otherwise indisposed. I was just going to have to put on my big girl panties and deal.

CHAPTER 60

I didn't know what to do with myself. I was supposed to be getting undressed and waiting for him naked, but I couldn't stand before him in all my nude, diamond-less glory. He'd see the missing jewel at some point, of course, but I'd rather it not be in the first three seconds, with him clothed and me squirming and naked.

So I paced the room, looked out the window at the disputable glories of Downtown, and waited with an anticipation that lacked sex in its tension. When the door clicked open, I wanted to run out, but Jonathan blocked the way.

He looked me up and down, in my black jeans and T-shirt, then tilted his head as if trying to figure me out. "Something's not adding up here," he said, dropping his keycard on the dresser. He didn't seem angry, just stern. Even when I smiled and shrugged, with a finger in my cheek like a pure innocent, he didn't crack. He stepped so close to me I felt his breath on my cheek. "Naked, Monica."

I shuddered. I wanted to obey. My hands twitched for my buttons and snaps, but I held them down and looked into his eyes. There was a smile there, buried under the rigidity. I couldn't tell if it was humor or enjoyment, but there was pleasure. If I could get him to take my clothes off so fast or messily he didn't notice, I'd consider this a success.

"Is this the submissive thing?" he asked. "You're proving you're not?"

I kept my mouth closed. I couldn't speak, so I had the perfect excuse not to answer. I just kept my face close to his, feeling the heat come off him in waves.

He brushed his hand across the top edge of my jeans. "Are you taking that belt off, or am I?"

I gave my twitching hands something to do, yanking my leather belt though the loop and snapping it off. I was about to drop it on the floor when he caught it.

"Thank you," he said.

He slipped his fingers in my waistband, and I gasped as he unbuttoned my jeans, then pulled down the zipper. He folded back the corners of the fly.

"My intention was to get you to use your voice one way or the other. You chose the other." He took a handful of hair at the back of my neck and threw me on the bed, face down.

I landed with a bounce. He was on me before I had a chance to inhale, straddling me, his knees pressing my thighs together as he grabbed my arms at the elbows.

"Anything that sounds like 'no' or 'stop' is effective. But you have to say it." He pulled my elbows together behind my back.

The restriction brought a tingle between my legs, a sensation that started deep in my gut and ran to the very tip of my crotch. When he wrapped the belt around my arms just above the elbows, I gasped from the sudden rush of arousal that nearly blinded me. He pulled it tight. I couldn't move.

"You have to use your voice. Do you understand?"

I nodded, looking back at him, half my face on the bedspread, the other half covered with a mass of hair. He gripped my jeans at the waistband and yanked them down over my ass, taking my panties with them. I thought he was going to pull them all the way off, but he only got them down to mid-thigh before he stopped to raise my ass up and back until my knees were under me.

He moved the hair from my eyes, looking deeply into them as he brushed his fingers over my vagina. "You're wet, Monica." He circled the outside of it, pushing the lips aside.

I felt how wet I was in the way he touched me, moving smoothly. Watching my face, he drew his hand away, and in the half second I missed it, I thought he'd take off his pants or kiss my pussy, but instead, his hand landed on my ass with a hard *slap*. A *hah* left my lungs. Then he did it again, higher up. Hard.

The sting was intense, and the rush of arousal was undeniable, like the tide coming in. My arms tensed against their binds, but I wasn't going anywhere. I was under him completely, confined, aroused, controlled. I had no will of my own, just the enslavement of his palm on my ass as he stroked it once across, down to my folds, then brought it back up to slap me again.

"You okay, baby?" he asked.

I nodded, admitting to myself that I felt more than okay. I felt safe. He kept at it. Stroke, slap, caress, slap. I lost myself in the sting and heat on my ass, submitted completely to what was happening, what I allowed to happen. The seconds between his palm slapping me and the stinging whacks themselves were hot with anticipation, and he timed them so they came when I didn't expect, thrusting me forward. My breathing got harsh and guttural as he moved down my thighs, one side, then the other. I knew he was going to hit the center. I knew the next slap was going to cut right into my pussy, and as if he knew I knew, he held it back an extra second, then whacked the backs of my thighs and my soaking clit.

I grunted.

"Monica, was that you?" He was breathless himself.

I couldn't make the noise again until he slapped my cunt twice, hard and fast, and the sting, then the rush of pleasure pulled one long vowel sound from my throat.

"There it is. That beautiful voice."

I felt the pressure on the mattress as he took off his pants. I couldn't see what he was doing, but those seconds of anticipation were rewarded when I felt his cock against the raw skin of my ass. He pushed it down along the slick wetness of my crack, and it slipped in as if meant to be there.

"Jonathan," was the only word I had as I felt him glide so slowly into me. He felt better than he ever had, smoother, silken almost, and I groaned, using the vocal cords that never could or would have damaged my life.

He dug his fingers into my waist and pushed himself deep, hard. A grunt left his lips. He took me, owned me, used me, and I was going to come right there with my back to him.

"No," I said. "Not like this."

He stopped and laid himself along the length of my back. "How do you want it?"

"Be sweet," I whispered.

"I need to hear your voice."

"Make love to me," I said, more embarrassed to ask for that than to beg for a hard fuck. But after the spanking, I needed his arms around me, his face in my neck, his breath in my ear.

He undid the belt that held my arms in one motion and turned me around. When I was on my back and my ankles were in the air, he pulled my jeans off the rest of the way. His dick never left me. Once I saw his face, I knew something had just happened between us. The rigidity in his eyes was gone, replaced by a mask of longing, and the openness to reveal it. He kissed me as I wrapped my legs around him. We moved together, and the urgency between my legs turned into a fire. He put his hands on my cheeks.

"Look at me."

I took him in, all of him. We slid against each other, his cock rubbing my sensitive, reddened lips while he pressed my clit against his belly.

"Oh." I had not another syllable.

"Look at me when you come." He rocked back and forth, drawing his dick out just enough so my sore pussy felt the pain and pleasure of him thrusting back in.

I took his hair in my hands, bringing his face to mine, as I spread my legs as far as they'd go. My pussy became a bag of marbles dropped on the floor, as it opened and the feeling spread all over me, across the floor, and into the corners. Ice-cold and white-hot at the same time, to my toes in undulating waves, I pressed myself against him and screamed as the marbles reversed themselves and landed everywhere his dick touched me. Nowhere else. I couldn't feel another thing, hear another thing, not even my own cries as I came, my cunt clenching him over and over.

I was looking right at him, but I couldn't see a thing past my own pleasure or hear him over my own screams.

When I finally opened my eyes, his face had drooped, and his eyes closed, and he said, "Ah, no," as he jerked into me like a reflex.

I felt close to him, tuned together, breathing in sync. He would tell me what happened when he was sixteen.

He'd tell me about Westonwood Acres, and I promised myself I wouldn't care. We were bound.

"I'm sorry, Monica." He pulled out of me, and from the way it felt and the slew of liquid that followed, I knew we had a problem.

"You weren't wearing a condom?"

"I was going to put one on, but when you asked me to flip you, I thought I had another minute. But you came and then—"

"Jesus *Christ.*"

"We'll handle it, whatever happens."

"This is not about you keeping me and a baby in a nice lifestyle, Jonathan." I felt shrieky. That moment between us had been so short before it was broken, and I already felt withdrawal pangs. "How many women have you been with?"

He straightened his arms, separating himself further. "I'm always careful."

"How is that supposed to help me sleep at night?"

"Monica..."

I pushed him off me and rushed into the bathroom, closing the door behind me. Alone. Finally. I could think about what the fuck I was doing. Crazy. It was all crazy. I turned on the shower and leaned against the door, sliding down to the floor.

I was involved with a womanizing slut who got over his wife fifteen minutes ago, who just spanked me because he thought I was ball-gag submissive, and who had spent time in a mental institution. Was I fucking *nuts?* Kevin was more stable.

I stripped off my T-shirt and bra and stepped into the shower. I'd worried about that diamond. I didn't even give a shit anymore. That thing was going back in the box and getting sent back to his doorstep. I couldn't return it personally. I couldn't let my knees get weak for that controlling, irresponsible, manipulative moth-erfucker.

A vision of him came to me, at the club the second time, when I was so worried about Jessica. I saw him straight and tall in his suit and tie, ginger hair finger-brushed back, and that slip of a smile when he spotted me, because the smile I felt in my heart when I saw him was ten times the size of the one on my face.

I turned up the heat on the water, cleaning between my legs as if that was going to do a damn thing. But I had to get him out. The scent of him, the taste, every cell of his had to be gone. Of course, the problem was that I wasn't involved with him. I wasn't dating him. I wasn't casually fucking him.

I was falling in love with him.

And when I realized that, I felt the warmth of peace because I knew what I was contending with, and my choice was clear. Stay with him, love him, and deal with the consequences, or end it with the commitment to make sure it stayed ended.

When I got out of the shower, I hadn't made a decision.

Jonathan was gone.

CHAPTER 61

J sat in the Echo Park Family Clinic, checking my phone. I tapped at the letters, considering a message to him, but with nothing to say about what I wanted from him, how could I show him the disrespect of a message? And with no word from him, maybe he was going to make my decision for me.

Darren texted:

—Are we cleaning Gabby's room?—

Lately, he and I only discussed practical matters. I thought that would be okay for a while. Eventually, we'd have to discuss what had happened.

—Can we do later in the week?—

—k—

—BTW I got my voice back—

—good—

—I want to use one of Gs comps. I'll credit her as author so the estate gets the royalties—

346

There was a long pause after that, then:

—*You're a good and honest person*
with an incredible right hook—

"Monica Faulkner," called the Hispanic woman behind the desk. She wore pink scrubs and slippers. I stepped forward as she took a triplicate paper from a sleeve. "Okay, you had a dose of postinor for emergency contraception and a depo-provera shot. Sign here. Did the doctor give you a date to return for another shot?"

"Yeah."

"Anything else?"

"I don't know if this guy is worth it."

"They never are, *mija*. Not one of them."

CHAPTER 62

We wove words under popsicle trees,
The ceiling open to the sky,
And you want to own me
With your fatal grace and charmed words.
All I own is a handful of stars
Tethered to a bag of marbles that turns

WILL YOU CALL ME WHORE?
    Destroy me,
    Make me lick the floor,
    Twist me in knots,
    Turn me into an animal?
    Will I be a vessel for you?

SLICE OPEN our lying box
    Through a low doorway for our
    Shoulds and oughts.
    Choose the things I don't need,
    No careless moments, no mystery.
    And you need nothing.
    My backward bend doesn't feed.

. . .

WILL I EVER OWN YOU?
Tie you?
Can I ever collar you?
Hurt you,
Hold you, and own you?
Will you ever be a vessel for me?

"THAT," said Jerry from behind the glass, "is exactly what I'm talking about. That is a *song*."

"Thanks," I said into the mic as I took off my headphones. I'd laid down the piano track first to get the tempo down, then I'd sung over it as I listened. "I'd like to do that second chorus again."

"It's that or you lay in the theremin. We're short on time."

My little electromagnetic box sat in the corner. The second chorus was going to have to stay the way it was. I needed to lay in a track with an instrument played without touching it, or the whole song wouldn't work. The lyrics were the culmination of all my fears, but there had to be a portion of the music that was comforting and sweet. Anything less would have been unfair.

Jerry didn't know that I hadn't actually composed an accompaniment for the theremin. I told myself I hadn't had time, but the fact was, I didn't know what I wanted out of the thing. The sounds it made were the opposite of Gabby's percussive composition, and the two things together made no sense at all.

As I stood in front of it, listening to my voice and the piano together in my headphones, I reached for the instrument. My hand crossed the electromagnetic field and made a note. I moved the other hand between the metal poles, stroking the music, not touching a thing, the vibrations caused by the lack of physicality. The hand dance became a sensual thing, as if I touched an imaginary man who had come too close to me when I felt vulnerable, who had touched me when I hurt, and who had made the mistake of caring about me when I asked him to. For those sins and the mistake of letting his skin touch mine in a dangerous way, I'd shut him out.

"Can I start over?" I asked Jerry, who was flipping dials in the control room.

"Yep."

Then I played the thing with all my anger and sorrow, flicking my fingers into the air to create notes of apology in measures of longing.

CHAPTER 63

I got back from the studio feeling as though I'd just played to a stadium crowd. Jerry was going to remix the whole thing and review it with me in the next few days. Until then, I was high. I had to shower and change before meeting Kevin and Darren about the Vancouver piece.

A Fiat was parked in front of my house. I recognized it as the one that had been parked in Jonathan's driveway the second night we were together. On my porch stood his assistant in all her blond sullenness.

"Hi," I said. "I don't think we've met?"

"Kristin." She didn't shake my hand or smile, just handed me an envelope. "I'm supposed to wait until you read it."

I tore it open. Inside was a sheet from Trend Laboratories. In the top right corner, Jonathan had scribbled, *Sleep well.*

Under the header were the words TEST RESULTS. Smaller words lined up beneath that. Many were no more than jumbles of consonants, each with two checkboxes. Positive and negative. Negative boxed were checked all down the line. I did a purposeful check for HIV, and when I saw the Negative box checked, I breathed a sigh of relief.

"Do you want to come in?" I asked.

"I'm late."

"Can I give you something to pass back to him?"

"Sure." Though the word itself implied that giving Jonathan a note would be her pleasure, and though her tone was completely professional, her posture and stony face told another story. She was probably a Harvard MBA passing notes between her boss and his mistress.

I unlocked the house. "This won't take a second."

I had a box of receipts, and I dug through it until I came to the one from the Echo Park Family Clinic. I circled the prescription for my morning-after pill and wrote, *You too*, in the upper right-hand corner. I stuffed it into the envelope, went back outside, and handed it back to her. I knew what I wanted to do.

He hadn't texted or called since he'd spanked me pink in the hotel room. I knew he was giving me space, taking the pressure off. He'd broken a cardinal rule by entering me without a condom, but I wasn't such a child as to think I had no responsibility to protect both of us. I could have checked. I could have been more diligent. When his dick felt so good in me, I should have known. It wasn't as if I'd never felt an unwrapped penis before.

I held my phone, feeling the heft of it in my palm. I could call him. I could reach out to him, and we could discuss him tying me up and hitting me with riding crops. Or chocking my mouth open so he could fuck it. Or sharing me with his buddies. How far did it go? How deep was the kink? I had no idea. I'd shut him down pretty quickly.

I put away the phone, deciding to give it an hour. I

wanted him to have that receipt in his hands before I called.

CHAPTER 64

"*W*hy should the space be limited?" Darren asked. "Space is visual, and it's your problem. Time is aural, and that's between Monica and me."

"This is a representation of human limitation," Kevin said, his posture twisted like a spring, leaning forward, fully engaged as always. "We have no authority over space and time in reality, and any control we wrest is, by its nature, false."

"So Monica and I will dictate the space, and you'll dictate the tempo. We work from there."

I leaned back, arms crossed, legs stretched, and ankles twisted. I had nothing to add. They were in an epic intellectual pissing match. None of what they said mattered, and it ran counter to the original vision, which was to remove the intellectual from the emotional. But they'd started the minute we entered Hoi Poloi Hog, also known as HPH.

The furnishings were found objects rescued from street corners and thrift stores. That included the lighting, the sockets of which had been fitted with bulbs that seemed specifically designed to cast as little light as possible. The sunless, dark blue sky of the October evening didn't help the lighting situation at all, burnishing the faces of my two companions a deep bronze.

It was lost on no one that I sat with two of the three men I'd shared my body with, but it wasn't discussed. Art was discussed.

"Either of you guys need more coffee?" I asked. They were both on their second espressos.

"I'll get it," Darren said. "You guys got the last two." He got up and went to the bar.

Kevin didn't say anything for a second, and neither did I. He'd get to it if I didn't try to fill the empty space.

"You need a partner for this?" he asked. "Because I didn't ask for a team."

"You would have had three of us if Gabby hadn't gone swimming while overdosing."

"Was that a cheap shot?"

It was my turn to lean forward. "I don't work well alone. You know that. I do my best work with other people."

"You have to get over that."

"You're not feeling threatened, are you?"

He leaned back in his seat and gnawed on a lemon rind. "You do *not* like being challenged, Tweety Bird."

My phone blooped, and I glanced at it. Jonathan.

—*Jesus Christ, the Echo Park family clinic? Are you serious?*—

—*Problem?*—

—*Let me count the ways*—

I was considering what to reply when it blooped again.

—*Can we stop this and talk before I have an accident?*—

I had a wisecrack at the ready regarding the meaning of the word "accident" and possible incontinence problems that could be serviced at the Echo Park Family Clinic for a nominal fee. I kept it to myself. "I'll be right back," I said to Kevin, not responding to his questioning look as I took the phone outside.

The street was active with dog walkers, phone talkers, deep kissers, and loud laughers. The traffic was loud, and I had to pinch one ear shut when he picked up.

"Hi," I said.

"You walked out of there with more diseases than you walked in with."

"You're being a snob."

"Snobbery is a defense against low social position. *Ego sum forsit.*"

"I can't believe you just said that. Even without the Latin part."

"Which I botched, really. Because I feel like I've botched everything with you."

I let the silence hang for a second, checking in with my memory of him, the way he moved, the way he spoke, his scent, his breath. Then, I thought of Carlos's blacked-out page from the institution, the ex-wife he may still love, the woman in San Francisco, and of course, the submissive thing.

I took a deep breath before I broke the silence. "We're both not saying the same thing."

If there was a way to hear a smile on the other end of a phone line, it would have deafened me. "I'll be home at ten or so, unless you want me to come there."

It hadn't occurred to me to do anything at my house, and the idea was appealing, except for Gabby's empty room and Carlos's envelope, which made a huge mental racket for an inanimate object.

"Ten is fine."

He breathed. Was it a sigh? "I look forward to it."

I went back in to watch the other two great fucks of my life talk about the dialectics of emotion.

$\mathcal{I}$ got out of there at nine forty-five with a head full of multi-syllabic words and no solutions. The boys were still talking about what it all meant in the grand scheme of things and seemed to be enjoying each other's company more and more as the espressos went down. As I got into the Honda, I decided that if they ended up sleeping together, I'd promptly become a lesbian, then banished the thought.

Jonathan's gate was open like a mouth ready to swallow me whole. I parked in his driveway and shut the car, sitting there for a second and watching the bougainvillea vine swing in the autumn wind. The yellow pad I'd been working on stuck out of my bag. I'd dashed off some notes during my talk with Kevin and Darren, but the page with my fears about Jonathan remained.

What if he collars me? Slaps me? Spanks me? Bites me? Fucks me in the ass? Whips me? Hurts me? Displays me? Gags me? Blindfolds me? Shares me? Humiliates me? Ties me down? Makes me bleed? Fucks me up? Chocks my mouth open. Pulls my hair. Fucks my face. Calls me whore. Tells me to lick the floor. Destroys me. Makes me hate myself. Turns me into an animal.

I dug around my bag and found a pencil. I leaned the pad against the steering wheel and crossed out some things. It was probably wildly incomplete, but a starting point.

What if he ~~collars me?~~ ~~Slaps me?~~ Spanks me? Bites me? Fucks me in the ass? ~~Whips me?~~ Hurts me? ~~Displays me?~~ ~~Gags me?~~ Blindfolds me? ~~Shares me?~~ ~~Humiliates me?~~ Ties me down? ~~Makes me bleed? Fucks me up? Chocks my mouth open.~~ Pulls my hair. Fucks my face. ~~Calls me whore. Tells me to lick the floor. Destroys me. Makes me hate myself. Turns me into an animal~~.

My remaining list didn't leave him with much room to maneuver, but I didn't see any of the crossed-out stuff as negotiable. The front door opened, casting a brighter light on my paper. Jonathan stepped out and went to the edge of the porch. Clutching my little pad, I got out of the car.

He leaned over the railing. "I thought you'd passed out in there." His hand gripped the railing, and in the light, each vein, each bone, each hair came to life as I imagined it on my body.

"I'm fine." I went up the porch steps as I'd done twice before, more guarded than the first time and more turned on than the second. He stood to the side of the door, waiting for me to pass. I didn't.

"You're not coming in?" he asked.

"I want to say something first."

He leaned in the entryway. "Okay."

I had words. I had plenty of words, but they all ran together and made no sense. I handed him the pad. He glanced at me, then down at it. I'd never felt so naked in front of him, even fully clothed in pants and long sleeves. He was looking at my limits. I couldn't imagine anything more intimate. I felt tingly heat all over my chest and cheeks when he glanced back up at me.

"You forgot to cross off anal sex."

"I tried it once. Didn't like it. If you're better at it, I'll have another crack." I paused. "No pun intended."

He pulled his lips between his teeth. I blinked hard twice, but that was as far as we got before we started laughing. The joke was terrible, but the release of tension turned what should have been a groaner into a belly laugh. He tried to look at the list again but started laughing, which made me unable to stop, and we were both wiping tears before he reached for me. I took his hand.

"Your list is good," he said.

"Really? It seemed like I didn't leave much."

"Monica, this should be fun. If we're not having fun, we're doing it wrong." He looked at our clasped hands and softened. "The other day, I said everything in the worst way possible. I like playing, and I know how to do it safely, but I haven't made a lifestyle out of it. I wasn't out looking for a submissive, and I haven't set hooks in the ceilings."

"So no dungeon?"

"The Historical Society wouldn't allow it," he joked.

"Oh please, you could buy and sell the Historical Society."

I tilted my head up, and he took the signal, kissing me. He wrapped his arms around my shoulders and pulled me close. "Jessica was the last woman I cared about that I discussed this with, and it didn't go well. None of it did. I was scared you'd run away."

"And I did."

"Sure as fuck you did. I was pretty upset."

"You didn't seem upset."

"I have a rich inner life, but that's where it stays."

"Really? Nobody gets in?" I slipped my arms around his waist.

"Can you live with that?" He puts his hands on my cheeks and kissed me. His stubble scraped my face, a rough counterpoint to the softness of his lips and the slickness of his tongue.

"No. Not for long."

"I'd like to see how long." He kissed me in earnest, pressing his body to mine. He felt good. Delicious. Warm and supple with his hands on my back and his open mouth on mine.

I could have kissed him for hours, but I didn't have the luxury. I kept my body close to his while moving my mouth away. "I need a test night. Like a trial run. To see if I'm scared."

"Boo." He dragged his lips down my neck and pushed his hands up my shirt.

"I mean it."

"Okay. You just smell perfect. And also..." He pulled far enough away to look into my eyes. "I'm blocked. I have everything I want from you, and I can't think of anything to do. I have too many options."

I pushed him away, smiling. "You're supposed to stand in the doorway and tell me to get undressed."

He laughed and stood framed in the warm light of the open door. He looked me up and down. I'd come from the meeting in tight jeans, boots, and a woven long-sleeved shirt with a daunting number of buttons.

"That outfit's bulletproof," he said.

"Sorry." I started unbuttoning the shirt.

"No," he said, his smile an infectious disease spreading all over his face. "Stop. Let's start over. Come up the steps."

He slipped into the house and closed the door behind him. Okay. He wanted to start over in the right frame of mind. I went down the porch steps and back up slowly. I knocked on the door and stepped back, clearing my throat. It seemed like two full minutes before the door opened, and he was there again, wearing the same shirt and linen pants, in his sock feet, smile in dormancy, but there at the corners of his mouth.

"Monica."

"Jonathan."

"It's good to see you."

"And you."

"Turn around."

My breathing immediately got heavier, pooling between my legs as I turned my back to him.

"Unbutton your pants." His voice had gotten half an octave deeper and more staccato at the hard consonants. The change in it made laughter impossible.

I yanked my belt loose, unbuttoned my jeans, and pulled down the zipper, then put my hands back at my sides.

"Good girl."

I felt him get closer behind me. He stuck his thumbs in my waistband and tugged down my jeans. In three heaves, they were mid-thigh, with my panties still protecting my ass.

"Now," he said, putting his hand on my back, "when I say bend over, you do it from the waist."

"Okay."

"Do it."

I bent over until my nose was inches from my knees. He put his hand on my ass and a finger in my panties, slipping under them to feel me. I gasped.

"You're wet."

"Yes."

"What were you thinking about while you were waiting out here?"

"Nothing."

"This is only fun if we're honest." He pulled my underwear down and circled my opening with his finger. "So say it."

Through my knees, I could see his legs behind me

and the open door of the house. I closed my eyes. "I was imagining you'd come through the door. You put your hand at the back of my neck and grabbed my hair. You kissed me. Then you pulled me down until I was kneeling. You had your dick out. I don't know how, but it's a fantasy, and you did it really fast. And you put your cock to my lips, and I took you in my mouth. You sighed really loud."

"Then what?"

"I started over. Did it a little differently. Maybe more kissing. Or I went to one knee instead of both."

"So it was that moment."

"Yes."

He put two fingers in me. I groaned.

"Another time. Maybe. When you trust me completely." He leaned over, brushing his free hand against my neck and shoulder, and pulled me up to standing, telling me what he wanted with a slight pressure. He pulled out his fingers and reached around me with his other hand, cupping my chin. "Open."

I opened my mouth, and he put in the two fingers he'd just removed from me.

"This is what I taste when I eat you."

I sucked his fingers, savoring the sex on them, the taste of arousal filling my mouth, my tongue licking his hard fingers. His erection pressed against my ass. His other hand pressed against my belly, pulling me against him. He took his fingers out of my mouth and put them back on my cheek, leaving dampness in their wake.

"You turned on?" he asked.

"Yes."

"If I do anything that changes that, you let me know."

I nodded.

"I didn't hear that."

"Yes."

363

"Yes, what?"

At once, I rebelled against the suggestion that I call him by an honorary, but at the same time, I wanted desperately to complete the act of surrender. "Yes, sir."

"You just gave me a little palpitation."

"I am at your service."

He brushed my hair from my ear and spoke softly. "Your knees, darling. Turn around and make use of them."

I stumbled a little as I tried to get on my knees in my half pulled-down pants. He took my elbow and helped me. Kneeling eye-level to his crotch, I watched him undo his pants and pull out his dick. I wanted it. I wanted to suck it dry. He took me by the back of the head and put his cock to my lips. I waited a second before opening my mouth and giving him complete power over me.

"Like you did it at the club," he said. "Open all the way for me."

He pushed his hips forward, and I took him, all of him, down my throat. I groaned for him, vibrating, concentrating on keeping open, accepting, concentrating on his pleasure, which peaked my own. It wasn't long before his thrusts became less gentle, more erratic.

"God, Monica. Get ready..." He groaned loudly, and the sticky bite of his semen filled my mouth and throat. He slowed, still coming.

I couldn't close my lips, so my mouth dripped his fluid. He thrust twice more then fell out of me. I looked up at him as he stroked my hair.

"Thank you."

"You're welcome, sir."

He whipped out one of those expensive hankies and wiped my mouth. It felt smooth and warm. "You change when you call me sir," he said as he helped me up.

"It turns me on."

"It's only for when we're together like this."

I nodded. He pulled me to him by the waist and kissed me hard and deep. I didn't know if I was supposed to put my arms around him, so I kept them at my sides until he lifted them over his shoulders, and I embraced him fully.

"You're both the best and worst submissive I've ever met."

"And you're the only dominant I've ever met."

"I want to be your last. I want to ruin you for other men."

"Better get cracking then, Drazen."

"Sir."

"Drazen, sir."

He smirked. "Leave your clothes on the porch. Then, upstairs with you. There's one door open."

He watched as I pulled my boots off, wiggled out of my jeans, then unbuttoned my shirt. I didn't do it in a lascivious way, using only the most functional movements to complete the task. When I was naked head to toe, he moved to the side so I could get past him. He took my hand, and I went upstairs in front of him.

My heart beat so hard I could barely breathe. I was doing it. The thing on the porch was an appetizer. Upstairs, I'd be his completely. I could do it. I had to. My soaking pussy demanded it. My hard nipples insisted on it. My come-covered throat required it.

I felt his eyes on my ass as I got to the top of the stairs. All the hall doors were closed except one, and it wasn't the one I'd been to twice before.

"Go on," he said.

I went through the open door. The difference between the two bedrooms I'd been in was more than the size, with the new one being bigger by fifty percent. The room was finished, lived in, and full of personal objects and photographs. The rug was worn where a man might lay his feet in the morning and night. The night table on one side held books, a half-empty glass of water, and a box of tissues.

"This is your room."

"Yes, darling." He ran his fingertips down my arms. "Get on the bed. On your back, please."

The bed was higher than the other. I crawled up and rolled over. The down comforter was cool on my back, soft on the feather bed.

Jonathan put his hands between my knees and spread them apart, then pulled them up, bending them until my heels touched my ass. I groaned from his touch and the act of obeying it.

"Stay there," he said. He got undressed, tossing his things on a leather chair while I lay on the bed, pussy and asshole up in the air. I watched his biceps tighten and release as he got his shirt off. His cock bounced out of his pants again. Naked, he slid on top of me and kissed my breasts and the diamond in my navel. I put my hands on his head, trying to push him down, but he wasn't being moved.

"So, the receipt from the clinic?" he started.

"Yes?"

"When does that birth control thing kick in?" he asked, coming face to face.

"Because of when I had my period last... uuuuuhm.... I have to figure it because the doctor said it was real important." I pretended to count on my fingers and tapped my cheek like I was thinking, screwing my eyes around.

"Monica, please." He played at annoyed, but he was smiling.

"Immediately."

He buried his face in my neck. "And I'm clean. What do you think?"

"You're the boss."

"This has to be more of a consensus."

I touched his face. He'd already ruined me for other men. "Yes," I said. "I want to feel you."

"You've overwhelmed me twice in one night."

"Don't freeze up on me on my first night of submission."

He straightened his arms, holding his body over me. "What happened to freaked-out Monica?"

"She turned into aroused Monica."

He shifted to my side and sat up. "Roll over then, aroused Monica."

I rolled over onto my stomach, holding myself up on my elbows. He placed his palm on my back, dragging it down my shoulder blades and the curve of my spine, landing on my ass, which he squeezed before standing up behind me.

"Okay, I'm going to show you something." He picked my ass up off the mattress. "Bend your knees under you."

I did it. I had one side of my face against the down comforter, watching him as he touched me and shifted my body the way he thought necessary.

"Now, pick up your butt. All the way up."

I did as I was told, straightening my knees to right angles.

"Higher." He gave my ass a slap that made me groan, then drew his hand along my back again, as if feeling for the right curve. "Put your hands under you, between your knees."

I wiggled to get them under me. "Touch your ankles."

"Like this?"

"Exactly like that."

He touched me all over, and I did feel like his work of art, his living opus with my ass in the air, so far up and bent out that my cunt must have been saluting the room.

"Physically," he said, "are you comfortable?"

"No, not really."

"And emotionally?"

"Not scared, but I feel exposed."

He kissed my ass, using his tongue along my cheeks. My pussy twitched in anticipation. But he stood up. I heard fabric shifting behind me and his movements, but I didn't look. When he came into my field of vision, he was wearing sweatpants.

"Stay there," he said. "Don't move."

"Where are you going?"

"You don't get to ask questions. You get to wait."

And he left me there, butt up, bedroom door open behind me. I wasn't scared, but I should have been. My ass tingled. Was he getting something to spank me with? Some rough tether? Cuffs? Hooks? Yes, I thought I should be terrified, but all I could think about was how much I wanted him to come back and fuck the living shit out of me.

I heard clicks and steps from downstairs, then nothing.

Your ass is out to a psychopath.

You don't know that. He could have been in the institution for anything.

At sixteen? Drugs. Suicide. Depression.

Violence?

I heard him on the creaky wood stairs, then his feet padding down the hall, then I smelled his sawdust scent.

"Very good." His voice was close behind me. "When I tell you to go upstairs and be ready, this is what I mean, okay?"

"Yes, sir."

"How was it? Waiting?"

"Not my favorite. But also kind of good because I just stewed, wondering what you were going to do to me."

He stroked my ass, letting his fingertips brush the crack, inside the cleft, touching where I was wettest. "It turns me on knowing you're up here doing what I tell you." He put both palms on my cheeks. I felt something in his right hand.

He put his mouth on me, and I groaned when he kissed between my legs. He flicked his tongue over my clit. I bucked a little. I knew I wasn't close, but I felt as though I could come from a warm breeze.

He moved me onto my back. He had a length of brown leather twine in his right hand. It might have made a fringed bag or a shoelace, but long. He looked at me clinically again, as if I were a problem to solve, then he went back to my eyes. "You ready?"

"The anticipation is killing me."

"Me too." He took my left wrist and placed it against my left knee, then looped a length of leather around them, making a figure eight, binding them together. "Too tight?"

"No."

He knotted it off, then picked up my back while he ran the rest of the spool under me. He pulled, playing with the length until my tied knee and wrist were splayed. "I want to say," he said as he placed my right wrist and right knee together, "if you say stop, it's good enough for me, but we might want to set a safeword." He spread my legs to get the right length under my back and tied my right side together, letting the rest of the loop drop off the edge of the bed.

"Tangerine," I said.

"Tangerine?"

"I doubt you can keep doing whatever it is you're doing if I say tangerine."

"Fine, wiseass." He leaned over me and kissed my lips so sweetly I wanted to put my arms and legs around him, but I couldn't.

He got off the bed and looked at me. I couldn't close or lower my legs, nor could I move my arms. A trickle of wetness dripped down my crack, and the discomfort of it was exquisite. He bent over and kissed between my breasts, dragging his tongue across, to my nipple, sucking it gently. "I'm listening," he whispered. "I'm listening to your breathing, your heartbeat. I'm listening to your skin on the sheets. If you need something, just say it. I'm all ears."

"I'll let you know."

"In words." He sucked the other nipple, which was hard and tight. He pressed his lips around it and pulled.

"I'll say, 'Get the fuck off me and untie me, you animal,' but not when you do that. That's good."

"And this?" He kissed down, circling my diamond crusted navel and down to my left thigh. He ran his tongue over my folds to the other thigh.

"That needs a safeword."

He licked my clit with the pointy part of his tongue. "What should it be?" he asked before licking again, then giving it a light suck.

"Oh, God."

"'Oh, God' it is." He got on top of me, his dick just touching my exposed pussy.

He kissed me. I moved my hips against him, and he shifted away, keeping the head at the entrance to my vagina, waiting. He watched me gasp as he pushed a little. He must have felt the way I closed in around him, as if I'd suck him into me.

"Please," I said. "Please fuck me. Sir, please."

He slid his cock inside me so slowly it felt ten feet long. Inch by inch, skin to skin, soft against slick, until he hit the end, and he pressed against me, rocking while my clit exploded. Then he pulled out just as slowly, and the feeling was devastatingly sharp in the pleasure of its loss. The heightened torment continued as he slid in again, and I couldn't grab him or move. All the other stuff was dress rehearsal for the control he took as he tortured me with the measured, unhurried thrusts and slow rocks of him against my clit.

"Jonathan, Jonathan, Jonathan...." I forgot to call him sir or anything else but his name.

He sped up, dropping onto me, a splayed thing, open, bound, servile, utterly compliant mass of nerve endings and clutching, wet flesh. His movements turned to pounding, slamming fucking that brought me close enough to cry out.

He slowed, straightening his arms above me and changing the rotation so I felt his cock, but not enough to stimulate me to orgasm.

"No," I said in a voice so desperate I was shocked to hear it.

"Easy, Monica."

"Jesus."

"You're mine. Your orgasms are mine. Your pleasure is mine to give."

I wanted to rail at him. I wanted to demand it. But not only would that not get me what I wanted, it wasn't how I wanted it to go down. I wanted to be fully compliant. "Yes, sir." Saying it calmed me.

"Breathe slowly."

I did as I was told.

He moved against me, gradually, as before. "Look at me."

I did, seeing the sweat on his brow and the pleasure in his face. That pleasure brought me the greatest satisfaction. I had done that. I gave him what he was giving me.

As if sensing my thoughts, he leaned down and

kissed me. "Will you come for me?" he asked, his voice low and growling.

"Yes, it's yours."

"Mine," he whispered.

He fucked me in earnest, then. He fucked me like he meant it, roughly, hitting the right places as if it was what he did to get himself off. My breasts bounced with the motion. My cunt was a pulsing strip of flesh under him, a swath of need. Then, like a rush from a firehose, I came, ass and pussy clenching over and over as I screamed and released it all. He kept going, hovering over me, thrusting, and the release continued to the point where pleasure met pain, and I came again, pushing my hips into him as he opened his mouth and grunted hard, then moaned. He slowed, rotating again, then dropped on me with a heaving chest and hot breaths on my neck.

He reached behind with his left hand and untied my right wrist and knee. They separated with a cramp. Sitting up, he untied the other side. I rubbed my wrists.

"So?" he asked.

"So, a needle pulling thread. You've ruined me."

He brushed the hair off my face, and I did what I'd been wanting to do. I put my arms and legs around him.

CHAPTER 66

I awoke slowly to a few sensations: the light of the sun cutting past my eyelids, my sore pussy, and Jonathan's fingertips stroking my hand as it rested on his chest. When I opened my eyes, he was looking at me.

"Good morning."

I grumbled and shifted closer to him.

"Are you working today?" he asked.

"Lunch shift." I spread my hand out on his chest, pushing it forward, brushing the hairs between my fingers. "Then I have to go to Frontage and see if we can work something out. I don't want to gig there without Gabby, but I don't want to be stupid."

He pulled me on top of him. "There's nothing stupid about you."

I kissed him, and that kiss got deeper and more urgent. My sore pussy twitched when I felt him harden. He ran his hands all over me, then over my arms which he guided to the headboard, until I was stretched over him.

"Oh, Jonathan. I'm so sore."

"Is that a no?"

"Just be gentle."

He guided himself into me, and it hurt, but with the most delicious pain. I used the headboard to leverage myself, and Jonathan guided my hips and then rotated his finger on my clit until I gave him a sweet orgasm that felt more like a long breeze than a tornado.

With his face beneath me, falling apart under his own pleasure, I knew something for sure, and I whispered it to myself as he came. *I love you, I love you, I love you.*

CHAPTER 67

*M*y clothes had been washed again and were waiting for me when I got out of the shower. Living on a hill in a crap neighborhood my whole life, I'd never had industrial-strength water pressure, and it seemed a good water heater was pretty important if you wanted a nice, skin-scalding shower. I got into my clothes, and feeling so refreshed, I almost skipped down the stairs, where I saw Ally Mira sweeping the corners.

"Hi," I said.

"Good morning." Her English was accented.

"Did you wash my clothes?"

"Mister Drazen left them for me. I get up early and do it."

"Thank you. It's very kind of you."

"You're welcome. I have tea for you in the sitting room."

"The what?"

She leaned her broom against the wall and motioned for me to follow her. We went downstairs, into the living room and through an arch I hadn't noticed before, past a short foyer, and into an enclosed porch on the side of the house overlooking a flower garden. A silver tea tray sat on the low table. I could hear Jonathan talking on the phone in another room I couldn't identify. Ally Mira indicated the couch.

I sat down. "Thanks." I picked up the teapot to let her know I'd do the pouring.

She nodded, smiled, and slipped out. I realized Jonathan's voice was coming through the wood sliding doors on the side of the room. The sound of the morning birds was deafening, and though it was a lovely white noise to distract me from Jonathan's phone call, his voice cut through. He did not seem happy. I tried to tell myself I wasn't eavesdropping, but when I heard her name, I stopped pretending I wasn't listening and made an effort to shut out the sound of the bird's chirping.

"Jess," he said, "this is you being afraid of being alone." Pause. "No, you don't. That's right. I'm telling you how you feel."

There was a longer pause, during which I sipped my tea and hoped the conversation ended soon, but Jonathan's voice got stronger.

"Don't you dare." Pause. "Jessica, let me be clear. If you do anything like that, I will destroy you. I. Will. Destroy. You."

That voice. It was the sawdust and leather voice, the voice that got me to unquestioningly spread my legs or bend at the waist. I'd never heard him use it outside of a sexual context. His voice got too low to hear after that, then the doors slid open.

He walked in looking as if a blanket of sadness had been thrown over him and tied at the neck. "You're up," he said.

"There's tea left if you want some."

He stepped forward until he was standing over me. "How much of that did you hear?"

"I know who it was but not what it was about."

He paused, then kneeled in front of me between the couch and the table. I put my hand to his cheek and leaned forward. His eyes shone a troubled green, and his mouth set itself in a line.

"Jonathan, what's wrong?"

"I won't let anyone come between us. I want you to know that."

"She won't if you don't let her."

"If she says anything to you, you need to come to me with it right away. Do you understand?"

"What happened, Jonathan?"

"Just say you'll call me."

"I don't understand." I held his face in my hands, stroking his cheeks with my thumbs.

"Wherever I am in the world, before you think you know anything, you make sure you call me. Say you will." He wasn't using his domineering voice, but the voice of a man who needed, desperately, to be soothed.

"I will."

He rubbed his palms along the tops of my thighs and up around my waist. He laid his head on my lap and said nothing as I stroked his hair and hummed a melody that reminded me of the cadences of his voice.

We sat like that, me on the couch, humming, and him on his knees before me, long after my tea became cold and the morning birds silenced themselves for the day.

* * *

JONATHAN AND MONICA'S story continues in ONE YEAR WITH HIM and ONE LIFE WITH HIM.

GET BOOK 2 - ONE YEAR WITH HIM
GET BOOK 3 - ONE LIFE WITH HIM

* * *

To HEAR ABOUT SALES, freebies, bonus content and new releases, CLICK HERE to get on my mailing list.

Facebook fan-run group, go here. Most fun, guaranteed.

I'm on Pinterest, Tumblr, Twitter and Instagram with varying degrees of frequency.

My email is christine@cdreiss.com

Printed in Great Britain
by Amazon